DEAD
STOP

DEAD STOP

JAMIE DENTON

BRAVA

KENSINGTON BOOKS
http://www.kensingtonbooks.com

For Tony.
Without you, none of this makes sense.

Acknowledgments

A very special thanks to the following:

Trish Nolfi, for helping me keep my hierarchy facts straight, and not running screaming when I came at her with my questions.

Mandy Roth and Dianne Miley, for sharing your down-in-the-trenches knowledge.

Mary Ann Chulick, for reminding me that I do know what I'm doing. Thanks, toots! One of these days I might actually believe it.

Leslie Crossen, for being the friend who knows where to hide the bodies.

CHAPTER 1

THE BITCH HAD everything. Everything that should have been his, they'd given to *her*. Even their name. She was their princess, the charmed one, but she'd paid for it. He'd made sure of it. And she'd continue to pay, he'd make sure of that, as well.

He knew better than to try to force the anger and resentment aside. Keeping his emotions close like a faithful old companion, he concentrated on the task at hand.

He plucked a pink rhinestone necklace and pair of matching earrings from the jewelry box, then snapped it closed before strolling across the candlelit basement to the operating table, where she waited for him.

She had a name, but it was unimportant. All that mattered was that she would pay for her sins.

"So pretty," he said, his tone venomous as he slid the necklace in place. "That's what they say about you, isn't it?"

She didn't answer him. Probably couldn't even hear him in her current state of unconsciousness. But she'd awaken again soon enough.

He straightened and examined her. The necklace worked perfectly with the sweetheart neckline of the pink beaded gown, which enhanced her pale complexion and showed off her slender curves. Still, he frowned. The earrings would never do now. He'd been too hasty. He should've waited so she could wear the earrings.

With a slight turn of his head, he admired the way the candlelight played with the sparkles interwoven in the gown he'd chosen for her. Her round breasts rose and fell beneath the elaborate fabric, drawing his attention. Cupping his hand over the full mound, he closed his eyes, enjoying the soft play of flesh and sequins beneath his hands. His dick hardened.

He snapped his eyes open and snatched his hand away. He wasn't supposed to touch. Not like that. Only it was becoming more and more difficult to resist the temptation.

Drawing in a deep breath, he stared down at her. Perhaps he should've gone with the soft blue gown, to match her eyes. She'd had such an intriguing gaze. He'd especially liked the way she'd slid him a sidelong glance when he'd first seen her. Those eyes had been what had initially captured his imagination. Without a doubt, he'd known in an instant she'd been the chosen one, the one sent to him to pay for *her* sins.

Young. Beautiful. And filled with a sense of entitlement that enraged him. Luring this one had hardly been a challenge, he thought with a sudden sneer. She hadn't been shy like the last one, and she'd foolishly trusted him. They always trusted him, but then he gave them no reason to fear him.

Fear, the real kind, always came later.

He took such pride in his work, and he made certain they realized just how fortunate they were to be selected by him. Their moment of atonement had arrived. And he would make sure they were grateful.

"Time to wake up," he said as he selected a syringe and the large vial of Narcon from the metal table he kept next to the old operating table. After drawing the appropriate dosage, he then shot the antinarcotic directly into the IV port.

While he waited for her to regain consciousness, he reached behind him and pressed the power button on the audio equipment. An electronic whir filled the silence of the room, momentarily recording only the sound of his own breathing. That would soon change.

By the time he turned back to his subject, she'd awakened. His erection returned when he was met by her stunning blue gaze. Confusion filled her luscious depths, followed instantly by a combination of revulsion and fear.

He said nothing while trailing the tips of his fingers along her cheek. She attempted to turn away, but quickly stopped when the bonds he'd fashioned around her neck instantly tightened. Tears filled her eyes and ran down her cheeks.

He didn't give a damn about her tears. Bending forward, he breathed in her scent, an intoxicating blend of the rose-scented lotion he'd applied to her skin before he'd dressed her, and the tangy, acrid scent of fresh blood.

"Welcome to orientation," he whispered softly in her ear before taking her lobe between his teeth and biting down hard enough to rip away the dangling flesh that remained.

AINSLEY BRENNAN YANKED the earbuds from her ears and closed the lid to her laptop with a snap before she inched away from her desk. If this was someone's idea of a joke, she wasn't laughing.

Alone in her little cubicle at the *Serenity Heights Sentinel,* she sat back from her desk and, with a frown, stared at her closed laptop. The audio file she'd received had to be some kind of a sick and twisted joke. It just had to be. Otherwise those horrific screams were just too chilling, too filled with terror. Too real.

Her frown deepened. They couldn't be real. Could they?

With her heart still beating double time, she snagged the envelope that had contained the CD with the disturbing audio file and walked away from her tiny cubicle. She headed across the vacant newsroom to the front desk, where Lisa Williams, the *Sentinel*'s receptionist, sat filing her nails.

Dropping the envelope in front of Lisa, she asked, "Do you know where this came from?"

Shrugging, Lisa glanced up at her with deep brown eyes framed by the longest lashes Ainsley had ever seen. "Mail? It was here when I came back from my break."

"There's no postmark," Ainsley pointed out. The only thing on the padded envelope was a white label with the words "For Ms. Brennan" printed across it in bold typeface. "It couldn't have come in with the mail. Did we have any visitors here today?"

Ainsley had been out all morning. She'd attended freshmen orientation with her youngest sister, Cassidy, then helped settle her into her new dorm room at Serenity Heights University, or the "U" as the liberal arts college was referred to by the locals.

Lisa shook her head, then shifted her concentration back to the hangnail she'd been filing. "Just Mona's daughter, Grace," she said. "She dropped off some banana muffins this morning—which I didn't need after two biscotti and a mocha latte."

Grace was Mona Nolfini's only daughter and one of two local hairstylists in town. Mona was a staple at the town's weekly newspaper and Ainsley swore the woman had worked for the *Sentinel* since God was a boy, running the classified advertising and special notices sections of the paper.

"You're sure?" Ainsley pressed.

"I'm sure. Why?" Lisa glanced up again. "Something wrong?"

"I don't know . . . Maybe." Ainsley picked up the envelope and reread the label for what had to be the fiftieth time. "For Ms. Brennan." Someone definitely wanted her attention. Well, they had it. Now what?

And maybe she was just overreacting. Maybe she was so anxious for that big story, the one that would get picked up by the Associated Press and make national headlines, that she was reading something into the audio file that wasn't there. Like the screams of a woman being tortured.

So what was she supposed to do about it? She couldn't report on a strange audio file she'd received. She had no *who, when, where,* or even a *why* to develop a story. Although, her imagination certainly had no trouble filling in the blanks, the images filtering through her mind were more suited for a Hollywood horror script than an article in a small-town, weekly newspaper. All she had was the *what,* which was patently clear to her—a woman's tortured screams. Real or not, it wasn't a sound she'd be forgetting anytime soon.

"You have no idea how it was delivered?" Ainsley asked.

"Nope." The phone on Lisa's desk rang. "Sorry," she said as she reached for the receiver. *"Sentinel."*

No postmark. No return address. Nothing to indicate where the package had come from or who'd sent the CD labeled "Day One."

"She's right here, Cass. Hold on a sec." Lisa looked up at Ainsley. "Your sister."

Not exactly anxious to return to the quasisolitude of her cubicle, she went to one of the vacant desks on the other side of the room. "What's up, Cass? I'm a little busy right now."

"Oooh, let me guess," Cassidy said, her tone teasing. "One of Mrs. Greenway's Jack Russells was seen chasing cars down Main Street again and you have the exclusive."

That about summed up her career, all right. Now that Cassidy was in college, Ainsley supposed she was free to follow her own dreams. Dreams she'd set aside eleven years ago when her parents had been killed in a ten-car pile up on Interstate 80, and she'd been left to raise her two younger sisters, Paige and Cassidy. But even if she did occasionally suffer with a pang for something a little more exciting in her life, Serenity Heights was home. She couldn't imagine her life elsewhere.

"How'd you guess?" Ainsley countered dryly. She took a quick breath. "What do you need, Cass? Change your mind and want to have lunch with me after all?" She almost hoped so. She'd take all the diversion she could get at the moment, and lunch with the sister she'd left little more than an hour ago sounded like a grand idea to her. Anything other than having to listen to that damn audio file one more time.

"No. I just wanted to thank you again for this morning."

"What part? Lugging your stuff up four flights of stairs to your dorm room, or sitting through that pompous jerk Devin McElvoy's freshmen orientation speech?" She hadn't liked the associate dean of students all that much when she'd interviewed him last month. She'd written a piece on him and the newly appointed dean of students, Mary Ann Chesterfield, both of whom had been up for the same job. She'd liked Mary Ann and was glad the position had gone to her rather than McElvoy.

Cassidy's laughter was light and breezy. "All of it. Oh, and just so you know, my new roommate's boyfriend thinks my 'mom' is hot."

Ainsley would've laughed if her insides weren't still a jittery mess. "Gee, thanks." Last time she looked in the mirror she hadn't spotted a single gray hair. Not that Paige and Cassidy hadn't done their best to give her a few in the past couple years. At nineteen, she'd been ill equipped as a parental figure, but somehow they'd managed to tough it out and stick together despite the odds.

"I think he meant it as a compliment."

"Just what I needed to hear." Now that she thought about it, it was probably the only male compliment she'd received in months.

"Okay, well, I gotta run," Cassidy said. "See you for Sunday dinner. You do remember that Paige promised to come up from Cinci, right?"

"I remember," she lied as she slid a notepad across the desk and jotted herself a note to make a trip to the Giant Eagle for groceries. She'd completely forgotten about Sunday dinner. She and her sisters did their best to get together at least once every couple of months. Since Paige's schedule change at the hospital, they hadn't seen each other once the entire summer. "Anything special you want for dinner?"

"Whatever," Cassidy said. "But I'd love some of your artichoke casserole."

A half smile tipped Ainsley's mouth. There'd been a time when her sisters had begged her to stay *out* of the kitchen. A lot sure had changed in eleven years.

Just as she was about to hang up, she said, "Cassidy, be careful."

Her sister let out one of those put-upon sighs she'd perfected so well in her teens. "Stop worrying, Lee."

"It's my job to worry," she reminded her sister. Not one she'd welcomed, but one she'd assumed since there'd been no one else. Her sisters had been her responsibility for so long, she didn't know how not to worry about them. "The world can be a dangerous place. That's all I'm saying."

Cassidy laughed again. "Quit with the mom routine. I'm all grown up now, remember? Besides, it's not like anything ever happens in Serenity Heights anyway."

True, but after what she'd just heard, she couldn't help feel more than a little overprotective—and a whole lot nervous, at least until she knew for certain that the audio file was nothing more than a prank.

She said good-bye and hung up the phone, then headed down the hallway to the small break room. Snagging a diet soda from the fridge, she walked back to her cubicle, only to sit at her desk and stare uneasily at her laptop.

She twisted the top off the soda bottle and took a long

drink. She had no choice but to listen to the file again. All of it this time. Then, prank or no, she was taking it to the cops.

With a deep breath and a whole lot of reluctance, she opened her laptop. Hesitantly, she slipped the earbuds back into place and hit the Play button.

Just like the last time, at first she heard nothing, just the whir of the CD in the player. Finally, she heard a sound. This time, she hit the Stop button and inched the bar back a few clicks, then turned up the volume and hit Play again.

A moan. She'd definitely heard someone moan.

She cranked the volume up another few notches. Definite moaning. And not the pleasurable kind, either.

"No," a woman's voice pleaded. "Oh, please. No more."

A coldness ran though Ainsley as if her blood had turned to ice water in her veins at the sheer desperation in the woman's voice. Her hands began to tremble. Good God, what was this?

She waited, knowing what was coming next. The first scream. So horrifying, so bloodcurdling, followed by another, then another.

"Cassidy get all settled?"

Ainsley jumped at the unexpected sound of Mona's voice behind her. She yanked out the earbuds and turned to glare sharply at the older woman. "Geeze, Mona. Give me a heart attack, why don't you?"

Mona's grin was only mildly sheepish. "Sorry. I thought you heard me approaching."

Normally she probably would have, since Mona had all the grace of a baby elephant, but she'd been too engrossed in her own apprehension to pay attention. "Yes," she said, softening her tone. "Cass is all settled. She's already called to remind me about dinner on Sunday." Silly, really, now that she thought about it, since the U was exactly six blocks from home.

"It'll take her a while to get used to being on her own. Grace called me every day, sometimes twice a day, during her first semester at beauty school."

Ainsley wasn't surprised. Mona and Grace had a very special relationship. Mona's husband had died when Grace was a preschooler and Mona had never remarried.

"We were lucky to hear from Paige once a week when she was at Ohio State."

"Yes, but Cassidy is the baby. It's been just the two of you for . . . what? The last five, six years? It's different when the baby leaves home," Mona told her.

Mona shifted the straps of the large quilted bag in her hand over her shoulder. "I'll be at the Cast Off if anyone asks. Earlene has started a lunch-hour knitting club." She leaned forward and lowered her voice. "Maybe you should come with me. You don't get out enough."

Didn't Ainsley know it. She wasn't a nun. She even dated on occasion, but she'd kept her romantic entanglements light and purposely had avoided anything serious, telling herself she'd been responsible for her sisters and couldn't afford the added drama until she'd fulfilled her obligation to Paige and Cassidy. But all that was about to change now that she was technically a free woman. Of course, she had to meet a man she was interested in first.

"You go have fun," she told Mona. "I'll help Lisa man the fort until you get back." Not that she didn't have a way with a pair of knitting needles and some lovely yarn herself. In fact, she was an occasional customer of the Cast Off, but joining a knitting club didn't quite sound like her idea of having that life she'd put on hold when her parents died.

"All right. Suit yourself." Mona turned to leave, nearly colliding with Lisa.

"You might want to turn on your scanner," Lisa told Ainsley.

Ainsley had turned off the police scanner when she'd first listened to the audio file and hadn't bothered turning it back on again. "Oh?" she asked. "What is it this time?"

"Probably nothing more exciting than one of Mrs. Greenway's Jack Russell terriers biting the FedEx delivery guy on the ankle again," Mona said.

Ainsley wouldn't be surprised. The most recent crime spree to hit Serenity Heights consisted of a pair of high school boys who'd decided to play Robin Hood with the cable company by scaling poles and hooking their neighbors up for free premium services.

"I wish," Lisa said. "I just heard from Darla Fitzpatrick, who heard it from Nita Morgan over at the post office. A couple of boys ditching school stumbled on a dead body out at Big Rock Clearing."

"Oh, sweet heaven," Mona muttered as she crossed herself.

Ainsley's hands began to tremble. She drew in a deep breath, hoping to steady her racing heart, but she felt as if she were being suffocated. Oh, this wasn't good.

What if the CD hadn't been a joke? What if the voice on the recording was . . . ?

"Man or woman?" Ainsley asked. She glanced at the laptop. She had a feeling she already knew the answer.

"A woman," Lisa said.

The woman's tortured screams from the audio file weren't only frightening, but haunting. She doubted the likelihood that the audio file sent to her and the discovery of a woman's body on the same day was nothing more than a strange coincidence.

Someone was trying to tell her something. She only wished she knew what it was they wanted to say.

"HOW THE HELL are we supposed to get a positive ID?"
Deputy Chief of Police Beckett Raines crouched down

next to the corpse, wondering the same thing. All he and Captain Alan "Mitch" Mitchell had been able to determine about the body was that it was a woman who'd been dead for quite some time. Initially, Beck thought perhaps the local wildlife had gotten to the body, but upon closer inspection he realized the victim's fingers had been severed, not torn. He had zero hope of matching dental records since the victim's teeth had been pulled as well. From the amount of dried blood in her mouth, Beck knew without a doubt that particular deed hadn't been performed postmortem, either.

"Let's just process the scene, Mitch," Beck told him. The wind shifted and his stomach roiled.

"Nothing like a rotting corpse to ruin a man's appetite just before lunch." Mitch moved upwind. "How long you figure she's been out here decomposing?"

As a former homicide detective with the LAPD for twelve years, Beck had seen plenty that would have the average Joe sleeping with the lights on and a double-barrel clutched to his chest like a teddy bear. He'd seen DB's in worse shape, too, but no matter how many times he worked a violent crime scene, whether it'd been another drive-by shooting, domestic violence, or a robbery turned homicide, he couldn't help the waves of disgust that crashed into him whenever he thought about man's inhumanity against man. Today was no exception.

"Not long," he told Mitch. "Probably less than eight or ten hours. But she's been dead a helluva lot longer than that." Two, maybe even three or four weeks by his estimation, but the coroner would be able to narrow down the time of death for them.

Beck stood and tugged off the latex gloves. He'd seen enough for now. "What's the crime lab's ETA?"

Like most small towns in the area, the Serenity Heights Police Department lacked the budget for their own forensics team. Not that Serenity Heights ever had anything like this to process. So they relied on the Cuyahoga County Crime Lab in Cleveland, which was less than twenty-five miles to the east.

Nothing ever happened in Serenity Heights. That's what he'd been told. Wasn't that why he'd taken the job in the first place? He hadn't been all that close to burn out, but he'd seen it happen to the best of them. He'd wanted a change and considered his return to Ohio more of a preventative mental health measure.

Mitch glanced at his wristwatch. "Maybe another ten, fifteen minutes, at the most. Coroner should be here any minute now."

Mitch was a decent cop, and a good guy if slightly out of shape and nearing retirement. But as he'd admitted when requesting Beck's assistance at the scene, he lacked hands-on experience when it came to actual homicide investigations. Sure, he'd had all the training necessary, even attended a few seminars at Quantico as his position of captain of police demanded. However, Mitch's primary role was that of supervisor. He was responsible for one K-9 unit and the dozen patrolmen on the small police force who rotated twelve-hour shifts in a town with a low rate of petty crime, a few domestic violence disputes, and the occasional group of high school or college kids who got out of hand on a Friday night. To Beck's knowledge, Serenity Heights hadn't seen a murder investigation in over seventy-five years.

A patrolman was busy sectioning off the path leading to the clearing with yellow crime scene tape. Beck had assigned another cop to photograph the immediate scene. He wanted shots of everything—footprints, tire tracks. . . . If a leaf looked out of place, he wanted it photographed. A third patrolman, Charlie Gabriel, was standing guard over the police cruiser, where the pair of teenage boys who'd discovered the body were huddled in the backseat.

The boys, who'd been playing hooky after only a couple

of days into the start of the new school year, had already been questioned by Mitch by the time Beck had arrived on scene, and were waiting to be taken to the station to give a formal statement. Beck already knew the boys hadn't seen anything that could provide the force with much of a lead in the case. They'd merely stumbled on the body after taking the path through the woods to a place the locals called Big Rock Clearing, a small clearing in the woods on the edge of town with a very large boulder in the center. A place where pilfered cigarettes were smoked and swiped alcohol was consumed, and where virginity was no doubt lost.

There was the issue of where the boys had gotten the six-pack of beer. From the nervous glances the boys had kept shooting in his direction when he'd arrived, he suspected it was from the personal stash of one of the parents whom Mitch had already contacted from his cell phone.

"Hey, Chief," Mitch called to him. "Take a look at this."

Beck didn't bother to remind Mitch he was merely the deputy chief of the department. He knew from experience it wouldn't do any good. Chief Munson was temporarily out of commission on an extended medical leave after suffering a major cardiac event, leaving Beck as acting chief of police after only being on the job less than a month. Since then, everyone called him "Chief" anyway. Period.

Beck tugged on a fresh pair of latex gloves and knelt beside the body again to take a closer look. Using the tip of his pen, Mitch held the vic's blood-soaked, matted hair back from her neck.

"I didn't notice this before," Mitch admitted. "What kind of sick bastard chews off a woman's ear?"

The kind that enjoyed killing, Beck thought with revulsion. He'd already suspected this was no random crime. Someone had put a whole hell of a lot of thought into murdering the victim, and Beck prayed this would be the only body they discovered. Unfortunately, the churning in his gut said otherwise. Best he could hope for was the perp had merely used the clearing surrounded by woods as a dump site.

"Think it could've been an animal?" Mitch asked.

"Could be," Beck said thoughtfully, "but I doubt it." The body wasn't quite frozen, but he'd swear it had been thawing for a while. Which to him meant the body had decomposed, then had been kept frozen prior to being dumped. But why? In hopes that the vic would be discovered intact? And why here, where the body would eventually be found?

Mitch leaned closer for a better look. The fifty-something police captain apparently had an iron gut. "I'll put my Rose's hot fudge cake up against those brownies you got on your desk that these are human teeth marks."

Since word got out that the new Serenity Heights deputy chief was widowed, Beck had been the recipient of a steady stream of casseroles and baked goods, courtesy of the marriage-minded females in the small Ohio town he now called home. His fridge was packed with macaroni and cheese, two different types of tuna casserole, and three varieties of lasagna. There was still a disposable container of spaghetti and meatballs and a platter of fried chicken along with a batch of potato salad that rivaled his dead wife's. And that didn't include the baked goods being dropped off at the station, sometimes three or four times a week.

A definite iron gut, Beck thought, if Mitch could talk food while viewing a ravaged corpse that stunk to high heaven. "Let's not get carried away." Beck stood and took a few steps back, not that the distance helped much. "We'll find out for sure during the autopsy," he said, although he did agree with Mitch's conclusion. The teeth marks looked human to him, as well, like the trail left in an ice cream cone.

"Who uses this place?" Beck asked.

"Kids mostly," Mitch said. "Once in a while some couple

trying to recapture their youth. In my day, we'd swipe a bottle from the old man's liquor cabinet, come out here and hang out. Hasn't changed all that much."

"The UNSUB must either be a local or someone who knows about this place. He knew the body would be found relatively soon."

"I dunno, Chief. This is a small town. I think we'd know if we had a nut job on the loose capable of doing something like this."

Beck didn't bother to remind Mitch that the killer could be the guy next door. The quiet fellow down the block who kept to himself, the church deacon, or even the local pizza shop owner.

Mitch reached into his pocket and produced a small plastic bag, then plucked something from the body. "Hey, what do you think of this?"

Beck took the bag and examined the contents. "Could be anything," he said, looking hard at the long purple fibers Mitch had removed from the body. Whatever it was, he doubted it was the cause of the ligature marks on the vic's neck. They went too deep, as if they were caused by something hard, not soft as the fibers suggested.

"Have there been any formal dances at any of the schools? Any big weddings in the past couple of weeks?" Beck handed Mitch the plastic bag and turned his attention back to the body. The vic wore a royal blue satin gown, the kind worn to a prom or perhaps by a bridesmaid. An elaborate gemstone necklace was draped around the neck, just below the ligature marks, as if to underscore the perp's handiwork.

"Not that I know of," Mitch said. He pulled a handkerchief from his hip pocket and mopped at the sweat dotting his forehead. "Prom's usually not until late spring. Even if she's been dead a month, it doesn't figure."

"And we've had no missing persons in the past few weeks, right?"

Mitch shook his head. "Nope. None. Last person that went missing around here was Maribelle Kinsella from the nursing home."

Beck frowned. He'd reviewed all the open investigation files, little more than a dozen of them, and didn't recall any involving a missing person. "When was this?"

"Around ninety-seven, I think. Old Maribelle ran off to Atlantic City with Eldon Jablonski and got herself hitched. Pissed her family off big time, too, because Eldon got it all when Maribelle kicked the bucket a couple of months after the wedding."

"A con job?" Beck asked as he turned to see the coroner coming down the dirt and gravel path.

Mitch chuckled and thumbed a cherry Life Saver from the roll he always kept in his breast pocket. "Love at first sight, the way I heard it."

Beck shook his head. What he wouldn't do for a chance to oversee the case of a pair of lovesick geriatrics right about now.

Mitch crossed the clearing to speak with the coroner, leaving Beck temporarily alone with the body. Glancing down at what was left of the woman, he couldn't shake the feeling this wasn't the last they'd heard from the brutal killer who'd shattered the peace of a town where nothing bad ever happened.

CHAPTER 2

PARIS NOLAN DIDN'T have a family. At eighteen, she barely had a history, at least one that she was willing to claim. What past she did have, she'd just as soon forget. Life didn't totally suck, though, because what she did have was a fresh start. She had every intention of making the most of it, too. At least for as long as it lasted, because everyone knew that the good stuff was fleeting at best.

"Was that your mom?" Paris asked her new roommate, Cassidy Brennan. "She seems nice."

Cassidy flung herself onto the bed on her side of their shared dorm room and laughed. "She's not my mom," she said, reaching over to the desk at the foot of her bed to set her cell phone in the charging unit. "Ainsley is my oldest sister."

Paris didn't have a sister, or a cell phone. She'd just never seen the need since there weren't five people she could even put in her calling circle or that she wanted to call. Maybe her boyfriend, Zach, but since she couldn't afford the monthly service fee, she supposed it didn't much matter.

"Your folks couldn't make it?" Paris asked as she pulled her feet up on her bed and sat cross-legged. For the past two days since she'd arrived at the U, she'd seen a flurry of activity in the dorms. Parents came and went and came back again. Crying. Laughing. Being a family. She'd tried not to feel envious, but couldn't help herself.

Yesterday she and Zach had explored the little town they'd be calling home for the next four years. Zach had said it was Podunk, a nothing, pissant town in the middle of nowhere, but she'd liked the quaintness of Serenity Heights, the wholesomeness of it all. Probably because Ohio was such a far cry from the harshness of Oakland, California, where she'd lived all her life. Better yet, it was three thousand miles away from a past she swore she'd overcome.

"My folks died when I was little," Cassidy said. Paris had only known her new roomie for less than two hours, but she had no trouble discerning the sadness in Cassidy's wide, shockingly blue eyes.

"I'm sorry," Paris said, and meant it. She could sympathize, having lost her own father to an aggressive form of lung cancer when she was only eight years old. The first of many social workers had attempted to locate her mother, but seeing as Paris didn't even know the woman who'd given birth to her, she'd never held out much hope on that score. Jocelyn Nolan hadn't exactly left a forwarding address when she'd run out on her daughter and husband shortly after Paris was born.

"Ainsley raised us. She can be a pain in the ass, but she kept us together." A slow smile curved Cassidy's mouth. "I don't think I appreciated her much at the time, though. I was a real little bitch."

Curious, Paris asked, "Us?"

Cassidy nodded. "I have another sister, Paige. She's a nurse in Cinci."

"You're lucky you had family. Foster homes can really bite." Longing filled her chest. Maybe if she'd had a family to look out for her after her dad had died, her life would've been different. All she'd had were a long string of overworked, burned-out social workers who didn't give a shit so long as she kept her nose clean and didn't make waves with the foster family. She supposed it could've been worse. She'd only been in three different foster homes in ten years. One of the girls she knew had been in several homes, and she'd only been a foster kid for five years.

The way Paris figured it, that was just the way life worked out sometimes. Some people had all the luck—and then there was Paris. She wouldn't exactly say she had nothing but bad luck; she'd just never been all that fortunate. But as her last social worker had told her the day she and Zach had driven out of Oakland and headed east in Zach's teal green '95 Honda Civic, "Life is what you make of it."

She supposed she had it pretty good, especially compared to what some of the other foster kids had told her. At least she hadn't been bounced around too much and had even been in the same foster home all through high school. While she had lived in a pretty rough neighborhood, the home wasn't the stuff nightmares were made of and her foster parents had been kind. And she'd had Zach. It wasn't all bad.

She'd also worked her tail off to keep up her grades, and was awarded a full academic scholarship to Serenity Heights University. Well, almost full. All of her college expenses were paid for, but if she wanted spending money, she'd have to get a job, preferably on campus since she didn't own a car. She'd never seen a speck of real snow in her life and had no idea how to drive in the stuff. She did have an interview with the associate dean of students tomorrow morning. Not that she was getting her hopes up or anything. She'd do what she always did—hope for the best but expect the worst. No disappointments that way.

Cassidy stretched out on her bunk. "So, you hungry? Wanna check out the cafeteria? I hear the pizza's not half bad."

"How about we go to that coffee house I saw in town?" Paris had exactly $183 to her name. She should take advantage of the meal card she had tucked inside the new back-pack she'd bought at the bookstore yesterday with scholarship money, but she'd been dying to try the spice-flavored frozen coffee she'd seen advertised in the window. Zach hated coffee.

"The Java Hut?" At Paris's nod, Cassidy added, "Sure, why not. Then I'll take you by the newspaper office and introduce you around."

"You know the people at the newspaper?" Paris was good with computers. Maybe she could get a job there if the one with the associate dean didn't work out.

"Sure do. My sister's worked there for like, forever."

"Really?" Cassidy's sister had seemed nice and had acted as if she'd liked her. Maybe she'd even put in a good word for her.

Cassidy swung her feet to the floor. "I grew up here. My house is just a couple blocks away. Hey, my sister is cooking Sunday dinner. You want to come? She's an awesome cook."

Despite her surprise, Paris shrugged. "Okay. Sure." She'd only met Cassidy and she was inviting her to her house? Where she came from, you just didn't do that kind of thing. She could be a psycho for all Cassidy knew. Not that she was, but still.

"If you live so close, why are you in this dump?" Paris asked with a sweep of her hand around the room. Concrete block walls painted a dull eggshell and ugly brown floor tiles. Cassidy's sister had added a few throw rugs in a deep rich blue, which did look nice, and had even promised to order curtains for their window, but the place was still stark and institutional.

"The illusion of independence," Cassidy said with a quick grin. She crossed the small dorm room to the smaller closet, where she'd stowed her backpack. "I can't afford my own apartment, so this is the next best thing."

Paris slid off the bed and followed Cassidy out the door,

tugging it closed and making sure it locked behind her. She didn't have much worth taking, but what she did have she didn't want anyone stealing. When you didn't have much to lose, it hurt like hell when you lost it.

"So," Paris asked once they were out of the ancient brick building, "you got a boyfriend?"

"Had," Cassidy said. "He got a football scholarship to Texas A and M. Long distance relationships are the pits, so we decided to see other people."

"Meaning he wants to screw around and didn't want to feel guilty about it."

Cassidy slid a glance in Paris's direction. "That's what Paige said, too." Cassidy shrugged. "Whatever. Your boyfriend seems nice."

"Zach?" Paris thought about it for a minute, then said, "He's okay. But he can be a jerk sometimes."

They cut through the administration building, then took the steps down to the quad. Paris lifted her face toward the sun, enjoying the warmth on her skin. She'd never seen a sky quite as blue as the one above her. "Is it always like this? Always so clear?"

Cassidy laughed. "Wait until winter. You'll be dying to see a blue sky."

Sounded a lot like Oakland to her. That was one gray city. But all that was behind her now. She had her whole life to look forward to, and she was determined to make something of it. No matter what it took.

AINSLEY KNEW FROM the time she was eleven years old she wanted to be a reporter. The more generous folks in town had smiled, said she had an inquisitive nature, and paid a nickel for her computer-generated newspaper. Others, and there were a whole lot more of them, had called her Nosey Nell and plunked down their nickels anyway.

She'd started her career in print by creating her own weekly newspaper using her dad's computer. Filled mostly with local gossip tidbits, the paper was initially free. But when her dad had told her she needed to start paying for her own computer paper, she'd begun charging her customers. Her distribution had dropped a bit, but she hadn't been too discouraged. She'd just turned to more hard-hitting news and her circulation numbers grew.

Her article about the time one of Mrs. Greenway's earlier Jack Russell terriers had bitten the gas meter reader had caused quite a stir, especially when her neighbor, Mrs. Greenway, was issued a fine by the city for allowing her dogs to run without a leash. The piece she'd written about the time Tess Applebaum had kicked Jerry Bailey's sorry butt on the playground during recess had resulted in her friend getting into trouble with her parents for fighting. Tess had refused to speak to Ainsley for an entire month. Again, she hadn't minded—too much—since she'd made a nice profit that week on newspaper sales.

Once she'd been old enough to hold a job, she'd taken the next logical step and had applied for a position at the *Serenity Heights Sentinel*. Her delusions of grandeur had quickly been quashed, however, when Dylan Bradley, the *Sentinel*'s owner, had given her a part-time job as a general office clerk and not the reporter position she'd been so sure would be hers.

Disappointed but not discouraged, Ainsley told herself she was paying her dues by learning the newspaper business from the ground up. She'd kept writing her articles, sniffing out a story with all the skill of an olfactory-challenged bloodhound. Dylan had been amused by her efforts, but kindly offered advice, sending her back for rewrite after rewrite. Finally, during her senior year of high school, she'd had her first op-ed piece printed in the *Sentinel*.

By the time she'd gone off to college she'd been overflowing with even more dreams. Her first year at the University of Pittsburgh had been filled with journalism classes in addition to her general ed requirements, and a job on the school newspaper. But her ambitions came to a screeching halt early one spring morning when her parents got in the car accident.

Her father had managed to hold on for three days, and her mother had lasted another two months in a vegetative state before the doctors had finally convinced Ainsley there was no hope left. Regardless of how unfair it had been to lay that kind of burden on the shoulders of a nineteen-year-old, the decision, they'd told her, had been hers.

Thereafter, her life had been irrevocably altered. Both of her parents had been only children. There were no relatives for the Brennan sisters to rely on, so the care and responsibility for her two younger sisters, then thirteen-year-old Paige and seven-year-old Cassidy, had fallen to her. There'd been small life insurance policies, which had paid for the funerals and most of the copayments on the medical bills, so they hadn't exactly been destitute. Monthly Social Security payments for her sisters since they were still minors had helped cover the mortgage of the decades-old colonial her parents had bought the year Ainsley was born. Still, there were living expenses, the basics like utilities, groceries, and incidentals. Having no other choice but to give up her own dreams, she'd quit school, moved home, and become the primary caregiver for her younger sisters.

Life hadn't been easy back then, especially in the beginning. She'd been encouraged by a particularly unsympathetic social worker to place her sisters in foster care, but she'd adamantly refused. Paige and Cassidy were her sisters. They were a family and she'd sworn they'd remain together. She and her sisters had had their share of squabbles over the years, but they'd stuck together, a fact Ainsley couldn't help be proud of.

She'd gotten her old job at the *Sentinel* back, only this time as a secretary. After a few years, she'd enrolled at the U on a part-time basis to finish up her journalism degree.

While she'd officially been a reporter for the *Sentinel* going on four years now, her boss tended to treat her as if she were still his secretary. If she'd learned anything since her parents' death, it was how to play nice. She hadn't wanted to give social services any excuse to remove her sisters from her care, and she'd needed her job, so she swallowed her pride and smiled until her face ached, since it meant holding together what was left of her family.

As of this morning, Cassidy had finally entered college, giving Ainsley her first taste of real freedom in eleven years. And for the first time in too long, she planned to do exactly what she wanted, when she wanted. She loved her sisters and had proved time and again she'd do anything for them, but she wanted her own life, even if she was eleven years behind schedule.

Ainsley turned her ten-year-old Ford Taurus onto the dirt road that would take her out to Big Rock Clearing. Navigating the deep ruts dug into the well-used road, she passed under a canopy of trees still lush with green that wouldn't begin to turn with the brilliance of autumn for at least another month. As she rounded the final bend, she spied two police cruisers blocking the road.

A surge of adrenaline rushed through her, kicking up her heart rate. Excitement settled into her bones. This is what she loved about being a reporter. That sense of discovery about to happen, of finding answers to the questions that always seemed to be floating through her mind.

Too bad it didn't happen all that often. Not that she was thrilled that a dead body had shown up in their quiet little town, but she'd spent so much of her career reporting on grand openings, church bazaars, and the goings on at the U or the high school that she sometimes wondered if she would even know a *real* story when she saw one.

She parked to the left of the white cruisers, beneath the shade of a majestic old sugar maple with wide-reaching branches. Grabbing her digital camera out of the bag that contained her notepad and a tape recorder, she left the car and surveyed the scene.

In addition to the two cruisers blocking the road, she spied a white van with "Cuyahoga County Coroner" printed in big black block lettering on the side. There were two SUVs, one black with no identifying information that she could see, and a dark, marine blue Dodge Durango that she knew belonged to the new acting chief, Beckett Raines. To the far right of the vehicles was another police cruiser with two young boys in the backseat, and Charlie Gabriel, one of the cops on the Serenity Heights police force, leaning against the side near the rear door.

She snapped a few shots of the area, focusing on the two boys in the back of the cruiser and the coroner's van. Tucking the digital camera into the pocket of her cropped brown linen blazer, she grabbed her notepad and headed across the makeshift parking area toward the boys.

The windows of the cruiser were rolled down in deference to the warmth of the late summer day. "Hi, boys," she called out as she approached. They looked in her direction with wide eyes filled with apprehension, but didn't offer a greeting in return. They were young, probably had yet to see their thirteenth birthdays, and were undoubtedly spooked by their unexpected discovery.

Charlie turned and circled the vehicle, effectively blocking her view of the boys. He was as wide as an oak, and nearly as tall, physical traits that had served him well during his heyday as a defensive lineman with the Cleveland Browns. "Ainsley," he said with a slight inclination of his head. "What can I do for you?"

"I understand you're having quite an interesting morning."

Charlie's grin appeared just as quickly as it disappeared. "No comment."

She slipped off her sunglasses, tucked them in her jacket pocket, and gave Charlie one of her best smiles. "I already know a woman's body has been discovered," she said. "You got an ID yet?"

Charlie crossed his massive arms across his equally massive chest. "No comment," he repeated.

She let out a sigh. "Come on, Charlie. Give me something. I have a deadline." It was a stretch, since the upcoming issue of the *Sentinel* had already gone to press for release on Thursday, but she didn't bother to remind him of that minor detail.

"There is no story."

"Are you serious?" she asked with a laugh. "An unidentified body is discovered in Serenity Heights? That's news. Besides, anyone with a police scanner already knows about it. You think this town isn't already buzzing with speculation? I heard it from Lisa Williams, who heard it from Darla Fitzpatrick, who heard it from Nita Morgan."

Charlie let go of a windy sigh. "Look, Ainsley, I'd like to help you out, but the chief will have my ass if I talk to you."

Ainsley knew a blue wall when she smacked into one, and Charlie wasn't going to give her so much as the victim's hair color, not with the new acting chief looking over his shoulder. She'd met Beckett Raines. The guy was intimidation personified without even trying. It was his eyes, she'd decided when she'd interviewed him shortly after his arrival in town. He had a way of looking at a person with that clear green gaze filled with an intensity that made her feel as if she'd been stripped bare and exposed. Vulnerable. And *she'd* been the one asking the questions.

"Is he here?" she asked Charlie.

"Over at the crime scene." Charlie inclined his head toward the worn dirt path that disappeared behind a copse of trees leading to the clearing with the big rock, hence its name, Big Rock Clearing. "The captain, crime scene flunkies, and the coroner are with him."

And the dead body, but neither of them stated that fact.

"I suppose you won't let me talk to them, either," she said, looking pointedly at the two boys in the back of the cruiser.

"Sorry. They're material witnesses at this point."

"Can I at least get their names?"

Charlie frowned. "Come on, Ainsley. You know the rules. They're minors. Not without their parents' permission."

Well, this was going nowhere fast. The cops on the force liked her and until today had always been helpful, giving her the information she needed. Of course a dead body on their turf was hardly on the same scale as a couple of junior Robin Hoods or a frat party gone wild.

She reached into her pocket and her fingers brushed against the metal casing of her digital camera. She hid a smile as she pulled her sunglasses from her pocket and slipped them back on before taking out her camera again. "Mind if I get a few shots of the area?" she asked innocently.

Charlie shrugged. "I don't see what harm it'll do. No shots of the kids and stay off the path to the clearing," he warned.

She flashed Charlie another winning smile. "I wouldn't dream of going near it." With the exception of her brief time at Pitt, she'd lived in Serenity Heights all her life. There was more than one way to the clearing.

BECK WALKED FROM the edge of the clearing, steering clear of the trio of CSIs as they marked and photographed everything from footprints to broken twigs if they thought it could possibly be considered evidence. Julia Reiki, one of the coroner's pathologists, crouched near the body, with Nathan Eisner, a Cuyahoga County assistant district attorney, standing a good five feet behind her. Upwind, Beck noticed, too.

Julia, a petite forty-something half Asian, half African-American with sleek black hair and a figure that could put most twenty-year-olds to shame, stood and signaled for Beck to join her. "I can't determine time of death until I get her on the table," she told Beck as he approached. "But my unofficial estimate is at least two to three weeks. There's a lot of decomposition here, Beck, even though the body was frozen for a time and is definitely thawing out."

"He must've tossed her in the deep freeze when she started to stink," Beck said. A fact that caused him to wonder what kind of place the perp had that he could keep a body around that long without someone complaining of the stench. A place in the country? Serenity Heights not only consisted of quaint homes in quiet little neighborhoods, but also stretched as far as the Lorain County border with homes on acreage dotting the countryside.

"He?" Eisner questioned. "You know that for certain, Raines?"

"I haven't seen any footprints out here that could've been made by a woman," Beck explained.

Eisner said nothing, just nodded slowly. He also, Beck couldn't help noticing, refused to look at the body.

"Your perp must've swept the area," Julia suggested, carefully lifting the long, floor-length skirt of the dress to reveal a pair of silver, strappy sandals embellished with blue gemstones. "It's obvious she was carried here and dumped. You see the bottoms of her shoes? They're as new as the day they came out of the box."

Beck made a note of Julia's findings. He had a list of various items to piece together later that would hopefully give him a better picture of the unknown subject, or UNSUB, he'd be tracking. No detail was too insignificant in his opinion. The devil, as the saying goes, is in the details, and a break in a case often came from some obscure detail.

"He had to carry her from the dirt road," Beck said. "The path is too narrow for a vehicle."

"And no tire tracks?" Eisner questioned. "What about the parking area?"

"Plenty of tire tracks there," Beck told him. "The techs will photograph and measure. If anything stands out, I'll know about it."

"But you're sure the killer is male?" Eisner asked.

"As sure as I can be at this point," Beck told him. "The vic weighs probably one-fifteen, maybe one-hundred twenty pounds. This place is at least three-tenths of a mile from the dirt road. Most guys could easily carry a woman of that size, but it's doubtful an average-sized female would be able to do it."

Julia walked over to where Beck stood with Nathan. "We'll get her photographed, then I'll bag her and take her to the morgue. I'll call you later with a cause of death."

"What's your initial impression?" Eisner asked Julia.

Julia turned and looked back at the body again before answering. "Best guess is strangulation. But there's a puncture wound on her arm. Looks like from an IV, so maybe she was overdosed." She looked at Beck. "You do realize the damage to the body is extensive. And she was alive when it was done. Whether or not she was conscious, though, is anyone's guess. For her sake, I pray she passed out before he started in on her."

The response hovering on Beck's tongue stilled when he heard a sharp gasp, followed by a quietly spoken F-bomb. He turned to find the reporter from the *Sentinel* who'd interviewed him when he'd first come to town, Ainsley something, standing less than three feet away from the body.

Shit! Just what he didn't need or want. The damn press

snooping around. Okay, so maybe the *Sentinel* wasn't the *Los Angeles Times* or the *Herald,* and Ainsley whatever-her-last-name-was wasn't even in the same stratosphere as the news-hungry bastards he'd dealt with on a day to day basis, but he knew from experience reporters were still a pain in the ass regardless of where they worked. He had no desire to deal with the press at the moment, particularly the sexy as hell reporter who'd just contaminated his crime scene.

"Don't move," Beck ordered her before she could do any serious damage.

"Oh, I . . ." The color drained from her face, her big blue eyes wide as she looked at him. "I'm sorry," she managed on a strangled cry seconds before she spun around and tossed her cookies.

"Oh geeze," Eisner muttered, looking a little green around the edges himself.

"I'll see about getting that body transported," Julia said, not bothering to hide her smirk.

"Dammit." Beck crossed the clearing. "How the hell did you get here?" he demanded when he reached Ainsley's side.

Bent over, with one hand braced on her knee for support and the other holding back a length of wavy blond hair, Ainsley retched again. "I didn't expect that," she said, her voice muffled.

He reached into his hip pocket and pulled out a handkerchief. "Here," he said sharply, then let out an impatient breath. "You waltz onto a crime scene. What did you expect to find?"

"Thank you." She took the handkerchief he offered and gave him a curious look as she wiped at her mouth. "I didn't know anyone used these any more."

Yeah, he knew it was old school, but his mom had been an old-fashioned girl at heart and had taught him to always carry a handkerchief. The habit stuck. "What are you doing here? This area is off limits."

"I was only told to stay off the path."

Beck narrowed his gaze. "How did you get here?"

"Would you happen to have some bottled water?"

"You didn't answer the question." He didn't bother to ask her *why* she was here. That much was obvious. She was sniffing out a story, but he had no intention of making it easy on her.

"The north trail." She brushed a stray leaf from her jacket sleeve. "I don't think it's been used in years, but it's still passable."

"Show me."

"Over there," she said, pointing to a break in the brush at the far north end of the clearing.

"You stay put," Beck told her, then went to speak to one of the crime scene technicians, all the while keeping Ainsley in his line of vision. She pulled a notebook from her pocket and motioned for Eisner to join her. The ADA looked at Ainsley, then at the body a mere few feet away. He was having none of it. Neither was Ainsley for that matter. Julia was more than close enough, busy laying out a body bag next to the victim's remains.

Finished with the technician who headed in the direction Ainsley had indicated in search of possible evidence, Beck returned to Ainsley. "I'm going to have to ask you to leave," he said.

"I realize you have a job to do, Chief Raines, but so do I. Have you identified the victim?"

"Deputy Chief," he said automatically. "And no comment."

"Can you give me the cause of death?"

He crossed his arms over his chest. "Look, Ms . . ."

"Brennan," she said, not the least bit intimidated. "Ainsley Brennan. Do you have any leads in the case?"

He frowned, even though he secretly admired her determination. "When I have something to report, I'll give you a call."

One pale eyebrow hitched skyward. "Does that mean you have no leads in the case?"

"No comment," he said, deepening his frown.

She frowned right back at him. "You're not being very cooperative."

"And you're testing my patience, Ms. Brennan. I have a job to do and you need to leave my crime scene. Now."

"Actually, I came out here to talk to you."

"Maybe next time," he said, then crooked his finger at her. "This way."

"I have something you might find interesting."

Against his better judgment, he quickly swept her body with his gaze. She had plenty he might find interesting—if he was interested, which he wasn't. "Yeah? And what's that?"

"An audio file. I have a feeling it's from the killer."

CHAPTER 3

"WHAT DO YOU mean they aren't related?" Ainsley flung herself into the chair opposite Beck's desk and glared at him. Her blue eyes sparkled with a mixture of indignation and disbelief, catching his interest in ways he hadn't imagined possible. It was too soon for him to be interested in another woman. Especially the wrong woman. Especially a member of the press. Especially when they were natural born enemies.

"There is no evidence to link the audio file to the body found today," he explained as he dropped into his own chair. He did have his suspicions on the matter, he just wasn't willing to share that kind of information with the press quite yet.

She blew out a stream of breath indicating her frustration. "I suppose you're going to tell me that audio file is nothing more than a prank." Her gaze narrowed. "Well, it won't fly. Not after what I saw at the clearing today."

Beck wished the audio file Ainsley had received was nothing more than a sick prank, but after listening to it three times, even without conclusive proof, he knew it was no joke. Before calling her into his office, he'd had the CD dusted for prints, then packaged it up to be delivered to the crime lab, where the sound engineers could take a crack at it.

There'd only been one set of prints on the actual CD, which he suspected were Ainsley's. Same story with the envelope she'd also provided him—only two sets of prints, Ainsley's and most likely those of the receptionist at the *Sentinel*. Neither of which were in the department's database, but once both women volunteered their prints for comparison, he'd know for certain.

Her tote bag hit the floor with a thud. "It's real. Give me that much at least," she said, twisting the top off the bottle of water she'd purchased from the vending machine upon arriving at the station. She looked at him expectantly as she took a tentative sip of water.

Before he could respond, she narrowed those blue eyes of hers again and added, "And don't even think about insulting my intelligence by denying it or giving me that 'no comment' crap. It's real, dammit."

"I know you're looking for a story, but—"

"This isn't about a story," she interrupted. "This is about feeling safe in my own bed."

Beck shoved his hand through his hair; whether out of frustration or to erase the image of Ainsley in bed, he couldn't state with any degree of certainty. Unfortunately, he had his suspicions, which included visions of crisp sheets and tangled, sweaty limbs.

"You're a reporter. I'm a cop," he said. "It'll always be about the story." A lesson he'd learned the hard way and would do well not to forget, especially when she looked at him with those big blue eyes lined with a trace of fear, like she was doing now.

She remained silent, never taking her eyes off him as she took yet another sip of water. A strategy he was all too familiar with. Most people became uncomfortable and started rattling off information, anxious to fill the silence. Well, not him. He'd played this cat and mouse game with the press too many times to count. He had too much experience to be susceptible to such an obvious ploy.

As if he were nothing more than a greenhorn rookie, he asked, "Off the record?" Only a fool would believe that anything said to a member of the media was off the record.

Color me a fool.

She sat up a little straighter. "Do you promise to give me the exclusive on this story?"

She might be the most squeamish reporter he'd ever met, but he had a bad feeling she was determined to become the next pain in his ass, if the intent gleam in her eyes was any indication. "I don't see any other news agencies pounding down our door, do you?"

She leaned forward to set her water on his desk. The silky camisole she wore under her jacket gaped slightly, momentarily drawing his attention to a glimpse of creamy looking flesh.

He dragged his gaze away. It was too soon and she was the wrong person. If and when he finally felt ready to date again, it sure as hell wouldn't be with a member of the press. The fact that Ainsley could light up a room with her smile or dazzle him with her bluer-than-blue eyes meant squat.

Almost.

"You and I both know with a case like this, it's only a matter of time," she said. "Main Street will be clogged with news vans. Reporters will be swarming the streets."

"I don't see that happening," he said, although she did have a damn good point. Melodramatic, but a point, nonetheless. With the body at the morgue, it wouldn't take long before the Cleveland reporters working the crime beat started hounding him for a statement. Once word got out that the killer had sent an audio file, they could very well be overrun by the press as Ainsley predicted. The last thing he wanted to deal with right now was a media circus.

"Look," she continued, "I deserve the exclusive on this. The killer sent the audio file to me."

He really didn't like the way this conversation was headed. Hell, he didn't like that he was even considering her request. "What you are, Ms. Brennan, is what the prosecution will call a material witness. Isn't that a conflict of interest?"

"Ainsley," she said almost absently. "And no, it isn't. It wasn't a conflict of interest when Robert Graysmith reported on the letters he received from the Zodiac Killer, and neither is this. It gives me the inside scoop, just like it did Graysmith."

Beck leaned back in his chair. In his opinion, members of the press were nothing but a pack of hungry jackals, but he wasn't opposed to using the media to his advantage. Such a relationship always came with a price. What price would Ainsley exact from him? How would she betray his trust? He didn't doubt for a minute she would if it meant getting what she wanted—a story.

"What if I asked you not to report on the audio file just yet?" he asked. "Could you do that?"

She hefted her tote bag onto her lap and started rifling through the contents. "Mind if I ask why?"

"For one, we don't know that the audio file is even related to the victim discovered today."

She looked up at him, suspicion evident in her eyes. "Don't bullshit me. I saw the body. I heard the recording. How can they not be related?"

"Until I have evidence to prove otherwise, I can't assume these two incidents are anything more than a coincidence," he said. Forget the fact that when it came to murder investigations, he didn't believe in leaving anything to chance. If there was a connection he'd find it. "If we release this kind of information without conclusive proof that the two incidents *are* related, it's going to do nothing but get a lot of good people in this town upset and nervous."

She pulled a notepad from the tote. "People are already talking about the discovery of the body," she pointed out. "Believe me, the gossip mill is working overtime by now."

Didn't he know it. Raelynn, the department's administrative assistant and general go-to-girl, had peppered him with questions the minute he'd returned to the station, as had Joyce and Caroline, the two dispatchers currently on duty.

"I don't doubt it," he said. "But if we withhold the information about the audio file for now, then we might be able to avoid a panic."

"And releasing that information might make people at least think about locking their doors tonight. I don't see the harm if it keeps people safe."

"You don't see the harm because you've never conducted a murder investigation," he argued. "The last thing I need right now is a bunch of angry, frightened citizens demanding my time when I need to expend my efforts on capturing whoever did this."

"So you think the killer is a local?"

Beck rubbed at the knot of tension forming in the back of his neck. "Off the record?" he asked again.

She bit her lower lip, then finally nodded. "Okay," she said. "Off the record."

"Yeah," he said. "I think he *could* be a local. Maybe not someone who actually lives in Serenity Heights, but someone who's familiar with the area."

"Someone who chose the clearing because they knew the body would be discovered quickly," she surmised.

That hint of fear returned to her eyes, giving his protective instincts a hard nudge. Which had nothing whatsoever to do with the fact that he couldn't seem to keep his gaze off the gentle slope of her breasts. He was, after all, a cop. It was his job to protect and serve.

"All right," she said as she dug into her tote bag and produced a pen. "Nothing on the audio file, but do I have your word when you want the information released, I get the exclusive?"

"Agreed," he said. "You'll be the first to run with the story."

"Now will you answer some questions for me?"

If she hadn't presented him with the audio file, they wouldn't even be having this conversation. And she sure as hell wouldn't be sitting across from him looking all sweet and determined to get a statement from him. "I'll give you five minutes."

"Do you have an ID on the body?"

"No."

"What about cause of death?"

"The coroner's office will be providing me with the exact cause of death once an autopsy has been performed."

Her gaze turned skeptical. "I think you can do better than that. Weren't you a homicide detective before you came here?"

"I have my own opinions, but they aren't confirmed."

"What is your opinion on the cause of death?"

"Next question."

Her perfectly arched eyebrows drew together in a frown. "You aren't being very cooperative."

"And you're wasting precious minutes."

"What about time of death?"

"The coroner's office will be providing me with that information once the autopsy has been performed."

"Any idea on why the killer removed the victim's fingers?"

"You saw that?"

A slight blush colored her cheeks. "And then some," she said, her tone dry.

His lips twitched. "No comment."

"How about an estimate on the victim's age?"

"We'll know that once we get a positive ID on the body."

She shot him a look filled with irritation. "No ID. No confirmed cause of death. No time of death. Is there anything about this case you *do* know, Chief?"

He really didn't appreciate her sarcasm. Leaning forward, he gave her a hard stare. "I think we're done here."

"Wait a minute. You promised . . ."

He stood. "Good-bye, Ms. Brennan."

She let out a puff of breath filled with frustration. "It's Ainsley," she said. "And I still have two minutes left."

"Not any more you don't." He started for the door, nearly colliding with Raelynn as she barreled into his office carrying an aluminum cake pan.

"We got another one," Raelynn said, walking over to his desk to deposit the cake pan.

Dread rippled through him.

"Another body?" Ainsley asked.

"No, thank heavens," Raelynn answered. "Carrot cake. Emily Wilmont just dropped it off."

"I've heard you've been overrun with baked goods," Ainsley said, a becoming smile curving her mouth.

Raelynn laughed. "It's been ridiculous around here." She adjusted the wireless headset to slip a stray lock of chin-length, reddish-gold hair behind her ear. "Hey. I think I can get a sitter for Friday night. Wanna have dinner and hit the martini bar?"

"Sure," Ainsley said. "Sounds like a plan."

Beck frowned. So, Raelynn was Ainsley's "inside source" quoted in her articles about the petty crimes that occurred around town. He'd have to put a stop to that right quick. "I take it you two know each other."

"Oh yeah," Raelynn said with a nod. "Since before kindergarten. Our moms were close friends."

Ainsley flashed him a brief grin. "Welcome to Serenity Heights."

Yeah, he knew. A town where nothing bad ever happened and everyone knew your business.

Raelynn held up her hand, giving the universal "just a minute" signal before pressing the button on her headset. "Raelynn," she said, then paused. "Sure, I'll tell him. Thanks, Caroline."

Raelynn looked at Beck. Worry filled her doelike brown eyes. "A nonemergency call just came in from the dean of students at the U," she said. "A freshman girl has been reported missing."

MATTIE DAVENPORT PLAYED the cello, was a volleyball star, and collected ceramic frog figurines. Until she'd left home a week ago to attend the U, she'd never been out of the state of Mississippi.

While holding the cell phone to her ear, Ainsley jotted down the telephone number of Mattie's best friend from her hometown. "And you said Jackie hasn't heard from Mattie, either?" she asked Mattie's mother.

"Not that I know of," Erin Davenport said tearfully.

From the snapshot Ainsley had lifted from Mattie's dorm room when she'd gone to speak to Mattie's roommate, Mattie was a pretty girl, complete with megawatt smile and laughing blue eyes. She was young and petite with straight blond hair. And she was missing.

The photograph, placed in a whimsical frame surrounded by brightly colored musical notes, showed Mattie dressed in a royal blue cap and gown, flanked on both sides by parents beaming with pride. The two other young women in the photograph bore a striking resemblance to Mattie. One had a swollen belly, obviously in the late stages of pregnancy, but both looked tired, the kind of tiredness that belied their young ages.

The third of three daughters, Mattie had dared to buck family tradition and follow her own dream of becoming a concert cellist. She'd said no to marrying her high school sweetheart, and had refused to take a job at the local fishery like her older sisters. From the conversation Ainsley had with Mattie's roommate, Rebecca Rivers, Mattie had wanted as far away from the small Mississippi gulf town as she could get. She went against her parents' wishes that she at least attend Mississippi State, and instead had accepted a partial music scholarship to Serenity Heights University.

According to Erin Davenport, mother and daughter spoke daily. "We told her not to move so far away from home," Erin said. "I just knew something like this would happen."

Seated on a stone bench outside the dormitory complex where Mattie had resided, Ainsley tapped her pen against the notepad balanced on her thigh. A warm breeze stirred the leaves of the cottonwood above her and blew her hair into her eyes, but she ignored it and gripped her cell phone a little tighter. "You're sure Mattie didn't have a boyfriend?"

"Of course not," Erin said, sounding somewhat offended by the suggestion. "She's only been in Ohio less than a week. Mattie isn't that kind of girl. Besides, I spoke to her three days ago. She would've mentioned if there was some boy."

Right, Ainsley thought. And how many freshmen had she known from similar circumstances? Enough to know that when the mouse got away from the constantly hovering cat, she often went a little wild.

"What about friends?" Ainsley asked. "Did she mention any one in particular during your daily phone calls?"

"Rebecca," Mattie's mother said. "I don't remember her last name."

"Rivers," Ainsley supplied. "Rebecca Rivers. She's also a music major."

"That's right," Erin said, her voice thick with a Southern drawl. "Mattie said she was a fiddle player."

Mattie had been lucky. For the short time Ainsley had been at Pitt, her roommate had been a physics major with whom she'd had little in common. They'd gotten along fine, but had never been all that close.

"Mrs. Davenport, when did you first suspect your daughter might be missing?"

"Two days ago. Since she left for school, we talked every day," she said again. "When Mattie didn't call yesterday, I was worried. I called the school, but they weren't no help. Classes ain't started yet, so they got no official attendance records. I just don't know where she could've gone off to, or why she wouldn't call home. Not unless somethin' was wrong."

Ainsley had a pretty good idea and it sickened her.

Day One.

Was Mattie's voice the one she'd heard begging for mercy on that audio file? She glanced at the framed family photograph again and her stomach clenched. She wanted to offer words of comfort to Mattie's mother, wanted to say something to try to set the woman's mind at ease, but words evaded her. What could she possibly say that wouldn't sound hollow, especially when she, too, feared the outcome?

"We have a top notch police department, Mrs. Davenport," she managed. "I know they'll do everything possible to find your daughter." Hopefully alive, but Ainsley kept that thought to herself.

As if on cue, Beckett Raines exited the old brick administration building across the area known as the quad. By his side was Mary Ann Chesterfield, the recently appointed dean of students. Following closely behind, Devin McElvoy, the assistant dean of students, along with Reid Pomeroy, the head of the music department. They were headed in her direction.

Ainsley tucked the framed photograph back into her tote bag, then stood. "Mrs. Davenport, I'll call again if I learn something. In the meantime, if you can think of anything that might be useful, please don't hesitate to call me."

"I will. Thank you," Erin Davenport said. "And when will your paper print Mattie's story?"

"Our next edition," Ainsley said, hating the fact that it could be too late for Mattie by the time the next edition of the *Sentinel* was released. She'd have to speak with her boss. Maybe after she presented the facts he'd agree to run a special edition. "But we'll have Mattie's picture on our Web site by tonight."

She slung her tote bag over her shoulder and started toward Beck and his grim-looking entourage. "Thank you again for your time. I'll be in touch," she said, then disconnected the call before dropping the phone into her tote bag.

She exchanged her notepad for her tape recorder, hit the record button, and thrust the recorder at Mary Ann Chesterfield. "Do you have any idea when Mattie Davenport was abducted?"

The dean stopped short. "Abducted?" She cast a sharp glance in Beck's direction. "No one said anything about an abduction."

"That's because we don't know that it is an abduction," Beck said, his tone the epitome of cool detachment. She didn't understand how he could be so calm, given the circumstances.

"And how many other students have been reported missing?" Ainsley asked, thinking of the body discovered at the clearing. She immediately envisioned the ravaged corpse, only with Mattie Davenport's megawatt smile and laughing blue eyes.

The dean looked at Beck, then at the two men standing behind her. "What other students?" she asked, her confusion apparent. McElvoy shook his head at the dean's questioning glance. Pomeroy looked as confused and startled as Dean Chesterfield.

Obviously they didn't know about the body that had

been discovered that morning. *Strange,* Ainsley thought. She would've thought by now that the news would be all over town. "Then you're saying that the entire student body has been accounted for?" she asked.

When the dean merely stared at her, McElvoy stepped forward to answer her question. "That would be difficult, Ms. Brennan. Not all students reside on campus," he said. The wind kicked up again, ruffling his neatly combed blond hair, which then settled back down as if it'd never been touched. "But those in residence will be accounted for shortly."

"What measures have you put in place to protect the students?" Ainsley asked him. "Why haven't you ordered the U locked down?"

Suddenly Beck was standing in front of her, looking down at her with those green eyes of his boring into her. Her tummy fluttered.

"No comment," he said in that same cool voice she was beginning to detest. Only the hardness of those damn, tummy-flutter-inducing green eyes conveyed his displeasure.

McElvoy offered her a patient smile. "We'll be ordering additional security to patrol the dormitories," he said, ignoring Beck's unspoken warning to keep quiet. "As a precaution, of course. We believe Ms. Davenport's alleged disappearance is merely an isolated incident."

"So you think foul play is involved?" she asked him.

"We have no way of knowing that, Ms. Brennan. We only learned of Ms. Davenport's alleged disappearance." He turned slightly and gestured to Reid Pomeroy. "Perhaps Dr. Pomeroy can offer some insight. He met with Ms. Davenport the day of her disappearance."

"We really should be going," Beck said, attempting to steer the faculty away from Ainsley. He turned and started toward the dormitory. His entourage followed dutifully along.

Ainsley hurried after them, grateful to be out of range of

Beck's intense gaze. "Dr. Pomeroy," she said, thrusting her recorder at him as she trotted alongside the forty-something department head, "what's your relationship to Mattie Davenport?"

"I'm her advisor," he said.

"When did you last see her?"

"We had a meeting in my office two days ago," Pomeroy answered.

She zeroed her attention on Beck. "Chief Raines, is Dr. Pomeroy a suspect in this case?"

Pomeroy halted. "Suspect?" he blurted, alarm evident in his voice. His soft brown eyes rounded and he went pale. "I'm a suspect?"

"There is no evidence a crime has been committed," Beck said.

Ainsley's irritation with Beck climbed another notch. The man obviously didn't know the meaning of giving an inch. "Do you honestly think this is just another coincidence?" she asked him.

Dean Chesterfield suddenly looked as stunned as Pomeroy. "Coincidence? What is she talking about? What coincidence? Is there another girl missing that I don't know about?"

"It's nothing." Beck fired another heated glare in Ainsley's direction. "Why don't you go on to the dorm and find the RA. I'll be along in a minute." His long, warm fingers slipped around Ainsley's arm as he kept her from following the group to the dorm.

Electrical sparks traveled down her arm, making her fingertips tingle. She frowned.

"A word, Ms. Brennan."

"But . . ." But she couldn't think straight with him holding on to her. Why wouldn't he let go? And why in the hell wouldn't her body stop humming with unexpected awareness?

"Just what do you think you're doing?" he asked once the others were out of earshot. "I thought we had a deal."

She tugged her arm from his grasp. Her ability to string coherent phrases together depended on it. "Our deal was that I wouldn't run a story on the audio file."

"Our deal was that you'd keep it quiet."

"I didn't say a word about the audio file."

"You're dangerously close to causing an unnecessary panic. You have no facts to support the conclusions you're jumping to."

"Don't you dare tell me this is just another coincidence," she said. "And I have plenty of facts. A dead body. A missing girl. And an audio file with a woman's tortured screams."

"And there isn't a shred of evidence to connect any of it."

"These are not isolated incidents," she argued. He couldn't be that obtuse. Stubborn, she didn't doubt, but Beckett Raines was not a dumb guy. That much she did know.

"Stay out of my investigation," he said.

Her eyebrows winged upward. "Are you threatening me, Chief?"

He leaned toward her, which in her opinion screamed threat. In big ol' capital letters, too.

"No," he said, using that cool, detached voice that made her want to grit her teeth, or kick him in the shins. "I'm making you a promise. Interfere with my investigation and I'll arrest your sweet little ass for obstruction of justice."

"You can't do that."

He smiled then, the way a snake might smile at a nice fat little mouse it was about to swallow. "Ainsley?" he said leaning closer. "I'm the acting chief of police. I can do anything I want."

CHAPTER 4

AINSLEY STARED AT her boss, momentarily stunned. "A flyer?" she asked incredulously. She couldn't have heard him right. A young girl was missing and as the only newspaper in town, he was suggesting she make up a flyer?

"You mean like the kind people put up on telephone poles?" she asked. "Or in store windows when the family cat goes missing?"

Dylan Bradley tossed a stack of pink message slips on his desk, then draped his corduroy sport coat, complete with leather elbow patches, over the back of his big black leather chair. "I'm sorry, Ainsley," he said, not sounding the least bit contrite but very much like a tightfisted accountant. "Running a special edition isn't an option."

"But this is a good story," Ainsley argued, dropping into the worn guest chair opposite Dylan's desk. The kind of story she'd been waiting her entire career as a journalist to report.

"An important story," she continued. "I have a couple of facts to check, but I could have it ready in a matter of hours. Couldn't we at least do an insert for this week's edition?"

Dylan let out a long gusty sigh. "It just isn't cost effective."

"There's a girl missing, Dylan. Doesn't that mean something to you?"

Dylan's slim eyebrows collided in a frown that deepened the creases of his forehead. "Of course it does," he said, sounding insulted. "Look, circulation has been down for months. If it weren't for the loyalty of our regular advertisers, we'd be in serious trouble."

Didn't she know it. She couldn't remember the last time she'd had a raise. "People are going to be clamoring for information," she told him. "This is the most important incident we've had to report on in a long time. Between the missing girl and the body that was dumped at the clearing, we have real news to report for a change."

"I know," Dylan said.

"And if the *Sentinel* doesn't provide it," Ainsley said, "people are going to go elsewhere for the story."

She had a point, and they both knew it. If the Sentinel didn't give readers what they were looking for, then they'd be snapping up copies of the *Plain Dealer* or tuning in to the local news broadcasts for information on the hottest topic to climb the Serenity Heights grapevine in years.

Dylan really wasn't a bad guy. He'd taught her the finer points of reporting and how to get the most out of an interview or a witness. She had a lot of respect for him, but as the *Sentinel*'s owner as well as editor-in-chief the past couple of years, Dylan's view was that circulation figures and advertising dollars reigned supreme. Before taking over the *Sentinel* shortly before his father's retirement, Dylan had been a serious newspaper man working the crime beat for the *Plain Dealer,* the Cleveland area's major newspaper. Now he wrote sports features, the occasional op-ed piece, and kept the paper afloat with advertising dollars.

He shoved a hand through his thinning brown hair and blew out a stream of breath. "I know it's not perfect, but if you do up a flyer, we could insert it in Thursday's edition," he suggested. "At least that way we can let people know about the missing student."

It was better than nothing, but still wasn't enough, at least in her opinion. "But what about the story? There's more than just a missing co-ed here." She scooted to the edge of her chair and gave Dylan a level stare. "A woman's ravaged body was dumped at the clearing. I've got an audio file of what I'm convinced is a woman being tortured, and I'm betting there'll be another recording showing up soon. It's all connected, Dylan. I know it is."

He remained thoughtful, then finally asked, "Do you have proof?"

"I have a hunch."

A weary smile tugged briefly at Dylan's lips. He suddenly appeared every day of his fifty-eight years. "And it all starts with a hunch, doesn't it?"

Ainsley returned his smile. "So I've heard."

"Who's involved in the investigation?"

"Beck Raines." That weird tingle shot down her arm again, as if Beck had just touched her. She wiggled her fingers, but the strange sensation wouldn't go away and she frowned.

Dylan leaned back in his chair. "What about BCI? Have they been called in to assist?"

"The clearing was crawling with crime scene techs. Julia Reiki from the coroner's office was there, and someone from the DA's office. I'd have to check my notes."

"Will Raines confirm your facts?"

"The facts, probably." If she were lucky. Cooperation with the press wasn't exactly high on the acting chief's list of priorities. He certainly hadn't been too happy about her snooping around the U earlier today, either. "Whether or not the incidents are related—not a chance."

"All right," Dylan said, the resignation in his voice clear. "You get Raines to confirm that the incidents are related, and I'll approve a one-page insert. You've got until noon tomorrow to get the story on my desk."

Dylan glanced down at the message slips in front of him.

"Did you keep your appointment with the new owners of the Java Hut?"

"No," she said as she stood. "I heard about the body found at the clearing and went right out there. Then when I was interviewing Beck, I heard about the missing girl from the U. I've been busy chasing down the story."

Dylan crumbled the message slip and tossed it into the trash can beside his desk. "Go. I'll cover the Java Hut."

Ainsley grinned, then scooted out of Dylan's office before he changed his mind and sent her to cover the Java Hut interview. The situation wasn't perfect, but at least Dylan was willing to spend the money for an additional insert, provided she could get Beckett Raines to confirm that Mattie Davenport's disappearance and the body of the young woman found at the clearing were indeed related.

Right. And for her next miracle, she'd fix that nasty global warming problem.

BY ONE-THIRTY the next morning, Ainsley was no closer to solving the earth's global warming issues than she was to obtaining a statement from Beck connecting the disappearance of Mattie Davenport with the discovery of the young woman's body found at Big Rock Clearing. She'd left him several messages, but he had yet to return her calls. After she'd spent most of the evening perfecting her article, she'd even gone back to the station, but according to one of the night shift dispatchers, Beck was out of the office. She didn't buy it. Not when his SUV was parked in the lot out back of the station house after ten o'clock. The man was obviously avoiding her.

What she wanted to know was what he had against her. Okay, so maybe it wasn't her personally, at least as far as she knew, but he definitely had a beef with the press. Or maybe he just didn't like her?

Nah.

She'd caught him checking her out when she'd been in his office yesterday. And she hadn't really minded all that much. He was, after all, a pretty hot number. What girl wouldn't feel a little flattered?

She stifled a yawn. Too bad she couldn't do anything to ward off the chilly night air. She poured herself another cup of too strong coffee from the thermos she'd brought with her, then wrapped her fingers around the mug in a vain attempt to seek warmth.

Where was all that global warming when she needed it, anyway? Like tonight when she'd gotten the hare-brained idea to sit in her car, parked down the street from the *Sentinel* office where she could see the front entrance. Her digital camera was armed and ready to shoot on the off chance she actually spotted someone delivering another audio file to her office. She had a hunch that Day One implied this was only the beginning. Day One, at least in her mind, signaled the first of what she feared would be many. Thus, she fully expected to see the arrival of another CD, this time labeled Day Two.

The thought made her ill. She glanced down at the flyer peeking out of her tote bag. On it was a photocopy of a photo of a smiling Mattie Davenport that Officer Gardocki had handed her during the door-to-door search law enforcement had conducted earlier this evening. Tom Gardocki hadn't told her much, only asking her to contact the station if she had any information that might lead them to Mattie Davenport's whereabouts.

Another shiver rattled down her spine. Damn, but it had gotten cold, though she couldn't state with any degree of certainty that the tremor quaking through her had as much to do with the weather as it did with the thought of what could be happening at this very minute to the Davenport girl. Still, she refrained from turning on the heater since she couldn't do so without firing the engine or she'd end up with a dead battery.

She'd swear the temperature had dropped a good ten degrees while she'd been sitting in her car for the past two hours. Although it was only the last week of August, the overnight temperature had dipped to the low fifties, a sharp indicator that fall was just around the corner. And then winter.

She let out a sigh. Long, cold, dreary days, layered clothing, shoveling snow and chipping ice from the windshield of her car. Not exactly her idea of heaven, but other than relocation to Florida, she'd just have to keep shoveling snow. There was no way she'd move far from her sisters, anyway. Serenity Heights was home, and she'd struggled for too long to give it all up because of a few lousy feet of snow and freezing temperatures three or four months out of the year.

A pair of headlights suddenly flashed across her windshield as a car turned off Main Street and headed down Palm Avenue in her direction. Her heart rate picked up speed as the vehicle crept nearer. Scooting down in the front seat as it drew closer, she waited, then carefully craned her neck in an attempt to determine the vehicle make and model.

Another cop car. The third one tonight.

She let out the breath she'd been holding and straightened. What had she been thinking? She hadn't even brought a gun with her. Not that she even had ammunition for it, but that wasn't the point. How the hell was she supposed to protect herself if she did come face to face with the CD delivering creep? She did have a canister of pepper spray in her tote bag, not that she planned to get all that up close and personal with what she was convinced was a murderer, but something more deadly than pepper spray would certainly make her feel a whole lot more secure. Like a dog. And not one of those cute yappy types that her neighbor

Mrs. Greenway favored, but a real dog, with great big teeth and a scary growl. A dog who meant business.

She looked forward, keeping the door to the newspaper office in her line of vision as she quickly surveyed the area. With the exception of a porch light burning a block away, the end of the street was dark again. A dog barked somewhere in the distance, but quickly quieted down. Maybe she should just give it up and go home. With the extra patrols out tonight, there was the possibility that the killer was lying low anyway.

Someone rapped on the passenger side window and she jumped, slamming her knee into the steering column. She let go with a wicked curse as tepid coffee sloshed over her hand and dripped on her jeans. Oh God, he really was hand delivering the CD.

"Ms. Brennan? Roll down the window."

Relief rushed over her in waves the instant she recognized Beck's deep, commanding voice. She still muttered a few more choice words, just because he'd scared the crap out of her. He must've come up from behind her car, because she sure hadn't seen him or heard another vehicle. Yup, she needed a dog all right. One with better hearing than she obviously had, because she hadn't even heard Beck approach.

Instead of turning on the ignition to roll down the power windows in order to talk to him, she flipped the switch for the door locks, then moved her tote bag to the floorboard behind the passenger seat. "Come on in," she invited him when he opened the door.

He easily slid into the front seat. All of a sudden, her midsize car felt about as big as a cheap tin can.

"What are you doing here?" she asked him after a moment of temporary distraction, all because of the enticing scent of his spicy aftershave. How was it possible for the man to smell so darned good at nearly two in the morning?

"Funny," he said, a hint of mild amusement in his voice, "but that's what I was going to ask you."

She frowned at his attempt at humor—or had it been annoyance? "You scared the hell out of me."

"Consider yourself lucky," he said, amusement slipping to censure. "I could've been whoever it was you've been hoping to see."

The guy was good, she'd give him that much. From that arched brow and the all-too-knowing look in his intense gaze, she apparently hadn't fooled him one bit with her amateur surveillance routine.

"I was thinking the same thing," she admitted, then let out a breezy sigh. She indicated the thermos on the floorboard at his feet. "Coffee?"

"Thanks," he said. "I've had my limit."

Not much imagination was required for her to envision him sucking down the stuff by the gallon. Her story was important to her, but his job was easily a gazillion times more stressful. Especially now. "Was that you who drove by a few minutes ago?"

"No, it was Officer Jonas. He saw your car and called in to tell me you were still staked out by the newspaper office." He gave her another of those looks filled with censure. "Now, do you mind telling me what you hope to accomplish, other than getting yourself into a boatload of trouble?"

She drained what was left of her coffee. "Same thing you are, Chief," she said. "Looking for a bad guy."

He scrubbed his big hand down his face. "You're determined to interfere in my investigation, aren't you?"

She took exception to that, even if she couldn't deny the truth of it. "I have a job to do."

"So do I, and you're not making it any easier." That eyebrow winged upward again. "Twelve messages, Ainsley? You give new meaning to the word *tenacity*."

"I prefer diligent, but whatever," she quipped with a shrug. "Considering the stronger than usual police presence in town tonight, is it safe to say the door-to-door search didn't produce any leads?"

"Why is it every time you ask me a question, I get the feeling I'm being interviewed?"

She smiled at him. "Maybe you're paranoid."

"Maybe I know your type," he said without bothering to return her smile with one of his own.

The man had a grudge with the press. She could smell it. "Oh, and what type is that?" she asked. His type? she wondered, then frowned.

So the guy smelled good. Get over it.

A slow smile eventually tugged his lips, softening the sharp angles of his face. "Tenacious."

She smiled back. She didn't want to, but dammit, she couldn't help herself. When he wasn't frowning at her or giving her one of the I'm-a-cop-and-you're-bottom-feeder-media-scum stares he had down to perfection, Beckett Raines was a major hottie. Of course she noticed. She had a pulse, didn't she?

His smile quickly faded, but at least he wasn't giving her the scum look any longer. "I have a good idea of what you're doing out here in the middle of the night, but I'd like to know why."

She set her empty mug on the dashboard next to her digital camera. "Day Two," she said.

"You've received another audio file?"

"No," she said with a shake of her head, "but I fully expect to. There was no postmark on the first one, so it had to have been dropped off. I was hoping to get a shot of whoever was doing the dropping off."

A frown immediately creased his forehead. "Do I need to remind you how incredibly dangerous, not to mention stupid—"

"Don't bother," she interrupted him. "I kinda figured that one out already." She rubbed at her still sore knee.

"So what makes you think there'll be a Day Two?"

"Not exactly rocket science, Chief. Day One, Day Two. I just hope to hell I am wrong."

"It's Beck," he said. "And you're operating on assumptions."

"No, I'm operating on a hunch," she told him. "Don't you trust your hunches?"

He rubbed at the back of his neck. "I trust the facts, follow leads, collect evidence."

She issued a short bark of laughter. "Yeah. Right. And that's why your officers conducted a door-to-door search tonight, and why they've been heavy on patrols all night long, too."

"It wasn't a search," he said. "We were hoping for any leads that might tell us what happened to Mattie Davenport."

"Uh-huh. Sure," she scoffed. "You think the killer is a local and you were hoping your officers turned up something, anything that might tell them we have a crazed wacko in our own backyard. You didn't authorize overtime the city can barely afford just to have more patrols on the street tonight because of facts. Wanna try again?"

He leaned back in the seat, his head against the headrest. When he looked at her, she noticed he looked tired, the lines bracketing his eyes appearing slightly deeper tonight.

"And what makes you think the UNSUB is a local?"

"Because," she said, "the audio file was addressed to me personally."

"All the UNSUB had to do was use Google. The *Sentinel* does have a Web site, you know."

"What about the body dump?" she asked, ignoring his sarcasm. "The clearing isn't off some beaten path, but a place where kids tend to hang out. Someone knew the body would be discovered sooner rather than later. If your unknown subject wanted to hide the body, there are plenty of woods around here where he could've dumped her without her being found for who knows how long."

"Could've been an unfortunate for him coincidence," Beck countered. "Maybe he doesn't know the area and just picked the wrong place."

"Bull," she said. "Anyone can see the footpath to the clearing is well traveled. And how do you explain the missing girl? She's not a local, but she attends the U. She's only been in town a few days and poof, she's gone. I think whoever is responsible knew Mattie wasn't a local and it could be days before she was reported missing."

"There aren't enough facts to support—"

"That's a load of crap," she argued. "Every single incident is related. I know it. You know it. Why won't you admit it?"

"Because I'm not in the habit of discussing an ongoing investigation with the public, let alone the press."

So she figured, twelve unreturned calls later.

Another vehicle turned down the street and she automatically slumped down in the driver's seat. She peered over the side of the door, then let out a slow stream of breath when she recognized the car as yet another police cruiser.

Beck shook his head and cast a pointed look at the digital camera resting on the dashboard. "You're sure to get a good shot at him from there," he said as the cruiser pulled to a stop next to her car.

She gave him a sour look and straightened. "I didn't want to be seen," she murmured as she turned the key so she could roll the window down. Her cover was blown anyway. "Hey, Steve," she said to the officer, whom she'd known most of her life. Steve Jonas was only a year older than her, married to a sweet girl he'd met while attending Nebraska State on a baseball scholarship that resulted in a degree in criminal justice and not the pro career he'd hoped for. He was the father to a pair of adorably mischievous twin boys that Cassidy had babysat for on several occasions.

"Ainsley," he said with a slight inclination of his head. "Chief. Quiet night."

Beck leaned forward. "Good. Let's hope it stays that way."

"You gonna be much longer?" Steve asked.

"I'll see Ms. Brennan home, then I'm heading home my-self for a couple of hours. I'll be back in time for morning roll call."

"Right. See you then," Steve said, then looked back at Ainsley. "Night, Ainsley."

"Good night," she said, before she rolled the window up again as Steve drove away. She turned back to Beck. "I ap-preciate the chivalry but really don't need an escort."

"You need a keeper, is what you need," he muttered.

She shot him a frown. "You don't like me much, do you?"

"I don't like that you keep sticking your nose into my in-vestigation," he said, his tone filled with annoyance.

"Like I said, I have a job to do."

"So do I," he fired back, "and you have a bad habit of getting in the way. We've been keeping an eye on the news-paper office all night, front and back. With you parked out here, do you really think the UNSUB is going to waltz up to the front door and drop off another CD for your listening pleasure?"

"No one knew I was here. Until you showed up."

"I've known you were here since you first pulled up over two hours ago," he said, his own frown deepening. "But when you showed no signs of coming to your senses, I fig-ured it was time to send you home. What the hell would you have done if the UNSUB had shown up?"

She wasn't sure whether she should be offended or touched by his concern. "All I planned to do was take his picture, then bring it to you. I'm not an idiot."

"Then do us both a favor, Ainsley, and stop acting like one," he said, his tone turning harsh. "Let me do my job. I'll find this guy. It's what I do."

Since her jig was up, she started the engine and turned the heater to full blast. A shiver raced through her and she trembled. "We could help each other, you know."

He let out a sound that could have been a laugh, but was more reminiscent of a grunt filled with annoyance and disbelief. "Yeah? And how's that?"

The heater's efforts were paltry at best, so she rubbed her hands over her arms to generate more warmth. "You confirm that the disappearance of Mattie Davenport and the discovery of the body are connected, and I'll share with you what I've learned about Mattie Davenport."

He let out a frustrated stream of breath. "There is no evidence to connect either incident. When are you going to understand that?"

She gave him a sour look. "And when are you going to get it that nothing ever happens in Serenity Heights? *Ever*. This is the most boring town in the state of Ohio. Yet within the past twenty-four hours the mutilated body of a woman has shown up and another woman has gone missing. Plus, there's the CD that could very well be Mattie's voice begging for mercy. The two incidents have to be related. There *is* no other explanation."

"I can think of a few dozen."

"And none of them will pan out. I'm telling you, evidence or not, they *are* related."

"And when the evidence confirms it, I'll let you know." The irritation in his voice was audible.

She didn't care. She needed a confirmation.

"Will you at least admit on the record that the possibility exists?" she pushed.

A full minute ticked by before Beck answered her. "All right," he conceded, albeit reluctantly. "The possibility does exist, but there is no solid evidence to confirm a definite connection. And your story better state that piece of information, or I swear, you'll never get another statement from me again. Got it?"

"Got it." She only hoped it was enough for Dylan to run her story.

She shifted in the seat to look at the space behind her car, which was empty. In fact there were no other cars on the street besides her own. "Where's your car?"

"I was at the station and walked over," Beck said. "Just drive home. I'll walk back."

"I really don't need you to see me home. It's only a few blocks from here."

"Humor me," he said, fastening his seat belt, then shot her a pointed look until she did the same.

She stepped on the brake, shifted into drive, and pulled away from the curb. A right turn onto Main, past the stop sign at Central, where the police station was located, then an additional three blocks before she reached Eucalyptus Lane. After she pulled into the drive, she cut the engine and turned to face Beck. "You didn't ask me what I know about Mattie Davenport."

He unfastened his seat belt. "You probably know as much as I do. Music major, five feet four, thin, blond, blue eyes. Never been out of Mississippi until she came to the U."

"Did you know the last person to see her was Reid Pomeroy?"

"That's unconfirmed."

"Did you know that she left Pomeroy's office at four forty-five PM?"

That got his attention, if the sharp glance he tossed her way was any indication. "You can confirm that?"

Ainsley grinned. "I can."

His hand stilled over the door handle. "How do you know that?"

"Text message."

"We're still waiting for her cell phone records."

"I spoke to her best friend back home. Jackie Bolton received a text message at four forty-seven PM, just two minutes after Mattie left Pomeroy's office."

"What did the message say?"

She didn't need to look at her notes. The text message had been stuck in her head all night. " 'Pomeroy is a perve. Ewwww.' "

"That doesn't prove anything."

"Maybe not, but when Mattie's friend called her back, all she got was Mattie's voice mail. It's all she's gotten since, too."

"There could be a dozen explanations," Beck said.

Only one explanation made sense to Ainsley. "But it does give you a suspect," she said.

"Pomeroy?" Beck chuckled. "Nice try, but he doesn't fit the profile."

Ainsley shrugged, then opened the car door. "And everyone thought Ted Bundy was just a nice guy," she said, snagging her tote from the backseat. She tossed her camera and the empty mug into her tote, then slid from the vehicle.

"Give it a rest, Nancy Drew," Beck said after getting out of the car. "Let the pros handle this one."

She slung her tote over her shoulder, then hit the lock button as Beck circled the car and came toward her. "You should leave a porch light on," he said, handing her the thermos.

She frowned and looked over her shoulder to the porch. "I did," she said. Who knew the last time the bulb had been changed, but that thought didn't stop the hair on the back of her neck from standing at attention.

"Give me your keys," he said, keeping his voice low.

Alarm skirted over her skin as she dug into her tote bag. "The bulb probably burned out," she said, but handed him her house key anyway.

"Wait here." He gave her another of those hard stares. "I mean it."

She nodded and backed up until her rear end came in contact with her Taurus. All this cloak and dagger stuff was getting to her. She was tired and her imagination was short-circuiting. Until Beck pulled a weapon from beneath his jacket.

Her eyes widened when she looked at him. "You don't think . . ." But she couldn't finish the sentence. Oh, God. Had the killer been to her home?

"Just stay put until I give you the all clear," he said, then took off toward the porch.

CHAPTER 5

WEAPON DRAWN, BECK crouched low and moved across the damp lawn, keeping his head beneath the trimmed hydrangeas lining the front porch railing. He didn't necessarily expect to find a crazed killer at Ainsley's, CD in hand, waiting to be captured. But, as everyone was so fond of pointing out, for a place where nothing ever happened, they were certainly in the middle of what was quickly becoming a nightmare.

He slipped his flashlight from the holder on his belt and turned it on before he crept up the wooden steps. With the light positioned in one hand and his weapon in the other, he flashed the beam into the shadows, finding nothing but a few pieces of outdoor furniture situated at the far end of the porch.

With no rubber gloves on him, he approached the front door and carefully opened the screen door. He heard a light crackling sound followed by a gentle thwap as a package landed near his foot.

"What is it?" Ainsley asked from the bottom of the porch steps.

"Didn't I ask you to stay put?" He flashed the light on the package. A plain brown padded envelope, identical to the one Ainsley had given him yesterday afternoon. A white label adhered to the front indicated, "For Ms. Brennan."

Shit.

He didn't need to look inside to know it contained another recording, more than likely labeled "Day Two." Just as Ainsley had predicted. Her instincts were as good as, if not better than, half the cops on the force. At this rate, he ought to give her a badge and deputize her.

"It's another CD, isn't it?" she asked, her voice tinged with apprehension. Not that Beck could blame her. An anonymous package delivered to her office was one thing. One left on her doorstep in the middle of the night made it a helluva lot more personal. And dangerous.

"Go back to the car, lock the doors, and stay there," Beck ordered her. He tried the front door, but it was locked. A good sign, but that didn't mean the UNSUB wasn't waiting inside for her. He doubted the probability, but he wasn't about to take any chances with her life. So far, he had a body count of one and he hoped to keep it that way. But, unless they caught a break, he fully expected that the missing Mattie Davenport could end up the UNSUB's second victim.

"But—"

"Go. You'll compromise the crime scene."

"Crime scene?" she blurted loudly. "This isn't a crime scene. It's my home."

His patience, not that he ever had much in great supply, started to slip. Turning, he glared at her. "Do it," he said more harshly than he'd intended. Dammit, just once he wished to hell she'd listen to him.

The look she gave him could've frozen the balls off a snowman. "Fine," she huffed, then stalked off across the yard.

A twinge of guilt pierced him, but he didn't want to put her in any more danger than she was already in just by being the recipient of the UNSUB's twisted calling card. Then again, maybe he should follow his own advice and listen to what she had to say for a change. She'd been insisting all along that the UNSUB was a local. Tonight's delivery at her home might not be concrete proof of that fact, but it was enough to make him think he shouldn't so easily discount her instincts. An outsider wouldn't know where she lived. Sure, anyone could ask around town, but with what he knew thus far of the residents of Serenity Heights, he seriously doubted anyone would willingly give out that kind of information to a total stranger.

He left the package where he found it for the time being, then unlocked the front door and pushed it open. Dim light spilled onto the patterned linoleum floor of the foyer from a small lamp sitting atop a tall, oblong table. He repositioned his gun so the barrel pointed upward and stepped into the foyer.

The light scent of cinnamon hung in the air, stirring memories he couldn't afford to indulge in at the moment. He pushed them aside for the time being and stood quietly, scanning the immediate area, listening for any sound of movement. Nothing but the ticking of a clock in the distance.

He checked the living room, then the formal dining room, the kitchen, followed by a family room and a bathroom. He walked back into the kitchen. Two dark loaves of homemade dessert breads sat on a wire rack on the island where Ainsley had apparently left them to cool. That explained the cinnamon.

After checking that the back door was locked, he backtracked and returned to the foyer to head up the stairs. Three bedrooms and a bathroom, all clear. He even checked the closets and shower to make sure no one was hiding there, then went back downstairs and out to the porch. After closing the storm door, he pulled out his cell phone and dialed Mitch's home number.

The captain picked up on the second ring. "This better be

good," Mitch complained, his voice scratchy and groggy. "It's after two in the morning."

"Do you know where Ainsley Brennan lives?" Beck asked him.

"On Eucalyptus," Mitch answered, sounding more alert. "Why?"

"Who is it?" Beck heard Rose's voice, Mitch's wife, in the background. "One of the kids?"

"No," Mitch answered his wife. "The chief."

"I'll go make coffee," Rose said, the resignation in her voice clear.

"What's going on?" Mitch asked him.

"Bring a print kit," Beck said. Dusting for fingerprints was more than likely an exercise in futility. Chances were they wouldn't find so much as a single smudged print. The UNSUB had been damn thorough when it came to the last CD. Beck imagined he'd taken just as much precaution tonight when delivering the package to Ainsley's door.

"Ainsley's not—"

"No," Beck quickly assured him, a little stunned by the relief he felt in that single word. Ainsley was a reporter, the enemy. He should feel nothing but contempt for her kind, but instead he'd been having flashes of an attraction he was nowhere near ready for—regardless of her occupation.

"While she was off staking out the newspaper office tonight," he said, "the UNSUB left a package on her doorstep."

Mitch issued a muffled curse. "Another CD?"

"Most likely," Beck told him as he holstered his weapon. "I haven't opened it yet."

"I'll be there in ten," Mitch said, then hung up.

Beck called dispatch next and requested a pair of uniforms to be sent to Ainsley's home. She might not like it, but a crime scene was a crime scene. Considering he didn't have squat so far on the case, he couldn't afford to overlook the possibility of a single clue that might provide him with a viable lead.

Ainsley kept hounding him about making an official connection. There was little doubt in his mind that each and every incident was in fact related, but that didn't mean he wanted it printed in the town's newspaper. In LA, as sad as it was, no one paid all that much attention. Murder happened all the time and rarely made headlines unless it involved a celebrity. Not the case in Serenity Heights. Once Ainsley's article was printed, he easily imagined the department being stormed by a mob of angry citizens, sans the pitchforks and fiery torches, demanding the killer be brought to swift justice.

He left the porch and walked over to the car. She'd only half done as he'd told her. Standing by her car, she clutched her tote bag to her chest. Her lips were set in a firm line, and those bluer than blue eyes shot daggers at him as he approached. Damn if she didn't look sexy as hell standing there glaring at him as if she wanted to kick his ass into next week.

"I told you to wait in the car," he said, pocketing his cell phone.

"He brought the next CD here, didn't he?" The tremor in her voice belied the irritation simmering in her gaze.

For the space of a heartbeat, he thought about placating her with his standard line, but decided against it. "There's a package, yes. I didn't open it, but I imagine it does contain another recording."

"Oh, God," she whispered, and clutched the tote bag tighter. As she looked up at him, the anger evaporated from her gaze, replaced by the glimmer of gathering moisture. "Why here? Why me?"

He wished he knew why the UNSUB had targeted Ainsley, but he didn't have any answers for her. If it was attention the UNSUB was after, why not involve The *Plain Dealer*, with a wider distribution than a local weekly newspaper, or even the television news out of Cleveland?

"I'm sorry," he said lamely.

She shrugged her slim shoulders and looked away as she visibly struggled to regain her composure. He took a step toward her and settled his hand on her shoulder. For the flash of an instant, she stiffened beneath his touch, but before he could pull his hand away, she dropped her tote bag and moved closer. He didn't think twice about what he was doing, or even why, but he pulled Ainsley into his arms and held her close.

She slipped her arms around his waist and held on tight. A tremor passed through her body and he tightened his hold. The scent of her perfume distracted him, making him think only of the woman in his arms and her gentle curves pressed against him as she sought comfort. He wanted to keep her safe, wanted to protect her, and he wasn't thinking in terms of his professional duty.

Why her? And why now? He couldn't say, except he was definitely physically attracted to her. He sure as hell hadn't been looking for anything remotely romantic when he'd left LA. He had a few demons locked in the closet he had yet to come to terms with, but apparently they weren't enough to stop his body from responding to her closeness.

"We'll find him, Ainsley," he said, gliding his hands up and down her slender back, hoping to ease her fears. "He probably saw you parked outside the newspaper office."

She pulled back and looked up at him. Fierce anger brightened her gaze. "The bastard knows where I live. Do you have any idea how that feels?"

Beck let out a long, slow breath. As a matter of fact, he did. "Is there somewhere you can stay for a few days?"

She slipped out of his arms as a pair of squad cars came barreling down the quiet street, alternating blue and red lights flickering, coming to an abrupt halt in front of Ainsley's place. "I don't know. Maybe," she said.

"Kill the lights," Beck called out as Steve Jonas climbed from his cruiser. At this rate, the street would end up crowded with curious neighbors, asking questions and possibly contaminating the scene.

As the officers cut the lights, Mitch pulled up in his wife's silver Toyota Avalon and parked in the driveway behind Ainsley's car. Mitch exited the vehicle, fingerprint kit in one hand, a travel mug in the other, and a plastic zippered bag, filled with what looked to be homemade cookies, balanced atop the mug. "Rose sent them," Mitch said, offering the bag to Ainsley. "She thought they might help."

"What is it with baked goods in this town?" Beck groused, relieving Mitch of the fingerprint kit.

"We're born with a strong affinity for comfort food," Ainsley said.

"Small town DNA," Mitch quipped.

Ainsley accepted the bag, opened it, and took a whiff. "Hmmm, oatmeal raisin. Thank Rose for me," she said to Mitch.

Beck left Ainsley with Mitch, who instructed the two patrolmen to search the backyard and small garage. Heading back up the front steps, Beck started dusting for prints. As he suspected, the place was clean.

HER WHIMPERS EXCITED him. Thrilled him to the point of arousal. He so wanted to touch her. To touch himself and feel the joy of release, but he kept those thoughts locked firmly in the back of his mind. He was in control. In charge. That meant controlling his need to make her his with his body.

She was barely aware of her surroundings now as she floated in and out of consciousness. The pain had become too much for her earlier and she'd passed out cold, but a few passes of smelling salts under her nose had brought her back to him. But her end was near. She would pay the ultimate price for her sins.

She would pay with her life.

He looked down at her, at the pleading expression in her soft blue eyes glazed with pain and misery. Anger mingled with a strange primal satisfaction throughout his entire body. His hand trembled with it as he smoothed her hair back from her face. "It didn't have to be this way," he whispered to her. "You did this to yourself."

She shed no tears. The pleading left her gaze, replaced by sheer hatred.

He pulled his hand away and balled it into a fist. He didn't see Mattie Davenport, the sweet little freshman who slid him sidelong glances, then blushed prettily when he glanced her way. No, he saw the evil bitch responsible for destroying the life that should have been his. The one responsible for taking everything that had belonged to him.

The urge to strike her overwhelmed him. With a great deal of concentration, he brought his rage back down to a manageable level.

"Bitch," he spat at her, unable to keep the venom from his voice. Hatred for her crept through his veins. "You had everything. Everything you didn't deserve."

"Fuck you." Her hateful words were nothing more than a raspy, mumbled whisper of sound, but he felt her contempt just the same.

"Silence," he ordered sharply.

She continued to glare at him, her loathing for him palpable. He didn't care, tried to tell himself her feelings meant nothing to him, but deep inside, down in the place he rarely examined, the truth resided. In truth, he did care. He'd always cared that he was so hated, only he couldn't allow himself to wallow in those emotions. To do so meant an exhibition of weakness and the opening of wounds that had never healed. Wounds that had scarred him for too many years. Wounds unattended that festered and oozed with fury.

He concentrated on the anger now. Let it bubble up and held it at a low simmer. Felt it slide through his veins. Mentally controlling it.

He smiled down at her. Her time had come. Turning, he hit the series of buttons on the equipment shelved behind him that would record her ending, then picked up a pair of gardening sheers.

CURLED UP IN her favorite chair, Ainsley sipped chamomile tea from a delicate china cup, hoping to calm her rattled composure. She'd never been the type to spook easily, but with a psychotic murderer leaving packages on her doorstep, she figured she was entitled. She wished Beck and his officers would leave, yet wanted them to stay so she wouldn't be alone in the big old colonial with only her overactive imagination for company.

She glanced at the antique mantel clock. Only another hour or so until sunrise. As silly as it made her feel, maybe Beck and his officers could hang around long enough so she wouldn't have to worry about being left alone in the dark.

She hadn't been at all surprised when Beck had finally opened the package to find a CD labeled *"Day Two."* He hadn't asked to play it and she'd been grateful. She knew what it contained. More of the same, no doubt, and in all honesty, she just didn't think she was that brave.

There was a reason she stayed in Serenity Heights. Unlike Paige, she just wasn't cut out for the big bad city. Small town life was in her bones. Sure, she might crave a little excitement on occasion, wonder what it was like to live in the fast lane, but her place, such as it was, was here where she'd spent her entire life.

She took another sip of tea, then set the cup back on the matching saucer and placed them on the end table beside her as Beck came into the living room. "You look tired," she said. As bone tired as she suddenly felt. She wondered when he'd last slept.

He took a seat on the worn sofa she'd been swearing she'd replace one of these days, but never got around to doing. There was always something else that needed to be taken care of first. Like replacing the upstairs windows or having the garage roof redone. Or paying Cassidy's tuition because the money set aside from their parents' estate hadn't been enough to compensate for the rising costs of a secondary education.

"It's been a long day," he said, and leaned back.

She rested her head against the back of her chair and offered him a weary smile. "Well, you know what they say, right?"

He managed a small, tired smile of his own in return. "No rest for the wicked?"

"No," she said. "No rest for a cop with a serial killer on the loose."

That hint of a smile faded and she instantly regretted her choice of words. "Sorry. Bad joke."

At that moment, Mitch walked into the living room, looking as exhausted as Beck did. "We're all done here, Chief," he said. "Unless there's something else, I'm gonna send the boys back out on patrol."

"Where are you headed?" Beck asked Mitch.

"To the station," Mitch answered, "to start logging in evidence."

"You found evidence?" Ainsley asked. She hadn't thought the killer had been in the house. At least that's what Beck had initially told her after he'd issued an all clear and allowed her inside.

"Just the CD," Beck quickly explained. He looked back to Mitch and added, "I'll meet up with you there."

"Good enough," Mitch said, then gave Ainsley a brief wave before leaving.

The click of the front door closed, and Beck looked over at her. Her heart did a funny little flip at the concern in his eyes, a not completely unpleasant feeling.

What was she thinking? She wasn't. She was tired. That's all. No way in hell was she attracted to Beck. Yeah, so what if the man oozed sex appeal? That didn't mean she had to go and get all gooey inside just because he was doing his job.

"Do you have somewhere to go for a couple of days?" he asked.

"I've been thinking about that since you brought it up earlier," she said. She could probably stay with Mona for a day or two. Or perhaps Raelynn and her daughter, but Raelynn's house was a microscopic two-bedroom. On the outside of town was a small, twelve-room motel where she could stay—if it became necessary. The only problem was, she didn't like the idea of being chased out of her own home. She didn't much like the thought of being afraid in her own home, either. But no way was she going to possibly endanger someone else's life because she'd suddenly turned wimp now that her private domain had been targeted as a drop off location for the local lunatic's sick game.

"And?" Beck prodded.

"You found no evidence that he was in my house."

He frowned. "I still think it'd be wise for you to find another place to stay for a few days."

"Oh, and that's going to stop him from bringing me those recordings? Just because I'm temporarily displaced?"

"No. But do you really want to answer the door and find him standing there? Or worse? Come home from work and find him inside your house?"

She shuddered at the thought. "Not really," she admitted. "But I do think it's unlikely."

"And how'd you come to that conclusion?" he asked, his tone once again laced with annoyance—which was really starting to bug the crap out of her.

"Well, for one, he isn't exactly leaving his name and address on those CDs."

His frown deepened. "What does that have to do with anything?"

"Probably nothing. But . . ." She stood and walked across the room to the rolltop desk in the corner, opened the top drawer, and pulled out the .38 snub-nosed pistol. "I do have this."

He rose from the sofa and walked toward her. "Is that thing loaded?"

"Don't be silly." She rested her backside against the edge of the desk. "Of course it isn't."

"A whole lot of good it'll do you." He took the gun from her, flipped open the chamber, and verified that it was indeed empty. "This thing registered in your name?"

He sounded way too much like a cop all of a sudden. "Not really," she admitted. "It belonged to my dad."

"Do you have ammo?"

She shook her head. "I never saw the need until now."

He let out a long, gusty sigh. "Do you even know how to use a gun?"

"Uh . . . not exactly."

"Never fired one in your life?"

"Nope."

He set the .38 on the desk and gave her a level stare. He was so close she could make out tiny gold flecks in the irises of his forever green eyes. And then there was that aftershave that kept tickling her senses.

Something in his eyes changed. His pupils dilated and she could have sworn he moved his head a fraction of an inch closer. His gaze dipped to her mouth. She held her breath. Waiting. Hoping?

"Then you're going to learn," he said suddenly. He took a step back, breaking whatever spell they'd both been under. Exhaustion, no doubt.

"I'll pick you up at three and take you to the shooting range," he said. "If you're going to have a gun in the house, then you should at least know how to use the damn thing."

She didn't have time to ponder what had just happened because his do-as-I-say attitude irritated her for about two seconds—until she realized he was absolutely right. What good was a gun if she didn't have the first clue on how to use one. Aim and shoot was about all she knew, and that's just what she saw on all those cop shows on TV. She'd just never given it much thought—until now.

CHAPTER 6

EVERYWHERE PARIS WENT on Wednesday morning, people were talking about Mattie Davenport. She'd heard so many stories, anything from a kidnapping to running off with a guy, she didn't know what was real or what was nothing more than a by-product of some way overactive imaginations. The truth, she figured, was probably somewhere in the middle.

"Do you really think it could've been a kidnapping?" Paris asked Zach, who dug into the pile of scrambled eggs and greasy hash browns on his plate. She'd met him for breakfast in the cafeteria before her interview with Assistant Dean McElvoy, and almost wished she hadn't. He was in a crank-ass mood, but wouldn't say what had crawled up his ass.

Zach could be a jerk that way sometimes. Usually, she just ignored him, but today, his attitude really irritated her. How anyone could have such a negative outlook when they were about to embark on an adventure that could change their lives forever was beyond her.

Zach shrugged his wiry shoulders. "Who knows?" He shoveled more food into his mouth, then added, "Who cares?" before he even bothered to swallow.

Paris cared, but she didn't tell Zach. He'd just call her a fucking bleeding heart or offer some other smart-ass comment about looking out for "*numero uno*" that would no doubt piss her off.

That bleeding heart crap was starting to bug her, too, something he'd started doing since she'd told him she wanted to be a social worker and planned to get her BSW. Zach was a foster kid like her, but he hadn't been as lucky as she had been. He'd really seen some shit, and she supposed she couldn't blame him for his bad attitude. She was just getting a little sick and tired of its being aimed at her. He also thought social workers weren't worth a damn, and she couldn't help wondering if he'd already started to lump her in that category, too.

Appetite lost, she pushed her plate with the half-eaten Denver omelet aside, picked up the cup filled with Seattle's Best she'd bought from the cappuccino machine, and took a sip. The instant stuff wasn't half bad, and the caffeine jolt felt good to her system since she and Cassidy had stayed up late talking. She much preferred the frozen coffee concoction she'd bought yesterday at the Java Hut with Cassidy, though, but until she landed a part-time job, she was guarding her limited cash supply.

She checked the inexpensive Timex on her wrist, a graduation present from her foster parents. Half an hour until her interview. She wasn't nervous, just a little anxious, hoping she'd get the job. Cassidy's sister hadn't been at the newspaper office yesterday when they'd stopped by, but the place had been a tomb, which didn't bode well for the possibility of potential employment. Still, if she didn't get the position in the associate dean's office, she'd talk to Ainsley on Sunday when she went with Cass to dinner. If the paper wasn't hiring, maybe Cass's sister had a line on where she could find part-time work.

"Well, I hope nothing bad happened to the girl," she said.

Zach looked up from his food, an impatient scowl on his face. "Did you know her?"

Paris shifted in her chair. "Well, no."

His scowl deepened. "Then what the fuck do you care?"

"I dunno," she said, her tone snippy. "A little thing called compassion, maybe?" She shoved her chair back. "I've gotta go."

She snagged her backpack and slung it over her shoulder.

"Whatever," Zach grumbled, then shoveled another forkful of hash browns into his mouth.

"Later," she said, then took off for the exit before she said something she'd regret. Like *fuck off, asshole.*

She trotted up the stairs and pushed out the heavy glass doors. A gust of wind hit her, blowing her hair into her face. She brushed it aside, then shielded her eyes from the sudden harsh glare of the morning sun as she attempted to find her bearings.

The university wasn't one of those humongous campuses, but it was still foreign enough to her that she might get lost if she didn't pay attention to where she was going. She spied the big brick admin building in the distance and headed across the quad. She was about twenty minutes early for her interview, but with any luck that just might work in her favor. Hopefully she'd look eager, and not as desperate as she felt.

She entered the building to find the main corridor packed with students standing in various lines at the multitude of open windows. Some were in line for adding classes, others in a longer one for dropping a class. The financial aid office overflowed with bodies, the line winding down the hall and disappearing around the corner.

She trudged through the mass of bodies, turned the corner, then another until she finally located the associate dean's office. She dropped her backpack between her feet, tugged her blue tank top up a fraction, then gave a tug to the pink overtop. Dragging her fingers through her hair, she attempted to bring a little order to the windblown strands.

"You look great."

Startled, Paris looked over her shoulder in the direction of the smooth, deep voice. "Excuse me?"

"I'd hire you."

Who was this guy? Other than incredibly hot with eyes as dark as chocolate and a smile that could melt steel. He probably had a girlfriend. Several of them.

"Um . . . thanks, but I don't think your opinion counts," she said, then frowned. "How did you know I'm here for a job interview?"

That movie star smile never faltered as he inclined his head toward the paper in her hand. "I gave that to you, remember?"

No, she didn't. And she was certain if she'd laid eyes on this guy before, she'd have definitely remembered. He was that drool worthy.

"Well, not me personally. I work part-time in the student employment office," he said, pointing to an office at the end of the corridor. "I saw you come in yesterday."

"Oh." She picked up her backpack. "Well. I . . . um, gotta go."

He stepped in front of her, blocking her path to the door. "Wanna go for coffee later?"

She really shouldn't. But boy, was she tempted, even if she did have a boyfriend.

Who treats you like shit.

"I really shouldn't," she said, then added, "I don't even know your name."

"Gavin," he said, and thrust his large hand at her. "Gavin Chesterfield. And you're Paris."

She couldn't help but feel flattered that he'd obviously taken the trouble to find out her name. "I have a class. . . ."

She shook his hand and felt a flurry of tingles race up her arm. "I could meet you at the Java Hut around one-thirty." Those tingles must've short-circuited something in her brain. But Zach was being a jerk and this guy was kinda sweet, in a slick, I'll-break-your-heart kinda way.

He turned and opened the door to the associate dean's office for her. "Good luck," he said in a low, rumbling tone as she walked past him.

The door closed behind her, but the gentle hum of awareness kept simmering in her veins. She was still smiling like a goofball when she approached the woman sitting at the desk. "Hi. I have an appointment with Mr. McElvoy."

The woman, probably in her fifties or sixties, glanced at the open calendar on her desk. "Paris?" she asked with a warm smile.

Paris nodded. "Yeah. Uh . . . yes, ma'am."

"You're early," the woman said. "Have a seat. He'll be along shortly."

"Thanks." Paris took one of the wooden chairs near the door to wait. She checked her watch again. She had an hour until her first class, and two and a half hours until she met Gavin for coffee. She had to be crazy to agree to meet up with a total stranger, even one as drop-dead gorgeous as Gavin Chesterfield. There was a student missing and a whole lot of rumors as to what might have happened to her.

Well, her foster mom had told her she'd meet new people and had encouraged her to be open to new possibilities. *Translation:* she'd meet someone better than Zach. Her foster mom had made no secret of the fact she thought Zach didn't always treat her all that great. Not that she thought her foster mom had specifically meant someone like Gavin Chesterfield, but what harm could there be in meeting the guy for a cup of coffee? She was eighteen. Didn't that mean she was free to make her own choices? Still, with the disappearance of Mattie Davenport, she decided to play it safe and stop by her dorm room to leave Cassidy a note before heading over to the Java Hut.

The heavy wooden door opened and Mr. McElvoy walked into the room. Paris recognized him from orientation. He didn't so much as glance in her direction, or that of his secretary, but went directly into his own office and closed the door with a sharp snap.

Great. Another moody jerk. Not that she cared—too much. She needed money. She'd put up with the devil himself if it paid enough.

Not ten seconds later, the phone on the secretary's desk rang and Paris was whisked into McElvoy's office. The secretary quietly closed the door, leaving Paris alone with the associate dean.

McElvoy stared at his laptop screen. "Have a seat, Ms. Nolan," he said, without looking at her.

Paris took the chair in front of the desk and set her backpack between her feet. She settled back, then, feeling awkward, sat forward and rested her hands on her knees.

Stop fidgeting.

She leaned back in the chair, then two seconds later, scooted a little forward.

"You're a scholarship student," McElvoy stated. He looked up then, but didn't smile. He just stared at her. Sizing her up?

She struggled not to squirm under his intense scrutiny. "Yes, sir."

"Aren't all of your expenses covered by your scholarship?"

"Only my college expenses," she told him. "I need a job for other stuff."

He nodded slowly. "I see." He leaned back in his chair, never taking those black as midnight eyes off her. He had dead eyes. Like a shark. She decided she didn't think she liked him very much. He wasn't exactly creepy, just ... sorta odd.

"The position is only ten hours a week at minimum wage. You do have computer experience?"

"Yes, sir. I took a couple of computer classes in high school." And what she hadn't learned there, one of her foster sisters had taught her. She wasn't exactly at the level of a hacker, but she definitely knew her way around a computer and then some. "I'm pretty good with computers," she added.

"The job entails a bit of data entry, filing and running errands for my secretary, Deborah, as she needs them. Does that sound like something you'd be interested in?"

She'd shovel horseshit if it meant she'd have at least a little financial freedom. "Yes, sir, it does."

He leaned forward suddenly, folding his hands on the desk in front of him. "So, Paris," he said, a slow smile starting to curve his thin lips, "tell me what's not in your student file."

Oh, God, she *hated* questions like that. She never knew what she was supposed to say. That she had a boyfriend who was becoming more of a jerk every day? That her mother hadn't wanted her? She supposed the latter was already in her student file since her social worker had written a letter of recommendation for her. So that left what? That her greatest goal in life was to be self-sufficient and never have to depend on anyone but herself?

"Well . . . um . . . this is the first time I've ever been out of California."

"And how do you like our sleepy little town, Paris? It must seem quite boring compared to Oakland."

Boring? She didn't think so. Okay, so maybe Serenity Heights wasn't exactly a hotbed of excitement, but she'd already made a friend and had a coffee date with a major hottie. What wasn't to like about that?

"It's nice," she said. "The people are friendly." God, could she sound any more lame? She smiled at him because she didn't know what else to do.

He pushed back from the desk and stood. "Thank you for coming in, Ms. Nolan."

Her heart sank. He'd started calling her Paris, now they were back to the more formal Ms. Nolan. That didn't sound like a job offer was coming her way, even if she did find how he kept using her name kinda creepy.

"I have two more students to see this afternoon," he said, coming around the desk, "but I promise to be in touch soon. I take it you can start right away?"

"Oh, yes, sir," she answered, her hopes rising.

"Tomorrow afternoon wouldn't be too soon?"

"No. Tomorrow would be fine." She had two classes in the early morning, but her afternoon was free until her two-hour biology lab at four-thirty.

"Good. I'll let you know this afternoon."

His smile widened slightly and he extended his hand toward her. She took it, and with a firm grip, shook his hand. "Thank you, Mr. McElvoy."

"It's been my pleasure," he said, and slowly let go of her hand.

She tried not to be creeped out by the way he held onto her hand a little too long. Maybe it was a small town thing, but she still thought it was weird. Scooping up her backpack, she said good-bye, then left, stopping to ask Deborah directions to Morton Hall, where the English Department was located.

She hadn't been offered the job on the spot as she'd hoped, but the brief interview had at least ended on a positive note. For now, it would just have to be enough.

"THERE'S NOTHING HERE," Mitch said in disgust, tossing a sheaf of papers in front of Beck. "A couple of text messages and incoming calls from four different Mississippi exchanges. That's it."

Beck looked up from the laptop screen as Mitch pulled

out the chair closest to Beck and sat. The captain looked tired and pissed off. Beck knew the feeling. For the past hour he'd been searching the database for similar crimes in the area and hadn't come up with dick.

"What about the GPS tracking on the cell phone?" Beck asked him. "Any luck?"

"Not so much as a freaking bleep," Mitch complained. His scowl deepened. "I have three daughters. Not a one of them goes anywhere without her cell phone. And they'll put the damn things on vibrate rather than turn them off."

He didn't know all that many teenage girls, except maybe his neighbor's daughter, Zoe. Whenever he saw her, her cell phone was usually glued to her ear.

"We know the Davenport girl had it with her when she left Pomeroy's office," Beck said. He leaned back and lifted his arms over his head, stretching the kinks from his back. "She exchanged text messages with a friend in Mississippi."

"It's there," Mitch said, indicating the phone records. "Listed as the last activity. The UNSUB must've tossed Davenport's cell."

"We'd have at least gotten a location from the GPS."

"Then the bastard yanked the battery," Mitch said. "Son of a bitch is thorough, isn't he?"

Too thorough, Beck thought. And careful. Which in his opinion, made him twice as dangerous. The guy knew what he was doing, left nothing to chance. The CD that had been dropped off at Ainsley's place last night was as clean as the first one, as far as fingerprints were concerned, and was a common brand purchased from any retailer. The audio file itself had contained more of the same, too. He'd couriered it over to the engineers at the crime lab as he had the first one, hoping they could come up with something.

"You hear from the coroner yet?" Mitch asked.

Beck stood and walked to the coffee maker Raelynn had set up this morning in an empty office they'd turned into a makeshift task force room. "I spoke to Julia about twenty minutes ago. She's changed her mind about the estimated time of death. We're looking at two months minimum."

"Two months!" Mitch shifted in his chair to look at Beck. "Where the fuck did he keep the vic for two freaking months?"

Beck poured himself another cup of coffee. It was strong, hot, and black and wasn't doing squat to stave off the exhaustion. After leaving Ainsley's house, he'd gone to the station to meet Mitch as promised when he really wanted to go home and crash for a few hours.

"Tucked in a freezer," Beck told Mitch. "One big enough that the vic could be laid flat."

"Jesus." Mitch scrubbed his hand down his face. "I don't like this."

Neither did Beck. He eyed the platter of brownies and brightly decorated cupcakes, contemplating adding a sugar boost to his caffeine rush, but decided against it. What he needed was sleep, something he didn't see happening anytime soon.

"We're going to need some help," Mitch said. "My guys aren't trained for this kind of shit."

"No, but you are," Beck reminded him as he returned to his chair and sat.

"There's a hell of a difference between training and on the job experience, Chief. What I've learned about this crap came out of a goddamn textbook."

"I've already notified the FBI office in Cleveland to set the wheels in motion," he told Mitch, "but as of right now, the Behaviorial Analysis Unit isn't involved."

"Why the hell not?"

"Because we haven't met their criteria for a serial crime." Beck took a sip of coffee and winced. Strong didn't begin to describe the black mud in his mug. But if it kept him going for another hour or two, he'd keep guzzling the stuff.

"We have one DB and a missing person. Two separate incidents," he said. "Until we have more than gut instinct to link the crimes, we're on our own."

Mitch shook his head. "That's about as useful as a restraining order."

Beck agreed, to a certain point, but he also understood the rules a little better than Mitch did, given his own homicide experience. And they did have access to the national database. Most departments did these days, so it wasn't like they were taking stabs in the dark. More like needles and haystacks, but it was all he had to work with at the moment. They just didn't have much to go on at this point.

"So what do we do now?" Mitch asked. "We've already canvassed the neighborhood. I've got two officers questioning students at the U this morning."

"We keep going over the facts. We follow every lead," Beck said.

"And we hope like hell this bastard makes a mistake?"

Beck set the mug on the table in front of him. "Something like that," he said. "Who do you think would have access to a large freezer?"

Mitch blew out a stream of breath and leaned his beefy forearms on the table. "Butchers. Meatpackers. Grocery stores. Ice cream parlors." Mitch frowned. "Nix the ice cream parlors. Those freezers are small. Oh, cemeteries."

"Cemeteries?"

"Yeah," Mitch said. "Anywhere there's a hard winter, most cemeteries have a deep freeze where they store bodies while the ground is too frozen to dig. You have the memorial service, wake. Everything except the planting. Those are done in the spring after the ground thaws."

Well, that put a whole new morbid twist on the matter. Beck hadn't even considered that possibility, and he'd grown up in Ohio.

He downed more coffee and mentally ran through the list

of possibilities. "The closest meatpacking plant is where? Cleveland?"

"Yeah. But we do have a butcher in town. Plus two grocery stores nearby. A Heinen's and a Giant Eagle. There's a Super WalMart off the main highway, too."

"What about the convenience stores at both ends of town?"

"One's independent, the other part of a big regional chain."

Beck wasn't about to completely discount the large chains, but doubted the ability of the UNSUB to keep a frozen body hidden in such an environment. The butcher shop and the independently owned C-store on the edge of town were definite possibilities. With one exception . . .

He looked at Mitch. "Any chance the butcher or the C-store owner has a working knowledge of dental practices?"

"SOLD?" Ainsley could not have heard right and blamed her suddenly bad hearing on a lack of a decent night's sleep. No way would Dylan Bradley sell the *Sentinel*. It just wasn't possible.

Mona nodded, her expression grim. "That's what I said. Sold. I heard it from Valerie Turner over at the bank not twenty minutes ago when I went in to make a deposit for Grace. She said that Dylan and a pair of big shots from Tricor Publishing had been there with a whole squad of lawyers most of the morning. Apparently I'd just missed them."

So that's where Dylan had been all day instead of waiting around in his office to approve her story. At the bank. Finalizing the sale of her livelihood. Her noon deadline had come and gone, but her story was sitting on Dylan's desk, waiting for approval.

"Do you think they'll shut us down?" Lisa asked Ainsley.

"No," she said. "Of course they won't." She hoped, but had serious doubts on the subject. Tricor Publishing owned or had been buying up most of the independently owned newspapers in Western Pennsylvania, Kentucky, and West

Virginia for the past few years. She supposed it really had only been a matter of time before they set their sights on Ohio and the *Sentinel* blipped on their radar screen. Problem was, she just never really gave it a whole lot of thought, since their paper had been owned by Dylan's family for three generations.

"I wouldn't hold your breath," Mona said. "Val told me her sister-in-law worked for a small paper down in Ashland. Tricor came in, fired everyone except the janitor, and replaced them with their own people."

Lisa started to cry.

Ainsley wanted to cry.

"Do you know for certain Dylan actually sold the paper?" Ainsley asked, grasping for the tiniest shred of hope. If she lost her job, she'd have to move, and she didn't want to move. This was her home, dammit. And she was a mere ten payments away from paying off the mortgage. "Did anyone see any papers being signed? Any transfers of money?"

"I didn't ask," Mona said. "I was in shock."

So was Ainsley.

She knew Dylan had been out of the office more than usual the past few weeks, but she'd just assumed he'd been out trying to stir up advertising dollars. Never in a million years had she imagined he'd actually sell the paper.

Mona shook her head. "I've been with this paper for forty years. You'd think Dylan would've at least had the common decency to say something."

Lisa snuffled. "What am I going to do?"

Ainsley plucked a tissue from the box on Mona's desk and handed it to Lisa. "We don't know for certain that Dylan sold the paper. Try not to worry until there's something to worry about." Great advice from someone who was already close to panic herself. "For now, it's just a rumor."

Mona made a sound that said otherwise.

Lisa blew her nose.

Ainsley wanted to throw up.

She sat on the edge of Mona's desk. "Who else do you know at the bank? Is there anyone who can verify what Val told you?"

"Walter Simmons—he's the bank manager and would know for sure," Mona said. "But you can't ask him. Val could get into trouble."

Ainsley understood. The only reason Val told Mona in the first place was that the two women had been friends since before God was a boy.

Of course, Ainsley *was* a reporter. And a reporter always protected her source. Just ask Raelynn, who'd been feeding her information about the goings on at the police department for the past few years. No one, not even Dylan, knew for certain that Raelynn was her source.

Ainsley plucked another tissue from the box and handed it to Lisa. "You're running," she said, indicating the black streaks of mascara dripping down Lisa's checks.

Mona rolled her eyes. "Get a grip, kid," she said to Lisa. "You're all of twenty-two years old and can easily get another job. Try it when you're my age."

"I heard the box factory over in Lorain is hiring. Maybe they need help in the office or something," Lisa said after another round of sniffles. "Think Dylan would mind if I took off early to go fill out an application?"

"No one is going anywhere," Ainsley said, forcing a conviction in her tone she was nowhere near feeling. "We could all be jumping to conclusions based on what is nothing more than rumor at this point. Until we hear from Dylan, let's not assume anything, okay?"

"I guess you're right," Lisa conceded. "But if it's true, I'll be late tomorrow."

"I'll be out of the office the rest of the day," Ainsley said after glancing at the clock radio on Mona's desk. "Call me on my cell if you hear anything." She had two hours before she met Beck for her first lesson at the shooting range. That gave her plenty of time to do a little investigating of her own. Starting with Val at the bank.

CHAPTER 7

AINSLEY RACED THROUGH the door with five minutes to spare before Beck was due to arrive to take her
to the shooting range. She dropped her tote on the padded
bench, tossed her keys on the hall table, then stuck her head
back out the door, intending to grab the mail out of the box
when she slowed down and took a deep breath, hesitating.
What if the killer had delivered another CD?

Day Three.

Was she being silly? Overreacting? Probably, even if those
feelings were justified. The killer *had* delivered two CDs to
her already. Day One. Day Two. Didn't it make sense that
Day Three would be delivered as well?

Closing the screened door, she stood, staring out through
the screen. A trio of laughing little girls ran down the street,
backpacks strapped to their backs, completely oblivious to
the fact that someone was watching them. Not all that long
ago, that could've been Cassidy and her two best friends.
Cassidy, all grown up now and a college freshman, the same
age as the missing Mattie Davenport. The thought had a
deep chill settling in her bones.

Was it Mattie's voice pleading for mercy in those audio
files? She hadn't listened to the second CD, but had let Beck
take it and catalog it as evidence in his investigation. For

reasons she couldn't really explain, she trusted him to tell her if the killer had left a personal message for her in the audio file. She doubted there would be one, but you just never knew. The person they were dealing with obviously wasn't wrapped all that tight, so she figured anything could be possible.

Despite the dread inching up her spine, before she could change her mind, she quickly opened the screened door and snatched the mail from the box. No thick, padded envelopes awaited her.

Thank God.

Letting out a hefty sigh of relief, she quickly sifted through the mail. Nothing more frightening than her AmEx card statement, along with the renewal notice for her car insurance, the cell phone bill, and a sales flyer from the local grocery store.

She dropped the mail on the hall table and walked into the kitchen. With trembling hands, she yanked open the fridge and snagged a bottle of Diet Coke from the shelf, knocking over a bottle of ketchup.

"Get a grip, Brennan," she chastised herself, twisting the cap off the soda bottle.

It wasn't like the guy was walking up to her in broad daylight and handing her those horrific audio files in person. So far, he was operating under a cloak of anonymity, which suited her just fine. But that didn't stop the inexplicable case of nerves quaking her insides after having just picked up her mail. It pissed her off. She shouldn't be afraid to reach for something as common as her own mail.

She took a long drink. The soda burned, doing zilch to alleviate the lump in her throat or settle her nerves. A shot of rum mixed in with her Coke might help, but seeing as she was about to go with Beck to the shooting range for gun handling lessons, she didn't think he'd appreciate her judgments being impaired.

A loud knock on the door sounded and she jumped a good foot, letting out a squeal of fright.

"Ainsley?" Beck called out. The tenor of worry in his voice did more funny things to her insides.

"In the kitchen," she called back. She ripped a paper towel from the holder and wiped up the splash of soda she'd spilled on the counter when she'd practically jumped right out of her skin. Sheesh! When did she become such a wimp?

"Are you all right?" he asked when he walked into the kitchen. The worry in his voice was evident in his gaze as he looked her up and down.

"Just a little clumsy," she said, tossing the paper towel into the garbage can under the sink. "Soda?"

"Thanks, no." He looked around the kitchen, then at her. "You sure you're all right?"

She set her half-empty soda bottle on the small, tiled kitchen island. "I guess I'm a little jumpy, is all," she admitted with a quick shrug of her shoulders.

A half smile canted his lips, drawing her attention to his mouth. He had such perfect lips, she thought. For kissing. Lots of kissing.

"Understandable," he said. "You ready?"

Boy, was that ever a loaded question, especially for a woman who hadn't been kissed in . . . She lost count how long it'd been. Obviously she was still tired after getting only a few hours of sleep this morning after Beck had left. But staring at that very kissable-looking mouth, she couldn't help thinking about that tiny space of a moment between them last night, those few seconds when she'd been so certain he'd wanted to kiss her. She wasn't sure what had her more confused—that she'd even noticed, or the fact that she wouldn't have objected if he *had* kissed her.

Now she was definitely being silly. They'd both been exhausted last night, lack of sleep affecting their ability to think clearly. And her emotions had been running high what with the killer dropping that CD off at her home. She was probably just imagining things.

But there *had* been a moment. She'd been sure of it, had felt the anticipation humming between them. Not that it mattered. She was so not interested in a cranky cop with serious interpersonal communication issues.

She dragged her gaze away from his lips and glanced down at her skirt suit. "Do you mind if I change first?"

"No. Go ahead."

"The family room is through that door." She pointed to the open French doors at the rear of the kitchen, then realized he already knew where it was since he'd searched her house the night before. The family room and downstairs bathroom had been additions made by the previous owners and were in desperate need of updating. But with Paige's college expenses and now Cassidy's, she didn't see a chance of upgrading so much as her nail polish for the next four years. "Make yourself comfortable. I'll just be a minute."

As soon as Beck headed toward the family room, she left the kitchen and bolted up the stairs to change into something more appropriate for learning how to handle a firearm. She had her skirt unzipped by the time she reached her bedroom, wincing when she saw her unmade bed. Not that she planned on anyone seeing her bedroom—namely Beck—but still. A girl who hadn't even been kissed in who knew how long was entitled to a runaway fantasy or two, wasn't she?

She had bigger issues to worry about than an unmade bed or the image of Beck there among the floral sheets and matching comforter. In the few hours she'd been out of the office, she hadn't learned anything new with regard to the rumor of the paper being sold. Val hadn't been willing to share any information with her, and when she'd asked to see the bank manager, he'd met with her, for all of three seconds. The minute she brought up Dylan's name, he'd claimed he had a meeting and had ushered her out of his office.

So much for the reliability of the small town gossip mill.

She'd called Mona to check in and had learned that Dylan had scheduled a staff meeting for first thing tomorrow morning. Two text messages had arrived shortly thereafter. One from Cass telling her she'd invited Paris to join them for dinner on Sunday, and the other from her boss, advising her he was running her story in a special insert in tomorrow's paper.

Thank heavens for small favors, she thought as she peeled off her skirt, then dug through her closet for a pair of comfortable jeans. Finding another job without a few hard-hitting articles to accompany her résumé would be tough at best. Hell, finding another job as a reporter wasn't going to be easy, period, especially if she wanted to stay in Serenity Heights. Since she had no intention of leaving, her employment options in journalism were going to be severely limited.

She tugged on her jeans, quickly changed her top, grabbed a pair of socks from the drawer and darted back into the closet for her gym shoes. She thought about touching up her makeup, but decided against it and quickly made her bed instead before rushing back downstairs.

She didn't know what she was so nervous about. This wasn't a "real" date. Beck was only teaching her how to shoot a gun. Why she'd even agreed, she still hadn't quite figured out, except perhaps common sense. Beck was right. If she owned a gun, she should at least know how to use the darn thing.

When she reached the kitchen, she heard the television in the family room. ESPN or CNN? Probably CNN, she decided. Beck didn't grab her as the sports fan type. He was too serious all the time.

She made a quick stop at the phone and picked up the receiver. Just a normal dial tone, no quick series of beeps to indicate she had voice mail waiting. She returned the phone to the base, then headed into the family room, stopping in the doorway at the top of the three short steps. Beck was in one of the mismatched recliners, remote control in his hand, fast asleep. She glanced at the television set and smiled. No ESPN or CNN, but instead Comedy Central, airing an ancient episode of *Saturday Night Live,* with John Belushi dressed as a Samurai warrior, whacking the hell out of a watermelon with a wicked-looking sword.

So much for Beck being serious all the time. She liked knowing that about him. Liked knowing that he had a softer side, one that included humor.

"Beck?" she called softly.

He didn't move.

She tried again. "Beck?"

Still nothing.

She crossed her arms and rested her shoulder against the doorjamb. Now what? The guy was obviously beat. She wasn't exactly perk central herself, but at least she'd managed to catch a few hours' sleep this morning. She couldn't help wondering if he'd been able to do the same. When Mitch left last night Beck had said he was going to meet him at the station. He probably hadn't slept at all, considering he'd managed to crash in the few minutes she'd been upstairs changing clothes.

She pushed off the doorjamb and walked quietly into the family room. Pulling a chenille throw from the back of the sofa, she carefully covered Beck, then curled up on the sofa, chuckling when Belushi gave equal treatment to more fruit with that nasty-looking sword.

BECK AWOKE MOMENTARILY confused. Not only did he not immediately recognize his surroundings, but the most tantalizing aroma wafting into the room had his empty stomach grumbling. Loudly. Embarrassingly so.

"Oh good," a bright and cheery voice said. "You're awake."

Ainsley. He couldn't see her actual smile, but heard it in

her voice. With the light from the kitchen behind her, her features remained a temporary mystery, but he admired the slender curves of her silhouette just the same.

Awareness stirred inside him. He frowned and kicked the recliner down a notch. "I'm sorry." He dragged his hands through his hair, fingers combing the short strands. "I usually don't do that."

"You mean fall asleep in a strange woman's home?" The hint of amusement in her voice was refreshing after the day he'd had, one filled with more questions than answers in regard to the unidentified body at the coroner's office and the missing freshman. The only new piece of information today was a cell phone battery one of his officers found in the plant bedding to the rear of the building that housed the music department at the U. They had no proof the battery came out of Davenport's cell phone, but it was one that was commonly used in the brand the missing girl owned. That was enough for him to suspect Davenport's disappearance wasn't voluntary.

"I guess I was tired," he said sheepishly. He took the recliner down the last notch so he was sitting completely upright. Other than the bluish tint from the television set bathing the room in an eerie glow and the light from the kitchen spilling into the family room, the room was dark. "How long was I out?"

"A little over three and a half hours," she said, and flipped a kitchen towel over her shoulder.

Beck winced. Obviously he'd needed the rest, but he felt bad about crashing the way he had, especially since he'd promised to take her out to the shooting range and show her how to use a gun.

His stomach grumbled again. "Something smells really good."

"Hungry?"

"A little."

"How does Salisbury steak, mashed potatoes, and roasted asparagus sound?"

Like she went to a whole lot of trouble. "Like you've been busy."

She flicked a switch and the den was suddenly bathed in a soft golden glow from the mismatched lamps on a pair of end tables, old, but not exactly antique. "There's a bathroom through that door," she said, pointing to the right. "Dinner's just about ready. Coffee or iced tea?"

He had another long night ahead of him, so the jolt of caffeine would be appreciated. "Coffee."

She turned and walked back into the kitchen. He hit the remote to turn off the television, but remained in the chair for a moment more than he should, enjoying the gentle sway of her curvy backside encased in a pair of snug jeans. A feeling that was more than awareness stirred when she reached into an overhead cabinet, stretching to lift something from a high shelf.

That wasn't awareness stirring in his khakis, but flat-out sexual interest. Attempting to ignore the sensation, he pushed out of the recliner. Obviously, the long hours were getting to him, he thought as he crossed the den to the small guest bath. Either that or the fact that he'd been living like a monk for the past couple of years.

What the hell was he supposed to do? He'd loved his wife. He missed her, not to mention the fair amount of guilt he still carried with him over her death. Besides, she'd only been gone a little more than two years. It was too soon to start dating someone else. Wasn't it?

You can't hide out forever.

Maybe not. But with a murder investigation, and a missing person who more than likely had met with foul play, now was not the time to be thinking with the head not above his shoulders. And if he ever did consider dating again, it sure as hell wouldn't be with a reporter. Trust was paramount to the success of any relationship. In his experience, trust was a concept beyond a reporter's comprehension.

A few minutes later he joined Ainsley in the kitchen. The aroma of fresh-brewed coffee mingled with the hunger-inspiring scents already permeating his senses. She'd set a couple of place settings at the small round dinette table in the corner, and motioned for him to take a seat while she carried a platter of Salisbury steaks to the table.

"Dig in," she said, returning with a fat mug of steaming coffee, which she set in front of him.

"Wow," he said, taking in the delicious-looking meal. "You didn't have to go to all this trouble."

"You're a means to an end, my friend," she said. "I was hungry and tired of frozen dinners. It was nice to have an excuse to actually cook for a change."

He spread his napkin in his lap and reached for a hot, steaming dinner roll. "It looks good."

Ainsley laughed. "Trust me on this, practice does indeed make perfect. Or at least a damn good effort."

He helped himself to a steak, then handed the platter to her once she was seated across from him. "So what you're saying then, is that this is the only meal you know how to cook well."

"Hardly. But if you'd met me eleven years ago," she said as she set a tall glass of iced tea at her place setting, "we'd be having Hot Pockets, frozen pizza, or scrambled eggs for dinner. And you probably wouldn't have appreciated the eggs all that much."

"Everybody has to start somewhere," he said, adding a helping of mashed potatoes to his plate. "At least you could do scrambled eggs. My wife couldn't boil water when we first got married."

Dammit. He hadn't meant to say that. Hadn't meant to

open the door to questions he didn't care to answer. But Linda had been on his mind—a lot lately. Mostly, he suspected, because of his attraction to Ainsley.

She cut into her steak and dragged it through the gravy on her plate. "How long have you been widowed?" she asked.

"A little over two years," he said, then braced himself for the wave of pain that inevitably followed. Time, some claimed, healed all wounds. Not that he'd ever been one to waste time and energy believing in clichés. He had to admit there was a nugget of truth to the old saw, but some pain was just too difficult to face. Easier to ignore it and go about his day on autopilot. The endless pain that had once gripped his heart whenever he thought about Linda wasn't as fierce and aching as it had once been. Oh sure, his heart still hurt to some degree, but he realized he could breathe again whenever he thought about her.

"I'm sorry," Ainsley said. "I do understand loss. We all grieve differently."

He poured mushroom gravy over his mashed potatoes wondering if he had grieved. He liked to think so. He liked to think he'd left all that behind when he'd returned to Ohio, too. Only he was no longer sure if he'd left the past behind, or whether he was hiding behind it.

"You're widowed?" Funny, but he hadn't heard any rumors on that score.

"No." Ainsley laughed, but the sound held a bitter edge that piqued his interest. "One must date first to find a suitable husband. I lost both of my parents when I was nineteen. I've been raising my sisters the past eleven years," she said. "That's a bit much in the baggage department for most guys."

"Would it help if I told you they were jerks?"

"No, because they still are." She grinned and her blue eyes sparkled. "But I appreciate the sentiment."

"It couldn't have been easy," he said, glad for the diversion from his own confused thoughts. "You were just a kid yourself."

"You don't know the half of it." She snagged a roll for herself. "Scared. Grieving. We were a mess."

"But you stayed together. That's admirable."

"It wasn't always easy, but we managed to get through it somehow. Paige was thirteen with all those freaky hormones girls suffer with at that age, and almost impossible to live with. Cassidy was only seven."

"Where are your sisters now?"

"Paige is an RN, living in Cinci. Cass just started at the U." A hint of sadness entered her eyes. "I guess my job is done."

A thirty-year-old suffering with a bout of empty nest syndrome. Now there was a concept even he couldn't get his mind around. "What about you? What do you do now?" he asked wondering if someone who spent the last eleven years raising her sisters would even want children of her own. He'd wanted a couple of kids, but the timing had never been right. He'd gone from patrol to detective and had spent almost double the hours at work. Linda had gotten a promotion and was working almost as many hours, plus she'd had to travel often for her job as an advertising executive. And then she'd gotten sick and all bets were suddenly off.

Ainsley let out a sigh. "I'm still trying to figure that one out." A troubled light entered her expressive eyes when she looked at him, making him curious. "I like Serenity Heights. It's home. I can't imagine living anywhere else."

"Seriously?" That surprised him. He could easily see her working the crime beat for the *L.A. Times*. She definitely had the tenacity for it, even if she was squeamish. "No dreams of being an ace reporter in the big city?"

"I did once," she admitted with a wispy smile, then took a sip of her iced tea. "Life had other plans and now I'm settled here. The house technically belongs to all three of us, but ten more payments and it's free and clear. That kind of security is hard to walk away from."

He suddenly realized what he found so attractive about Ainsley, aside from the obvious, all those slender curves, her big blue eyes, and that megawatt smile. Her strong sense of responsibility combined with a maturity and selflessness he hadn't seen in a lot of single women her age. Granted he was only six years her senior, but he'd seen plenty. Too much, sometimes.

Ainsley Brennan was a combination of sensuality and sensibility he found way too attractive. The kind of woman who stuck. And that made her dangerous.

THEY HADN'T FED him for three days. That had been his punishment. Three days of nothing but stale bread and water because he'd dared to speak his mind. Because he'd dared say she didn't deserve their love. And they'd punished him for it.

He drove the dark blue cargo van slowly, trying to keep the jarring from the deep ruts in the service road to a minimum. Not that his passenger cared one way or the other. She was, after all, dead.

He made a sound reminiscent of a snarl when the van hit another rut. She'd laughed at him. The bitch. She'd laughed and called him weak. A spineless pervert. But he'd punished her. He'd cut out her tongue.

That thought brought a smile to his face. In the end, he'd shown her who was spineless. The pretty little useless beauty queen hadn't been quite so pretty when he'd finished with her.

Oh, how they'd mourned. It had killed his mother, who'd overdosed on a combination of sleeping pills and vodka. His father had gone off the deep end then, but he hadn't stuck around to find out just how far the old man had gone off the reservation. He'd hated the bastard almost as much as he'd hated the little bitch who'd taken everything from him. He hoped the fucking prick was alive, rotting in his own personal hell.

He drove past the transmission tower and deeper into the shadows, eventually stopping by the field with the sloping hillside. No trees shielded him this time, so he carefully scanned the area to be sure he wasn't seen. The old service road was traveled, but usually by kids on foot taking a shortcut from their homes on the far edge of town. It could be days before his previous conquest was discovered, which suited his purposes.

Certain he was alone, he cut the ignition and slid from the driver's seat, moving into the back of the van. She lay on the floorboard, a tight-fitting red sequined gown clinging to her still-frozen body. Flashy red and white rhinestones encircled her neck, just below the deep rut on her throat, and a matching earring dangled from her remaining earlobe.

After checking the rear windows, he opened the door from the inside and climbed out, dragging his conquest with him. He hefted her cold body into his arms and carried her to the side of the road, where he carefully laid her, arranging the skirt of her dress and making sure the red satin strappy sandals remained on her feet. He'd painted her toenails a bright, shimmering red.

Perfection.

He stood and studied her one last time. Satisfied with what he saw, he climbed back into the van and drove away. He had more work to do. More preparations. More planning for the message he was compelled to deliver.

CHAPTER 8

SLUMPED AGAINST A hollowed-out tree stump, Zach Toomey took another hit on his second to last joint and held the smoke in his lungs. His head swam for a brief moment, then he slowly let the smoke float from his mouth as he sucked it back in through his nostrils. The blue van he'd been watching the past ten minutes crept past, the driver oblivious to his presence. He thought about strolling over to see what the guy had dumped in the field, but couldn't muster much enthusiasm. Probably just some dumb ass too cheap to pay for garbage pickup, saying fuck you to Mother Earth by dumping his trash where it would rot or be picked apart by whatever creatures happened upon it. God knew, he'd passed enough of the shit on his hike out to the middle of nowhere.

If Paris were with him, she'd want to check it out and would drag him with her. She was like that. Nosy, sometimes. She wasn't exactly a goody-goody, but she was conscientious. She'd have said something to the guy dumping his trash, that's for sure. Caused a scene and been a pain in his ass.

He'd called her earlier to see if she wanted to join him for a little high, thinking he might get lucky while he was at it, but she'd gone all bitchy on him again, saying she had a lot of reading to do for a class. He didn't know what had crawled up her ass again, but he'd about had it with her ragging on him. She'd really turned into a fucking bleeding heart lately, too, and it was starting to piss him off. Maybe it was time to ditch the bitch.

He took one last hit, then pinched off the end of the joint and tucked the remainder inside the half-empty pack of Marlboros in his jacket pocket. He only had a joint and a half left from the small stash he'd brought with him from Oakland, and would need to score soon. His roommate was cool enough, but he didn't know yet if the guy partied. Even in this Podunk town, someone had to be dealing pot, or at least know where he could score some decent weed. Otherwise, he'd take a drive into Cleveland over the weekend.

He had a couple of books to crack tonight himself, and now that he had a nice buzz going, maybe it wouldn't bore him to tears. He'd always been good in school, aced just about every class he ever took, but nothing seemed to excite him much these days. Still, he was smart and it had gotten him a free ride to college. He'd really wanted to attend the University of Southern California just because they had a kick-ass football team, but the academic scholarship they'd offered had only been a partial. Even with grants and a part-time job, he wouldn't have made tuition, let alone living expenses. Since he was no Bill-fucking-Gates, he gave up on the Trojans and took the offer from Serenity Heights U. After a couple of years, he hoped to transfer to a university someone had actually heard of.

Paris might think he didn't give a shit about anything but getting laid and getting high, but she was wrong. He had plans. Plans to be somebody some day. Exactly how, he wasn't sure, but that's what college was for, right? To figure out what he wanted to be when he grew up.

He craned his neck to see where the van was and spotted the red taillights in the distance. The van stopped just before it slipped out of sight, around a row of trees at the far end of the field. Zach reached into his pocket for the pack of Marlboros and lit up, keeping his eye on the van.

He couldn't hear their voices, but he did see some chick with long dark hair walk up to the driver's side of the van. They talked for a minute and then she rounded the van and disappeared from view. The van remained idling for another couple of minutes, then took off around the trees and out of sight, obviously with the chick since she was nowhere to be seen.

Zach shrugged, then stood. Deciding he was safe from a bust, he started off in the opposite direction the van had taken, and hiked back to the dorm. What did he care if some jerkwad was picking up chicks in a field half a mile from the U? Maybe this was a place where hookers hung out. Not that he gave a rat's ass. It wasn't his business. And if he'd learned anything on the streets of Oakland, it was to mind your own.

BECK COULDN'T REMEMBER the last time he'd felt so content. He couldn't move, and wasn't exactly certain he wanted to, but his cell phone was ringing and he had no choice but to get off his ass and answer it. He'd enjoyed the company tonight probably more than he should have. And since he'd been in a self-indulgent mood, he'd gone and eaten far too much, too. Running on nothing but a couple of brownies and a handful of M & M's, he'd been hungry for real food.

"Excuse me," he said to Ainsley as he got up from the table. He walked into the family room, where he'd left his cell resting on the end table, and checked the display before punching the Call button. It was Mitch and he didn't expect the news would be good. "Raines."

"Hey, Chief," Mitch greeted him. "Thought I should check in before I call it a night."

Beck was glad to hear it. At least he'd gotten a few hours

of unexpected sleep on Ainsley's recliner, but Mitch had been going strong since Beck had called him in last night.

Beck heard the rustling of papers. "You got anything new for me?"

"Just a couple of updates." Mitch sounded tired and Beck could've sworn he'd just heard him attempt to stifle a yawn. "Coroner's office called. No ID yet on the body, but Dr. Reiki believes a combination of materials were used to strangle the vic."

Beck walked to the worn sofa and sat. "Any idea what he used on her?" Remembering exactly where he was, he kept his voice low. The last thing he wanted was his conversation showing up in the next edition of the *Sentinel*.

"Something soft. Could be a velvet cord," Mitch said, "combined with a more restrictive material. Which might explain those purple fibers I pulled off the body. But get this—Reiki doesn't think strangulation was the ultimate cause of death."

Beck frowned. "Then why go to the trouble?"

"Probably to get his jollies off." Mitch's disgust was obvious. "This is a real twisted fuck, Chief. Reiki says she won't know conclusively until the toxicology report comes back in about five days, but she's pretty sure a 'potent opiate analgesic drug' was used to overdose the vic."

"Morphine?"

"Morphine, maybe even heroin. She found a puncture wound on the arm and thinks whatever he gave her was through an IV."

"It could've been administered through a syringe."

"Not according to Reiki." More papers rustling. "Too much organ damage, particularly to the liver, and no track marks to coincide with the amount of drugs she believes were given to the vic, just the IV insertion point."

"Anything else?"

"Yeah. She thinks he kept the vic alive for a while. This

wasn't a one-night party, Chief, but one that went on for a few days."

Shit. He didn't like this. The UNSUB wasn't only dangerous, he was smart. He knew things. Like how to use an IV. How to get his hands on morphine. "Did she confirm the damage to the body wasn't postmortem?"

"Yeah," Mitch said. "She did."

Was that why the UNSUB pumped his victims full of morphine? To deaden the pain? Or did he use it just to render them incapacitated? Either way, it didn't make much difference if they couldn't bring this guy to a dead stop.

Mattie Davenport's smiling face floated through his mind. Beck scrubbed his hand over his jaw, but the image refused to waver.

More papers rustled. "Raelynn took a call from the sound engineer at the crime lab. He thinks he might have something for you."

"What?"

"A bell."

Beck's frown deepened. "A bell?" He'd listened to both audio files and hadn't heard anything but the victim begging, followed by several minutes of her tortured screams.

"Yeah. A church bell, maybe," Mitch said. "It's really faint, but he picked up the sound when he stripped everything else away on the second file. Once he did that, there were two distinct bells."

Two AM or PM? Did it matter? Probably, but Beck didn't have a clue yet about the exact significance. All he knew was they were looking for someone with access to a large freezer who had a working knowledge of dental practices, and now with access to morphine and who quite possibly lived near a church. Or perhaps a train station.

"Tell him to keep working on it."

"I'll call him back before I head home. You're going to be around for a while tonight, right?"

"If he's still in, give the engineer my cell number. If not, leave him a message. I'm not sure where I'll be yet."

"You know, we should probably expect another CD delivered to Ainsley tonight."

Beck looked into the kitchen to where Ainsley was busy stacking dishes near the sink. "I'm expecting it," Beck admitted. Which was why he'd decided it might be best if he stuck close to her for a while tonight. She was strong and independent, and probably wouldn't appreciate his hovering, but that was just too damn bad. The only pattern they had to go on at the moment was the UNSUB's delivery of those CDs to Ainsley. He might feel better about leaving her alone if he'd taken her to the gun range as he'd promised her he would.

Or not.

"How many patrols did you put on the street tonight?" Beck asked, not liking the road his thoughts were determined to travel.

"Not that the added presence did us much good last night," Mitch said, "considering the UNSUB walked right up to Ainsley's front door, but I've got officers working double shifts. For the time being, we'll have a fifty percent increase in our usual presence. You know the city council is gonna be all over your ass when they hear of all the overtime."

"They'll have to get over it," Beck said. That was one part of his new job he didn't care much for, dealing with the bureaucrats. He didn't appreciate a bunch of unqualified suits telling him how to do his job.

"I put two patrolmen over at the U. We're checking IDs on anyone seen on campus after dark."

"Good." The solution wasn't perfect, but it was all they had for now. They were a small police force without a detective unit. But he had the word of every officer on the payroll that they would do their part and then some until they

brought the sick bastard down. For their sake, and everyone else's, he hoped it was sooner rather than later.

"Make sure dispatch knows to contact me if the officers
request it," Beck instructed. "I'll be by the station later."

"You got it, Chief." And with that, Mitch disconnected
the call.

"Bad news?"

Beck looked up as Ainsley came into the family room,
two mugs of coffee in her hands. "Not exactly." But at least
he had more information than he'd had an hour ago. Not
that it gave them the break in the case he'd been hoping for
in finding Mattie Davenport or identifying the UNSUB. But
they were inching forward, one microscopic step at a time.
Only problem was, he needed a four-minute mile.

He flipped his cell closed and slipped it into his pocket
before taking the mug of coffee she offered. She walked to
the built-in bookcase on the far wall and pressed the power
button on the small stereo unit. A song from a country music
station filled the room as she took a seat in the glider rocker
closest to the sofa.

"You know," she said thoughtfully, "maybe we need to
make a pact."

He leaned back and took a drink of the hot, steamy brew,
watching her over the rim of his mug. "What kind of pact?"
he asked cautiously when she continued to stare at him.

"You don't bullshit me, and I won't print anything about
the case without running it by you first."

A deal with the devil. That's what she was asking.

"Okay, so maybe I'm no mental health professional," she
said when he didn't answer, "but you need someone you
can talk to. This case is going to make you crazy."

He lowered the mug. "What makes you think that?"

She flashed him a brief smile. "You've got that whole
weight of the universe thing going on. And it's not healthy
to keep it all in, you know."

Beck chuckled and shook his head. Since when had he become so transparent? Maybe always. Most people just thought he was a prick, but Linda had always been able to tell when a case was getting to him, too.

"So do we have a deal?"

She looked so earnest he didn't have the heart to tell her he couldn't trust her. Not her, per se, but her kind. The reporter kind.

"I don't think that's a good idea." He took another drink of coffee. "Let's talk about something else."

"Okay." She slipped a coaster from the holder and set down her mug. "Not that I don't appreciate the company, but how about you tell me why you don't seem to be in any big hurry to leave? And don't you dare tell me it's because you consider it rude to eat and run, because I won't believe you."

He attempted a smile. "Maybe I just like your company."

Her expression turned skeptical. "Nice try. I'm thinking it's because you're waiting for someone to deliver another CD to me. Like, oh, I don't know. A whacked-out killer, maybe?"

All right, so he was transparent. Like fucking cellophane. "The thought had crossed my mind."

She pulled her feet up onto the chair and wrapped her arms around her upraised knees. "Appreciated, but I can take care of myself."

He had his doubts on that score. She had a gun in the house, didn't have the first clue how to use it, and even if she did, she didn't have any ammo. "Excuse me, but wasn't it you who puked all over my crime scene yesterday?"

She wrinkled her nose. "I was taken by surprise is all."

"Don't come across too many dead bodies in your line of work, huh?"

She rolled her eyes. "In Serenity Heights? Puleeze. Until yesterday, the biggest story in weeks, if you can even call it that, was the nail biter about who would be named the new dean of students at the U. Chesterfield got the job, by the way."

"No place is safe, Ainsley."

She shrugged. "This town used to be. And it will be again. Just as soon as you nail this S.O.B."

He appreciated her faith, but not her rose-colored view of the world. He wasn't jaded, just a realist. "You need to be more careful."

A light frown tugged her eyebrows down. "Don't lecture me, Beck. I am careful. When I'm in the city, I look in the backseat of my car before getting into it. I park where it's well lit, and I even carry my keys so they can be used in self-defense if necessary. I do know how to take care of myself."

"In the city, but what about here in town? I'm willing to bet your doors aren't even locked."

She swung her feet to the floor and stood. "Ha! You'd lose that bet." To prove her point, she marched into the kitchen and checked the back door.

He set his mug on the coffee table and followed her. Sure enough, the door was closed, but not locked. The dead bolt hadn't even been secured. "You lose," he said.

She flipped the knob and locked the door. "That's odd. I thought it was locked."

"Thought. But you never checked to make sure." He folded his arms over his chest and gave her a smug look. "Care to check the front door?"

She let out an exasperated huff of breath and took off toward the foyer. He followed, distracted by the sway of her ass encased in those snug-fitting jeans. The urge to slide his hands over her hips and pull her to him suddenly overwhelmed him. To skim her curves with his hands, to taste her.

"Locked," she said, and turned, flashing one of her megawatt smiles that had his heart tripping over itself. God, he wanted her. It made no sense. He didn't even know her all that well.

Sex. That's all this was about. The timing was lousy and she was the wrong woman. But that didn't stop the sharp, intense need from clawing at his gut.

She looked up at him as he neared and her smile slowly faded. A delicate frown lined her forehead, and she tipped her head slightly to the side, her long blond hair falling over one shoulder.

He slipped his hand along her hip, drawing his thumb along that microscopic space between her jeans and the bottom of the top she wore. He pulled her close before his common sense took over and he changed his mind. He'd felt the same clawing need last night. Had wanted to taste her then, but he'd ignored it. He wasn't about to make the same mistake twice. "You know this is probably a bad idea."

She slipped her hand behind his head and urged him toward her. "I know it is," she said, but lifted her face to his anyway.

The moment his lips touched hers heat shot through his body and simmered in his veins. She made a sexy little sound in the back of her throat, then angled her head, deepening the kiss and bringing their bodies closer together.

Nothing made sense to him any longer. Every reason why he shouldn't be kissing Ainsley shattered when her arms wound around his neck and her breasts pressed enticingly against his chest. Through her thin top, he could feel her nipples bead and scrape against him. He didn't care if it was a mistake, he had to have her.

He turned then and pushed her up against the wall, pressing into her, surrounding her with his heat, with his body. Her breath caught, then she let go a deep, sensual moan of pleasure that had his dick throbbing painfully. He nudged her legs apart with his knee and she rubbed against his thigh. A tremor shook her body and he nearly came out of his skin.

He dragged his mouth from hers and trailed a hot path down her throat to the opening of her top, dipping his tongue beneath to tease the swell of her breasts. Her back arched and she sucked in a sharp breath. Shoving her hands into his hair, she held him to her.

He wanted her naked. Naked and hot beneath him. If one of them didn't come to their senses soon, that's exactly where they'd end up, too. Of that he was certain.

There was a ringing in his ears that annoyed him. He tried to ignore it, but . . .

Ainsley pushed at his shoulders. "Your phone."

"Huh?"

"Your cell phone." Her breathing was as labored as his own. "Shouldn't you answer it?"

Shit. He pulled the phone from his pocket and checked the display. Damn. "Raines."

"Chief, this is Loretta from dispatch. You'd better get over here."

"What's wrong?"

"There's a Mr. and Mrs. Davenport in the lobby demanding to speak with you. And the mayor and associate dean from the U are here, too."

Great. Just what he didn't need. But that explained why all he'd gotten when he called the Davenport home today was an answering machine. "Tell them I'm on my way." He flipped the phone closed and slipped it back into his pocket.

"I'm sorry," he told Ainsley. "I have to go."

She wrapped her arms around her middle and nodded, not looking at him. He wished she'd say something. Wished she'd look at him.

"Lock the door," he said. "Keep the porch light on. I'll be back later."

She turned and opened the door. "That's really not necessary," she said stiffly. "I'll be fine."

He didn't feel good leaving her alone. There would be another CD showing up, but he was pretty sure that wasn't the only reason he was so reluctant to leave her alone. "Humor me."

She finally looked up at him. A half smile quirked her mouth and she made a sound that almost resembled a laugh. "Go. You have people waiting for you."

He did, but it wasn't until he was halfway to the station that he realized she hadn't even bothered to ask him who was waiting for him.

CHAPTER 9

"OKAY, I'VE BEEN patient long enough," Cassidy said. She closed her world history text with a sharp snap and pushed away from the small wooden desk on her side of their shared dorm room. "Are you going to tell me what happened today or not?"

Paris hid a smile and looked up from her own reading assignment on narrative text for her freshman comp class. "Tell you what? That I got the job in the associate dean's office?"

Cassidy flung herself onto Paris's bunk. She grabbed the pillow there, hugging it to her chest. "Good for you, but . . . Duh!" she said, with an accompanying eye roll. "I wanna know about your date with Gavin."

Paris turned her attention back to the paragraph she'd already read four times. She understood the concept of narration, that was fairly elementary in her opinion. But the example she'd been studying was just plain dull and failed to hold her attention. "It was no big deal," she said with a shrug.

Only it was a big deal. Just not in the way Cassidy was thinking.

Cassidy let loose with a long drawn-out sigh. "Coffee with Gavin Chesterfield? Are you kidding me?"

"It wasn't like a real date," Paris said, closing the book

and pushing it aside. She turned in her chair and kicked her feet up on the edge of her bunk. "We met for coffee. That's it."

One of Cassidy's pale eyebrows rose a fraction. "Okay, so how was your meeting for coffee, with like, the hottest guy at the U?"

Paris smiled then. Gavin was hot, no doubt about it. And he was so her type. Tall, dark hair, nicely built but not like those big gorilla football players that had no neck. And he had the most amazing eyes—ever.

"Nice," she said. A lot better than she'd imagined, too. Gavin wasn't only incredible to look at, he seemed like a really nice guy. In her limited experience, most of the good-looking guys she knew were, well, dickheads.

Like Zach.

"Maybe better than nice," Paris added, remembering Zach's crappy attitude that morning. "He's not dumb as a post, that's for sure." And he'd appeared interested in what she had to say, too. Unlike Zach, Gavin hadn't belittled her concern over the missing student, but had actually expressed concern, as well.

Cassidy sat up a little straighter and crossed her legs. The most ridiculous pair of multistriped socks peeked out from beneath the length of her fleece pajama bottoms. "Did he ask you out again?"

"Yes," Paris admitted.

"Very cool. Where are you going?"

"I told him I had to think about it."

Paris had the urge to reach over and pick Cassidy's jaw up off her chest.

"Are you freaking nuts? Why?" Cassidy asked.

Probably, but she did have standards. "Zach."

"Hmmm," Cassidy mused. "I guess that would complicate things, huh?"

Yes, it did, especially because Paris did like Gavin. Not that she expected anything to happen because of one coffee date. She might only be eighteen, but she wasn't totally naive. She and Gavin came from different worlds. His included a silver spoon and an aunt who was the dean of students at the U, while hers was more of a picnic-ware kind of existence with no family ties.

And then there was Zach. He'd called her earlier to see if she wanted to get high with him. She told him she had too much homework, but the truth was, she was still mad at him for being such a jerk to her that morning. And she'd never really liked getting high all that much anyway. If Zach had ever bothered to pay attention to her, he would've realized that by now.

"So, what are you going to do about it?"

Paris shrugged. "I don't know. But I think I should probably talk to Zach."

"You're going to tell him about Gavin?"

"There's nothing to tell. I only had coffee with Gavin. He asked me out again, but I don't think I should go. At least until I see if things can be worked out with Zach. We haven't been getting along, anyway. Maybe it's time we explored other opportunities."

Cassidy giggled and slid off the bed. "You read that somewhere."

Paris grinned. *"Cosmo."*

"So you got the job working for McElvoy?" Cassidy strolled across the room to her desk, where she stacked up the books and notebook she'd had spread out there. "That guy gives me the creeps."

Paris thought so, too, but the job was easy money. It was better than working in the dining hall. "Did you have any luck?"

"Yup. I'll be working in the financial aid office two afternoons a week." Cassidy wrinkled her nose. "Yuck. I hate numbers."

Paris laughed. "I've heard the dining hall is always hiring."

"Yeah, because nobody wants to work there. I worked the last two summers at the Pizza Pit in town. The money was okay, but the job was gross."

Cassidy turned off her desk lamp, then grabbed the remote for the small color television set sitting atop an old chest of drawers in serious need of a paint job. "Will it bother you if I watch some TV?"

"No. Besides, I'm done." Paris turned off her own small desk lamp and crawled onto her bunk, adjusting the pillows behind her against the short headboard. Without cable, which she knew neither of them could afford, they couldn't get much, only the local network affiliates out of Cleveland. But it was better than radio all the time, so she was grateful Cassidy had brought the small television set.

Cassidy settled on a reality competition, but instead of watching, she turned to Paris and asked, "Have you thought about pledging to a sorority?"

Paris tugged on the covers. "I don't think I can afford it. Aren't the dues something like a few hundred dollars every semester?"

"Most are around five to seven hundred." Cassidy brushed her hair from her face and flipped the long length over her shoulder. "I've heard of some that are over a grand, but they're at the bigger schools."

"That's two thousand dollars a year." That was an almost decent used car, not to mention way out of her price range.

"My sister, Paige, was a Theta, and she says it wasn't too expensive. And your scholarship money would pay for the housing, which I've heard is actually cheaper than living in the dorms."

"Are you going to pledge?" Not that it mattered to Paris.

Not really. But she did like having Cassidy as a roommate. Cass was easy to talk to, and they got along pretty well—so far. And then there was the possibility of the occasional home-cooked meal to look forward to, as well.

Cassidy snorted. "Like I have two grand sitting around. But we could check it out if you want. There are only four here at the U. The parties are supposed to be pretty cool."

Paris thought about that for a moment. "I dunno, Cass. Do you really want to be judged by a bunch of strangers who probably think they're better than you are?" Even if she wanted to pledge to a sorority, which she didn't, she didn't especially like the idea of an exclusive girls' club. More than likely filled with little rich bitch snobs she'd have nothing in common with, anyway. Besides, she didn't have the money to spare. Her new job would help cover extras, but it wasn't in any way enough to cover the semester dues of a sorority. And then there were the formals and all the other expenses that would be required, all of which spelled money she didn't have. "It'd be a waste of time for me. I just don't have that kind of cash."

"Yeah." Cassidy let out another sigh, then snuggled under her covers. "You're probably right. Who wants to hang out with a bunch of snooty bitches anyway?"

"Exactly. Why get our hopes up for something that we can't afford?"

And that pretty much summed up not only Paris's life, but her philosophy, as well. If you kept your expectations low enough, then there was a lesser chance of disappointment. It wasn't perfect, but it was all she knew.

"WHY HAVEN'T YOU found our daughter? What are you people doing up here?"

"Mr. Davenport," Joe Cummings, the town's mayor, spoke. "I'm sure Chief Raines is doing his best to find your daughter."

Condescending prick. It wasn't that Beck didn't like the

guy, he just wasn't fond of politicians. They not only made promises they knew they wouldn't keep just to get elected, but were a pain in law enforcement's ass with their unrealistic demands. Cummings was proving to be no exception.

"Well, his best isn't good enough," a red-faced Hank Davenport railed, and smacked his fist on the table. "My daughter has been missing for going on four days now. Why haven't you people found her?"

Because they didn't have a single lead, that's why, but Beck kept that fact to himself. Of all the students and faculty he and his officers had interviewed, not a one could remember seeing Mattie Davenport after she'd left her advisor's office. Even her own roommate hadn't bothered to report her missing. All they had was a cell phone battery tossed into the bushes that might or might not have come out of Mattie's cell phone. No one saw Mattie talking to anyone, never saw her leave campus with anyone. She'd simply vanished.

"We have extra patrols on the street, we've interviewed faculty and staff at the university," Beck told Davenport. "We've even gone door to door. We're doing everything we can to find your daughter."

"We heard you found a body," Mrs. Davenport spoke up in a strained, wavering voice.

Despite the red eyes and tearstained cheeks, Erin Davenport's resemblance to her daughter was remarkable. Beck had no trouble imagining what Mattie would look like in twenty or so years. If she lived that long.

"I can assure you, it's not your daughter," Beck told her.

"Are you certain?" Devin McElvoy asked. The associate dean had been quiet throughout the entire meeting. Beck wished he'd shut the hell up now. "It's my understanding the description could be a match."

Beck shot the dean a sharp stare. "And how would you know that?" He'd quickly read Ainsley's article when he'd arrived at the station. Raelynn magically had an early copy waiting for him on his desk. Even if McElvoy had gotten his hands on a copy, there was no mention of the fact that the physical description of the body matched that of the Davenport girl. Ainsley hadn't printed anything about there being a link between the two incidents, although it didn't take much for people to draw their own conclusions and connect the dots, which he guessed was her intent.

She hadn't made any mention of the audio files, either. In other words, she'd kept her promise to him. He'd have to remember to thank her.

McElvoy offered up a smooth smile. He reminded Beck more of a used car salesman than a college dean, even dressed in a pair of crisp jeans with a dark smudge on one knee and a button-down Oxford shirt, neatly tucked. "This is a small town, Chief Raines. People do talk."

So he was learning. The Serenity Heights rumor mill was one well-greased machine.

"Perhaps the good people of Serenity Heights may be of assistance," McElvoy said to the Davenports.

Mrs. Davenport dabbed her eyes with a ragged tissue. "How so?"

"An intense ground search of the surrounding area," McElvoy suggested. "We have many wooded areas and open fields surrounding our town. I've heard only a cursory search has been conducted. We could very easily organize a search party, say, by noon tomorrow."

"That's an excellent idea," Cummings said, and pushed out of his chair. "Chief, you'll see to it, won't you?"

As if he had a choice in the matter now. "Of course," Beck agreed.

"I'm sure the students and faculty of the university will gladly volunteer their time," McElvoy said. "Bud Jenkins has a pair of tracking dogs. Bloodhounds, I believe. Shall I see if he's available?"

"Leave the scent dogs to me," Beck said. They didn't

need scent dogs, they'd need cadaver dogs, but he wasn't
about to voice that particular opinion in front of the Davenport girl's parents.

"I'll be in touch with the county's search and rescue team
first thing in the morning," Beck said before turning his attention back to the Davenports. "Where are you staying?"

"The Northeast Inn off the interstate," Hank Davenport
said.

"There's a lovely B and B right here in town," McElvoy
said. "It's quite nice. I'm sure you'd be so much more comfortable there, and closer."

"Uh . . . thanks, but no," Davenport declined. "We're fine."

One look at the Davenports and it didn't take a rocket
scientist to realize they weren't rolling in money. The early
model faded red Dodge pickup truck with Mississippi plates
in the parking lot looked as if it wouldn't make the trip back
to Mississippi. Hell, Beck was surprised it made the drive
up to Ohio.

He shot a smug glance in the mayor's direction.
"Mr. McElvoy has a point," he said. "The department will
be happy to pick up the tab while you're here. Wouldn't we,
Mayor Cummings?"

"Oh, but of course," the mayor agreed, while shooting
daggers back at Beck.

Beck smiled. Like the mayor could decline without looking like a first-class asshole. Not that Beck gave a rat's ass
what the mayor thought, even if he was technically his boss
while Chief Munson was off on an extended medical leave.
But that ought to teach the stupid son of a bitch to try to
make him and his department look incompetent in front of
a pair of distraught parents whose daughter was more than
likely dead.

"Thank you," Davenport said, standing. "Your hospital-
ity is appreciated."

"Yes, thank you," Mrs. Davenport added as she also

stood and moved to her husband's side. She certainly was a tiny thing, but Beck wasn't fooled by her petite stature. While the woman was understandably distraught, he sensed an iron will behind those red-rimmed eyes.

Beck reached out to shake Davenport's hand. "I promise you, sir, we are doing everything we can to find your daughter."

"Thank you," Davenport said again.

Beck scribbled the address for the B and B on a yellow sticky note and handed it to Mrs. Davenport. "I'll call and let Ms. Carson know to expect you within the hour. You'll be much more comfortable there."

Mrs. Davenport took the note and tucked it in her purse.

"I'll see you out," McElvoy said, then ushered the Davenports from the room.

"We'll be in touch," Cummings called after the couple, then waited until the small, formal conference room cleared before turning to Beck. "That was uncalled for, Raines. You know your department can't afford to put those people up at Carson's Bed and Breakfast for who knows how long."

"Too bad," Beck snapped at him, "because it's done."

"And now we have to pay for the county's search and rescue team?" Cummings's voice rose sharply. "How could you let that happen? And just exactly how do you think the city is going to pay for that kind of expense, Raines? We're a small municipality. We don't have that kind of money."

"I'm calling search and rescue," Beck fired back hotly, "when I should be calling in the cadaver dog team. And how you pay for it is not my concern, but you better fucking find the funds, because it's too late now."

"Now you wait just a minute—"

"No, you wait. We have a missing girl, an unidentified body in the morgue that has been grossly mutilated. I have two audio files of a woman being tortured, which I'm thinking could very well be Mattie Davenport." Beck pulled in a deep breath and let it out slowly, trying to calm his rising temper, to little avail. "If you think I'm going to ask for permission for every penny spent to conduct an investigation, then you're dead wrong, Mayor."

"But I thought you said the two incidents weren't related."

"Don't believe everything you read in the paper." The moron. "I don't have concrete proof yet, but I know in my gut they're related."

The mayor returned to his seat. He looked over at Beck and for the first time Beck saw honest concern in the mayor's dark gaze. "Are you saying this is the work of a serial killer? Right here in Serenity Heights?"

"It's possible," Beck admitted.

The mayor shook his head. "This is bad, Raines. Bad for our city's economy. Bad for the U. What if parents start yanking students? Homecoming is in six weeks. That's parents weekend, too. Do you realize how much potential revenue is at stake?"

Beck made a sound that could've been a laugh, only there was nothing funny about what the mayor was saying. In fact, it was downright ludicrous. "This isn't about revenue, Joe. It's about keeping the citizens of this town safe. It's about putting an end to what could be just the beginning of a vicious murder spree."

Joe Cummings nodded solemnly. "Yes. Yes, you're right. Do what you have to do," he said. "I'll handle the city council the best I can. We'll find a way to make sure the department has the funds available to do its job."

"Thank you," Beck told him. "The sooner we nail this bastard, the less collateral damage you'll have to deal with."

Cummings stood again and extended his hand to Beck. "I appreciate that," he said.

"What was McElvoy doing here?" Beck asked Cummings. "Did you call him?"

"No. The Davenports went to the U. Mary Ann was at a fund-raiser with the university president, and so security called McElvoy. Why do you ask?"

"I don't like it when Joe Citizen tries to stick his nose in my investigations. It's a distraction none of us needs right now."

"And what about Joe Mayor?"

Beck managed a small laugh. "Him, either."

The mayor chuckled and headed for the door, stopped and turned back to Beck. "Have you talked to Munson about any of this?"

"No," Beck said. "I was waiting to hear back from his wife to see how he was holding up first."

"Last I heard, more bad days than good ones. Maybe you shouldn't bother him," Joe suggested. "At least for the time being."

"I'll keep that in mind." Beck sure as hell hoped the chief made a full recovery because he had no desire for his temporary position to become a permanent one.

THE HARRINGTON FARM, as everyone in town referred to the place, had been established in the 1830s by Patrick Harrington and his bride, Juliet Morrissey of the Morrissey Shipping empire. Juliet's father, Jasper, had made his riches transporting slaves across the ocean. Sweet, delicate Juliet had given her husband four strong sons to work the farm along with a willful daughter, Jasmine, who'd gone on to shame her Southern-sympathizing family when she'd eloped with an abolitionist out of Pennsylvania. It was rumored that Jasmine's mother had died the night of her daughter's elopement, presumably in a state of such complete and utter despair that her heart had stopped beating within minutes of learning the news.

With his sons dying off one by one while fighting for the

cause, and what slaves he had owned confiscated by the Yankees to fight for the North, Patrick Harrington had no one to help with the two hundred acres of farmland, so the place had gone to seed. Some said Patrick had taken to his bed with some good ol' Kentucky bourbon before shooting himself in the head, while other accounts claimed Harrington accidentally shot himself while cleaning his perfectly matched set of pearl-handled pistols.

Upon reading the news of her father's death, Jasmine and her abolitionist husband returned to Harrington Farm with the goal of using the place to help escaped slaves from the South start a new, free life in the North. But because the great state of Ohio was one divided by their beliefs, there were those who didn't appreciate the good work Jasmine performed, so she and her husband did their best to make the good townspeople of Serenity Heights—then known only as Serenity—believe that Harrington Farm was exactly what her father had intended when he'd purchased the land, a farm.

By day, Jasmine and her husband worked the land on a much smaller scale, putting in few crops and making even less money. But once the sun set, they went about their life's ambition, to help those less fortunate by seeing them safely to freedom.

They made use of underground tunnels and underground rooms beneath the enormous barn to hide those who came their way, doing their best to feed and clothe the many who passed through their hands. Once the war ended, and when their services were no longer needed, Jasmine and her husband sold Harrington Farm and traveled west, where they lived out the remainder of their days.

Since then, Harrington Farm had passed through many hands. At the turn of the century, it had been lost to the bank holding the mortgage, but had quickly been bought at auction by young Benjamin Piedmont, a cattleman from Texas, rumored to have been disowned by his family because of a certain unfortunate incident with a young lady of substantial wealth and standing. Piedmont died, alone and childless during the Great Depression. When the place went up for auction, this time to pay the back taxes on the land, Edwin Middlefield, a merchant looking for a quieter way of life, and who'd come into a small amount of wealth through an inheritance from an uncle he hadn't known existed, had purchased the land and stock for a song.

Unfortunately, Middlefield didn't have the first clue how to raise cattle, but he certainly knew how to eat beef, as did his six children, ranging in age from three to twenty-three. So he hired a young drifter passing through looking for a hot meal, who possessed excellent skills with a knife.

Middlefield not only learned how to butcher beef, he also hired another drifter to tend to the cattle, and thus was the birth of Middlefield Beef and Processing. After the Depression, Middlefield built a much larger meatpacking plant and moved his family back to the city and away from Harrington Farm. The place changed hands a few more times over the years. Most of the land had been sold off by previous owners until only a small ten acres, a few outbuildings, and the house and an old barn were all that was left of Harrington Farm.

Two summers ago, *he'd* purchased what remained of Harrington Farm. The real estate agent hadn't cared that he was a single man intent on living on such a large piece of property or in a house meant for a large family, because, after all, a sales commission was a sales commission. Just as it had for Jasmine and those who followed, the place suited his needs perfectly.

He turned his vehicle down the long driveway, but drove past the old farmhouse and out to the barn, which had been converted into a deep garage and butcher shed by Middlefield. The workshop had been where Middlefield's small meatpacking operation had started. Upon one of his many explorations of the place, he'd discovered that the locals had also used the services of Middlefield to have their game dressed, as evidenced by the boxes of antlers he'd found in an upstairs storage room. Most of the meatpacking equipment was long gone, but certain items had remained. Items he'd found quite useful for his purposes.

He hit the switch and the automatic garage door slowly lifted. His work had been interrupted tonight, which had irritated him immensely at the time. Now, he wasn't quite so disappointed. In fact, by the time he'd crawled back inside his vehicle and drove home, he'd been surprisingly elated.

Chief Raines hadn't appreciated his interference during the meeting with the Davenports, that much had been obvious from the scathing glances he'd kept shooting his way. In fact, it had appeared to him as if the man had actually squirmed a time or two, particularly at the mention of an intense ground search. He'd had to stifle the laughter threatening to bubble up inside him when those bloodhounds had been brought into the conversation. He knew what the chief had been thinking. They wouldn't need bloodhounds to track *her* scent, they'd need cadaver dogs.

Not that they'd ever find her. At least not yet. Not until he was ready for them to find her.

The garage door open now, he drove through and parked beside the dark blue cargo van, then cut the engine. He listened for any sign of life, but all he heard was the quiet ticking of the warm engine. Not trusting that his knockout blow would keep his other interference of the night out of commission until he'd returned, he'd had to improvise and had shot his little hitchhiker full of a heavy dose of morphine to ensure she'd not awaken until he was able to return to her.

He grabbed a flashlight from the glove compartment, then climbed from his car and strode to the van. Opening the back, he flashed the light inside. She was exactly where he'd left her—slumped in a heap on the paint-stained floorboard in the rear of the van.

He stood looking at her for a moment, collecting his thoughts. She was all wrong. Too tall, breasts too small, and hips as narrow as that of a young boy. Her eyes were brown and set too far apart. And her hair was an ungodly shade of mousy brown. But her skin was creamy and unscarred. He thought her passably pretty, but wrong. He flashed the light on her hands, bound behind her back. They were ugly. Not long and graceful, but short and stubby. From the looks of it, she chewed her nails.

He shuddered.

Not that any of it really mattered, he thought. He did, after all, possess the power to change all of those inconvenient imperfections to suit his needs. When he was done with her, she *would* be perfect. She had to be, because she wouldn't be permitted to draw her last breath until she *was* perfect.

He turned off the flashlight and reached into the van, dragging her body closer to the opened rear doors so he could heft her into his arms. Turning, he left her and walked the length of the garage, stopping in front of a large sliding door. He lifted the latch and pulled the heavy door back, then bent and peeled up the faded red and gold shag carpet to reveal another door, this one in the floor. Lifting the door took all of his strength, but he managed to pull it up and secure the hatch door with the metal rod hanging on the back wall. He grabbed the large meat hook next to it and reached down to flip on the light switch before going back to the van for his prize.

He hefted her in his arms. Given her height, she was lighter than he'd first thought, so carrying her down the steep staircase to the multitude of rooms below ground was easier than he'd anticipated. The table where he brought them to the perfection he required remained occupied—by the blond beauty who'd reached perfection because of him.

He carried the brunette to one of the old bunk rooms that had once housed runaway slaves, and dropped her limp form on the thin mattress of a small antique bed. Cutting off the plastic cording he'd used to bind her hands and feet, he then positioned her spread-eagle on the bed before duct taping her hands and feet to the metal head and footboards. She would have to wait for his attentions. There were more pressing matters requiring his attention yet tonight.

He double checked the bindings on her hands, tugging to make certain she couldn't escape. Reaching down for the bindings holding her ankles, he noticed that her left sandal was missing.

Alarm ripped through him. A mistake? He didn't make mistakes. He'd learned early on that he would be punished harshly, not only for his own mistakes, but *hers* as well.

He let out a bellow of frustration, then slammed out of the room. Anger boiled inside him as he shoved the bolt home, locking the brunette inside her small, dank prison. He retraced his steps and wasted the better part of an hour looking for that missing brown sandal, only to come up empty-handed.

He sat on the floorboard of the van and rubbed at the pain throbbing at his temples. It didn't matter, he told himself. He would find that sandal, dammit. If she'd lost it when he'd picked her up tonight, wouldn't she have said something?

Yes, of course, she would have. He was overreacting. He'd find it. That sandal was here somewhere, and he *would* find the damn thing.

He took a few deep breaths to calm his still-racing heart.

It helped to tell himself he couldn't afford to waste time thinking about a stupid sandal, especially because he had much more work to accomplish, not only tonight, but tomorrow afternoon, when he led the police exactly where he wanted them.

CHAPTER 10

ANSLEY COULDN'T SLEEP. Whether her current bout of insomnia was the result of the brief nap she'd had earlier, or the very real fear that she could wake up and find another CD on her doorstep, she couldn't say for certain. More than likely the latter, since she was afraid to even change out of her clothes into something more comfortable. What if she had to run for her life? She'd get a lot more traction in a pair of gym shoes than she would a pair of fuzzy blue bedroom slippers.

Curled up on the worn sofa in the family room with the throw she'd tossed over Beck this afternoon, she sipped on chamomile tea while watching her favorite of the late night news broadcasts. Ten minutes into the broadcast and not a word about the missing college student or the unidentified body found out at the clearing.

She set her tea aside and tugged the throw more tightly around her. She breathed in, taking in Beck's spicy scent. Well, that was a mistake, she thought with a frown. She'd been trying to forget about that toe-curling kiss all evening, but she didn't even have to close her eyes to imagine the feel of his warm lips pressing and demanding against her own.

She let out a groan and dropped her head against the

back sofa cushion. Kissing Beck hadn't been her smartest move, that's for sure, but damn, it'd been good. Real good. The kiss hadn't lasted more than a minute, but wow, what a minute. Her entire body had come vibrantly alive. Nerve endings she'd forgotten existed had tingled, sparked, and sprung to life. The sharp tug of desire had been so overwhelming, if Beck had even hinted that he'd wanted to have sex, she probably would've stripped right then and there and done him in the foyer.

Abstinence sucked. Having no real relationship for way too long wasn't exactly a party, either. But what was worse, she couldn't state with any degree of certainty that she wasn't attracted to Beck simply because it'd been ages since she'd had sex. She had to face facts. She was horny and she'd be willing to bet he'd have been ready, willing, and more than capable of scratching that particular itch if his cell phone hadn't gone off.

He'd said he was coming back, but that'd been over three hours ago. Was he coming back to finish what they'd so recklessly started, or because he was concerned she'd receive another audio file tonight? Did it matter? She didn't think so. What was wrong with wanting to kill two needs with one hot police chief? That didn't make her a bad person, did it?

No, she thought. Just a woman who hadn't been laid in forever.

She let out a sigh, then took another sip of the tea that wasn't doing squat to help her relax enough to fall asleep. Whatever happened with Beck, she knew it couldn't last forever. Especially since she faced the very real possibility of losing her job and would probably have to move away from Serenity Heights.

By the time the weather reporter came on, predicting more of the same, warm days with chillier nights, for the

next five days, there'd still been no word about the unidentified body found in Serenity Heights. She frowned over that.
Surely news of a body turning up in their quiet, sleepy little
town would at least garner a blip on the radar screen of the
local television media.

Or maybe not. It wasn't like Cleveland wasn't rife with
enough of its own crime. The city council was being bom-
barded by neighborhood watch groups demanding they do
something about the elevated murder rate and the rise in
gang violence in the downtown area in recent months.

Another commercial break, followed by sports filled with
updates and happenings for the Cleveland Browns, along
with speculation of the team's chances of a win in their final
preseason game. The topic switched to a discussion of baseball between the female anchor, an avid Cleveland Indians
fan, and the sports reporter on the team's chance at landing
a spot in the play-offs again this year.

She shifted on the sofa to find a more comfortable position. The gun that had been resting on her lap slid to the
floor and landed with a loud thwack, causing her to flinch.

A lot of good an unloaded gun would do her, especially
when she really didn't know how to use it. But having the
non-lethal weapon near gave her an odd sense of comfort.
She thought again about getting a dog, but with her employment up in the air, a pet wasn't a logical choice at the
moment. So she'd opted for the unloaded gun and prayed
she wouldn't be forced to admit to a crazed lunatic she didn't
have a single bullet in the house.

She set her tea on the coffee table and bent to pick up the
gun. That's when she heard it. The distinct creak of the back
door screen.

Her heart thundered in her chest and she hit the mute
button on the remote. Could've been the wind, she tried to
tell herself, only there hadn't been much of a breeze all

night. Or maybe one of Mrs. Greenway's dogs, but last she knew, Mrs. G's dogs weren't all that bright and she doubted their ability to open her screen door.

She could turn on the light. That might scare off whoever was skulking around her kitchen door. Or maybe he'd think she was offering an invitation.

Slowly, she untangled herself from the chenille throw and got up off the couch. She took the gun, grabbed her cell phone and flipped it open, dialing Beck's cell number single-handedly.

As she crept up the steps from the family room into the kitchen, she heard the ringing of a phone—in her ear and coming from outside her kitchen door. Realization instantly dawned and she opened the door just as Beck answered his cell.

"Well, don't I feel silly." She set the empty gun on the counter before flipping her phone closed, then opened the screen door and motioned him inside.

"I should've called first," he said, tucking his own phone back into his pocket.

She shut the door and locked it this time. "Yes, you should have," she said, securing the dead bolt on the kitchen door. "You scared the hell out of me."

"I didn't mean to. I am sorry."

He looked so adorably contrite, her heart did a little flip in her chest and she instantly forgave him. "It's okay. I'm just a little jumpy tonight."

"Understandable."

She nodded, because all of a sudden, she didn't know what to say. She felt—awkward. Funny, but she hadn't felt that way with him earlier. No, she'd been all over him and would've had no qualms about doing him. But she didn't know why he was really here, and that made her uncomfortable. Had he come to play guard dog or to play—with her?

"I made a small pot of chamomile tea," she said, hating that her voice sounded so stilted all of a sudden. She flipped on the overhead light. "Would you like some?"

"Thanks, no. Something with caffeine would be better."

"Coffee? Diet Coke?"

"Soda."

Glad for something to do, she walked to the fridge and retrieved a bottle of pop. "Ice?"

"No."

"Glass?"

"No."

"Okay," she said, and handed him the plastic bottle. God, she hated their monosyllabic conversation. "How was your meeting?" There. That was five syllables. If he said "good" she'd kick him.

"The Davenports are in town."

Seven. They were making progress.

"I spoke to Erin Davenport on Tuesday," she told him. "I felt bad. She was so worried."

"She still is." Beck twisted off the cap. A shadow entered his gaze. "Her daughter looks just like her."

"I know," she said, staring at his mouth as he lifted the bottle to his lips and took a long drink. "I have a photo of them together."

He lowered the bottle and gave her that hard stare, the one that clearly said she was butting in where she wasn't wanted. "Mind if I ask how you managed that?"

She shifted her feet a little, then moved over to the stove to turn the heat on under the tea kettle. "Well . . ."

"Ainsley?"

She let out a sigh and stuffed her hands in the back pockets of her jeans. "I swiped it from Mattie's dorm room, okay? It's in my tote bag if you want it."

He frowned at her. "You tampered with my crime scene?"

"It wasn't a crime scene," she defended. "It was her dorm room. One, that I might add, she shared with another girl, so it was hardly an uncorrupted scene anyway."

He let out a sigh and shook his head. "Did you take anything else?"

"No."

He offered a brusque nod, then took another long drink before setting the half-empty bottle down on the counter. "I read your article," he said. "Nicely done."

"Really?" she asked, surprised. Not that she didn't have confidence in her ability, but that he'd already seen it. "It's not supposed to be available until tomorrow."

He leaned his backside against the counter and crossed his arms over his chest. "Raelynn managed to scare up a copy for me."

"I wasn't sure my boss would run it since I couldn't officially link the incidents. Maybe it'll at least make people aware that there's something going on in this town."

"I wanted to say thanks."

She waited, but he didn't seem compelled to expand on that particular sentiment. "For . . . ?"

"For keeping your word. That hasn't always been my experience where the press is concerned."

"Oh. That." She shrugged. "I guess I lack the killer instinct."

That made him smile. He really needed to do that more often. The guy was a looker anyway, but when he loosened up, even a little, he was practically irresistible.

Needing a bit of space, she went to the family room for her tea cup, then turned off the fire under the kettle when she returned to the kitchen. Using a pot holder, she poured herself another cup. "Sure I can't interest you in one? It's chamomile."

"No, I'm good."

She added a spoonful of artificial sweetener and stirred, keeping her eye on Beck. "Surely you didn't come over at this hour just to thank me for keeping my word," she said.

"No. Not especially."

She set the spoon on a paper towel. "Then why are you here, Beck? Is it to play night watchman, or something else?"

"Ainsley, I don't . . ."

"Don't what?" she prompted when he looked as if he'd suddenly lost the ability to speak.

"It's probably not a good idea."

She crossed her arms and rested her hip against her side of the counter. "I think we already established that, but it didn't seem to make much difference three hours ago, now did it?"

He shifted, bracing his hands behind him on the counter. Not, she thought, because he was uncomfortable with the sharp turn she'd taken in their conversation. Quite the contrary. He looked as confident, and sexy, as ever. Which she figured could actually bode quite well for her if she were going to see some action tonight.

When he didn't seem inclined to answer her, she asked, "Are you attracted to me?"

That smile made a comeback, and his eyes darkened. "Yeah, as a matter of fact, I am."

Damn if her knees didn't go just a little weak. "Any thoughts on what you plan to do about it?"

He pushed away from the counter and circled to her side of the kitchen island. "Has anyone ever told you that you ask too many damn questions?" Heat simmered in his eyes. His hands settled on her shoulders, his fingers slowly inching toward her neck.

"I'm in the business of asking questions," she reminded him.

"Why? Does it bother you?"

"Everything about you bothers me."

She wasn't sure if he'd just insulted her, or complimented her. Before she could ask for clarification, he lowered his head and kissed her, long and slow and deep, making her nipples bead and her toes curl in one shot, with one sweep of his tongue over hers.

Definitely a compliment, she decided as she wreathed her arms around his neck, and angled her body with the length of his. For the first time in her adult life, the only person she had to worry about was herself, and the sensation was intoxicating. Whatever happened tonight was between her and Beck—and only her and Beck.

With that knowledge guiding her, she felt free—free of the responsibility of her actions affecting her younger siblings. She could fuck Beck right here on the kitchen floor if she wanted to and the only recriminations she might suffer would be her own morning-after regrets.

With freedom came a sense of power, a sense of rightness in taking what she wanted. And right now, all she wanted was Beck.

His hands skimmed up and down her sides, over her hips and down to her backside, where he nudged her closer. The havoc he created with her senses was a massive turn-on that had heat pooling in her belly, filling her with need. The man was pure sexual attraction and she was quickly becoming lost in the wild sensations rippling through her.

Not that she cared. Wasn't that what she wanted? Wasn't that why she was rubbing up against him now, because the only thing that mattered to her in this moment was the pleasure she knew without a doubt they would bring to each other?

Hell, yes.

Without breaking the bone-melting kiss, he backed her up against the counter and easily lifted her onto the tiles. Without so much as a thought as to what she was doing, she wrapped her legs around his hips and drew him closer. She wiggled forward until the hard ridge of his desire was pressed against her. She groaned into his mouth and held on tight.

Suddenly his hands were everywhere, urgent, questing fingers reaching beneath her top and skimming along the surface of her skin. He cupped her breast in his hand, his thumb rasping back and forth across her nipple, sending her senses into an even deeper spiral.

God, it had been so long since she'd been held like this. Kissed like this. Beck touched her in a way that aroused her with such a ferocity that it spooked and delighted her at the same time.

And yet it wasn't nearly enough. She wanted so much more. That intimate contact of his flesh against hers, of their bodies finding that perfect rhythm. She wanted to explore his body with her hands, her lips, and her tongue. She wanted Beck and she wasn't ashamed to admit it.

He dragged his mouth from hers and she whimpered at the loss of heat, then sighed when he nuzzled her neck. "My god, you're amazing," he said, his voice deep and husky, vibrating against her flesh. His words were filled with the same wonder, passion, and desire clamoring through her.

He caught her mouth again, his kiss breath-stealing and insistent. The man was lethal, and she was loving every blessed second of it. She didn't care that they were in the kitchen and not in the warmth and comfort of her bed. She didn't even care that the overhead lights were blazing and he could see all of her flaws, or that Mrs. Greenway could easily catch them doing the nasty if she happened to be snooping out her own kitchen window, which was entirely possible. She didn't care about anything except the give and take of pleasure.

And that damn insistent barking.

It had to be Lily, she thought. She was the most vocal of Mrs. G's dogs, who would yap if the freaking clouds moved.

Ainsley broke the kiss and hooked her fingers around his belt loops. "Let's go upstairs," she suggested with a little tug, "where we can have a little more privacy." If Lily was out, that meant her neighbor probably was as well.

Beck rested his forehead against hers, his breathing as hard as her own. But before he could answer, a high-pitched yelp pierced the silence, followed by a horrible series of agonizing cries.

Lily was hurt. Her heart took a dive at the sound of that poor little animal being hurt. She pushed Beck away, hopped off the counter, and bolted for the back door.

His hand clamped on her shoulder. "Wait," he said, and reached around her to flick off the lights. "Wait here."

She shrugged off his hand, turned on the back porch light, then tugged open the door and was outside before Beck could stop her. She heard him swear, but she didn't waste a second arguing with him. "Lily," she called out. The dog's cries had quieted to a pitiful whine and Ainsley followed the sound around to the back of the house. There, at the edge of the garage, was Lily, hunkered down and whimpering, holding up her front leg, which was set at an odd angle.

"Oh my God," she said, going down to her knees in front of the dog. "Who did this to you, baby?"

Sweet little Lily licked Ainsley's hand as she reached for the dog. Careful not to jar the leg, she lifted Lily in her arms and held her close, petting her and murmuring words she hoped comforted the dog.

"What's going on out here?"

Ainsley looked over her shoulder at the sound of her neighbor's voice. She didn't see Beck and suspected he was scouring the area.

"It's Lily," Ainsley said, standing. She carried Lily over to where Mrs. Greenway stood leaning over the railing of her back porch. "She's been hurt."

"What did you do to her?"

Ainsley didn't appreciate the accusation, especially when she'd been the one to come to poor Lily's rescue. "Nothing," Ainsley snapped at the cranky old woman. "I found her this way."

"Give her to me," Mrs. G demanded, her arms outstretched.

"What was she doing out here all alone?" That fact alone was highly unusual. Mrs. G rarely let her babies out, even at night, without her constant supervision.

"That's none of your concern, missy."

Ainsley lost her patience. "Go get dressed," she told the woman. "I'll drive you to the emergency vet in Avon. Lily's leg is broken and she needs a vet."

Mrs. Greenway shot her a sour look, then finally nodded in agreement before disappearing into the house. She and her neighbor might not always see eye to eye, particularly when it came to the way Ainsley raised her sisters. Through the years, she'd been hard pressed many a time not to tell Mrs. Greenway to mind her own business, but Ainsley knew the older woman did care, in her own misguided way. She had her better moments, too, times when she'd been almost friendly. And the woman did dote on her trio of Jack Russell terriers. Anyone who loved her dogs as much as her neighbor did couldn't be all bad.

Carrying Lily, Ainsley walked to her car, parked in front of Beck's Durango. She needed her purse, and her keys. Dammit. Where was Beck? She needed him to move his truck.

Walking back to the house with Lily still cradled in her arms, she managed to open the screen door. She walked to the closet in the foyer where she kept her purse, dragged it out, then snagged her keys from the table.

"How's the dog?"

She jumped at the sound of Beck's voice. Lily showed him her teeth. "You scared us."

Beck looked rather apprehensively at the little terrier in her arms. "Sorry." He stretched his hand toward the dog and let her sniff his fingers. "How is she?"

"I think her leg is broken. Did you see anything?"

When Lily didn't look as if she'd take his fingers off, Beck gently rubbed her head. "Nothing."

"Someone hurt her," Ainsley said, looking down at the dog in her arms. The pooch let out a breathy little sigh and rested her muzzle on Ainsley's forearm. "Who would do something like this?"

He didn't say anything, and that irritated her. "It wasn't a rhetorical question," she said.

"Don't start jumping to conclusions," he warned.

She frowned at him. "Given what's been going on around here lately, what do you expect?"

"I searched the area and didn't find any evidence of an intruder."

"Someone broke this poor little girl's leg, Beck," she argued. "It didn't just happen."

"There could be a dozen explanations."

She hiked up an eyebrow. "Name one."

There was a loud rap on the back door. "Ainsley? You coming?"

"I'll be right there," she called back to Mrs. Greenway. She looked at Beck. "I need you to move your truck. I'm driving my neighbor and her dog to the twenty-four-hour emergency vet over in Avon."

He pulled his keys from his pocket. "Take mine."

"Don't be silly," she said. "There's nothing wrong with my car."

"Ainsley?" Mrs. Greenway called again. "Are we going or what?"

"Just a minute," she called back.

"I need you to leave your car here."

"Why?"

"It's evidence."

"Evidence? What are you talking about?" That made, like, zero sense. "Why is my car evidence?"

He scrubbed his hand down his face, then blew out a long stream of breath. "Because," he said, "there's a package addressed to you on the driver's seat, inside your locked car."

CHAPTER 11

BECK DRAGGED THE headset off and tossed it on the desk in disgust. God, he hated this bastard. Hated the sick game he was playing. Even more, he despised the fact that he didn't have squat insofar as a solid lead was concerned. The bastard was that fucking good.

Leaning back in the worn office chair, Beck rubbed at his tired eyes, grainy from lack of sleep. Tough cases weren't new to him, nor were the long hours. Hell, he had more assistance now than he'd ever had in LA, where it'd been only him and his partner, so he didn't have a damn thing to bitch about on that score. His only complaint, other than zero leads, was that he'd thought he'd left that life behind when he'd packed up and moved to the other side of the country.

That's what he got for thinking.

His cell phone rang, and he snagged it off the desk. Squinting, he checked the display. Ainsley. He pressed the Call button. "Yeah?"

"Hi, it's me. How's it going?"

Nowhere fast. "No comment."

She laughed, just a short little breezy sound, but it was enough to lighten his mood half a notch. At least someone had managed to hold onto their sense of humor, because he sure as hell had lost his the moment that body had been found at the clearing.

"That wasn't an official question, by the way." That hint of laughter disappeared from her voice when she asked, "How are you doing?"

"Tired," he admitted. Tired. Disgusted. Feeling damn inept. He could go on, but what was the point? He had a job to do, a killer to stop, and a missing student to find, all of which took precedence over his own comfort. "But that's not why you called, is it?"

"I'm still with my neighbor."

Code for she couldn't really ask the questions she wanted to ask him. Which meant he could easily blow her off, if he wanted to, or spend time playing a guessing game he was in no mood to play.

He didn't know what to do about Ainsley, didn't like the tightrope he had to walk when he was with her, but dammit, he liked her. A lot. She was sweet and sassy all at the same time. Smart, sexy, and he couldn't stop thinking about her. Every rare, stray moment he'd had to himself the past couple of days, she'd managed to creep into his thoughts. And damn, he wanted her. Badly, based on his behavior tonight. Or was it last night? It was all becoming such a blur, he didn't know any longer.

But she was a reporter, he reminded himself. If he let his guard down, anything he told her could easily end up as front page news.

Regardless, he was still attracted to her. She turned him on beyond belief, reminded him that he was alive.

And that filled him with fifty different shades of guilt.

"How much longer do you think you'll be?" He glanced at the clock on the wall. A little less than three hours until the next shift change. He could use some sleep, but had a ground search to coordinate, a coroner to pressure for faster results, and the sound engineer at the crime lab to meet with, not to mention dealing with the anxious parents of a missing girl, now residing six blocks away. None of which he could start in motion for another few hours.

"We should be heading back in a few minutes," she told him.

"How's the patient?"

"Her leg wasn't broken, but her shoulder was dislocated. The vet didn't seem to think she did it jumping off the porch, either."

Neither did Beck. "I think your little friend surprised some-one."

"Yeah, me, too," she said. "So, um, what's new?"

"More of the same," he told her, knowing she was refer-ring to the package found on the front seat of her car. But that wasn't exactly the truth, because the latest audio file had contained more than the cries and screams of pain of the victim recorded on the two previous CDs. There were other sounds on this one, some that he could guess at that had turned even his stomach. There were other sounds, as well, but he wasn't exactly certain of their origin. One thing had been patently clear, however—the killer's words.

Stop me.

Had it been a plea for help? Desperation? Or something more sinister, like a dare? The words had been whispered, so there was little chance of his identifying the voice. God knows he'd tried. He'd replayed those two words over and over again, hoping to pick up something, the trace of an ac-cent, any type of inflection in the killer's voice, only to come up empty-handed. With any luck, the sound engineer would pick up something when he broke the audio file down. He could only hope.

"I had to impound your car," he told her. He'd felt bad about that, but it couldn't be helped. He'd wanted a thor-ough search of her vehicle, and hoped against hope that the crime lab would unearth at least a partial print, a fiber, a hair. Anything. Any piece of trace evidence that could give him the much needed break in the case.

"You did? Why?"

She didn't sound angry, just curious. "It's been towed to the crime lab," he said.

"They're giving it a thorough look, then?"

"It was necessary. He broke into your car, Ainsley."

"I wasn't complaining. Not in that sense, anyway. How long?"

"A few days, at least."

"Do you think I'll have it back by the weekend?"

"Probably not."

"Well, that's inconvenient." She let out a sigh. "Ah. Lily's ready to go home. I'll drop Mrs. Greenway off, then bring your truck over. Are you at the station?"

He really could use some sleep, even if he only managed to catch a couple of hours' worth. If he saw Ainsley, he couldn't guarantee that sleep is what he'd be getting.

"Keep it," he said out of pure self-preservation. "I'll pick it up later."

"Are you sure?"

There was a sudden note of vulnerability in her voice that made him pause. He didn't expect the UNSUB to be waiting for her when she returned home, but the bastard was becoming more bold in his deliveries. Ainsley wasn't stupid. She had to be thinking the same thing.

"Better yet," he said, "meet me at my place." So much for self-preservation. "Do you know where it is?"

"On Mulberry," she confirmed. "Third house from the corner, on the left."

"I'll see you there."

"I'm on my way," she said, then disconnected the call.

He flipped his phone closed. He knew he'd just made a

huge mistake, fully understood that he was asking for trouble. But damn if he had any desire to step back from that particular ledge . . . regardless of the consequences.

HER HAIR SHINED like spun gold. Long, almost entirely straight save the slight curl at the ends that looped around his finger. Beautiful. Perfect. Just as he'd made her.

He hummed an obscure melody while he dragged the brush through the length of her hair over and over again, smoothing each stroke with his hand. His fingertips lingered at the ends as he gently rubbed the silken strands with the pad of his thumb and forefinger. So soft.

He adjusted a large section of her hair over her shoulder and spread it so it covered one breast. Her nipple peeked out over the top of the tight corset and through the long, golden strands. He smiled.

He'd needed to redress her. The gown she'd been wearing for her exit had been ruined beyond hope, splattered with the blood that had dripped from her discarded fingers. He'd have no choice but to destroy the gown now, and that irritated him. The color had been so perfect for her.

Instead, he'd brought down a royal purple and silver sequined dress for her. The dress wouldn't show off the color of her eyes or make her skin glow the way the pink gown had, but it would fit her slender curves and enhance the gentle flare of her hips. And there were those sequined pumps to match.

He set the brush aside and unzipped the garment bag, removing the gown. Careful not to damage it, he crouched down and, starting with her feet, slowly eased the gown up her cool legs. The warmth had left her by the time he'd returned from delivering the latest record of his work. When they found her, they'd remark how beautiful she was. They'd say it was such a shame. The good people of Serenity Heights would be openly horrified and frightened, fearful that one of their pretty little blond daughters could become his next victim.

He chuckled as he slowly eased the gown past her hips. They'd make guesses about him. They'd make wild assumptions as to his identity, about his mind. They'd call him a crazy fuck. And he'd sit beside them at the Java Hut on Main and ponder with them. He'd discuss the news with the morning regulars at the Parkway Café over on Palm Avenue, speculate about what the police were doing to stop the lunatic on a killing rampage, destroying the serenity of their quiet little northern Ohio town.

Outwardly, he'd show them nothing other than concern for those poor tragic victims. He'd share their outrage that a killer dared to walk among them. Inside, he'd celebrate his victory. He'd praise his intelligence. And scorn their stupidity.

He stepped behind her and inched up the zipper that stopped at the base of her spine. Lifting her bagged wrist, he slipped it through the sequined cap sleeve, then did the same with the other sleeve. He moved back to her front and adjusted the gown until it was in place. A perfect fit, just as he'd imagined.

She'd been perfect before, too, but he'd been too hasty. He'd had a delivery to make tonight, and had been so angry that his plan hadn't gone as smoothly as it should have gone that he'd rushed. All thanks to that goddamn mutt. He'd made a mistake.

He liked Ms. Brennan. She didn't look down her nose at him like that cunt he had to answer to at work. When Ms. Brennan had come to interview him for her newspaper, she'd been kind and had shown sincere interest, which was why he continued to gift her with the record of his accomplishments.

The affinity he'd felt with the reporter hadn't been misplaced. They came from the same place. Perhaps not geographically, but he knew how it felt being forced to be the one wholly responsible for the happiness and well-being of someone else. How their mistakes became your mistakes, how you were the one punished for their wrongdoing. How it felt to be taken advantage of in ways unimaginable. They understood each other.

Finished with his tasks for the night, he stood back to admire his handiwork. He cupped his hands together and blew into them in an attempt to ward off the chill, but to no avail.

He was pleased. She was perfect once again.

He turned and walked to the control panel, then pressed the appropriate button. Nothing happened, so he pressed again. The conveyor made a few grinding noises, then eventually started moving, carrying her away until the time for her unveiling.

Empty meat hooks that had decades ago moved monstrous sides of beef clanked and rattled throughout the old meat locker. He pressed the large red button to stop the conveyor when she reached the end, where she would remain with the others until it was her time to shine.

SHE'D DIED ALONE. A truth that continued to weigh on Beck's mind. A truth he'd been unable to forgive himself for, even though he hadn't been the cause of his wife's death. No, ovarian cancer held the blame for taking her, but she'd been alone when the end had finally come for her, and that ate at him.

Tonight the guilt he continued to carry with him was stronger than most nights. He wanted to blame Ainsley, or rather, his attraction to her, but she wasn't the cause of his dive into the deep end of the guilt pool.

Out of habit, he stripped off his weapon and put it in the lock box he kept in the closet, then hung his shoulder holster on the hook inside the door. He'd thought he'd moved

on, had convinced himself leaving LA and putting some distance from the constant reminders of his failure as a husband
would finally enable him to put the past to rest and get on
with his life. Apparently he'd been wrong about that, too.

He turned off the light, then walked back to the front of
the 1930s style bungalow left to him by his father's sister, to
wait for Ainsley. The house was old, but his aunt had made
improvements over the past twenty years, with updated
electric service, replacement windows that hadn't compro-
mised the integrity of the home, and modernized plumbing.
That didn't mean he didn't have work to do on the place.
The boiler in the basement could stand an upgrade, as well
as the roof. A coat of paint wouldn't hurt, either, and he
needed to start thinking about hiring a landscaper to bring
some order to the overgrown gardens in both the front and
back yards.

The list of to-dos faded from his mind when the headlights of his Durango splashed across the living room windows. He thought about putting up a pot of coffee, but
what he needed was sleep. Besides, he'd been strung out on
caffeine the past three days. His gut could use the break.

He flipped on the porch light and opened the front door
just as she trotted up the steps. "Come on in," he said, feeling himself inching closer to the ledge.

She walked inside and handed him the keys. "Thanks for
the ride. I like your truck."

"It's an SUV."

"Whatever," she said with a quick smile. "It's still a nice
ride compared to my antique."

He motioned for her to precede him into the living room.
"About that," he said as he turned on a lamp, "I'm sorry,
but it was necessary if we hope to find any trace evidence
that could help us identify the UNSUB."

She tossed her tote bag on the floor beside the sofa and
sat. "Forget about it. I'll get a rental and send you the bill."

He chuckled when she flashed him that hundred-watt smile. "That ought to make the mayor's day." He sat on the other end of the sofa and faced her.

She leaned back until her head rested against the back cushion. "Is he giving you a hard time?"

He hesitated and she frowned and said, "You really have to get past this whole 'I'm a reporter, you're a cop' thing."

A part of him, the part that wanted to haul her gorgeous, curvy little ass off to his bed, knew she was right. But lessons learned were hard to ignore. His attraction to Ainsley aside, he couldn't stop worrying about every word he said to her having the potential to come back and bite him publicly on the ass.

She let out a gusty sigh. "Look, Beck, our private conversations are off the record. Period. Does that help?"

He shifted on the sofa to face her and rested his arm along the back cushions. "Not really," he admitted. "I was burned by the press once."

"I'm sorry about that, but we're not all blood-sucking vultures waiting to swoop down on the next headline."

He laughed at that. "You really are small town, aren't you? You trust everyone, take them at their word, don't you?"

"Yes, I do. And I'm damn proud of it, too." She flashed him another of those brief smiles before her expression turned serious. "You know, you're not in LA any longer. Maybe you need to start thinking that not everyone is out for number one. Haven't you ever heard of midwestern integrity? Our word means something to us. I promise, it's not gonna hurt if you learn to remember that from time to time."

He wished he could be more like her. More trusting. More accepting of people at face value. Only he knew it'd be a waste of time. He'd spent too many years wrapped up in the darker side of humanity to be able to see the brighter side.

He knew the viciousness of the human race, the damage people could do to one another. The world was an ugly place.

"I'm more pragmatic," he told her. "But feel free to keep wearing your rose-colored glasses, Pollyanna."

"*Cynical* is the word I would use." Her ever-present smile softened the sarcasm.

"How do you feel about *obtuse*?"

"Me?" She laughed. "Because I trust someone unless they prove otherwise? That's not obtuse."

"You're right. *Naive* might be more appropriate."

She picked up the throw pillow next to her and tossed it at him. "God, you're such a hard ass."

He grabbed the pillow and chucked it to the floor. "Like I said. Pragmatic."

She stood suddenly and reached her arms overhead, stretching. The bottom of her top crept up, giving him a peek at her slender waistline. The urge to pull her to him and press his lips to that tiny bit of exposed flesh overwhelmed him.

Her attempt to stifle a yawn failed miserably. "I should get home. I have a meeting at the office in"—she glanced at her wristwatch—"less than six hours."

He should let her go. Anything else would be a mistake, but that didn't stop him from reaching out and taking hold of her hand. "Stay."

"Why?"

She didn't frown, didn't look surprised or startled by his request. She simply looked at him with those big blue eyes and waited for his response.

He didn't believe in making excuses. Wasn't the type to waste time with platitudes or some bullshit line about it not being safe for her to be home alone. He wanted Ainsley, wanted her in his bed. "Because I want you."

The color of her eyes deepened. "Damn," she said, her voice tinged with nervous laughter. "Direct, aren't you?"

"Life's too damn short." He smoothed his thumb over her fingers. "Stay with me, Ainsley."

She sucked in a long, slow breath, but didn't answer him. He could practically see the wheels turning in her mind as she weighed the consequences. Wondering what it all meant, if anything at all. He prayed she wouldn't ask him, because damn if he knew. He wanted her, and hadn't thought much beyond that point.

"And if I say yes?"

He stood and pulled her to him. Taking her face between his hands, he dipped his head and kissed her. He didn't waste precious time with gentleness or coaxing, but swept his tongue inside her mouth and tasted her deeply.

She melted against him and moaned, a tiny murmur of sound that had his libido redlining in three-point-two seconds flat. As far as he was concerned, that sexy little response was answer enough for him.

He teased her, tempted her, and demanded more from her with just his lips and tongue. And she gave it to him, too. Her arms wreathed around his neck and she held on tight, pressing her sleek curves against him. He wasn't playing fair, but dammit, he didn't care. He had to have her. Right here, right now. Tonight, or what was left of it.

He slipped his hand beneath the hem of her top and spread his fingers over the small of her back. Her skin felt warm and soft against his rougher fingertips as he dipped his thumb below the waistband of her jeans.

She pulled back and ended the kiss. Desire clouded her lush gaze as she looked up at him. "I need a shower."

He smiled. "That can be arranged." He took her hand again and led her from the living room down the hall toward his bedroom.

CHAPTER 12

AINSLEY DIDN'T BOTHER to pretend shyness. Considering she was naked and about to slip into a hot and steamy shower with Beck, that was just stupid. She wanted him. It was enough for her—for now.

Closing the shower door behind her, she took one look at Beck and stopped breathing. The man was gorgeous, no two ways about it. From the top of his short, cropped dark hair all the way down to his feet. She'd never realized a man's feet could be so sexy.

She refused to question the whys of what she was doing. Wasn't about to waste a second of their precious time together on what ifs. She wanted Beck and saw no reason why they shouldn't have sex. Now. Later she'd deal with the ramifications of her actions—like when she didn't have a gorgeous, naked man dripping wet and wanting her only eighteen inches away.

He stood with his back to her, his head bent beneath the spray, his hands braced against the tiled walls. Water sluiced over his shoulders, down his back to his supremely nice ass. Grabbing the bar of soap from the holder, she rubbed it between her hands until she had a good lather going, then started at his shoulders. She smoothed her soap-slicked hands over the hills and valleys of his muscled back, along his sides and over his ass, enjoying the touch of all those dips and hard planes of his body beneath her fingertips.

She brought her hands to his front, over his ribcage and upward to his chest. Her breasts rubbed against his back and she closed her eyes, enjoying the feel of her flesh against his.

He covered her hands with his much larger ones as she smoothed her way over his chest. She marveled at the contrasts, the smooth skin, the hard muscle. Dragging her fingers through the light furring of hair on his chest, she slowly followed the trail down, past his navel and lower still.

He sucked in a sharp breath when her fingers brushed the tip of his erection. Before she could explore further, he turned to face her. His gaze was dark, intense. "No turning back," he said.

She shook her head. "No," she agreed. "No turning back."

He kissed her then. Hard. Hot. Demanding. She gripped his firm biceps for balance, certain if she let go, she'd slide into a puddle at the bottom of the shower floor.

He took hold of her arms and looped them around his neck. She clung to him, not so much for balance now, but because the glide of their bodies made her hot. And then there were his hands, which were everywhere—cupping her breasts, his thumbs teasing her nipples into hard points. He slid his hands down her back and gripped her bottom, urging her closer. The hard, rigid length of his very impressive erection rubbed against her. The sharp tug of desire pulled at her, filling her with need.

He broke the kiss and kissed a blazing path down her throat to her breasts. Her world tilted when he pulled her nipple deep into his mouth and suckled her. With her head tossed back, she dug her hands into his hair and held him to her, enjoying every wanton sensation racing through her. The heat surrounded them, from their bodies or the steam from the shower, she didn't know which, but her breathing came in hard pants as she struggled for air.

He shifted and pushed her up against the steam-covered tiles of the shower stall. His lips never left her body when he went down on his knees in front of her. With his hand, he gently nudged her thighs apart, then carefully opened her labia and pressed his thumb against her clitoris while sliding his finger deep inside her. Her breath caught, then slid out on a moan of pleasure so erotic she hardly recognized the sound as her own.

With one hand holding her hip, he nuzzled her sex with his mouth, then exchanged his thumb for his tongue. She nearly came out of her skin at the intimate contact, and cried out as he continued to stroke her with his fingers. He used his tongue to drive her absolutely insane. Her need intensified, and the pressure built so hard and fast she couldn't think. Before she drew her next breath, she flew apart with a strangled cry as a hard orgasm rocked her.

Her head thumped against the hard tiles, but she didn't care. The muscles of her legs tightened. Her arms felt as if they were weighed down. Her mind split and shattered into a million unrecognizable fragments. She couldn't think, could only feel, and what she experienced was nothing short of heaven.

Slowly, he brought her back to earth. He stood, kissed the side of her neck, then gathered her in his arms and held her close. His hands swept up and down her back, and her heart twisted and tightened at such tenderness. When was the last time someone had held her like this? She simply couldn't remember, then realized the reason she had no memory was because she'd never experienced anything like it before.

Which made Beckett Raines one helluva dangerous man.

Only if she let him be, she thought as she looped her arms

around his waist and held on to him for support. She rested her head against his chest, heard the thumping of his heart, and reminded herself that she wasn't some silly, lovesick girl. She was a grown woman with responsibilities. There wasn't a damn thing wrong with her having a hot fling with a man she found wildly attractive. Just so she remembered that in the light of day, she'd be fine. One mind-blowing orgasm did not equate to ridiculous notions of anything beyond their physical attraction for each other.

So why did she feel as if her heart had just bloomed like a flower on a high-speed camera shot?

The water turned cold suddenly. Beck let go of her long enough to shut off the tap, then pushed open the shower door. In one swift move, he lifted her in his arms and carried her, both of them still dripping wet, to the bedroom. He laid her on the bed and quickly joined her, covering her with his body. She didn't have time to think about the air chilling her skin, because he'd caught her mouth in another one of his hot and deep kisses that scattered her thoughts and had her wanting him again.

She opened her legs and cradled him between her thighs. Just when she was certain he'd turned her brain to mush and her body into liquid fire, he ended the kiss. He nibbled, laved, and kissed the side of her neck until he had her trembling beneath him.

He leaned up and looked down at her. "You're so beautiful," he said quietly, then kissed her again, long and languidly.

"Tell me what you want," he asked when he'd come up for air.

"You," she whispered. She did. Again and again. Until she couldn't move.

He smiled and her heart did a flip in her chest. "That's a cop-out."

"It's the truth." She reached up and laved at his chest with her tongue.

He pushed her back down, then dipped his head and teased her nipple with his tongue. A fresh wave of desire slammed into her. How that was even possible after the orgasm she'd had only moments before, amazed her. Was Beck that good, or was she that hard up? She didn't really give a rip, just so long as he finished what he'd started.

He lifted his head again and looked down at her. His green eyes were dark, almost black in their intensity. "Tell me," he demanded gently.

"Everything."

His smile turned wicked, causing her pulse rate to go ballistic. Slowly, he slid off her to his side, then reached over her to the nightstand. He tugged opened the drawer and withdrew a small box of condoms. An unopened box.

She couldn't help herself. She smiled.

He caught her smiling and his expression turned adorably sheepish. "It's . . . uh . . . been a while," he admitted.

Her smile deepened. "Since we're being honest," she said, "same here."

A satisfied expression entered his eyes before he nuzzled her neck again. "Think we'll remember how?"

She really loved this playful side of him. She laughed and turned in his arms. "Any chance of me believing that went down the drain a few minutes ago, pal."

She plucked the box of condoms from his grasp, ripped it open and emptied the contents on the bed between them. She gave him what she hoped was a disappointed look. "Only three?" she teased.

"They'll have to last until one of us gets to the drugstore." He chuckled when she wrinkled her nose at him, the sound as warm and inviting as the comfort of his arms around her. "Feeling ambitious?"

"Try ravenous." She tore open a wrapper with her teeth and removed the condom. "Or adventurous." She held the condom to her lips and blew gently.

His Adam's apple bobbed when he swallowed.

She flashed him a wicked grin of her own. "Or both," she added, then pushed at his chest, urging him to his back.

She climbed up and straddled him, then bent forward and traced the tip of her tongue around his areola. "My turn," she whispered, then kissed and laved her way down his chest to his abdomen.

Beck was in deep trouble. He knew it and there wasn't a damn thing he planned to do about it except enjoy every lasting second of making love to Ainsley. She got to him, plain and simple.

He hadn't seen it coming. Not really. Oh sure, he'd noticed the attraction. He'd have to have been a dead man not to notice. But this—*thing*—between them extended beyond mutual attraction. He couldn't exactly say he was falling for her, but he sure as hell wanted to see more of her. And not just naked and wanting in his bed.

She made him laugh, something he'd thought he'd long forgotten. She made him crazy with need. She made him remember what it was like to be alive, to feel, to desire, to want.

To care.

Fuck.

He didn't want to care about her, about what happened to her. He didn't want to care that they were possibly embarking on a relationship and not just a few hours of hot sex. Worse, she filled him with hope, and that was the scariest prospect of all.

Hope meant there could be more tomorrows—with her. Hope meant he had no choice but to move forward, to take that final step in letting go of a past he couldn't change.

He laid his head back against the pillows, concentrating

on the feel of her hands and mouth on his body. Her cool, slender fingers wrapped around his dick. He opened his eyes and looked down at her. Light from the bathroom splashed softly into the room, making her skin glow with warmth. With her hands wrapped around him, she raised up on her knees and lowered her head.

He caught sight of the condom between her lips and forgot how to breathe. Gently, she slid her hands up and down his shaft and carefully placed the condom over the tip of his cock with her mouth. Using her tongue and lips, she eased the protective sheath down his length.

His control took a nose dive. His dick pulsed and throbbed. He tried to think of anything except the exquisite torture of Ainsley applying the condom with her mouth, but his efforts were futile.

He reached for her, but she shrugged off his touch. "Come here," he said, his voice a harsh rasp of sound.

"Uh-huh," she murmured, the tenor of her voice vibrating over his cock.

Good God, he was going to come. He pushed up and reached for her waist. With her mouth still over him, she looked at him curiously when his fingers dug into her flesh.

"Come here," he said again, urging her around until she straddled him. He gripped her bottom with both hands and slid his hands forward, teasing her folds open, and slid a finger from each hand into her sweet, slick center. He stroked her deeply, retreated and slid upward to cover her with her own wetness.

Her deep moan of pleasure vibrated through him, pushing him closer to the edge. She took him deeply in her mouth. He circled her clit with his wet finger as he slid his tongue inside her, tasting her. She was sweet, creamy, and her groans of pleasure grew louder as he stroked and teased her toward another orgasm.

Her mouth did incredible things to him and honestly, he

didn't know how much more he could take before he lost it. He rolled them over, so she was flat on her back, then he twisted his body around so he was the one giving her pleasure. He pressed her thighs open and lifted her bottom, then continued to drive her wild. She lay open and fully exposed, vulnerable as he loved her with his mouth. She clawed at the comforter, twisting the fabric in her hands as her head thrashed back and forth. Her cries of pleasure built until she called out his name, the sound desperate and needy and so fucking sexy he nearly came.

The tension in her body grew tighter. His own control was already shot and he knew he couldn't hold out another minute. With her bottom still gripped in his hands, he came up on his knees and thrust into her. Her legs clamped around his waist, drawing him deeper inside.

They didn't bother with slow and gentle. They'd gone beyond that point the minute she'd used her mouth to apply the condom. He drove into her, over and over again, taking them closer and closer to the ultimate fulfillment, their lovemaking fierce and intense.

Her legs clamped around his waist like a vise. The sounds coming from her were pure, primal. Her body contracted around him until the final shred of his restraint crashed and burned. Holding her to him, he thrust into her one last time and came in a hot rush. A groan ripped from his throat and he held her tight against him, pulsing into her.

He didn't know how much time had passed before his senses returned, but he rolled to his side and gathered her in his arms. He kissed her slowly, languidly, and before the ringing in his ears quieted, understood that it'd been far too long since he'd felt so content. For a guy intent on punishing himself, the realization was hard to swallow, but he knew he had Ainsley to thank. Without her, he couldn't help wonder if he might never have experienced such total and complete contentment again.

She ended the kiss and rested her head against his chest. "Wow," she whispered. "I can't move."

He tipped her head back and planted a quick hard kiss on her lips. "You're welcome."

She made a sound that was as close to a laugh as her exhaustion would allow. "Go ahead. Strut and pound your chest. You earned it."

"I would, but I don't think I can move, either."

She tucked her head against him again and snuggled closer. "You're welcome," she said sleepily.

He chuckled, then winced when something sharp poked his side. Rolling slightly, he found the source, one of the two remaining condoms. He felt around for the other one, then tossed them both on the nightstand behind him.

He looked down at Ainsley, already fast asleep. So much for ambition, he thought. She was dead to the world.

Careful not to awaken her, he climbed out of bed, disposed of the condom, then grabbed a blanket from the chair in the corner. He rejoined her, but she rolled to her other side. Spreading the blanket over her, he climbed back in beside her and pulled her against him so that her back was against his chest.

He glanced at the bedside clock. He had to be back at the station soon. There was a laundry list of tasks he needed to accomplish today, but for now, the outside world could wait. Closing his eyes, he held her close and fell asleep listening to the sound of Ainsley's deep breathing.

MAYBE THEY'D CALL her a throwback to an era long before the women's movement. A disgrace to her gender. Ainsley didn't care, because there was just something utterly delicious about waking up next to a big strong man who knew how to please a woman. Especially one intent on doing so first thing in the morning.

Florida could keep its orange juice, and Folgers its beans. This is what she called starting the day off right.

With her backside pressed against him and her leg hooked over his, Beck slowly stroked her with his fingers. No pressure, just long easy strokes that made her feel all lazy and languid, yet incredibly hot at the same time.

She reached her arms over her head and stretched, pressing her bottom against his erection and widening her thighs to give him deeper access. He groaned as she rubbed up against him, a low sound from deep within his chest. If she wasn't careful, she really could get used to this. At least for a while—however long that might be.

She didn't think having Beck hanging around would be much of a hardship. Not really. What could it hurt? They were both consenting adults here. So she'd slept with him. Big deal, right? It wasn't like she was falling for him, so her heart was definitely not at risk. Her pride might end up taking a beating, but her heart was absolutely safe.

Right.

God help her, she knew better. Not once in her adult life had she ever embarked upon a relationship that was purely physical. She just wasn't a booty-call kind of gal. Before she dove between the sheets, she'd always had to feel some kind of emotional connection. Her relationships, albeit few and far between, had all mattered to her.

Last night had been her first exception. Oh, sure, she liked Beck. A lot. And she was wildly attracted to him, obviously. But this was the first time in her life she'd ever let passion overrule her common sense, or her sense of duty and responsibility. She'd leapt without looking beyond the moment, and that wasn't like her.

Stop the presses! Ainsley Brennan did something for herself for once in her adult life.

Shocker!

They'd been passionate last night, so incredibly hungry

for the other. Their actions equally demanding and responsive. This morning he was taking his time, drawing out the pleasure, building it slowly, and damn if she wasn't enjoying every erotic second of it. Considering she was operating on less than three hours' sleep, she didn't think she was exactly in the right frame of mind to dissect the matter. And there were all those deliciously distracting moves he was putting on her, too.

Ever so gently, he rolled her to her back and moved between her thighs, entering her slowly. She wrapped her legs around his hips and clung to him, lifting her bottom to take him more deeply into her body. With her arms stretched above her head, she grabbed hold of the wooden rungs of the Mission-style headboard. She gave herself up to the wondrous sensations rippling through her with each long, measured stroke of his body inside hers, and forgot about everything but making love to Beck.

The pressure climbed as he pushed her closer to the brink of no return. He must've felt her body contracting because he upped the tempo, became more demanding until she finally flew apart. Her body bowed and she cried out, the ferocity of her orgasm taking her completely by surprise. She opened her eyes in time to see Beck, his head tossed back as his own body was wracked by the intense pleasure of his own release.

With her heart thundering in her chest, she loosed her death grip on the rungs of the headboard and pulled Beck down to her. He collapsed against her and buried his face in her neck. His breath came in short, hard bursts, like her own.

She wasn't sure how long they lay like that together, but eventually he rolled to his side and tucked her close. They dozed for a short while until the alarm clock on the bedside table buzzed, shattering the silence and intruding into their quiet bliss.

Beck reached over her and smacked the buzzer on the alarm clock. He looked down at her, his smile lazy and adorable, stilling her breath. He planted a quick kiss on her lips. "Good morning," he said, his voice all rough and scratchy and way too sexy.

She chuckled, considering he hadn't bothered to say "boo" when he'd woken her earlier to make love to her. "It's been a very good morning," she said, and wound her arms around his neck.

"Coffee first or a shower?"

The world was already intruding, and she resented it. It wasn't fair. Why couldn't they stay like this all day? Happy. Satiated. Teasing.

"I'll shower while you make coffee," she said.

"Why don't I make coffee, then join you in the shower?" he suggested, then added a lascivious wiggle of his eyebrows that made her laugh.

"Because we'd both be late for work, and you know it," she said, although she was certainly tempted. "Besides, I have a meeting to go to and you have . . ." Her smile faded.

"Yeah." He rolled away from her and off the bed, then pulled on a pair of sweats and headed for the door. "Coffee coming right up," he said, and left her alone in bed.

Smooth, Brennan. Geeze, talk about a buzz kill.

She kicked off the covers and hurried across the room to the bathroom for a shower for one. Reality sucked, especially since she'd been the one to reintroduce it so rudely into what had been the best few hours she'd ever shared with a man.

Maybe there'd be more, maybe there wouldn't. She didn't know, except this sure didn't feel like a one-night stand to her. And that, she realized, was only the beginning of her problems.

CHAPTER 13

A INSLEY STARED AT the contents of Beck's fridge and
shook her head in disbelief. She'd heard the rumors, she
just hadn't expected them to be so in her face. The lengths
that the single female population of Serenity Heights had gone
to by inundating Beck with baked goods and casseroles was
nothing short of astounding. Not to mention downright
ridiculous.

All that home-cooked food made her feel just a tad silly
after the supper she'd made last night. Like she was as desperate for a man as any one of the barrage of women sub-
scribing to the old saying about the way into a man's heart
being through his stomach.

Unearthing a small carton of half-and-half behind a platter of fried chicken, she tried not to think about the variety
of casserole dishes she had to reach around to find it. She
added a splash to her coffee just as Beck sauntered into the
kitchen. He wore a shoulder holster over a dark green polo,
complete with weapon, reminding her that he was every
inch a cop.

His hair was still damp, and he was clean shaven and
dressed in fresh clothes, ready to start his day. She still had
to go home and change, then get to the newspaper office in

time for a 9:00 AM meeting that could very possibly end up changing the course of her career. And her life.

Her day might have started off with a bang, but she couldn't help worrying that it was headed downhill from there. If Dylan had indeed sold the paper as Mona had theorized, she'd just have to figure what to do next. And it'd have to be quick, since she had a sister in college to help support for the next four years, and a year left on the mortgage. She could use a newer car, but with Cass in college, she wasn't sure she could swing the payments. Especially now that her future employment could be up in the air.

If worse came to worst and she did need to find a new job, she'd figure out something. Didn't she always?

She returned the half-and-half to the fridge, then walked over to the breakfast bar to join Beck. He sat on one of the barstools, cell phone in hand, reading what looked like a text message.

She climbed up on the barstool next to his, then took a sip of coffee. "Damn, you're hired," she said, determined to keep it light between them this morning. "This is really good coffee."

Not that she regretted for a second making love to him, but she didn't want their time out of bed laden with the usual morning-after bullshit. She liked him. A lot. Spending more time with him wasn't something she'd object to, either, but she did believe it best to proceed with caution. She'd had her heart stomped before and it wasn't much fun. Granted, she no longer had the same concerns she'd carried with her into her previous relationships, but as long as Cassidy was in college, she still had a responsibility to her sister. Most guys didn't want or appreciate that kind of baggage, and to be honest, she couldn't say the same wouldn't be true for Beck.

Yet.

Until she knew differently then, she planned to keep their

relationship light and breezy. And if she protected her heart in the bargain, that was okay, too.

"When you put in the kind of hours I used to, you learn." He turned off his cell phone and reached for his own mug. "It's either that or you're stuck with the rotgut the department likes to call coffee."

"Doesn't seem like much has changed," she said. "The hours, I mean."

He shrugged, then finished off the last of his coffee. "Comes with the territory," he finally said, then shifted in his seat to look at her.

His expression turned serious and her heart started to pound. Here it came, the old I-had-a-great-time-but . . .

"There's probably going to be a ground search today," he said. "If you call Raelynn once you get to the newspaper office, she can give you the details so you can cover it for the paper."

She let out the breath she'd been holding when he didn't deliver the kiss-off she'd been expecting. She even appreciated the tip, which surprised her considering his still unexplained aversion to the press.

"Why the ground search?" she asked, setting her half-empty mug on the counter. She kept her fingers wrapped around the warm ceramic so she wouldn't fidget. "Do you think you'll find Mattie Davenport's body?"

"I don't think it's likely, but . . ." He ended with another shrug.

"But what? What aren't you telling me?"

He hesitated and it irritated her that despite the intimacy they'd shared, he still didn't trust her. "Off the record," she reminded him, surprised she'd managed to keep the annoyance out of her voice. "But what?"

"But it's possible," he finally said. "After what I heard on the last audio file, we should be calling out the cadaver dogs, not the search and rescue team."

"The one you found in my car?" She'd heard more than enough on the first audio file she'd received from the killer. She'd been grateful. Beck had told her the second recording had been similar to the first. "How was this one different from the first two?"

"The UNSUB spoke."

A chill passed over her. "I'm afraid to ask."

"He said, 'Stop me.' The rest was his usual M.O."

Meaning more tortured screams. She shuddered. "Is that what makes you think he's killed her? Or was there something else?" Something else she probably didn't want to know.

"He hadn't spoken in the two previous recordings," Beck said. "That he did in the most recent makes me think he's killed her."

"But you don't know that for certain." There had to be some hope that Mattie Davenport was still alive.

"No, not for certain."

But his instincts said otherwise. She got it.

"Beck," she laid her hand over his, "you have to stop this guy."

The sigh he let out was a long one. "You think I don't know that?"

"What I mean, say he has killed the Davenport girl. What's to say he hasn't already targeted another victim?"

Slowly, he pulled his hand from beneath hers, then slid off the barstool. "I'm on top of it," he said as he shrugged into a lightweight sport coat that effectively hid his shoulder holster and weapon from view.

She didn't doubt that he was, but she didn't understand the trace of resentment suddenly evident in his voice. Taking the hint that it was time to go when he snagged his keys off the counter, she slid off her own barstool. She carried their empty mugs to the sink, where she rinsed them. "Is that why you're doing a ground search today?" she asked. "Because you think you'll find the Davenport girl's body?"

He pocketed his cell phone. "We're doing a ground search because that jackass from the U suggested we conduct one, and the mayor jumped on it to look good in front of the girl's parents."

She ripped a paper towel from the holder and dried her hands. "Which jackass?" There were several employed at the U, in her opinion.

"McElvoy," Beck told her. "Pompous little prick. He was at the meeting last night with the Davenports and the mayor. Apparently he's organizing students and staff from the U to help with the search. Ready?"

She nodded. "I'm sure he's just trying to help," she said, following Beck. She made a quick stop in the living room to pick up her tote, then met him at the front door. "Besides, something like this doesn't look good for the U. I'm sure he's only wanting to protect the university."

"It doesn't help us," he complained as he yanked open the front door. "All it's going to do is get a lot of people upset and worried, not to mention frustrated when we don't find a damn thing."

She stepped outside and immediately shielded her eyes from the early morning brightness of the sun. There wasn't a single cloud in the sky, a sure indicator they'd be enjoying another warm end-of-summer day. "You can't know that."

He crossed the walkway to the driveway where she'd left his Durango parked, then unlocked the passenger door and held it open for her. He waited until she climbed in, then said, "I wouldn't be so sure," before closing the door.

She set her tote on the floor by her feet and waited for him to climb in on the driver's side. Frowning, she asked, "What did you mean? You know something."

He slipped the key into the ignition and fired the engine. The alternative rock station she'd been listening to after dropping Mrs. Greenway off last night blared through the speakers.

He gave her one of his tolerant looks with a slight lift of one eyebrow. Whether he was questioning her musical tastes or the obnoxious decibel level, she couldn't be sure.

As he backed out of the driveway, she reached over to turn down the radio. "Sorry about that."

She waited, impatiently, for him to continue. By the time he reached the corner of Mulberry and Dogwood, he still hadn't said a word. "Beck? What do you know?"

He made a left on Dogwood. "This isn't for public consumption," he said with a warning in his voice she couldn't possibly mistake. "The body at the morgue wasn't a fresh kill."

"How do you know?" She wasn't so sure *she* wanted to know.

"The estimated time of death is several weeks." He shot her a quick glance. "The body was thawing when it was discovered."

"Oh my God." She didn't know what else to say to that gruesome bit of news, so she sat back and kept her mouth shut for once. Her mind still spun with questions she wasn't sure she had the courage to ask.

By the time Beck pulled into her driveway, she still hadn't peppered him with the questions she should be asking. Dammit, she was a reporter. Asking the hard questions was supposed to be her job, but she'd promised him their conversation was off the record. And on a personal level, she wasn't sure she wanted answers.

He turned off the ignition. "You're unusually quiet."

Didn't she know it. "You've stunned me into silence. Give me a minute."

"Mind if I enjoy it while it lasts?"

She didn't appreciate his lame attempt at humor at a time like this, and shot him a glare. "Jesus, that means he's killing and storing the bodies." She unfastened her seat belt, then turned to face him. "Are there more girls missing? Do you know? Have you checked ViCAP? Have you checked with the surrounding towns?"

"Whoa," he said, and held up his hands. "Slow it down, Nancy Drew. Believe it or not, I've done this kind of thing before."

She let out a short puff of air. "Not in Serenity Heights."

"No, in Los Angeles. If I can catch a bad guy there, I sure as hell can do it here."

"But you'll need help."

"I have an entire police force at my disposal."

"Get real," she scoffed. "You have a captain counting the weeks until his retirement, and a dozen patrolmen who've probably never fired a weapon outside of the shooting range or during hunting season. And I seriously doubt your one K-9 has ever chased down a suspect who wasn't dressed in protective bite gear."

"I have complete faith in Mosley," he said, speaking of the department's German shepherd.

Her frown deepened. "Stop patronizing me, Beck. I'm serious."

"So am I. Mosley's a damn good K-9." He unbuckled his seat belt and leaned toward her. He tucked his finger beneath her chin and tilted her head slightly, then bent forward and kissed her slowly, gently.

If his intent was to distract her, his ploy worked. Her pulse even kicked up a notch. The kiss was sweet, tender, and she was so on to him.

He ended the kiss, which was probably a good thing because she easily imagined Mrs. G peeking out her kitchen window at them. "Stop worrying," he said.

"I wasn't worried." Well, a little.

"Okay." He did that half-cocked eyebrow thing again, a clear indicator he didn't believe her for a second. "Do you have plans for tonight?"

Nothing other than updating her résumé, she thought. "That depends on what you had in mind."

The look he gave her was nothing short of sinful. "Why don't you pack a bag and stay at my place tonight?"

"Stop trying to protect me." She appreciated his concern, but she was not going to be chased out of her own home. Besides, if Beck was right and Mattie Davenport was already dead, there wouldn't be another audio file showing up tonight.

"I wasn't," he said, attempting an innocent look that failed miserably. "I was just hoping to get you out of your panties again."

She didn't believe him for a minute. "Well, in that case . . ." She leaned over and kissed him quick. "What time do you want me and my panties there?"

"The sooner the better," he said, then turned the key and fired up the truck. He reached into the console, then handed her a key. "Make yourself at home until I can get there. I could be late."

She understood. Unfortunately.

She slipped from the vehicle and he pulled out of the driveway. As she walked across the lawn to the front porch, she frowned. For a guy who was apparently worried about her being alone in her own home, he sure took off in a hurry. She'd half expected him to come in and search the house first.

By the time she climbed the front porch steps, she saw the reason that he'd left her alone—the patrol car parked across the street, two doors down. And even she had to admit, the police presence did make her feel just a tiny bit safer.

BY THE TIME Beck reached the station, he walked in on a flurry of activity. Mitch was frantically manning the phone, which was ringing off the hook, and Raelynn looked just as frazzled.

And it was only half past seven.

Beck approached Raelynn's desk. "What's going on?"

"Ainsley's article," she told him. "The phone has been ringing nonstop."

Mitch covered the receiver with his hand. "We've got half of the Sigma Pi sorority sisters in the conference room," he said, then quickly switched his attention back to the caller. "Yes, sir, we are."

Beck looked to Raelynn for confirmation.

"Megan Conner didn't come home last night," she said. She scribbled something on a pink message slip and added it to the growing stack on her desk.

"And who's Megan Conner?"

"A junior at the U. According to the girls, she went out for a walk last night and never came back."

Beck glanced at Mitch, who offered a helpless shrug as he answered yet another call. "Yes, ma'am. I understand your concern," he said to the next caller.

"I'll talk to the girls," Beck told Raelynn. "Ainsley Brennan will be calling later for information on the ground search. Go ahead and let her know where we're mobilizing."

"And where will that be?"

Shit. He still had to call in the search and rescue team. "I'll let you know."

Raelynn scooped up the stack of pink message slips and handed them to him. "She's not the only reporter interested in the story."

Great, just what he didn't need. More press. Press he might not be able to control. Not that he thought for a minute he could *control* Ainsley, but they did have an uneasy alliance where their respective positions were concerned. He'd never be foolish enough to translate that into a matter of complete and total trust. Her job was to inform the public, his to protect them—and that didn't exactly put them on the same side.

"Who else has been sniffing around?" he asked, flipping through the message slips.

"So far, I've only had calls from a reporter at the *Plain Dealer* and one reporter as far as Columbus."

"Any idea how they heard about the story?"

"I'll bet either someone from the coroner's office or the DA's office has a big mouth, or they spied the copy of Ainsley's article on the Web."

Beck had known once Ainsley's story hit, it'd only be a matter of time before the larger newspapers in the area picked up on it and started snooping around. He'd just hoped it would be later rather than sooner.

"Yes, ma'am," Mitch said to the caller. "We appreciate that. Thank you." He hung up the phone. "It's been like this since I walked in the door an hour ago. We're gonna need some help to field calls."

"What the hell is going on?" Beck asked. He'd expected a few phone calls, but nothing like the volume they were being hit with this morning. "We didn't even have this much activity after the door-to-door the other night."

"It's Ainsley's article," Raelynn said again as two phone lines rang simultaneously. "People are nervous, Chief."

"Not just that," Mitch added. "Word's gotten out that we're conducting a ground search today and they're asking what they can do to help."

"I can call the employment office at the U and see if they have any available bodies willing to answer phones for a few days," she offered. "It's the beginning of the school year. Kids are always looking for part-time jobs."

"Do it." He'd worry about the budget concerns later. "Just make sure they know they're not to give out any information you haven't authorized."

"You got it," she said, then hit the call button on her headset to answer one of the ringing lines before it bounced back to dispatch.

Mitch picked up the other phone, and Beck went to his own office to place a call to the county's search and rescue people. Thirty minutes later, he had the search scheduled with two teams of four coming in from Cleveland to assist and help organize. There were dozens upon dozens of acres of old, unused pastureland and open fields in between the town and the more densely wooded areas. In other words, a helluva lot of ground to search that would take more than a day. They'd divide the area into four sections, with him and the rescue team leader, Trace Holt, manning a command center and organizing volunteers.

He placed a call to the sound engineer, but had to leave another message, then returned a call to Julia Reiki of the coroner's office. He dispensed with pleasantries quickly. "I got your text message. What's up?"

"The wound on your Jane Doe's back could be from a bale hook."

"Could you repeat that?" Beck dropped the pen he'd been using to take notes and sat back. He wasn't certain he'd heard Julia correctly.

"A bale hook," she repeated. "One of our pathologists worked summers on a dairy farm in Wisconsin. He said the injury on your vic's back looks like it came from one of those hooks they used to hoof around hay bales."

"How the hell would he know that?"

"He showed me the scar," Julia said. "He got in the way once and was nailed in the bicep. The scarring around entrance of the wound is similar."

"But it wasn't the cause of death?"

"No," Julia confirmed. "And neither is strangulation. This damage is definitely post mortem."

"All right." He let out a sigh, made a few more notes. "Do me a favor and e-mail me the autopsy photos."

"Will do. I'll fax a copy of the preliminary report as well. You calling in the Feds?"

"Not yet," he said, but he would be making use of ViCAP to check for similar crimes. "What about the tox report? Can you speed it up?"

"I'll try to lean on the lab. Best I can probably get for you is tomorrow afternoon."

Not perfect, but better than having to wait a week or longer. "Thanks, Julia. Much appreciated."

"Beck? Catch this bastard, would you? I really don't want to see any more of his work on my table."

Neither did he. "We're doing all we can," he told her, then thanked her and hung up the phone.

He then headed to the conference room, where the sorority girls were waiting to be questioned on the disappearance of their friend.

"EFFECTIVE next Monday, the *Sentinel* will be owned by Tricor Publishing."

Ainsley stared at her boss, half in shock, half in a rising state of panic. So Mona's source had been right, after all. Dylan really had sold the paper.

Lisa started to cry again.

Mona just looked pissed.

The older woman sat back in the blue conference chair and crossed her arms, glaring at Dylan. "So where does that leave us?" Mona asked him, her tone surprisingly calm despite the anger in her gaze.

"I don't want any of you to worry," Dylan told them. "None of you will be losing your jobs."

"Yet," Mona scoffed.

"Of course, there will be some changes," Dylan continued. "The *Sentinel* is being absorbed by the *Daily Tribune,* so we can expect things to get busy around here. We'll be going from a weekly publication to a daily." He looked around the conference room at each of them. Lisa wept. Mona glared.

Ainsley played with her travel mug, not knowing what to think.

Dylan frowned, obviously perplexed by their reaction. "Come on, guys. This is good news," he said.

Mona mumbled something under her breath that Ainsley didn't catch.

Lisa dabbed her eyes with a worn-out tissue.

"Exactly how is this all supposed to work?" Ainsley finally asked. "I scrounge for stories as it is. There's barely enough news in this town to fill a weekly, let alone a daily."

"Exactly," Mona added. "Did you see this week's classifieds? They barely filled two columns."

Dylan's frown deepened. "I don't get it. I thought you'd all be happy about this."

"Well, you obviously thought wrong," Mona complained.

"The *Trib* is a larger, regional paper. That means more opportunities." He shot Ainsley a pointed look. "Especially for you."

"Me?" She supposed Dylan had a point, except she wasn't all that happy about the sale of the paper, either. Worried pretty much summed up her feelings on the matter. A bigger paper required bigger stories, and with the exception of the past seventy-two hours, Serenity Heights was hardly a hotbed of breaking news.

"Come on, Ainsley. You seriously don't want to cover bake sales and Little League fund-raisers for your entire career, do you?"

Now that he mentioned it, regardless of the subject matter, she had enjoyed the challenge of her most recent article. "I guess not," she admitted. Where to find those meatier stories, however, was another matter.

"The story you just did on the missing college student and the unidentified body found was excellent reporting," Dylan told her. "Clean, tight, and to the point."

"Thanks," she said, even though she couldn't help be a

little surprised. Dylan rarely praised, other than the occasional "nice job."

"What about you?" Mona asked suddenly. "Are you leaving us to the mercy of the corporate bean counters?"

"Not right away," Dylan said. He reached for the bottled water in front of him and took a long drink.

Buying time? Ainsley wondered. "You're retiring, aren't you?" she asked him.

"Retiring?" Mona blurted. "Don't be ridiculous. He's too young to retire."

"Ainsley's right," Dylan admitted. "I'll be leaving at the end of October. That should give everyone time to adjust to the transition."

"You mean time to find new jobs," Mona complained. "I've heard the rumors. We all know how Tricor works, Dylan. They come in and pretend nothing has changed, then they fire the staff and close the paper. No more *Sentinel.* No more local coverage. No more job."

Lisa started sniveling again.

"No one is going to close the paper," Dylan said in a placating tone. He glanced nervously at the tearful Lisa, then back at Mona. "It's true, we are being absorbed into the *Daily Tribune,* but that will give us wider distribution. We'll have a daily section for local news, advertising, and classifieds. Nothing will change except we're now part of a larger newspaper with wider distribution."

"No one cares about what happens in Serenity Heights except the people who live here," Mona argued. "People in Columbus or Pittsburgh don't give a damn about our quiet little town."

Ainsley traced her thumbnail along the rim of her travel mug. "Has the sale been finalized?"

"What do you mean?"

She looked up at Dylan. "Is it a done deal?"

"I haven't signed on the dotted line yet, if that's what you mean."

Slowly, she nodded. "When will that happen?"

Dylan's frown returned. "Tomorrow. Why?"

"Just curious," she said with a careless shrug.

Reckless would've been a more appropriate description, considering where her thoughts were headed. But she couldn't help wondering, exactly how much did a small town newspaper sell for—and could she raise the money to buy it herself?

CHAPTER 14

CHARLIE GABRIEL DIDN'T need to be a cop. He sure as hell didn't need the money even though his pro football career had ended early, but Beck knew the former defensive lineman liked his job. Liked feeling that he was helping people.

If the current situation weren't so grave, Beck might have laughed at the sight of big and burly Charlie, helplessly inept amid a room full of college women in varying stages of tears, worry, and frustration.

"Why aren't you out looking for her?" a tall, lithe, dark-haired girl demanded.

"She's right," another, this one short, blond, and curvy, piped up. "You're wasting time asking us the same questions over and over again."

"Excuse me, ladies," Beck said to them. "We're here to help, but Officer Gabriel can only answer one question at a time."

Six pair of eyes shot in his direction. Charlie's wide shoulders slumped in relief at the sight of Beck.

"Why don't you all have a seat," Beck suggested, "while I speak privately to Officer Gabriel. I'll be with you in a minute."

The look Charlie shot Beck was one of pure relief. "Damn,

they're vicious," Charlie said when Beck closed the conference room door.

"They're scared," Beck said. "What did you expect?"

"You'd never guess I have four daughters," Charlie said, casting a wary glance at the closed door.

Beck would've liked to have interviewed the girls separately, but there just wasn't time. He had the search and rescue teams scheduled to arrive in a couple of hours and he needed to pay a visit to the U. He wanted to question Pomeroy again, and McElvoy. The bastard had insinuated himself into his investigation and Beck wanted to know why. Was the U's reputation his only concern? Or something else?

"Can you give me a quick rundown?" he asked Charlie.

"Megan Connor, twenty years old, a junior, poli-sci major," the officer said. "About five-foot-seven, slender, long brown hair. According to the girls, Megan had an argument with her boyfriend yesterday evening. They claim she was pretty upset and said she was going for a walk to clear her head. No one thought much about it until this morning when they realized Megan hadn't come home."

"Any idea what the argument was about?"

"Apparently the boyfriend's a bit of a player."

Beck nodded. "I'll question the girls. You brief Mitch, then call Steve Jonas to meet you at the Sigma Pi house. See what you can find out, then call me."

"Will do, Chief," Charlie said, then headed off down the hall. He stopped and turned back to face Beck. "What about the boyfriend?"

"Let's bring him in for questioning."

Charlie hesitated.

"Is there a problem?"

"Depends on what you consider a problem."

Beck frowned. "What now?"

"He's Gavin Chesterfield. His aunt is the dean over at the U."

* * *

"HEY, PARIS, DID you see this?"

Paris looked up from her breakfast of soggy pancakes and overcooked sausage links to take the flyer Cassidy thrust at her. "What is it?" she asked as she scanned the black and white photograph of Mattie Davenport.

"They're asking for volunteers to help with a search." Cassidy plunked down in the chair across from Paris. "I'm going over to McElvoy's office now to sign up. Wanna come?"

"Sure," Paris said, pushing the rest of her breakfast aside. Zach was supposed to have met her for breakfast, but he'd stood her up. He hadn't even bothered to call, which told her he was probably still ticked at her for blowing him off last night. "I have to work this afternoon, so I don't know how much help I can be."

Cassidy plucked a piece of sausage from Paris's plate. "Even if you're only handing out bottled water to the volunteers, it's something."

"We'd better go sign up now," Paris said, standing. She hefted her backpack over her shoulder. "I have a Western civ class in twenty minutes."

Cassidy stood, then reached over and snagged the last piece of sausage, dragging it through the syrup puddle on the plate. "I've got freshman comp and earth science, then I'm done for the day." She slung her own backpack over her shoulder, then said, "Let's go."

Paris disposed of her tray, then followed Cass up the steps and out into the bright morning sunshine. It was only midmorning and already the day was heating up. She was used to warm summers, but without that nice thick layer of city grime and smog, the sun was a lot hotter than she was accustomed to. By the time she and Cass reached the admin building, a thin layer of sweat had her shirt sticking uncomfortably to her back and her wishing she'd worn something a little lighter than jeans.

The corridor wasn't half as crowded as it'd been when she'd come to interview for the job. There were still plenty of kids milling around, standing in lines at the various windows, adding or dropping classes. They wound their way through the corridors until they reached the associate dean's office, where the sign-up sheets were being manned by Deborah.

"Good morning, girls," Deborah said solemnly as they approached her desk. "Are you here to volunteer today?"

"We thought maybe we could help," Paris said with a shrug.

"It'll be appreciated."

Deborah handed her a clipboard with the sign-in sheet attached just as the door to Mr. McElvoy's private office swung open. Her new boss walked over to Deborah and set something on the desk, then gave Paris a curious stare. "Paris," he said without smiling. "You're a little early for work, aren't you?"

"We're just here signing up to volunteer," Cassidy told him, then took the clipboard from Paris and added her own name to the list.

"I figured I could help until I need to be here," Paris said, not wanting him to think she was blowing off her first day of work, regardless of the cause.

"That's fine," he said, still not smiling. He was looking at Cass. Staring at her, actually. "Any help at all is appreciated."

He gave Paris the creeps. She'd have to ask Cass's sister about the possibilities of a job at the newspaper. She didn't think she'd like working for this guy. He was just—weird.

"So?" Cass handed McElvoy the sign-up sheet. "Where are we supposed to meet?"

Mr. McElvoy quickly shifted his gaze away when Cass kept looking at him. "All volunteers are meeting at noon at the front entrance," he said. His gaze dipped to the sign-in sheet. "Brennan? Any relationship to Ainsley Brennan?"

"She's my sister," Cass said.

"Well, uh, thanks," Paris said, then nudged Cass to get going. Cassidy shot her a strange look, but turned and reached for the door. "I'll see you later," Paris added, then quickly followed Cass out the door.

"What's up with you?" Cassidy said once Paris pulled the door closed.

"Did you see the way he was staring at you?"

Cassidy shrugged. "So? The guy's a perv."

"I guess," Paris said, but she still thought it was weird the way he'd looked at Cass. She'd gotten a strange vibe, and it made her uncomfortable.

"My first class is on the other side of campus. I gotta run. See you at noon?"

"Yeah. Noon," Paris said, then tried to shrug off the weirdness as Cass took off down the hall. Her own class was upstairs on the third floor, so she spun around to head to the stairwell and practically smacked into Gavin.

"Hey, there," he said, grabbing hold of her shoulders so she didn't fall on her butt. His voice all smooth and kinda sexy. "I was going to call you, but you didn't tell me what dorm you're in."

"Oh." She smoothed her suddenly sweaty palms on her jeans. She liked the idea that he'd wanted to call her. "I'm in Davis Hall."

"Wanna have lunch with me today? I have a break between classes around noon."

"I can't," she said regretfully. She liked Gavin, but she didn't think it was right for her to go off on coffee or lunch dates until she'd officially broken things off with Zach. Not that she was actually planning on hooking up with Gavin, but she didn't want to start seeing any guy, even casually, until she'd broken up with Zach.

Funny, she thought, but until this very second, she hadn't even realized that's exactly what she'd been wanting to do. Her decision to end it with Zach didn't have anything to do with Gavin. Not really. She liked him, but that was beside the point. All Gavin had done was make her realize she didn't deserve to be treated like a convenience, which is exactly what Zach had been doing for months.

"I signed up to volunteer, then I have to be at work," she told him. "Some other time, maybe?"

"Uh-oh," Gavin said. "This doesn't look good."

Paris turned to see what he was talking about, surprised to see his aunt, Dean Chesterfield, walking hurriedly toward them. She didn't look too happy, either. Two campus security guards and a cop accompanied her.

"Gavin, a word please," his aunt said, her expression tight.

"I'll catch up to you later," Gavin said to Paris, then gave his aunt his full attention.

Curious, Paris lingered, but took a few steps back to hopefully give the illusion of privacy. She crouched down and unzipped her backpack as if she were looking for something.

"What's up?" Gavin asked, his gaze darting between his aunt and the cops.

"Gavin Chesterfield," the big cop said, "I need you to come with me."

"What? Am I under arrest for something?" He laughed, but sounded way too nervous to carry it off.

"Of course you're not," his aunt reassured him. "Officer Gabriel just has some questions for you about Megan."

Gavin definitely looked worried. "She's all right, isn't she?"

Paris frowned. Who the hell was Megan? His girlfriend? So much for her not being a convenience.

"I need you to come with me, son," Officer Gabriel said

in that cop voice Paris bet they all learned at the academy. The one that said ain't no way in hell you'd win an argument with him.

One of the campus security guards grabbed hold of Gavin's arm. "This way."

The dean stepped between Gavin and the security guard. "That isn't necessary," she said coldly.

Gavin shrugged off the guard. "Tell me she's all right," he demanded. He looked to his aunt. "What's happened? Where's Megan?"

"No one has seen her since last evening," Mary Ann Chesterfield told her nephew. "Go with Officer Gabriel. I'll be along shortly."

Gavin nodded, but when the campus security guard attempted to grab hold of him again, Gavin shrugged him off once more and went willingly with the cop. The two campus guards followed close behind.

Paris stood and slowly walked to the stairs, not knowing what to think about what she'd just witnessed. Who the hell was Megan Conner, and why was Gavin being questioned about her disappearance? And worse, could Gavin have anything at all to do with the disappearance of Mattie Davenport?

HE SEETHED AS he read the article in this week's edition of the *Sentinel* for a second time. There'd been a huge spread on the missing girl as well as the girl he'd left for them in the clearing. But not a single word about the very special gifts he'd presented to Ainsley Brennan. Nothing. As if what he'd done for her didn't matter.

How dare she dismiss his work like that? Didn't she realize the importance of what he'd bestowed upon her? He'd allowed her to witness his power. Surely she had to understand that much.

Maybe he'd been mistaken about her? Could he have misjudged their connection?

No. That simply wasn't a possibility.

Dammit, they'd understood each other. He'd felt it, and he was never wrong about such things. They'd come from the same place. Last place. Others had always come first in their lives, leaving them with nothing but whatever paltry scraps remained. She knew all about sacrifice, just as he'd known.

They were connected on a deeper level. Perhaps he only needed to make her realize that fact. She might have given so much of herself that she had little left inside her to recognize how in tune they were to each other.

He would help her. When the time was right, she would know.

A knock at the door sounded. Carefully, he folded the newspaper and stuffed it in the bottom drawer of his desk. "Come in," he said, as he turned on the computer monitor.

The door opened and his *boss* breezed into his office. The bitch. She'd stolen the job that was to have been his. He knew why, too. She'd slept with half of the board of governors. Women like her always fucked their way to the top. It probably didn't hurt that she was related by marriage to a cousin of the university's president, either.

She looked flushed, upset about something as she paced in front of his desk.

"What can I do for you, Dean Chesterfield?" he asked, maintaining an even tone.

"Got any miracles up your sleeve?" she asked. "We're in trouble, Devin. We have another missing student. And my nephew was just taken in for questioning. This is not good for the U."

"I hadn't heard about the second missing girl," Devin McElvoy lied smoothly. "I'm sorry."

But he wasn't. Not really. She'd brought it upon herself, the little cunt, snooping around where she wasn't wanted. He'd had no choice but to take her, even if she was all wrong. Megan Conner had been in the wrong place at the wrong time, and he would make her see the error of her ways, just as he had the others.

Dean Chesterfield stopped pacing and rubbed at her forehead. "It's a girl my nephew has dated," she said. "I know Gavin. He wouldn't hurt anyone."

"Do the police know?"

She shot him an impatient glance. "I just told you they took him in for questioning," she snapped. She let out a quick breath. "I'm sorry. That was uncalled for. It's just . . ."

God, he hated her. She was just like *them*. Taking, taking, and taking, not caring about anyone but herself. Full of self-entitlement. The bitch.

"You're upset." He stood and circled the desk, crossing his office to the cabinet on the far wall, where a small refrigerator was hidden. Retrieving a cool bottle of water, he handed it to her. "Why don't you have a seat and collect yourself?"

"Thanks." She took the bottled water and twisted off the cap. "But I can't. I need to call Megan's parents, then get over to the police station. Can you field any calls we might receive on this matter? Please, try to keep the damage to the U to a minimum."

He resented her implication that he wasn't capable of doing his job. "You know I will," he said, careful to keep his anger in check.

She nodded, then left without further insult.

He returned to his desk and sat. Slowly, he smiled. So the police thought the dean's nephew was a suspect?

He chuckled.

What a lovely distraction for the police. He couldn't have

planned it better himself. How utterly perfect, and what a marvelous method to inflict suffering on the bitch who had taken what should have been his.

And he hadn't even been trying.

BECK TUCKED HIS cell phone back into his pocket. He'd just finished talking to the sound engineer, who informed him the two words spoken by the UNSUB probably weren't enough for a speech expert to work with. He was having a bitch of a day, and it wasn't even noon yet.

The sorority sisters from Sigma Pi had given him a headache, but with some effort, he'd managed to calm them down long enough to get the answers out of them that he'd needed. Megan Conner had had a heated argument with her boyfriend, Gavin Chesterfield. Still agitated a couple of hours later, she'd said she was taking a walk to cool off. No one noticed that she hadn't returned until this morning when one of the girls had stopped by Megan's room to borrow something. She'd noticed Megan's bed hadn't been slept in and had sounded the alarm.

What the hell was wrong with these kids, he wondered? You'd think with a student already missing they would pay a little more attention to what was going on around them. That they would go wandering off alone was damn stupid of them. When would these kids learn they weren't invincible?

"So what did you and Megan argue about?" Beck asked Gavin Chesterfield. According to one girl, Megan's arguments with Gavin weren't all that unusual, and more often than not were centered around Gavin's dating habits—with other girls.

"Megan thought I was seeing someone else," the kid admitted.

"And were you?"

"I had coffee with a freshman yesterday," Gavin said. "It wasn't a big deal, but Megan found out and got all freaky about it."

In Beck's opinion, Chesterfield wasn't a bad kid. He knew the type, too. Young, privileged, and good-looking, a hell of a triad when it came to picking up chicks. The kid wasn't doing anything that he or half the guys at the station hadn't done once upon a time. Chesterfield had simply been taking advantage of his youth the way boys often did. Hell, he'd been that age once himself, and God knew no one would have ever called him a saint.

Beck leaned back in the metal folding chair and crossed his arms over his chest, leveling a hard stare at the kid. "Do you do that often?" he asked. "Have coffee with freshmen girls?"

Gavin shrugged. "Sometimes. Megan and I weren't exclusive."

"Did Megan know that?"

Gavin looked away. Apparently not.

"So tell me what happened after you left the Sigma Pi house yesterday."

"I went back to my apartment, did some reading for a class, then met up with a few of the guys down at the Pizza Pit."

Beck knew the place. A regular hang-out for the high school and college kids. A place where they could stay out of trouble, shoot some pool, and waste quarters on a few video arcade games. The pizza wasn't half bad, either.

"Then what?"

"I left just before it closed at eleven. My roommate was home when I got there."

"Did you leave?"

"No. My roommate and I had a brew, then I went to bed."

"You didn't try to call Megan?"

"No way," Gavin said. "She was rippin' pissed, so I figured I'd let her cool down."

Beck understood that philosophy all too well. There was just no reasoning with a woman when she was fired up enough to want to rip your head off.

He slid a yellow legal pad in front of the kid. "I'll need the name of your roommate, and the guys you were hanging out with last night."

"Then I can go?" Gavin asked hopefully. "I'm not under arrest?"

"You can go once I check out your alibi," Beck said. "So you might as well make yourself comfortable, kid."

"Dude, I have a class."

Beck didn't believe the kid had anything to do with the Conner girl's disappearance, but he wasn't about to take any chances. How many times had he heard of the cops having the perp in their custody and letting him walk? Too damn many to count.

"I'll bet there will be plenty of pretty girls who'll gladly share their notes with you," Beck said, standing. "Press that buzzer over there by the window when you're done."

Beck left the interrogation room. Waiting outside the one-way glass were the kid's aunt, Mary Ann Chesterfield, and Mitch. The captain looked tired, as if he'd gotten little sleep last night. Beck knew the feeling, but his lack of rest had more to do with Ainsley and less about his thinking about the investigation.

"We'll let him go just as soon as we can check out his alibi," Beck told the dean.

"Is that really necessary?" she asked. "Keeping him, I mean."

"It shouldn't take long," Beck reassured her. "I can have someone call you when he's ready to leave."

Dean Chesterfield gave him a harsh stare. "The only thing my nephew is guilty of is infidelity."

Mitch coughed suddenly and looked down at his polished boots.

Beck ignored him. "You may be right," he said, "but we wouldn't be doing our job if we didn't thoroughly investigate any and all leads in the case, now would we?"

"And this is how you go about it?" Her tone bordered on shrill and grated on Beck's nerves. "By questioning my nephew and keeping him here when the real perpetrator is out there somewhere," she continued, "targeting girls from the university?"

"We don't know that anyone is targeting girls from the U," Beck said, but it was certainly starting to look that way to him. "Unless there's something you know that you'd like to tell us?"

"Like what?"

"Does anyone have a grudge against the U? Or you?" he asked. "Or any member of the staff or faculty, for that matter?"

"Don't be ridiculous," she scoffed. "How could we possibly know that?"

"It's something you'll have to think about." He'd be willing to bet she'd managed to piss off a few people in her lifetime. "At this point, just remember that no one is without suspicion. If you think of anything unusual, call me."

That truth sobered her, and her harsh expression softened. She drew in a breath, then let it out slowly. "If I think of anything, I'll be in touch."

"Good enough."

Mitch waited until the dean was out of earshot. "If you don't think the kid is guilty, why make him hang around here?" he asked. "Unless you don't think his alibi is going to pan out."

Beck braced his feet apart and crossed his arms, watching the kid through the one-way glass as he wrote down a list of names on the pad Beck had left him. "He's no more guilty than either one of us," Beck said. "But the longer we keep him here for questioning, the longer the UNSUB might think we're chasing the wrong suspect. He might start to feel complacent, and that's when he'll make a mistake."

"Whoa, back up a minute." Mitch looked up and down the corridor, then back at Beck. "You're convinced the UNSUB is a local? When did this happen?"

"Last night confirmed it. The third CD was found inside Ainsley's car. It happened sometime after I got there. I know because I looked inside her car before going inside." He'd also checked out the front porch before going inside, because like Ainsley, he'd also believed there would be more deliveries.

"So what does that have to do with the price of peanuts at the circus?"

"The UNSUB knows Ainsley." Something she'd been trying to convince him of all along.

Mitch scratched the back of his head. "I thought we figured that one out already, what with the delivery of the recordings addressed to her."

"It's more than that. This guy knows her habits, Mitch."

"You think he's watching her?"

"Possibly."

Mitch swore. Though he'd made a career out of investigating homicide cases, he'd never had a personal stake in any of those investigations—until now. And that scared the hell out of him.

"So what are you going to do about it?"

"Nail this fucker to the wall," Beck said. "The sooner, the better."

CHAPTER 15

AINSLEY KNEW IT was going to be a hot one when her linen pantsuit started to wilt before she did. Behind the wheel of a shiny, almost new, deep green Jeep Compass, she cranked up the AC and drove from the rental car office in Avon back to Serenity Heights. She'd spoken to Raelynn earlier. As Beck had promised, she'd been provided with the information on where the command center was being set up for today's search of the surrounding woods.

More worrisome was the news that Raelynn had also imparted to her. Another student was missing from the U. She'd also told her, confidentially, that the dean's nephew had been brought in for questioning. According to Raelynn, Gavin Chesterfield had unofficially been eliminated as a suspect, as had Reid Pomeroy, but the department was keeping that information under wraps for the time being.

The news of a second missing student had Ainsley worried. Both girls, one a freshman, the other a junior, had lived on campus, just as her sister did.

To hell with the rules. Effective immediately, she was moving Cassidy, and her roommate, too, for that matter, home with her until the sick bastard preying upon young girls at the U was stopped. There would be other students leaving, too, just as soon as word spread to parents that the U wasn't exactly the safest place right now for their daughters.

She figured she'd be in for a fight with Cass, but that was just too damn bad. She had enough to worry about without being in a constant state of fear that something could happen to her baby sister.

God, could this day get any crappier, she wondered? She hoped she would have better luck with Cass than she'd had when she'd spoken privately to Dylan following the bomb he'd dropped on her this morning. It had taken her boss all of three seconds to dash any silly hope she might have had of "saving" the *Sentinel* from big bad corporate fate. Tricor had not only met Dylan's asking price for the paper, but they were purchasing the building, lock, stock, and toner cartridges.

Now she didn't know what she was supposed to do. Should she listen to Mona and expect the worst, that they'd all be standing in line at the unemployment office in a matter of weeks? Or should she take Dylan's advice and look at the sale of the *Sentinel* to Tricor as a growth opportunity? Regardless of which ideology she chose to subscribe to, she still had no idea how they were supposed to go from a weekly publication to a daily. She hadn't been exaggerating when she'd told Dylan she had to scrounge for stories as it was.

By the time she pulled up next to Beck's SUV parked under the shade of a sugar maple tree on the southern edge of town, her emotions were still running the gamut, from her thin chance of continued employment, to Cassidy's welfare, and the upcoming search. She prayed they wouldn't be finding any more dead bodies today. But then, there was nothing like a corpse to give a story some zip.

Disgusted with herself for even thinking that way, she shut down the Compass, then slid from the rental. She easily spied Beck, standing beneath a large canvas cabana with a group of men and women she didn't recognize. From where she stood, he appeared at ease, in his element, but she couldn't help noticing the tension in his shoulders. His eyes were shielded by a pair of dark sunglasses, but it wasn't hard for her to imagine stress lines framing those incredibly intense green eyes.

Four large German shepherds rested quietly, seemingly oblivious to all the commotion, also beneath the shade the cabana provided. Farther away were several groups of young people, most seated on the grass under whatever shade they could find, along with a respectable number of residents from town that she recognized. She pulled her digital camera from her tote and snapped a few shots.

Shedding her jacket, she tossed it in the backseat, grateful she'd paid attention to the weather forecast this morning while she'd dressed for work and had put on a cotton tank beneath her blue linen suit. After gathering her tote, she started across the grassy area to the cabana, only to stop when she heard someone call her name. She turned to see Cassidy and her roommate, Paris, break from the crowd of students and head toward her.

"What are you guys doing here?" she asked the girls when they approached.

"We signed up to help," Cass said. She gave her a look, but kept the "duh" to herself this time.

"I can't stay long," Paris added. "I have to be at my new job in a few hours."

There was just something horribly wrong about these two young girls being part of a search party that could very well end with tragic results. They weren't supposed to be subjected to these kinds of life lessons. They should be getting their hearts bruised so they made smarter relationship choices in the future. They were supposed to struggle with algebra homework and biology midterms, and eat pizza by the pound, not be part of a search effort for disappearing classmates.

Ainsley glanced over at the group of students from the U. There had to be at least a hundred of them, possibly more. "No one would miss you if you left now," she told the girls.

Cassidy rolled her eyes. "I'm not a baby, Lee."

"Believe it or not, I've noticed. But I don't think you need to be out here."

"Excuse me," Cass said, shoving her hands in the back pockets of her jeans, "but weren't you the one always telling Paige and me that we needed to take an active role in the community?"

"Yes, but I didn't mean—"

"Well, the U is my community now. I'm going to help, so get over yourself."

Get over herself? That's what she got for taking care of her sister all these years? Get over herself?

She wondered if anyone would notice if she slipped her hands around her sister's neck and squeezed. Probably. Too many damn witnesses hanging around.

"I suppose you feel the same way?" Ainsley asked Paris.

"Yeah. I'd like to help," she answered.

"Okay, fine. But don't you guys dare call me at two in the morning when you wake up screaming from a nightmare. You're on your own."

Paris giggled. Cass rolled her eyes again.

"Listen, why don't the two of you grab a few things and come by the house for a few days," Ainsley told them.

Cass frowned. "Why?"

"Would you just humor me?"

"No," Cass said stubbornly. "Tell me why first."

Paris nudged Cass with her elbow. "She's worried about you, dummy."

"What's new? She always worries," Cass answered, sounding thoroughly disgusted by the thought.

"You're both right," Ainsley said. "Look, I don't know if you've heard, but there's another student who's missing."

Paris nodded. "I was there when the cops picked up Gavin."

Cass shot her roommate a sharp look. "You were? Why didn't you tell me?"

Paris shrugged. "I guess I forgot about it until now."

Ainsley wasn't certain if she believed Paris. From the narrowed-eyed stare Cassidy was throwing Paris's way, her sister didn't look as if she believed her, either. Regardless, the fact remained that she wanted the girls at home for the time being. "Why don't you both go back to the dorm and pack. I'll meet you there and take you back to the house."

"Nice try, Lee, but Paris and I are going to help first. Remember?"

"Fine. Help then," she said, her voice sharper than she'd intended. But dammit, her sister was frustrating the hell out of her. Independence was one thing. Stupidity was another matter entirely. "But promise me you'll come stay at the house for a few days. At least until things calm down. Paris can stay in Paige's old room."

"Won't we get into trouble?" Paris asked her. "There's some rule about freshmen living off campus."

"Let me worry about that," Ainsley reassured her, and tried to summon up a smile. Cripes, the dean's own nephew had been brought in for questioning. Surely Dean Chesterfield wouldn't dream of punishing the girls for her wanting them to be safe. Safe at home where she could protect them.

"We wouldn't have to share a bathroom with anyone but ourselves," Cassidy told Paris.

Paris shrugged her slender shoulders. "I'm cool with it."

"Okay," Cass said to Ainsley. "You win. We'll be there. After we get done here."

"Thanks," Paris said before Cassidy grabbed her by the arm and the two of them took off to rejoin the others as if nothing at all were terribly wrong with their world.

Cassidy was probably right, Ainsley suddenly realized. She did need to get over herself. But she'd never had a chance to be that young, that carefree. At their age, she'd been saddled with responsibilities she'd never asked for and had been ill equipped to handle, leaving her no choice but to grow up in a great big hurry.

Cassidy had no idea as to the horrors she might find today, and that, Ainsley supposed, was her fault. She'd done all she could to shield and protect her sisters. Obviously that hadn't changed, considering the invitation she'd just issued. But life had dealt them a difficult hand. As the oldest, the responsibility had fallen to her to see that her sister made it through safely into adulthood. Hell, now that she thought about it, she supposed it was a miracle they'd all turned out at least partially sane, productive individuals.

Letting go was a bitch, she thought. Especially when doing so left her with plenty of spare time to examine her own life. But she was imbedded in Serenity Heights. This was her home. Or was she simply using it as an excuse to hide out? Was she really afraid to finally spread her own wings now that her obligations had been met?

She frowned, unsure she liked the answer.

More curious was how Beck fit into her unplanned future. Incredible sex and a few mind-blowing orgasms didn't exactly constitute a relationship. But they did have a definite connection outside the bedroom, too. The question was how far, and how long, would it stretch? An even bigger question perhaps, was how far did *she* want it to go? The distance? Or for only as long as it lasted?

By the time she approached the cabana, she still had no answers. She received a few curious glances from the various personnel on site, but she kept quiet and stood off to the side, listening and learning. Beck acknowledged her presence with a quick glance in her direction. Otherwise, he was all business, as was the guy she determined was the team leader, who offered suggestions on the best approach to take with the search and making use of the volunteers.

In addition to the handful of officers, including Mitch, the associate dean was also present. McElvoy stood on the fringes, not quite a part of the group, but close enough to give onlookers the impression his position was as important as Beck's or the rest of the law enforcement personnel. He was out of place in his neatly pressed suit and shiny black dress shoes. He had a look on his face, as if he wanted to contribute to the conversation, but the others essentially ignored him.

Curiously absent, she couldn't help noticing, was the mayor. Mattie's parents were absent as well, but she hadn't really expected them to be here, considering what they might find today.

Ainsley pulled her notepad from her tote and made notes about the parties present, along with a few descriptions of the scene, from the college students to the residents of Serenity Heights. Fred Aames from the minimart had shown up to help as well, and had even brought several cases of bottled water for the volunteers. Delilah Staple from the drugstore was busy handing out sunscreen samples, urging everyone to make sure they were protected from the dangerous UV rays.

Decisions made, the volunteers were then called upon to split into four groups. There would be four search teams, each group consisting of volunteers, led by a K-9 team and two SHPD officers. Beck, Mitch, and the search and rescue team leader, whose name she learned was Trace Holt, would remain behind at the command center. McElvoy seemed displeased by this, but ended up joining Team Bravo. Paris and Cassidy were a part of Charlie Team.

Armed with sunblock and bottled water, the teams dispersed. Supplied with her own bottle of water, Ainsley went back under the shade of the cabana and sat in a vacant folding camp chair out of the way. She considered going out with one of the teams, but after her last run-in with a corpse, she decided she'd make better use of her reporting skills by hanging with the men in charge of the operation. Besides, if anything was found, Beck would be the first to know. She could always follow him out to the site.

An hour passed, then two. From her vantage point under the cabana, she could see the Alpha Team off in the distance. The group moved together through the open field in a straight line, the search painstaking and slow. Bits of information came in to the command center, but most finds were inconsequential and quickly dismissed as irrelevant.

She made more notes and attempted to frame her story, but every time one of the walkie-talkies crackled, she tensed and lost her train of thought. Although she and Beck kept their distance physically, they did exchange a few heated glances now and then. The last one Mitch happened to catch. The police captain coughed and looked away, which made her feel a little like a teenager caught necking. Beck chuckled when she blushed and buried her nose in her notes.

Halfway into the third hour, a call came in from one of the team leaders. "Bravo Team to Base. Come back."

"Base here," Beck answered. "Go ahead."

"Request a ten-seventy-nine, Base."

Ainsley frowned, then remembered that a ten-seventy-nine was a request for the coroner. *Oh no.*

"DB located approximately three hundred yards from the main road in the northern quadrant." There was a pause and more crackling sounds, followed by, "Stand by, Base."

"Son of a bitch," Beck swore. "Call Julia Reiki, see if she's available," he instructed Mitch. "If not, we'll take whoever they can spare. Better call Eisner at the DA's office while you're at it. He'll probably want to be here for this."

Mitch dragged his cell phone from his pocket. "I'm on it."

More crackling. "Delta Team to Base. Come back."

"Base here," Trace Holt answered the call. "Go ahead, Delta."

"We have an indication by the K-9 unit. A brown leather sandal. Hasn't been out here long. A woman's size eight."

"What the hell is going on out there?" Beck complained to no one in particular.

Trace held up his hand, which only made Beck's frown deepen. "What's your ten-twenty, Delta?" Trace asked.

"Eastern quadrant," the team leader replied. "We're on a dirt road about six hundred and fifty yards from Team Bravo. Officers are roping off the immediate vicinity. Await your instructions, Base. Go ahead."

Ainsley walked over to the folding table where Beck and Trace Holt were bent over the map spread out there. Trace drew circles on the map based on the information they'd received from the team leaders, then drew a heavy, dark line from one location to the next.

"I know this area," she said. "It was part of a big farming operation that had been abandoned and sold off during the farm crises in the early eighties."

"Do you know who owns it now?" Beck asked her.

"The city," she said. "Every once in a while the city council talks about turning it into a park, or maybe an overnight RV campground, but nothing ever happens. Mostly it's used by hunters to gain access to the woods"—she pointed to another location on the map—"here."

"Bravo Team to Base," another radio crackled. "Come back."

"Go ahead, Bravo," Trace Holt answered.

"Permission to dispense volunteers due to risk of crime scene contamination."

Ainsley knew what that meant, considering she'd been accused of doing the same thing just a few days ago. If this body was in anywhere near the same shape as the previous one, she easily imagined students losing their lunch all over the crime scene.

Trace looked to Beck.

"Send them back here for debriefing," Beck said. "We'll need to question them to see if anyone saw the body and could identify it. Instruct the officers to secure the scene."

While Trace relayed Beck's instructions, Ainsley thanked God that Cassidy and Paris weren't part of teams Bravo or Delta.

Beck pressed the button on the walkie-talkie. "Base to Bravo. Come back."

"Bravo. Go ahead, Base."

"Can you give me a description of the DB?"

"Stand by, Base."

Ainsley bit her lip as she waited along with everyone else for the brief description of the body that had been found. She sent up a quick prayer that it wasn't Mattie Davenport, hoping against hope that the cello player with the sweet smile and laughing blue eyes from Mississippi was still alive.

"Female. Blond hair, approximately five-foot-two. Age undeterminable at this time."

Ainsley wracked her brain, but she couldn't for the life of her recall Mattie's height. God, she should know this. She'd included it in her article. Had seen it on the flyer the police department had handed out. Frustrated, she tried to envision the photograph she'd taken from Mattie's dorm room, the one with her family, but it was useless without a point of reference. Why was it she could recall a stupid detail like a police code and not Mattie Davenport's height?

"Anything else?" Beck asked. He looked at Ainsley, his expression grim.

The radio crackled again. "Yeah. She's dressed up like a goddamn prom queen."

SEVEN HOURS LATER, Beck crouched on the floor, balanced on the balls of his feet, surrounded by grisly five-by-eight glossy photographs. Two sets of crime scene photographs were spread out on each side of him. To the left was their first Jane Doe. On the right, their second. Behind him were the corresponding autopsy photographs of Jane Doe I. He was still waiting on Raelynn to print up the batch Julia had e-mailed him for Jane Doe II.

He was tired, hungry, and buried up to his ass in paperwork and dead bodies. He needed a break, a bed, and food. Seeing Ainsley again wouldn't hurt, either. But all he had for the foreseeable future was three-hour-old coffee and a scant selection of leftover baked goods. The caffeine buzz would help, the sugar rush would probably kill him.

As Mitch walked into the conference Beck glanced up and said, "You look like shit."

"Don't go thinking you're gonna be winning any beauty contests anytime soon," Mitch fired back crabbily. He pulled out a cushy blue chair and sat. "I hate this fucking case."

"That makes two of us," Beck said, shifting his attention back to the photographs. "I take it you read Julia's preliminary report on our second Jane Doe."

"Yeah. More of the same. A whole lot of mutilation and no answers." Mitch looked at him curiously. "Wouldn't you be more comfortable with those on the table?" he asked with an inclination of his head toward the photographs.

"They stay in place better down here on the carpet."

"Just what are you hoping to find?"

"Anything I might have missed."

"Chief, I think we need to consider calling in BCI. This kind of thing is right up their Special Investigations Unit's alley."

Beck braced his hands on his knees and slowly stood. His back protested and his knees popped loudly as he rose. "What kind of thing?"

Mitch let out a long, slow breath. "They're better equipped to handle serial offenses. We're just a small-town department. Hell, we have every scrap of evidence farmed out as it is."

Beck dragged a chair out from the table and positioned it so he could still scan the photographs. He sat, then glanced at Mitch. "Two unidentified bodies does not a serial killer make."

"You're forgetting these," Mitch said, shoving two photographs across the conference table toward Beck. "Davenport and Conner."

"I'm not forgetting them." To prove his point, he snagged the two photos, then walked over to the wall, where he tacked them up by ramming in two pushpins.

"Raelynn filed reports with the FBI's Missing Persons Division today. Since we don't think that the girls have been taken across state lines, she was told there's not a lot they can do except offer support. Julia's office is working with the CSU to hopefully identify the two Jane Does." Beck dropped back into the chair and glared at the captain. "When I got in, I had a preliminary report on Ainsley's car. Nothing. Not so much as a fucking hair that didn't belong to Ainsley or her sister. We don't have dick on this case, Mitch. What do you expect me to do?"

Mitch gave him a hard, tired-eyed stare. "Call in BCI."

Beck leaned forward and braced his arms on his knees,

clasping his hands together. "You don't think I can bring this prick down?"

"It's not that," Mitch said. "Given enough time, I'm sure we'd nail him. But we don't have time, Beck. Time means more girls could go missing. More mutilated bodies could show up."

Bodies that more than likely wouldn't be those of the girls already missing. How many more would show up before the UNSUB finally got around to dumping Davenport and Conner's bodies?

"We need a profile," Mitch continued. "We're pissing in the dark here, and not even coming close to figuring out what kind of UNSUB we should be looking for."

Beck dropped his head into his hands. "Maybe you're right," he reluctantly admitted. Maybe he'd lost his edge. Maybe he'd been lying to himself and he no longer had the guts to do the job. Wasn't that the truth of why he'd left the Homicide Division and come running back to Ohio with his tail between his legs? Because he was sick and tired of being surrounded by death. Tired of being reminded that no matter how good a cop he once might have been, in the end, it was never good enough.

"You know I'm right," Mitch said, softening his tone. "Call BCI, Beck. They'll send someone out to assist in the case, someone who's worked cases like this before. We'll get a profile on the UNSUB and maybe, if we're damn lucky, we'll nail his ass to the wall before he strikes again."

Beck straightened. Leaning back, he braced his hands behind his head and stared at the photographs of Davenport and Conner. He frowned and slid his gaze to the crime scene photos of the two Janes.

"He prefers blondes," Beck said suddenly.

Mitch frowned. "That doesn't explain Megan Conner. She's a brunette."

"What if Megan saw him dump our second Jane Doe last night? Megan Conner knows our UNSUB."

"The brown sandal," Mitch said slowly as he nodded in agreement.

"Did her sorority sisters confirm it was hers?"

"Not one-hundred percent, but enough of a confirmation to believe it did belong to her."

"He dumped the body last night." Beck shot out of the chair, feeling a sudden burst of energy. "Megan was taking her walk to cool off after her fight with Chesterfield. She runs into the UNSUB as he's coming out of that field, after he's dumped the body."

"She lost a sandal," Mitch said. "Could mean there was a struggle."

"Nothing at the scene indicated a struggle." Beck stood and started sifting through the photographs on the table, searching for the ones of the area where the brown sandal was found. "There weren't any other recent footprints."

"No," Mitch said. "But maybe her sandal fell off when he knocked her out. He could've dragged her into the vehicle without ever getting out."

"He'd have to be relatively strong," Beck said. "Conner's slender, but tall. How much you think she weighed? Around one-twenty? One-thirty?"

"Maybe."

Beck located the photos with the sandal and spread them out on the table. The dirt road was hard, packed earth. There were some tire tracks in the area, all of which had been photographed and casted by the crime scene technicians. "He'd need a large vehicle to transport the bodies."

"Right," Mitch agreed. "Since he keeps them frozen, it's not like he can stuff them into the trunk of a car."

"Then we're looking for a large-profile vehicle. An SUV. Maybe a van."

"Could be a station wagon," Mitch added.

"Call the techs"—Beck glanced at his watch—"first thing in the morning. See if you can charm them into putting a rush on those tire tracks."

"If he's getting sloppy, we might just catch a break," Mitch said.

"Let's hope so," Beck said, because God knew, they sure as hell needed one.

CHAPTER 16

AINSLEY CLOSED HER laptop, then pushed away from the old rolltop desk and stretched her arms over her head. She'd been hunched over her computer for most of the evening and her neck and shoulders were feeling it.

After she'd finished her article reporting on the search and the resulting discovery of yet another body, she'd taken the time to update her résumé, then pulled together a sampling of her better archived articles. The list of the larger Ohio newspapers, ones not yet owned by Tricor, hadn't taken her long to assemble, and only served to remind her that her employment options were severely limited. Worse case scenario, she could always find a job as a secretary to pay the bills until something better came along. Regardless, Mona would nonetheless applaud her efforts, but she was simply being cautious. With Tricor stepping in on Monday, she wanted to be ready just in case Mona's predictions rang true.

Despite the lack of sleep the previous night, she felt keyed up and antsy. Perhaps a shot of something stronger in the tea she'd been sipping all evening would relax her enough to fall asleep. Preferably a deep, dreamless sleep.

She got up from the desk, left the living room, and headed into the kitchen. The sound of the television, turned low, drifted in from the family room. A peek through the open

French doors revealed Cassidy sprawled on the sofa engrossed in a sci-fi flick, while Paris sat curled up in the recliner with an open book balanced on her lap and a notebook situated on the arm as she made notes.

Ainsley set the kettle back on the stove, turned up the heat, then went in search of that little something to add to her tea. She was supposed to have met Beck at his place later tonight, but under the circumstances, she didn't think that was such a good idea. She didn't feel comfortable leaving the girls alone, not after she'd made such a big deal about their coming to stay with her. Since making the mistake of following Beck and the coroner out to the dump site, she just might be the one waking up at two in the morning, screaming from a nightmare.

Having a big, strong man to cuddle with afterward held mountains of appeal, however she'd still opted to stay home and had sent him a text message earlier to that effect. She hadn't heard back from him, but she imagined he was swamped with work at the moment.

A conversation with Mitch had revealed they still had no suspects in the case. Mitch hadn't stated specifically, but she suspected they had no leads, either. The coroner's office had confirmed there was still no ID on the dead girl found at the clearing earlier in the week. There were more questions than answers, and after the events of the past few days, she was beginning to believe there would be no end in sight. How many more girls would turn up missing? How many more ravaged bodies would they find?

On a high shelf in the pantry, she unearthed a couple of dusty booze bottles left over from who knew when. Considering the thin layer of dust, she imagined they were about two years old. She and Raelynn had gotten trashed doing watermelon shooters after Raelynn's divorce was final. Remembering the hangover from hell, she bypassed the vodka and opted for the half-pint bottle of Southern Comfort. She stepped out of the pantry and turned back to the stove, then let out a squeal of fright.

Paris winced. "I didn't mean to scare you."

Ainsley set the bottle on the counter with a thump. "You just took ten years off my life," she said with a nervous laugh.

Paris's smile was hesitant. "I'm sorry."

The tea kettle started whistling. Ainsley turned off the stove. "Do you want some tea?"

"Thanks, no." Paris leaned forward, bracing her forearms on the counter. "Um, thanks again for letting me stay here. It's a little nuts over at the U right now. A lot of kids were going home tonight."

"I'm hardly surprised." Ainsley wiped the dust off the bottle. "And you're welcome. Did you call your folks to let them know you'll be here for a few days?"

She hoped it was only a few days. Not that she didn't like having the girls around, but rather, she hoped it wouldn't take but a few more days until the person responsible for bringing terror into their quiet little town was stopped. Preferably with a terminal case of lead poisoning. Not that she didn't trust the justice system, but well, after what she'd seen recently, she couldn't help feeling a bit bloodthirsty.

She didn't need to close her eyes to see the ravaged body of the girl found today. It'd be weeks before she managed to get those horrific images out of her mind, if ever. She had no idea who the girl had been, and her last call to the coroner's office hadn't produced a name, either, but it hadn't been Mattie Davenport or Megan Conner, for which she'd been thankful.

"I don't have anyone to call," Paris said quietly. Ainsley looked at her and Paris shrugged. "I was a foster kid."

That news surprised Ainsley, but then it certainly explained Paris's higher level of maturity. Paris and Cassidy might be the same age, but in comparison, Paris was an old soul.

Ainsley poured the steaming water into her cup, then added a fresh tea bag to steep. "That couldn't have been easy."

Paris shrugged again. "It wasn't too bad. I got lucky compared to some kids I know." She traced her finger over the scalloped edge of the bowl filled with fruit on the counter. "Cass said you took care of her after your mom and dad passed."

Ainsley nodded. "You do what you have to do," she said. "I couldn't have lived with myself otherwise."

"You mean if you put her in the system." There was no resentment in her tone, only the acceptance of facts. "Cass was lucky. I don't think she realizes it though."

Ainsley chuckled at that. "Yeah, well," she said, "what are you gonna do?"

"Um, I wanted to ask you something."

Ainsley figured as much from the way Paris kept hanging around. "Shoot."

"Do you know if the newspaper office is hiring?" she asked. "I'm really good with computers. I took typing in high school, too."

Ainsley pulled the tea bag from her cup, then added about a capful of Southern Comfort. The tangy scent of lemon wafted in the air. "Are you interested in becoming a reporter?"

"Not exactly," Paris said. "I'm hoping to get my BS in social work."

Ainsley took her tea and walked to the table. "I thought you had a job."

"I do," Paris said, following. "I was kinda hoping for something else though."

"Where are you working now?"

Paris wrinkled her nose. "The associate dean's office. His secretary, Deborah, is really nice, but he's kind of a perv."

Ainsley hated to be the one to tell her, but there were a lot of men over thirty who would fall under that particular classification, especially when they were constantly surrounded by young, healthy females. "Well, I know as of today we're not hiring, but that could change next week. The newspaper has just been sold and if my boss is to believed, we'll be a lot busier. How about I let you know?"

Paris smiled. "Okay."

She really should do that more often, Ainsley thought. Her entire face lit up and her pretty blue eyes sparkled when she smiled.

"Don't get your hopes up," she warned, thinking of the résumé she'd just finished updating. "None of us really knows what's going to happen at the paper right now."

"Don't worry," Paris said brightly. "I won't."

Right. Of course, she wouldn't.

"Tell me, how do you know Gavin Chesterfield?" Ainsley asked her.

"I met him yesterday and he asked me out for coffee." Paris frowned suddenly. "I didn't know he had a girlfriend. Well, I kinda figured it was possible. Guys like that usually have a couple of them."

"Guys like what?"

"Rich. Good-looking." Paris shrugged, then gave her a knowing look well beyond her eighteen years. "Charm oozing from their pores."

Ainsley laughed. "I know that kind. We call them jerks."

"Yeah, but he didn't seem like a jerk," Paris said. "I really thought he was a nice guy."

"Aw, sweetie, you're going to meet a lot more jerks in your lifetime. It's called dating."

"How can you tell the difference?" Paris asked. "I mean how do you know when you find a really nice guy?"

"Good question." Ainsley sipped her tea and thought about

that for a minute before she finally looked over at Paris. "I'm not the best person in the world to answer that question. I don't have much of a track record."

Paris looked stunned. "No way. You're like, totally gorgeous. And smart." She shook her head. "No way," she said again.

"Sad as it might be, it's true." Pathetic, even.

Ainsley heard the scuff of her sister's slippers on the tiled floor. "That's because she's a homebody," Cass said from behind her. "She never dates."

"I've dated," Ainsley said, sounding way too defensive. Not much, but she did date. She just had responsibilities, is all.

Cassidy set a package of chocolate chip cookies on the table, then went over to the fridge, returning with a gallon of milk and two glasses from the cabinet, setting one in front of Paris. "Oh yeah?" She pulled out a chair and sat. "When was the last time you had a date?"

Ainsley glared at her sister. "Last night," she said without hesitation.

Cass slid her a sly look. "Your vibrator doesn't count, Lee."

Paris burst out laughing. Maybe if she kept laughing she wouldn't notice when Ainsley really did strangle her sister.

"So?" Cass ripped open the bag of cookies. "Who is he?"

"None of your business," Ainsley said snootily, then sipped her tea. The warmth of the whiskey slid down her throat and warmed her from the inside out.

"Is it that cop?" Paris asked, reaching into the bag for a couple of cookies. "The one at the search today?"

"How did you—?" Ainsley couldn't help herself. She blushed. Heat fired her cheeks, and she couldn't even blame the whiskey she'd added to her tea for her elevated temperature.

"What cop?" Cassidy asked.

"The tall one she kept looking at when we were talking

to her today," Paris supplied. "I think he was one of the ones in charge."

"The new guy?" Cass asked, clearly surprised. "You're going out with the chief of police, aren't you?"

"He's the acting chief. And never you mind," Ainsley told them.

"Not a chance. This is too good," Cassidy said with a giggle. "Really?"

Ainsley couldn't help herself. She actually squirmed under the girls' close scrutiny. "Someone tell me why I thought it'd be a good idea for you two to stay here for a few days."

"Come on, Lee. Give it up."

She let out a sigh. "There's nothing to give up," she told her sister. Mostly because she had no idea herself. And she refused to discuss her sex life with a pair of eighteen-year-old girls.

Paris poured herself a glass of milk. "Is he a nice guy?" she asked thoughtfully.

Was he? Beck was kind and thoughtful, if a bit surly on occasion. But from what she'd witnessed thus far, caring and compassionate. That he was an incredibly sensitive lover didn't hurt, either.

Finally, Ainsley smiled. "I think he is."

"Well." Paris grabbed another cookie from the bag and returned her smile, along with an understanding look. "Okay, then."

A knock at the front door caused Ainsley to frown. A quick check of the clock revealed it was just after nine. Probably Beck, she thought as she got up to answer the door, only to feel a big ol' stab of disappointment when she got there and found a grunged-out kid asking to see Paris.

"YOU ARE GOING to tell him to get lost, right?"

Paris shoved her arms through the hoodie and tugged it on before giving Cass a shrug. "We'll see," she answered.

She wasn't sure what she was going to say to Zach, but they definitely needed to talk. She didn't like the way he'd been treating her lately, and in all fairness, she had been a little bitchy herself. It was like they were feeding off the worst of each other, and that was a merry-go-round she didn't want to ride any longer.

Zach was a nice guy—some of the time. Lately, he'd been a real prick, and dammit, she deserved better than a some-of-the time nice guy. She might be young, but she knew what she wanted.

Cass suddenly threw her arms around her and gave her a quick hug.

Paris stiffened. "What was that for?" She wasn't used to people touching her. Displays of affection weren't handed out on a regular basis in her world.

Cass shrugged and grinned. "Emotional support."

"Uh . . . thanks," Paris said awkwardly, then slipped out the door and joined Zach.

She found him in one of the wicker chairs at the far end of the porch, leaning back with his feet propped up on the low matching table. When she closed the screen door, he looked over at her, but didn't smile or offer any sort of welcome, and that bugged her. If he'd come to bitch at her or call her caring what happened to another person stupid, she was so out of there.

For good.

With her back against the blue vinyl siding, she stood under the porch light and tucked her hands into the front pocket of her hoodie. "How did you know where to find me?"

"The RA," he said. "Your dorm is like a tomb."

Paris shrugged. If she said she understood why people were leaving, Zach would no doubt ridicule her for being compassionate, so she kept quiet.

"Are you going to sit down?"

She wanted to say no and stay right where she was, near

the safety of the door and a quick escape. Instead, she crossed the porch and dropped into the love seat facing him.

He drew in a deep breath. "It's good you're here," he said quickly.

What? Like he was suddenly worried about her? No, he was stalling. About what, she wanted to know. Had he come to dump her? A thought that should have made her feel sad, but surprisingly didn't.

"What do you want, Zach?"

"To make sure you're okay."

She laughed. "Oh, really?" Okay, now he was bullshitting her. Zach didn't give a rip about anyone but himself. She did get it, though. She was a foster kid, too, so she knew all about having to look out for number one. When you grew up in the system, there really weren't that many people standing in your corner, if any.

He shrugged. "Yeah. Look, I know I've been a dick lately."

"You think?"

His shoulders slumped. At least he had the decency to appear contrite. "So is this where you tell me to get lost?"

She leaned back and folded her arms over her chest. "I've been thinking about it."

He frowned and gave her one of his go-to-hell looks. "Yeah, well, don't think too hard. I wouldn't want you to hurt yourself."

"God, you are such an asshole." She stood and started for the door. If she didn't leave now, she'd say something she might even regret later. Like *fuck off, jerkwad*. "I don't know what I ever saw in you."

"A way out of Oakland."

She balled her hands into fists, because if she didn't, she might actually hit him for that crack. "Screw you, Zach."

"Paris, wait," he called as she reached the door. "Wait. I'm sorry."

He came off the chair and was across the porch to her side. He settled his hand on her shoulder and urged her to face him. "I'm sorry," he said again, sounding as if he really meant it.

She shrugged off his touch and glared at him. "Go to hell, Zach. I'm so tired of you treating me like shit."

"I said I was sorry," he said, but he didn't look sorry, he looked angry. With her. "What more do you want from me?"

"A little respect would be a nice start."

"Like the other guy you're seeing does? He has a girl-friend, you know."

So that's what this was all about? Gavin? He wasn't worried about *her*, he was ticked because some other guy had shown an interest in her. Forget that said guy had been hauled in for questioning because his girlfriend had gone missing after they'd had an argument. She wouldn't dream of going out with him again.

"I'm not *seeing* anyone," she told him. "I went for coffee. That's it."

"Were you gonna tell me?"

"Maybe if you'd bothered to show up this morning, I would have."

He looked away suddenly. "I overslept," he said, his tone somewhere between quiet and a hint of something else she'd never heard from him before—uncertainty.

"How convenient for you. But that doesn't give you the right to come over here and give me shit." She turned around and reached for the door again. "I gotta go. It's getting late."

He put his hand on the screen door, preventing her from opening it. She tugged, but it was useless.

"Knock it off, Zach."

"Did you volunteer today?" he asked.

Curious, she frowned. "I did. Why?"

"I heard they found something."

"Then you heard right."

"Another body?" he asked. "And a shoe that belongs to another girl that's missing?"

"I wasn't there when all that happened," she said. "I had to be at work, so all I've heard is the rumors." Rumors, and the reality of students who lived close to the U being moved out of the dorms by their nervous parents. She imagined more kids would be leaving in the next couple of days once word got out about the rising body count of Serenity Heights University students. "I thought you didn't care."

He shrugged, but didn't defend her accusation. This whole conversation was weird, especially when she considered his comments to her yesterday. "What's going on, Zach?"

"If I tell you something," he said, lowering his voice to an almost whisper, then looking around as if to make certain they were alone, "you have to promise not to say anything."

"Okay."

He grabbed her hand and led her back to the wicker love seat, where he sat down. He gave her hand a light tug until she joined him.

"What is it?" she asked. "You're making me nervous."

Still holding her hand, he said, "I might've seen the body they found today being dumped."

She wasn't sure what she'd expected him to say, but it sure as hell wasn't *that*. "Oh. My. God." She dragged her free hand through her hair. "How? When?"

"Last night," he said. "The town has been crawling with cops, so I took a walk."

To find a place to get high in hopes of lessening his chances of getting busted, no doubt. "What did you see?"

"A van pulled up on the dirt road maybe fifty yards from where I was. Some guy got out and dumped what I thought was trash. Now I'm not so sure it was garbage he was getting rid of."

"Did you see who it was?"

He gave her a get-real look. "Like I'd know."

True. They'd only been in town a week. The only people besides Zach that she knew were Cassidy and her sister. And Gavin, but she didn't really count him after what happened today, even if she had been right about his having a girlfriend.

"What color was the van?"

"Blue, I think. It was dark."

She blew out a stream of breath, not sure if he meant the night or the van. "Then what happened?"

"The guy got back in the van and drove off. I saw him stop and talk to somebody, then he was gone."

"Do you think it was Megan Conner?"

"Who the fuck is Megan Conner?"

"The other girl who's missing."

"I dunno," he said with a shrug. "Maybe. I don't know. I couldn't see. It was pretty dark by then."

"You have to go to the cops."

"No way."

"You have to."

"Forget it."

"Why not?"

"Because I ain't no rat."

"That's stupid."

"Not where I come from."

She understood. Really, she did. In their neighborhood, snitches often ended up dead. But this was different. This wasn't some gangbanger ripping off the corner liquor store, but an honest-to-God serial killer. "If you haven't noticed, we're not in Oakland any longer." They'd escaped, away from the gangs, away from the harshness of an unforgiving city.

Only to walk right into a nightmare.

"It doesn't matter," Zach said.

"Yes, it does. Someone's life is at risk. You have to go to the cops and tell them what you saw."

"Right. So they can bust me for smokin' pot?"

"This isn't about you. It's about you having information that could save someone's life." She had to find a way to get through to him. "I didn't see what they found today, but I heard people talking about it. Did you know this guy cuts off their fingers and rips their teeth right out of their head? I heard people speculating about him even doing it while they're still alive."

He said nothing, just looked at her with his jaw set in a stubborn expression.

"You could save Megan Conner from having to suffer," she continued, not caring to tone down the pleading note in her voice. Let him call her a baby or a pain in the ass bleeding heart. She didn't care. "That has to mean something to you."

He let go of her hand and stood. "I gotta go," he said, and hurried toward the steps.

"Are you going to the cops?" She stood. "I'll go with you."

"I gotta go," he repeated, then took off without another word on the subject.

Paris stayed on the porch, watching until Zach disappeared around the corner. She chewed on her thumbnail, trying to decide what to do. There wasn't a chance in hell she was keeping her word to Zach, that much she did know. She supposed she could tell Cass's sister about what Zach had told her. Didn't reporters protect their sources?

Zach would be pissed at her, might not ever forgive her, but she couldn't *not* go to the cops. She had to tell them what she knew, or rather, what Zach knew. Especially if it meant saving lives.

CHAPTER 17

"HER NAME IS Tara Iverson," Julia Reiki said. "She was a freshman at Kent State, Trumbull campus. She was reported missing almost five months ago."

"How'd you manage an ID?" Beck asked her. Forget that he'd gotten her call after ten PM, he was surprised she'd gotten an ID on the body so quickly.

The damage had been the same as their first Jane Doe, but according to Julia, the cause of death this time had been strangulation. She also suspected drugs had been used, but the murder weapon of choice was clearly a strong wire. At this point, she suspected a piano wire had been used, based on an imprint found on the vic's neck.

"She fit the description on a hot sheet of missing persons. The report was initially filed by the Trumbull County sheriff's office," Julia said. "We were able to ID her by her tramp stamp."

Tramp stamp, code for a tattoo on her lower back, something that had recently grown in popularity among young women.

"The parents left the morgue not twenty minutes ago," Julia continued. "They confirmed that it was their daughter."

Beck felt bad for the parents. He'd witnessed body identifications in the past, and even from an outsider's perspective, they were damn heartbreaking. He could only imagine the myriad emotions loved ones suffered having to endure a trip to the morgue.

"I'll give the Trumbull office a call, see what they know," he said. "Thanks, Julia. I appreciate the overtime you've put in on this."

"Just doing my job," she answered. "Still no word yet on your first Jane Doe. I did talk to the lab and they should have the tox report by noon tomorrow. I'll fax it over as soon as it's available."

"Much appreciated," he said just as the intercom line buzzed.

Now what?

"I'll be in touch," he said, and disconnected the call. He punched the blinking light. "Raines here."

"Chief?" It was Loretta, one of the night dispatchers. "There's a Paris Nolan here to see you."

"Do you know what she wants?"

"I don't know, but she's not carting any casseroles that I can see," Loretta said with a chuckle. "She's from the U and says it's important."

"Just send her back to my office," Beck said, and hung up the phone. At this rate, it'd be after midnight before he got out of here. As much as he was looking forward to seeing Ainsley again, he was almost glad when he'd received her text message advising him that she wouldn't be able to make it tonight. He needed rest, and that would be the last thing he'd have gotten if he'd climbed between the sheets with her.

The timing sucked. Starting something with her while he was elbow deep in a multiple murder investigation wasn't the smartest thing he'd ever done, but then, he hadn't been looking, either. Ainsley just—happened. Not that he was complaining. He was just so damn tired he couldn't think straight.

"Hi," a young girl, probably no more than seventeen or eighteen, said from the doorway in a hesitant voice. "Are you Chief Raines?"

Beck stood and circled the desk. "I'm Deputy Chief Raines," he said. "Come in and have a seat. And you are?"

"Paris Nolan," she said as she sat in the chair opposite his desk. She fidgeted with the strings on her hoodie and looked nervously around his office. "Um . . . I go to the U."

He sat on the edge of his desk and tried to appear welcoming. "What can I do for you, Paris?"

"Well . . ." She folded her hands, then unfolded them and tucked them in the front pouch of her bright pink SHU sweatshirt.

He struggled to hold on to his patience. "It's okay," he said, aiming for a calm he was nowhere near feeling, all under the guise of trying to set her at ease. The kid was obviously intimidated by her surroundings, but she'd come here for a reason and he didn't want to spook her because he was in a crappy mood.

"I didn't see it myself," she said in a rush. "Someone else did."

He leaned forward slightly. "See what, Paris?"

"A van. Last night. My friend saw a guy in a blue van out in the field near where that girl was found today."

She definitely had his attention now. "Who are we talking about?"

"I promised I wouldn't say anything."

He didn't want to go all Dragnet on her, but his patience was slipping fast. "Who did you promise?" he pressed, wanting to be certain there really was a "friend" or if she'd been the one to actually witness the blue van.

"My boyfriend." She frowned suddenly. "Ex-boyfriend. I think."

"Where's your ex-boyfriend now?"

She shrugged. "Back at his dorm, I guess."

He'd get the name out of her eventually. Right now he wanted to hear about this blue van. He stood and walked back behind his desk and sat. "Do you know what he was doing out there?"

She nodded. "I'd rather not say."

Beck could easily imagine. No doubt partaking in a bit of illegal activity. He wasn't concerned with the drug habits of an ex, possibly pot-smoking, boyfriend, but with the information he might or might not have that could help their investigation. "What exactly did he tell you he saw?"

Beck listened and jotted notes as Paris told him what she knew, which really wasn't much, but was still a hell of a lot more than they knew before this scared little blond freshman had shown up out of the blue. "Did he say what kind of van it was?"

Paris shook her head. "No. Only that it was blue."

"Was it light blue? Dark blue?"

"I'm not sure. He said it was dark, but I don't know if he was talking about it being dark outside, or if the van was dark blue."

"Okay. Good enough." He leaned back and regarded Paris thoughtfully. She was still a bit skittish, but nowhere near as hesitant as when she'd first walked into his office ten minutes ago. "So you want to tell me why you're here and not your ex-boyfriend?"

She let out a quick little sigh. "It's stupid," she said. "But where we come from, snitching can get you in worse trouble than going to the cops."

He knew all about the no snitches rule, having run into that particular brick wall too many times to count back in LA. "Where are you from?"

"Oakland, California."

That explained it. The area was rife with gang activity,

and the no snitch policy often meant the difference between life and death on the streets. "I'm from LA," he said. "Oakland's not an easy place, either, is it?"

"It's okay," she said with a shrug. "It's a lot nicer here, though."

It'd be even nicer when he nailed the bastard in the blue van. That explained how the UNSUB was transporting the bodies, a lead that could bring an end to the terror in their little town if he played his hand right. But they needed to talk to the boyfriend to see if the information was reliable and if the guy was even credible.

"I should talk to your ex," he said. "He might have seen something that could help us. Something besides the blue van."

"I know. I tried to get him to come see you, but he wouldn't."

Beck figured as much. "Will you tell me his name?"

She bit her bottom lip.

"Paris, it's important."

"I know," she said again. "But I promised."

He had the urge to shove a few autopsy photos at her to see if that changed her mind. "I made a promise, too. I promised to protect the people of this town, and that includes the students of the U."

She slumped a little in the chair. "So you're saying your promise is more important than mine?"

Exactly.

"Not exactly," he said, "but if you break your promise, it could save someone's life."

"And if you break yours, more girls could end up dead." Her blue eyes filled with distress. "Zach Toomey," she finally said. "And now he's really gonna be my ex-boyfriend."

He couldn't help her there, but if the guy didn't have the decency to come forward given the events of the past week, then in his opinion, good riddance. "Thank you, Paris. Any idea where I can find Zach now?"

"Probably in his room," she said. "He's in Carlson Tower."

He stood and snagged his keys. "How did you get here?"

"I walked."

"You walked?" With a nut job on the loose? Now he really was tempted to show her those autopsy photos. "Do I need to lecture you on personal safety?"

"No," she said, and offered him the first sign of a smile since coming to see him. "Besides, I wasn't at the U. And it was only a couple of blocks."

"I have to take care of something first, and then I'll take you home."

"Okay," she said. "Thanks."

He left his office and headed into the dispatch room, where he asked Loretta to run a DMV check of every blue van registered within the state, then to break it down by Cuyahoga County and Serenity Heights residents.

"Do you want an APB?"

"Not until we have more details," he said. "And keep it quiet. I don't want the press getting wind of this." Raelynn had been fielding phone calls half the day from the bigger news outlets around the state. Word had gotten out, and now all eyes were on Serenity Heights. He'd even heard a rumor that a local television news reporter had dubbed the UNSUB the Freshmen Strangler. Just what he didn't want, a media circus. If they didn't get this bastard and quick, their quiet little town would be inundated with news vans and reporters before much longer.

"Who's the most senior officer on duty tonight?"

"Jim Ellis," Loretta said. "Why?"

"Get him on the radio," he said, then gave Loretta the information about Zach Toomey so Ellis could question the kid. "If the kid's as obstinate as I think he might be, have Ellis bring him in and we'll cool his heels for a while."

"You got it, Chief," Loretta said, then turned back to the computer screen in front of her.

"I'll be out until the next shift change," he said, "but I'll have my cell on if you need me."

As he escorted Paris to his Durango, he felt hopeful for the first time since the case began. At least they finally had a lead. Whether it developed into anything concrete remained to be seen, but they had something to go on for a change.

"Where to?" he asked once they were buckled in.

"I'm staying with my roommate at her sister's place," she said, and shot him a sly glance. "You know where Ainsley Brennan lives, right?"

So she was the reason he wasn't getting laid tonight. He almost laughed at that, except he didn't like the idea of Ainsley and two teenage girls alone in a house that the UNSUB had targeted.

"Yeah, I know where it is," he said, wondering about the wisdom of insisting all three of them stay at his place for the time being. It wasn't like he didn't have the room.

God, he needed some sleep. He definitely wasn't thinking clearly.

Moments later he pulled into Ainsley's driveway and parked behind her rental car. "I need you to do me a favor," he said.

"Okay."

"Let's keep this information about the blue van to ourselves for the time being." If word got out, then their chances of finding the guy could easily go up in smoke. When the time was right, he'd release the information to the public, but for now, it was their only ace in the hole. "I don't want people speculating." Or storming blue vans and harming innocent citizens.

She shrugged her slender shoulders. "Sure thing," she said, then reached for the door handle. "Are you coming in? I bet Ainsley would like to see you."

Apparently his relationship with Ainsley was no longer secret. Not that he cared one way or the other what anyone thought. His personal life was his business. "For a minute," he said, then got out and followed Paris up the steps to the front door.

HE REMAINED ON a hard plastic chair, continuing to watch her motionless body, deep in a drug-induced sleep. For the past three hours he had sat quietly, just watching her. She was quite beautiful, and he appreciated her natural beauty in a way that he hadn't done with the others. Was it because she was so different, he wondered?

He shouldn't have taken her. She was all wrong. She was too tall, too dark. But he'd had no choice. She'd seen him. If he'd let her go, she'd have been able to identify him, would've told them that she'd seen him in the vicinity. No, he'd had no choice.

So what did he do with her now?

You kill her.

Yes, but she was all wrong. She wasn't even a blonde.

So make her right.

He could. Not much he could do about her height, but changing her hair color was a possibility. Colored contacts would fix her eye color, too. Isn't that what they'd done for the bitch who'd made his life a living hell? The one who'd taken everything that should have been his? They'd transformed her, made her into what they wanted.

And in the end, he'd made certain she'd paid the price for his suffering.

He stood and walked over to the bed where she lay. Her skin wasn't right, either. She wasn't pale, didn't have that ethereal look about her. He could bleach her hair, but not her skin.

You can't let her go.

"I know," he said quietly. She'd seen him, knew who he was. When she'd approached the van window, she'd addressed him by name. There would be no sparing her.

He should make it quick. Overdose her. That would be simple enough. No mess, no fuss. But then what would he do with her? He couldn't put her with his treasures. She was all wrong. That's why he kept her here, in this tiny room instead of moving her to where he performed his transformations. Where he brought out the truth of who and what they really were.

He turned and walked out of the room, switching off the light and locking the door behind him. He'd have to make a decision about her soon enough, but not tonight.

He climbed the stairs, then closed up the entrance. He thought about stopping for a visit with his treasures, but he was tired tonight. The day had been a long one, filled with excitement, and it had taken its toll on him. Instead, he locked up and walked to the house, where he would enjoy a brandy and perhaps plan his next presentation to the good people of Serenity Heights.

"WHY THE HELL not?"

Ainsley didn't much appreciate Beck's bullish attitude, or the harsh glare he was drilling her with, but he was being ridiculous, so she bullied and glared right back. She and the girls were perfectly safe right where they were, and had said as much. Twice.

"Because it's a dumb idea, that's why."

"What if the UNSUB comes back tonight? There could be another delivery. He's getting bolder every time. Risking your own neck is one thing, but now you've got two girls here with you."

The two girls in question were currently seated at the

kitchen table, quiet and no doubt listening to every word of her exchange with Beck. "I can take care of us."

"Right. With your unloaded gun that you have no idea how to shoot."

She planted her hands on her hips. "I've been taking care of my sisters since I was nineteen without any help from you. I think I can take care of us now."

He blew out a frustrated stream of breath, then scrubbed his hand down his face. "Dammit, woman. Are you always this stubborn?"

"Welcome to my world," Cass yelled from the kitchen.

Ainsley threw up her hands. "I give up."

"Good. Now go get packed."

"Beck, there are three of us. You really have no clue what you're asking."

"I'm not afraid of a little estrogen."

"It'd be an overload."

"Why doesn't he just stay here?" Cass asked. "We don't mind, do we, Paris?"

Ainsley looked past Beck to where Cassidy and Paris stood, in the doorway of the living room. She opened her mouth to protest, but her vocal cords refused to cooperate. She'd never had a man stay the night before, especially with her sisters in the house. Her first priority had always been to protect them.

Which is exactly what Beck was trying to do now, she suddenly realized. Protect her, and Cassidy and Paris, from some unknown crazy that might or might not show up to deliver another recording of proof of his viciousness. When she thought of the tortured screams and useless pleading she'd heard on the first recording, she caved.

"Cass is right," she relented. "It'd be easier if you just stayed here tonight." She didn't even add that she still thought it was completely unnecessary.

"Paris can bunk with me," Cass offered, only to receive an elbow to the ribs from Paris.

"What?"

"Excuse us," Paris said, and gently pushed Cass back through the foyer into the kitchen.

Ainsley smiled as she heard their hushed whispers followed by girlish giggles.

The first sighting of a smile teased his mouth, transforming the hard angles of his face, reminding her of how deadly gorgeous he was, of how attracted she was to him. "Is she really that naive?" he asked.

"No, just dense sometimes," Ainsley said, loud enough for Cass to hear. She looked up at Beck, at how the lines bracketing his eyes had deepened since she'd last seen him this afternoon. "You look exhausted." Which meant they probably wouldn't be having sex. Too bad. "Have you even eaten?"

He walked over to the sofa and sat. "I had something at the station earlier," he said, leaning back to rest his head against the cushion.

Cassidy poked her head through the doorway. "We're going to bed," she said with a wide grin on her face.

Ainsley rolled her eyes. "She's subtle, too, don't you think?"

Eyes closed, Beck chuckled.

"Come on, Cass," Paris called out, already halfway up the stairs. "Good night."

Ainsley heard the girls upstairs moving around as they readied for bed. She walked to the sofa and curled up beside Beck. "So are you going to tell me what was so important that Paris walked over to the police station tonight to see you without telling anyone where she was going?" A subject she'd planned to broach with Paris herself, until Beck had started grilling her about taking the girls and staying at his place.

"Later," he said, then hauled her close and kissed her senseless.

She was as close to exhaustion as he was, but that didn't stop her body from immediately responding to his touch. Later, she decided, was just fine by her, just so long as he kept kissing her.

CHAPTER 18

"COME ON," Ainsley said in a quiet voice. "We'll be more comfortable upstairs."

Beck was fine right where he was, but took the hand she held out to him anyway, rising when she gave him a tug. He turned off the lamp, then followed her from the living room, guided by the moonlight spilling in through the windows. Never in a million years would he have dreamed pink plaid pajama bottoms could be classified as sexy, until he enjoyed the way the soft fabric hugged Ainsley's ass as she climbed the stairs ahead of him.

He succumbed to the urge to slide his hands over her curvy bottom and gave her rump a squeeze. She stopped on the step ahead of him and looked at him over her shoulder. Heat smoldered in her eyes and he forgot all about the need for sleep.

Following her into her bedroom at the top of the stairs, he closed the door and pulled her to him. She wrapped her arms around his neck and pressed her sweet body to his, reaching up for a kiss. He happily obliged.

He'd never had trouble separating work from his personal life, and tonight with Ainsley was no different. The ugliness of the crappy day he'd had slipped away as he lost himself in her scent, in her touch, in the feel of her arms around him, holding him tightly.

Wanting more, he backed her up, moving them closer to the bed until the mattress abruptly stopped them, and they fell together onto the plush floral comforter. Anxious to have her naked and wanting beneath him, he yanked off his shirt. She quickly stripped off those sexy plaid pj bottoms. Her top was next, and went flying somewhere over his shoulder. As he toed off his shoes, her hands were on his belt, then his fly and finally, she was pushing the heavy denim past his hips. He kicked his jeans away, along with his socks, then rejoined her on the bed.

"I can't think straight when I'm with you," she whispered. She guided his mouth back to hers for another deep, wet kiss so erotic she had his dick throbbing painfully.

"You don't need to think," he said when they came up for air. He nibbled her ear lobe, then nuzzled her neck until she sighed. "Just feel and enjoy everything I plan to do to you."

His hand slid down her body, between her thighs to her soft, wet core. She widened her legs for him and he pushed into her with deep, long strokes. She moaned against his mouth, her hips rolling against his hand, pulling his fingers more deeply inside her. She swept her tongue over his, tasting him while her hands smoothed over his shoulders and around to his chest, where she played with his nipples using the tips of her fingers.

With his thumb, he teased her clit, applying the slightest amount of pressure. Her body instantly tensed, and he pushed her harder, building the pressure, then backing off to withhold her release. She whimpered. She moaned. She swore, then grabbed his hand and held him still as she took control and rode his fingers to completion until she lay spent and panting for breath in his arms.

He loved her sounds. He loved the way she moved against him. Thought she was sexy as hell when she was being stubborn and obstinate. There was an innocence about her that frustrated him as much as he adored that very quirk in her personality. She had a way of looking at him that made him feel as if he couldn't draw his next breath.

Ainsley was trouble. He'd known it from the minute she'd blazed her way onto his crime scene. There wasn't much about her he didn't adore, nor did he think he'd ever get enough of her. He wanted to protect her, to shield her from the harsh realities of a world gone crazy. Wanted to keep her close so nothing ever happened to her, but life had already taught him some hard lessons in that regard, and he understood no man held that kind of power. You loved, you lost. People died and not even medical science could stop the inevitable. He could easily stay buried in the past, but if he did, he'd miss out on whatever fate had yet to offer.

And that included Ainsley, and whatever the future might hold for them.

God help him, as crazy as it sounded, he was falling in love with her.

The realization startled him, but he knew there wasn't a damn thing he could do to stop the feeling. Yet, he kept the words to himself. For now, they were too new, too raw yet for him to share with her, so instead of telling her what was in his heart, he moved over her and slid his body inside hers.

Her eyes widened in surprise, and then she smiled up at him with a wicked, determined gleam in her big blue eyes. She wrapped her legs around his waist and pulled him deeper. Together they moved in perfect rhythm, each giving and taking pleasure from the other.

The tension built, the pressure pushing him closer to the edge. He ramped up the tempo of their lovemaking until her body clenched his as another orgasm tore through her. Unable to hold back another minute, he followed her over the edge into the sweet and blissful oblivion of his own release.

Oh yeah, he thought as his world slowly righted itself. He was a goner, all right. And he didn't even mind.

SOMETHING WOKE BECK. A sound he couldn't immediately identify from somewhere in the house. He struggled to shake off the vestiges of the deep slumber and find his bearings.

Immediately, he was conscious of Ainsley's nude body tucked close to his, of her quiet breathing as she slept on her side with her curvy bottom pressed snugly against his groin. Instantly he responded, but he ignored the demands of his body and lay still, listening for whatever had awoken him.

Then he heard it, the sound of water running through the pipes in the old house, followed by the closing of a door somewhere down the hall a few moments later. His heart rate slowed and he relaxed, realizing it was either Ainsley's sister or her friend.

A quick glance at the bedside clock indicated he should be getting up soon to head back to the station. Only he wasn't in any hurry to leave the warmth of the bed, or Ainsley for that matter.

"Hmmm, you're awake," she murmured sleepily.

She wiggled her bottom against him. He settled his hand on her hip to still her movements before she drove him completely insane. "It's early," he said. "Go back to sleep."

She ignored him and turned to face him instead. "Do you have to be at work soon?"

"In about an hour." He pulled her close to plant a quick, hard kiss on her lips. "Why? What did you have in mind?"

She sighed dreamily, then laid her head on his chest. "Do you think we'll ever be able to just spend a lazy morning in bed together?"

He certainly hoped so. If he had his way, there'd be many lazy mornings together in their future. "With any luck," he told her, "soon."

She lifted her head and looked at him again. In the pre-dawn light spilling into the bedroom, he could see the frown tugging her brow. "Don't talk to me about luck," she said. "Mine just might be running out."

"What do you mean?"

"Tricor Publishing just bought the *Sentinel*," she said. "I spent last night updating my résumé."

He had no idea what Tricor Publishing was, or why she felt the need to polish her résumé, but it sure as hell didn't sound promising. "I don't get it."

"Tricor has a habit of buying up small town newspapers, then either shutting them down or bringing in their own people to run the operation. Either way, I could be out of a job before much longer."

"Maybe you should look at it as a growth opportunity."

That earned him a sour look. "You sound like my boss. Or my former boss. Almost."

"Try not to worry until you know there's something to worry about." Advice he needed to remember for himself on occasion. "Why get all worked up about something that might not even happen?"

She pulled back and sat up, holding the sheet to cover herself. "Because I have to worry," she said, reaching behind her to turn on the beside lamp. "I have a mortgage and a sister to help through college. It's not like I can just pick up and move to wherever the big newspapers might be."

That wasn't something he wanted to see happen. He had no desire to embark upon a long distance relationship, no matter how much he cared for Ainsley. Nor did he like the idea of relocating again if she ended up having to move to wherever her career might take her. Besides, Serenity Heights was growing on him. Current circumstances aside, he liked the quiet simplicity of life out of the fast lane.

"Speaking of big newspapers," he said, "Raelynn was fielding calls from several papers yesterday, one as far as Cincinnati. I didn't see the broadcast, but I heard the local television news picked up on the story, too."

"Great," she muttered. "Just what I don't need right now. Competition."

"I'm not happy about it, either." He settled his hand on her leg peeking out from under the floral sheet, and rubbed the smooth skin of her calf. "The last thing I want to have to deal with now is a media circus."

"Yes, I know. We're all bottom-feeders unfit for polite society," she said with a teasing glint in her eyes. She dragged her hand through her hair, pushing the strands from her face. "You never did tell me why you hate the press so much."

He wasn't sure he wanted to tell her now. Those were memories better left in the past, but he could see from her curious expression, she probably wouldn't let the subject alone until he caved.

He let out a sigh. "Don't take this the wrong way," he said cautiously, "but in my experience, reporters aren't to be trusted."

"Yeah, I get that you don't like my kind all that much, but why? Specifically?"

Nope. No way in hell was she letting it go. "Like I said. They're not to be trusted."

She leveled him with those blue eyes. "Beck."

He sat up and adjusted the pillow behind his back. "I shared information with a reporter that was supposed to be off the record," he told her as he leaned back against the headboard. "He ran with it anyway, and we lost our only eyewitness in a murder investigation."

"I don't understand. Why would your witness refuse to testify? Was he afraid?"

"He didn't *refuse* to testify," he clarified for her. "He disappeared. To this day I have no idea if the guy went into hiding, or if he's buried somewhere in the high desert of California."

She winced. "There is such a thing as journalistic integrity, you know."

"Apparently it's not practiced much."

"I admit that is pretty low, especially if your conversation was off the record, but I don't think it's fair to disparage all of the media because of one unethical reporter."

Neither did he. But the wounds caused by that one unethical reporter, as she put it, ran deeper than she realized.

"So I take it you didn't get the conviction you wanted."

"No. We never did. We knew who the shooter was, but without our eyewitness and only circumstantial evidence, there was no way to get a conviction. The DA refused to budge without more."

"That had to bite."

"Yeah, well, it was a shitty time." Memories swamped him, but the pain he usually experienced when he thought about that fateful day didn't feel anywhere near as suffocating as it once had. The guilt was still there, but for the first time in months was nowhere near as overwhelming. He no longer felt strangled by it.

He let out a long slow breath. "Linda had been diagnosed with stage-four ovarian cancer. By the time we found out, it was too late. The cancer had metastasized and spread like wildfire through her. There wasn't anything anyone could do for her, except try to make her as comfortable as possible. She'd been in hospice care, and my partner covered for me as much as he could so I was able to spend as much time with Linda as possible. Toward the end, I honestly don't think she even knew I was there half the time.

"So, my wife was dying and the brass was all over our asses to bring in our prime suspect and make it stick. If I'd been focused on the job, I probably never would've said a word to the press. But I did and the bastard quoted me; then our witness disappears into thin air. The real icing on the cake came while my partner and I were getting our asses royalty chewed up one side and down the other for fucking up. The people at the hospice couldn't get in touch with me when Linda took a turn for the worse. By the time they finally did, it was too late."

"Oh, Beck. I'm so sorry. I know how difficult it is to lose someone you love."

He reached for her hand and urged her close. She snuggled up to him, her head resting against his chest. "It was a long time ago," he said.

"Not that long," she said, drawing her fingers along his chest. "Obviously it still bothers you. Loss hurts."

He let out a sigh. "What I regret is that it went down the way it did. Linda was a good woman. She deserved better than to die alone in a strange place."

"My mother hung on for two months after the accident," she said quietly. "But I was there when she left us. It didn't lessen the guilt in the decision I was forced to make, to let her go. That took a lot of time to get over, but being there really helped. Her passing was truly very peaceful. I think being with her then gave us all the ability to heal."

He thanked God he hadn't been forced to make that kind of decision regarding Linda. Although he'd have given anything to spare her the pain that had ravaged her small body. In the end, she'd been a shell of the young, vibrant woman he'd loved.

Still, he couldn't help appreciate that Ainsley understood. Or did she? No woman wanted to hear about the other women in a man's life. Especially one he'd loved with all his heart.

He tucked his hand beneath her chin until he could see her eyes clearly. Compassion and understanding lit the depths of her gaze, going a long way in setting aside his concerns. "I did love my wife, Ainsley. A part of me probably always will. We were married for ten years, and had a good marriage. I won't lie to you. It hurt like hell, and I went a little crazy when she died. A lot of it, I suspect, was guilt that I wasn't there for her at the end."

"It's okay, Beck. You don't have to explain."

"I just want you to understand that that's all in the past. But it doesn't mean I'm not capable of loving someone that deeply again."

She pulled back slightly and regarded him carefully. Cautiously, almost. "What are you saying?"

Hell, he didn't even know anymore. He wasn't even sure why he was telling her all this. "That I don't want you to confuse the past with what we have."

"And what do we have?"

Oh hell, he'd walked right into that one, didn't he? There was no getting out of it now. Except perhaps to tell her the truth. "I care about you, Ainsley," he said. "A great deal."

Okay, so maybe not the whole truth and nothing but the truth, but it was as close as he was willing to admit to her. For now, it had to be enough.

She nodded and a slow smile spread across her pretty face. "Me, too," she said. "A lot."

The muffled ringing of a cell phone saved them both from an awkward moment. "I think it's mine," he said, then reached over the side of the bed and dragged his jeans close, plucking the phone from the pocket. "Raines here."

Ainsley slipped from the bed and threw on a thin blue cotton robe before quietly leaving the bedroom. He glanced at the bedside clock. It wasn't quite six o'clock.

"Chief, it's Mitch. I came in and found a fax from an investigator at the Bowling Green Police Department. He thinks our Jane Doe could be a freshman from Bowling Green University name Sloan Westin."

"I'll be there in thirty," Beck said, already sliding from the bed. There were now multiple counties within the state involved. The girl from Kent State and now the very real possibility of one from Bowling Green. "We'll get BCI rolling on this when I get there."

"I think it's a good idea," Mitch said.

"Last night Jim Ellis was supposed to question a student at the U.—Zach Toomey. He may have seen our UNSUB."

"Hold on," Mitch said. There was a rustling of papers, then Mitch came back on the line. "It's here. The kid wasn't too cooperative until Ellis threatened to bring him in."

"What's the word on the blue van?"

"Dark or medium blue," Mitch read from the report. "Cargo type. No side windows."

"That narrows it down some. Did Loretta get the printouts from the DMV?"

"They're on your desk. I'll get started on them."

"Thanks," Beck said. "Any chance the kid got a look at the driver?"

"Only from a distance," Mitch said. "Not enough to give us an ID, but we have a general description. Medium height, light hair."

"That's not saying much."

"Hell, it's more than we had when I went to bed last night, so I'll take it," Mitch said. "I'll get on those DMV records and see you when I see you."

"Good enough." Beck flipped his phone closed. By the time Ainsley came back from the bathroom, he was already dressed. He made quick use of the bathroom, then headed downstairs to join her in the kitchen.

She added water to the coffee maker. "I hope that was good news so early in the morning," she said as she slid the basket holding the grounds into place.

"Maybe," he said, coming up behind her. He wrapped his

arms around her and rested his chin on her shoulder. "We might have a possible ID on our Jane Doe."

"Which one?"

"Both. I forgot to tell you, the girl yesterday was Tara Iverson, a student from Kent State Trumbull. And Mitch had a fax from Bowling Green this morning. The first girl could be a freshman from the university there. I'll know more later."

She turned in his arms, a deep frown on her face. "That's three freshmen girls," she said, her eyes filling with worry. "And the Conner girl."

"I know, babe," he said. "Look, try not to—"

"Worry? My sister and Paris are both freshmen, Beck. How am I not supposed to worry about them when it's starting to look as if freshmen girls are his primary target?"

"We'll stop him."

"But how? And how many more girls are going to die or go missing before you do?"

She wasn't being unreasonable, but her voice hinged on the edge of panic. Dammit, he understood her fears because they mirrored his own. And now, because of his involvement with her, the case was one misstep away from becoming personal.

"Hopefully, none. Look, we're calling in BCI today. There are three counties involved now. We'll stop him, Ainsley. I promise you that."

She folded her arms and gave him a hard stare. "Can I quote you on that, Chief Raines?"

He reached for her and gave her a quick kiss, catching her off guard. "Yes, you can. Keep in touch with Raelynn today. You just might get that exclusive you've been wanting."

If the other members of the press accused him of favoritism, fuck 'em.

*   *   *

IT HAD TAKEN some serious arm twisting, but Ainsley had eventually managed to convince Cassidy and Paris to skip classes today. She supposed she should be thrilled that her sister was so serious about her academic responsibilities, but the truth was, she would've been a basket case if the girls had been wandering around campus right now.

The entire population of Serenity Heights was jumpy. There was a quietness about town that was unusual and down-right eerie. People were cautious, and while they continued to be civil, the open friendliness had vanished, replaced by a cool politeness shrouded in suspicion. She hated that her hometown had been transformed. She hoped Beck made good on his promise, and soon.

She'd spent some time at the U today, and the place was practically deserted. Word around campus from the handful of remaining students was that many of the more local students had opted to return home temporarily. When she'd walked over from the newspaper office to the U earlier, she'd noted dozens of Pennsylvania, Kentucky, and Indiana license plates in the parking lot, with kids being packed up and brought home.

Officially the U wasn't closed, and according to Dean Chesterfield, classes were continuing as usual for the time being. Campus security had been stepped up, in addition to the heightened patrols by the police department. A strict ten PM curfew had been put in place, as well. Personal safety was being stressed by every professor and instructor, and the female students in particular were being urged to employ the buddy system and not travel anywhere alone.

She left Dean Chesterfield's office and nearly collided with the associate dean, Devin McElvoy. He was dressed just as he always was, polished shoes, pressed suit, and a matching tie.

"Miss Brennan," he greeted her. "How lovely to see you again."

"Hello," she said, and prepared to sidestep him. She wanted to stop by the Sigma Pi house to get some background information on Megan Conner before heading to the station.

"I suppose the recent events have kept you quite busy," he said, turning and walking with her.

"To say the least," she answered, wondering what he wanted with her. "If you'll excuse me, I have an appointment."

"I've been meaning to ask you. Have you heard if the police have any leads?"

Surely he'd heard the same rumors she'd been hearing all day. "No, not really," she said carefully. Was she merely being paranoid, or was he actually hinting that she might have inside information? She was sleeping with the acting chief of police, and in a town as small as Serenity Heights, she figured the speculation was already running rampant after Beck's truck had been parked in her driveway all night.

"I haven't heard anything specific," she said, "if that's what you mean."

"This kind of thing doesn't reflect well on the university."

Didn't she know it. Dean Chesterfield had been less than friendly with her, but Ainsley figured the stress of the situation was getting to the woman.

"I understand Paris Nolan is staying with you. Is that so?"

What business was it of his? "Yes, she is," she answered, struggling to hide her annoyance. "She's my sister's roommate. I thought it best, under the circumstances. Why do you ask?"

"Paris is a lovely girl," he said smoothly. "Quite bright. She works for me, you know."

Ah, yes. She'd forgotten about that. Ainsley just smiled, wondering exactly where this inane conversation was leading. She checked her watch. "I'm sorry, Dean McElvoy. I really do have to go."

"I met your sister yesterday," he said before she managed

to get away from him. "Tell me, does she appreciate all that you do for her?"

Okay, this had gone beyond annoying and was settling somewhere close to weird. Ainsley pasted a smile on her face and shrugged. "You know how teenagers are," she answered him. "I've gotta run. Bye."

She took off for the exit and thankfully made her escape. No wonder Paris was hoping to change jobs. She didn't know if she'd classify McElvoy as the perv Paris had called him, but he had made her feel decidedly uncomfortable with his bizarre questions. They weren't exactly personal, but they had definitely crossed a line as far as she was concerned.

As she hurried across campus to the Sigma Pi house, she thought about Paris's asking her about a job last night. She decided if she couldn't get the girl a job at the paper, then she would make it a point to talk to a few of the business owners in town once things settled down. Because in her opinion, McElvoy was indeed one strange dude and she'd feel a whole lot better knowing the girl was nowhere near the creep.

CHAPTER 19

NEVER IN HER life had Ainsley been surrounded by so much testosterone in one room. All those male eyes settled curiously on her was a little unnerving, too.

When she'd walked into the small conference room at the police station not five minutes ago, she'd expected Beck and possibly Mitch, but she'd been surprised to also find representatives from Trumbull County, an investigator from the Bowling Green PD, and the Wood County ADA, as well as ADA Eisner from their own Cuyahoga County. In addition, Gage Zimmerman, a special investigator from the state's Bureau of Criminal Identification and Investigation, or BCI, was also in attendance.

Aside from Beck, Zimmerman was easily the most commanding presence in the room. He was nearly as tall as Beck, had short-cropped, light brown hair and an engaging smile. When she shook his hand, she couldn't help think that Raelynn had been right—Special Investigator Zimmerman did have the most electric blue eyes she'd ever seen. Of course, in her opinion, they hardly compared to the intensity of Beck's clear green gaze, but hey, that was just her.

Once the introductions were out of the way, she took a seat at the far end of the conference table, then reached into her tote for her recorder and a notepad. She wasn't certain what they wanted from her, but she had a feeling this meeting was for more than just the exclusive Beck had promised her. When she'd checked in with Raelynn earlier today, all she'd been told was to be at the station by three o'clock for a meeting with Beck. She'd had no idea she'd be privy to what appeared to be an entire task force involving personnel from three counties and BCI, which had been formed in a matter of hours.

"Ms. Brennan," Gage Zimmerman started, "it's my understanding that you're a friend of the department."

Meaning she could be trusted, not that she was having a hot and heavy affair with the man in charge. She knew the vote of confidence came from Beck, and it meant a lot to her, especially after what he'd told her this morning.

"That's right," she said.

"With your help," the special investigator continued, "we'd like to do something a little unorthodox."

She glanced at Beck, who sat next to her. He gave her a barely perceptible nod. "Whatever I can do to help," she said, turning her attention back to Zimmerman.

"With Gage's help," Beck said, "we've developed a profile of the UNSUB. We'd like you to take it public."

Well, hell. There went her big exclusive break before she even had the chance to enjoy it. "I'd love to, but you're forgetting, the *Sentinel* is only a weekly paper," she said. "Our next scheduled edition won't hit stands until next Thursday. We are supposed to be going to a daily, but as part of the *Daily Tribune*. I have no idea when that's even going to happen. It could be as early as next week or a month or two from now." If at all, but she kept that thought to herself. "I could get it on the Web, but I don't think that's what you want."

"We were thinking about a press conference," Gage said.

"That's fine," she said, despite the huge stab of disappointment. "But I'm print media, not broadcast."

"We'd like you to be the one to go before the cameras," Beck explained.

They weren't kidding. What they were proposing definitely was unorthodox.

"We feel your presence could be very effective in drawing out the suspect," Gage said.

She put her hands up. "Wait a minute," she said. "Wait a minute. Do you mind if I ask why me?" Not that she wasn't willing to do whatever she could to help, but what they were asking was just downright weird. Press conferences were traditionally held by law enforcement or public officials, not other members of the press, and certainly not no-name reporters of a no-name weekly paper generally filled with news of bake sales and Little League scores.

"Because he's already targeted you, Ainsley," Beck said. "For reasons we're still unsure of, he's connected himself to you."

"The audio files," she said. "He sent them to me."

"Yes," Gage said. "Based on the profile we've developed, we strongly believe the killer is a local. He knows you. Perhaps he even feels an affinity to you, which is why he's chosen you to get the word out about what he does."

Her skin prickled. The very idea that the killer was someone she knew scared the hell out of her. Was it someone close to her? Someone she spoke to on a daily basis? The cook at the café? The guy who cleaned her chimney once a year?

Oh God.

"We feel if you present the information we're about to give you," Gage said, "he may view it as a betrayal of his trust."

"But I never reported on the audio files," she said. "Why hasn't he considered that a betrayal?"

"He may have," Gage explained. "But it's more likely he views that as you keeping his trust. You share his secret."

"But if you're right and he does know me, then he'd know I've gone to the police."

"Yes, but the fact that you haven't gone public with it would make a difference. You're keeping his trust. He shares a secret with you, and that gives him a sense of power."

She blew out a stream of breath. This whole scenario was crazy. But then so was the guy they were after, so she supposed it all fit somehow.

"All right," she said. "I'll do it."

"Good. I'll have my people set up the news conference," Gage said as he pulled a cell phone from the pocket of his suit jacket. "We'll shoot for six o'clock and hope for the best."

The others got up from the table. Some stretched, some stood brooding, talking among themselves. Beck remained seated by her side. Beneath the table, his settled his hand over hers and gave her a quick, comforting squeeze.

"Are you all right with this?" he asked her. "If not, say the word and I'll cancel it right now."

She looked at him, and her heart swelled at the deep concern for her in his eyes. He hadn't said he loved her, but he'd come damn close this morning. So close that she couldn't help wonder if that's exactly what he had intended all along. She didn't understand how she could have fallen in love so quickly with the man herself, but she chose not to question or analyze the emotion to death.

An affair with Beck complicated her life somewhat. Falling in love with him put her into a tailspin. There was the uncertainty of her job, for one thing. Plus, she couldn't help wondering how much he really trusted her. He had strong reasons for disliking the press, and even if she did have to take an interim job until she found another newspaper willing to hire her, would she always be a reporter in his eyes? Regardless, now definitely was not the time to ask that particular question.

"Do I really have a choice?" she asked him.

"We all have choices, babe," he answered in a hushed tone.

Sure, but most of them weren't life and death choices. "Just tell me what it is you want me to say."

THE CROWD OUTSIDE the Serenity Heights Police Department ran several people deep, with reporters and citizens in equal numbers. The press was out in full force, and that pleased him. Satellite news vans lined the street, and reporters and cameramen milled around, conducting man-on-the-street interviews with the locals. A podium had been set up in front of the police station with close to a dozen microphones attached. Even CNN and Fox News were there.

He stood on the fringes, watching and waiting with the rest of them for the press conference to begin. He scanned the crowd for familiar faces, and that's when he saw *her*. She stood with her friend, paying him no attention whatsoever.

She was subdued this evening, a worried expression clouding her clear blue eyes. He hadn't realized exactly how pretty she was, not really. Oh sure, he'd noticed she was attractive, but he hadn't realized until now what a very perfect addition she would make to his collection.

Sharp need gnawed at his insides as he watched her. The buzzing in his ears shifted to a roar, with all the ferocity of waves crashing upon the shore, violently, as if in the midst of the force of a hurricane.

She had no parents, no one to miss her, except perhaps her friend, but that one was shallow. She wouldn't be missed right away, of that he was certain. No one would even think twice about their leaving together, either.

He turned and nodded a subtle greeting to a plump, middle-aged woman he recognized from the minimart. Skirting the crowd, he slowly made his way to where she stood chatting with the other one, the one who'd dismissed him as unimportant.

Anticipation hummed in his veins. He imagined her with the others, perfect and transformed. Excitement bubbled up inside him.

He moved up behind the girls. Waiting. Listening to their inane chatter, wondering how difficult it would be to separate them.

She must've sensed his presence, because she looked over her shoulder at him. "Oh, hi, Mr. McElvoy."

He smiled. "Good evening, Paris."

BECK PACED THE conference room, which had been transformed into a command center. He was keyed up, anxious, and feeling borderline desperate now that Ainsley was more directly involved. He hated putting her in this position, but they were running out of options, and time. Mattie Davenport and Megan Conner were still out there. Somewhere.

A conversation with the mayor earlier in the day hadn't gone well, especially when Joe bitched about the cost of putting up the Davenports at the B and B in town indefinitely. Their daughter was missing, possibly even dead, and Beck had lost his temper, hanging up on the mayor before he'd said something that would've ended up with him looking for a new job.

Extra phones had been brought in, and would be manned by one of his on-duty officers for the duration. Faxes and printouts were spread on the table. Crime scene and autopsy photographs were pinned to a large bulletin board, which he'd turned to face the wall before Ainsley had arrived in deference to her squeamishness. A map had been tacked to the wall, complete with flags to indicate the locations where the bodies had been found, and where the two missing girls were last seen.

"Are you sure you want to do this?" he asked Ainsley. The more he thought about it, the more he disliked the idea of drawing the UNSUB's attention to her in this way. Granted, the UNSUB had already targeted her as they'd explained earlier, but this was different. They were about to tweak the bastard's nose and he could very well strike out—at Ainsley. The thought filled him with a coldness he felt clear to the bottom of his soul.

She looked up from the notes she'd been making. "I'm positive."

He stopped pacing and stood facing her, folding his arms over his chest. "Once we're done here, I think it'd be best if you and the girls stayed at my place for a while. If Gage is right about this guy, he just might come after you."

She set her pen down. "If he knows where I live, then chances are he knows where you live, too."

He frowned. "Then you'll have twenty-four-hour police protection," he said, his tone harsh.

"Beck, stop it," she told him. "Please. I'm nervous enough as it is, and you're not helping. Besides, you won't have the personnel to spare. After the press conference, this is going to turn into a manhunt and you know it." She indicated the telephones with a wave of her hand. "That tip line you've set up is going to be ringing off the hook. And now that the press is really here in force, someone from the department is going to have to act as a liaison between you and them. You can't expect your men to pull twenty-four-hour shifts and still be fresh."

His frown deepened. Every one of her arguments made perfect sense. But that didn't mean he had to like it.

"I'm worried about you."

"I appreciate that, but I promise you, we'll be careful," she said, her tone placating enough to grate on his already raw nerves. "We'll go stay at a hotel in Strongsville, Parma, I don't care where. We'll drive down to Akron or Youngstown if that will make you happy, but please, you've got to chill out so I can get through this."

"Ainsley?" Gage Zimmerman appeared in the doorway. "We're ready if you are."

She looked back at Beck, a determined glint in her eyes. "Let's do it."

He didn't say anything, just gave her a brusque nod. If anything happened to her, heads were going to fucking roll.

He wanted to pull her into his arms and hold her close, tell her how much he cared for her, but he couldn't. Now wasn't the time. Still, the ache persisted when she followed him and the others outside the station to the front steps for the press conference.

He stepped up to the podium, thanked the press for coming, introduced the interested parties, then read a short statement, indicating they would take questions at the conclusion. He then turned the press conference over to Ainsley.

As he stood off to the side with Zimmerman and the others, his admiration of her grew. He knew she was a wreck, but he doubted anyone present knew exactly how nervous she'd been just moments before. She was the epitome of calm, the total professional.

She chose her words carefully as she relayed the events of the past few days, starting with the discovery of Sloan Westin's body at Big Rock Clearing. She briefly mentioned receipt of the audio files, but played that aspect down and moved on to the search and the resulting discoveries of yesterday afternoon. As planned, she left out the information of the sandal believed to belong to Megan Conner as he and Zimmerman had instructed her.

She looked up from her notes and focused on the cameras. "The suspect is believed to be a white male, thirty to forty years old," she said, her voice clear and firm with the slightest hint of disdain. She spoke as if she were talking directly to the UNSUB.

The bells from the tower at the U sounded seven bells and she paused, waiting until the last one pealed before continuing.

"The suspect is not an authority figure," she continued, "although he probably sees himself that way. More than likely he has difficulty in his relationships with women, particularly women of authority."

She paused again and shifted her focus to the crowd as if searching for the man she described. Several cameras shifted their focus as well to the crowd, just as Zimmerman had predicted they would. The purpose was to give them a visual record since, as Zimmerman pointed out, their guy would more than likely be in attendance.

She waited until the cameras were focused on her again. "The victims have not been sexually assaulted," she said, looking directly into the cameras. "This tells us the suspect is not at all comfortable with the opposite sex. Quite possibly, he is impotent or suffers from some other sexual dysfunction. He may have been sexually abused by a parent or some other female authority figure."

She paused again and glanced Beck's way, then looked directly at Zimmerman. He gave her an encouraging nod; then she turned back to the cameras. "It is believed that the suspect is not an overly large man and is of average height and build. The experts tell us that his actions are cowardly, as he either takes the victims by surprise or uses coercion rather than physically overpowering them."

She concluded by offering physical descriptions of the Davenport and Conner girls. After giving the reporters the number for the tip line, she stepped aside and Gage Zimmerman took over for the wrap-up.

She stood next to Beck, then turned so her back was to the crowd and looked up at him. "I just publicly called the suspect a little dickless weaselly coward, didn't I?" she whispered.

"You did," he whispered back.

She briefly closed her eyes. "I hope to hell you guys were right about this."

So did he.

When Zimmerman started taking questions from the press, reporters jostled and pressed forward. Beside Beck, Ainsley started to tremble. Suspecting a possible meltdown now that the reality of what she'd done had started to set in, Beck signaled to Mitch, who escorted Ainsley back inside the station and away from the cameras.

The press conference went on for another thirty-five minutes, with Beck and Gage fielding most of the questions. By the time he rejoined Ainsley in the conference room, she'd calmed considerably. She looked up at him when he walked in, but her expression was closed. A survival tactic, he suspected. She was tough when she had to be, and he felt as if he'd been given a glimpse of the young girl who'd once faced tragedy and had remained standing in spite of the weight she'd been forced to carry on her own.

"You were perfect," Zimmerman said from behind Beck. "Good job."

"Thanks," she said weakly. "I think."

"You did good, kid," Mitch said, then gave her shoulder a rough pat.

"So what happens now?"

"Now we hope someone saw something suspicious. Or knows something about the suspect and comes forward. We watch for any unusual behavior," Zimmerman told her. "And we wait for him to make a mistake."

Ainsley frowned. "But how? The description I gave the press wasn't accurate. No one knows what he looks like."

"Actually, we do have a vague description," Beck told her. "Last night we questioned a witness . . ."

A commotion down the hall erupted. Beck heard what

sounded like two women arguing, one of them close to hysteria. Frowning, Beck went to investigate. Mitch followed.

Beck walked into the outer office and found Paris Nolan arguing with Raelynn, demanding to see Ainsley immediately. "I'll handle this," Beck said to Raelynn. "You'd better get Ainsley."

"I can't find her," Paris wailed hysterically. Her eyes were red and swollen, her cheeks stained by mascara drip. "I've looked everywhere and I can't find her."

"Whoa," he said, stepping past the counter that separated the lobby from the main office area. "Take it easy, Paris. What's going on?"

"Oh God." Paris cried harder. "Where's Ainsley? I need to see Ainsley."

Beck shot Raelynn a dark look, and she finally took off for the conference room. "She's coming," he told Paris.

"She was right beside me, then we got separated when those stupid reporters started shoving. Oh God. Oh God."

"Who can't you find, Paris?" he asked, but he had a sinking feeling in the pit of his stomach that he already knew the answer.

He turned just as Ainsley came charging down the hall toward them. "What's wrong?"

Paris started crying in earnest again. Once Ainsley made it into the lobby, Paris threw herself at her and sobbed uncontrollably.

"Shhh," Ainsley said, trying to calm the girl. "What's the matter?"

"I can't find her," Paris sobbed. She pulled away from Ainsley and, using the heels of her hands, swiped the tears from her face. "I looked everywhere, but I can't find her. I even went back to the house to see if she went there. She's gone, Ainsley. Cassidy is gone."

CHAPTER 20

"STOP TELLING ME to calm down." Ainsley dropped onto the sofa in her family room and wrapped her arms around her middle. Rocking forward, she hugged herself tighter, but the pain refused to go away. "That sick bastard has my sister."

"I know, babe." He sat next to her and slipped his arm around her. "We'll get her back."

He attempted to pull her close, but she stiffened and pulled away. She didn't want to be held, she wanted him to find Cassidy before it was too late.

Standing, she distanced herself from him. "How?" she demanded hotly. "You have no leads."

"We'll find her," he repeated. To give him credit, he appeared as anguished as she felt, but Cass was *her* sister, not his. He wasn't the one who'd nursed Cass through a horrendous case of chicken pox, or sat there helpless and hurting for her sister when the doctor had to set Cass's arm when she'd broken it by falling off the backyard fence. There were fights and tears, celebrations and milestones he'd never understand. So many memories, all of which swamped her at once. She felt as if she were drowning.

"Exactly how do you plan to do that?" she asked him. "You still haven't found Mattie Davenport. Or Megan

Conner, for that matter." She pulled in a deep breath, but her racing heart refused to slow. The fear clawing at her refused to ebb.

"Dammit, Beck," she said, lowering her voice. There were two investigators from BCI camped out in her living room, setting up recording equipment should Cassidy or her kidnapper call, with BCI ready to intercept and hopefully get a trace on the guy. Beck had tried to get her and Paris to stay at his place, but she'd insisted on coming home. If Cassidy somehow managed to escape, home would be the first place she'd come, and Ainsley wanted to be there.

"Those two dead girls were missing for months," she continued, "and no one found them until he dropped what was left of them on our doorstep. Excuse me if my confidence in your ability to find Cassidy is hovering around zero at the moment."

She turned away because she couldn't bear to look at him and see the truth in his eyes, that he had no idea who had taken her sister. She flipped open her cell phone, then snapped it closed again. There'd be no message from Cass. No text message to tell her that her sister was alive or how to find her. And even though she knew there wouldn't be, that didn't stop her from checking just the same. Paris had found Cass's cell phone in one of the planters lining the sidewalk in front of the station. The bastard had taken her right from under their noses.

While Beck had been questioning Paris, Ainsley called Paige, who was driving up from Cinci and should be arriving within the hour. There wasn't anything Paige could do, but just their being together now was important. Together they'd wait, and pray for word that Cassidy was still alive.

"God, why didn't Cass just stay home?" She fought a fresh wave of tears and lost the battle. "If she had, then she'd be here now. Safe. Scrounging in the fridge for leftovers or a Diet Coke. Bopping around the kitchen with her iPod."

"Ainsley, don't." He came off the sofa and approached her. This time when he slipped his arms around her, she let him hold her, and she greedily accepted comfort from the warmth of his embrace. "Don't do that to yourself."

She wasn't used to depending on anyone but herself. Eleven years of self-reliance, of being the strong one, the one to care for others, were too ingrained in her now for her to accept comfort from him easily. Yet with her head resting against his chest now, hearing the strong, steady beat of his heart, she drew a modicum of comfort from his strength.

A part of her wanted to curl up on the sofa against him and let him hold her while she cried until there was nothing left. She wanted numbness against the pain ripping through her, but she knew that wasn't possible. She'd be strong. She'd handle this. It was what she did.

She slipped out of his embrace. "You've got people waiting for you," she reminded him. "Paige will be here soon. Go. Please. Go find my sister."

He looked ready to protest, but she shook her head. "Go," she said again. "We'll be fine."

"I'll try to stay in touch."

She wouldn't hold him to that promise, but knew he'd do his best to update her when he could.

She walked with him to the front of the house. He stopped in the living room to talk to the two BCI agents Gage Zimmerman had requested to assist, then joined her at the front door. "Would you like me to send Raelynn to stay with you until your sister gets here? I don't like you being alone."

She shot a glance over her shoulder to the living room. "I'm hardly alone," she said. "Besides, Paris is here, and Paige should be arriving any minute now."

"How is she?" he asked, inclining his head in the direction of the staircase.

"She was asleep when I left her," she said, referring to Paris. The girl had been hysterical when she'd realized that Cass was missing, and the emotional storm had taken a toll on her. She'd ended up with a raging headache and had crashed almost as soon as her head hit the pillow. "Hopefully she'll sleep for a few hours."

He dipped his head and kissed her softly on the lips. "You should try to get some rest yourself."

Like that would happen.

He hesitated for a moment, then turned and opened the door. "I'll be in touch," he said, then left.

She locked the door behind him, then went into the living room, sidestepping the BCI agents and their sympathetic expressions. She went to the window and pulled the curtain back, watching as Beck pulled out of the driveway.

The sun had set hours ago, and the night sky was dark and cloudless. She looked up to the inky blackness and did something she hadn't done in a very long time. She prayed.

"THERE'S NOTHING HERE," Mitch said, shoving the DMV readouts across the table at Beck in frustration. "I've been over it and over it, and there's not a single dark or medium blue cargo van registered to anyone in this goddamn town."

"What about people who work here, but live in one of the outlying towns?" Gage Zimmerman asked Mitch.

"That, too," the captain groused. "I've checked and cross checked until I'm cross-eyed."

"Are you sure?"

Mitch glowered at the BCI investigator. "You're damn right I am. With the exception of the U, the businesses here are family owned and operated. There are two cargo vans registered to owners in town. One to the Secret Garden, a floral shop, and the other to French Creek Construction."

"Then we have to assume the van is either stolen, or even unregistered," Charlie Gabriel offered. He'd been manning the tip line they'd set up, but all they'd gotten so far were several dozen calls expressing concern from the good people of Serenity Heights.

"Which doesn't help us much," Beck added. It was one more brick in the wall they just couldn't seem to scale. "So what *do* we have?"

"Not fucking much," Mitch complained. He pushed away from the table and went to the coffee maker, where he poured himself another cup.

"While you were out," Gage said to Beck, "I looked at the tapes from the press conference. There are one or two glimpses of Ainsley's sister and her friend, but nothing unusual to jump out at me."

"I'll take a look," Beck said, then glanced over at Mitch. "Have we heard back from Bowling Green yet?" There'd been a symposium held at BGU the weekend Sloan Westin had gone missing, for college and university administrators and department heads throughout the state. The Westin girl had last been seen working the registration desk that weekend. "They were supposed to provide us with a list of attendees."

Mitch set his coffee mug on the table. "I'll check on it," he said, then left the room.

"Is he always this pleasant?" Gage asked, inclining his head in the direction of Mitch's vacant chair.

"We're all wound a little tight right now," Beck said, to which Charlie nodded in agreement. "But Mitch has known the Brennan girls since they were little." A fact Beck had always suspected by the almost fatherly affection the old captain showed Ainsley whenever she was around, but had only confirmed earlier tonight in a conversation with Mitch himself.

"He and his wife were friends of their parents," Charlie added. "When they died, he and Rose sort of stepped in as surrogate grandparents. He's taking Cassidy's disappearance personally."

"Under the circumstances, you should consider removing him from the case," Gage suggested. "His objectivity is in question."

"If I did that, I'd have to remove just about every officer on my staff from the case, myself included," Beck admitted. "You have to understand, this is a small community. These people's lives are intertwined. Cassidy Brennan used to baby-sit for one of my officers' chidren, and Ainsley went to school with at least two of the men at the force, that I know of. My administrative clerk is her best friend."

"Okay, okay." Gage lifted his hands in mock surrender. "Point taken," he said, then gave Beck a hard stare. "You're not from here, Raines. What's your connection?"

He looked dead on at the BCI investigator. "That's none of your fucking business."

Charlie coughed suddenly, then looked away.

Mitch returned, impervious to the tension in the room. He walked to the whiteboard and uncapped one of the blue markers. "Chesterfield," he said as he wrote the dean's name on the whiteboard, then added, "Pomeroy, Sylmar, McElvoy, Rhoades, and Given." He tapped the board with his knuckles. "They all attended the symposium at BGU."

"I take it these are all from your university here?" Gage asked.

"Right," Beck confirmed. "We can cross Chesterfield off the list." He looked to Gage. "She's the dean of students."

"Better remove Sylmar and Given, too," Charlie said.

Mitch drew a line through Sylmar's name, then paused. "Unless there's a possibility the UNSUB is female."

"No," Gage said, shaking his head. "We're definitely looking for a white male. Too much damage to the vics for it to be a woman. Besides, women tend to go with poison as their weapon of choice, and more often than not, financial gain is their primary objective."

"Okay, so that leaves us with Pomeroy," Mitch said as he underlined Pomeroy's name, "McElvoy, and Rhoades."

"Pomeroy was the Davenport girl's advisor," Beck said. "He was the last one to see her alive."

Gage reached across the table for the autopsy report. He flipped through the pages until he found what he was looking for. "The vic was strangled with piano wire," he said, tapping his pen on the section in question. "Same as the Iverson girl."

"Pomeroy is the head of the music department," Beck confirmed. "He'd have access to piano wire."

"Should we get a warrant?" Mitch asked.

"Not yet," Gage said. "What about the other two?"

"Rhoades is the university president," Charlie said. "He's pushing sixty, if not more."

"It's unlikely he's our man, then," Gage suggested. "Cross him off for now." He looked to Beck. "What about McElvoy?"

"Associate dean," Beck said, and looked to Mitch, who shrugged.

"He's not from around here," Charlie pointed out. "He came to the U a couple of years ago. Bought the old Harrington Farm, but that's all I really know about him."

"Do either of you know where he came from?" Beck asked.

"Columbus," Mitch said. "Cincinnati, maybe."

Gage slid his laptop closer. "Where was the Iverson girl from?"

"She was a student at Kent State—Trumbull campus," Beck said. "Why?"

"The beauty of technology," Gage said as he typed, "is access to state employee files."

Beck and Mitch both moved closer to get a look at the computer screen. A photograph of Devin McElvoy flashed on the screen.

"Cincinnati State," Gage read. "He taught Anatomy and Physiology."

Beck and Mitch exchanged a look over Gage's head. "What's his specialty?" Beck asked.

"Nursing studies," Gage read.

That made little sense. "How the hell does someone go from nursing studies to becoming an associate dean of students?" Beck asked.

"Maybe he sucked at teaching," Mitch offered. "The guy's a dweeb."

Beck couldn't argue with that assessment. The guy had been a pompous pain in the ass, poking his nose in his investigation since the Davenport girl's disappearance.

A few clicks of the mouse and they had their answer. "It says here," Gage read, "that he went into administration three years ago. There's an incident in his jacket." He made a few more mouse clicks. "Dammit. Which I can't access."

Beck swore. "It's sealed?"

Gage nodded. "I'll go up line and get it," he said, then shot an e-mail off to his supervisor requesting the hidden information on McElvoy. "But he's never taught or been associated with Kent State that I can see."

"I'll contact the Trumbull County sheriff," Beck said. "He might have some luck with the campus administrators. Maybe there was some event that McElvoy or Pomeroy attended around the time Iverson went missing."

"Let's check Pomeroy," Gage said, then started typing again.

Mitch straightened and returned to his chair, as did Beck.

"You won't find anything there," Charlie told them. "Pomeroy has been at the U for ten years or more. Honest to God, I doubt he's our guy, either. He's quiet, friendly to his neighbors, and keeps to himself."

"Right, there's a reason to eliminate him as a suspect," Mitch complained. "I can't tell you how many newscasts I've seen where some old lady in a moo-moo with curlers in her hair is telling reporters that the serial killer next door was such a nice man. A good neighbor. Yada, yada, yada."

"Single?" Gage asked, ignoring Mitch's tirade.

"Far as I know," Charlie said.

"There's still that piano wire connection, though," Mitch reminded them. "I vote we wake up a judge and get ourselves a search warrant."

Beck sat back in his chair and scrubbed his hand down his face. In the distance, the bell from the tower at the U pealed off the midnight hour. They'd been running in circles all night and in his opinion, they weren't any closer to solving the case or finding Cassidy Brennan than when he'd walked into the room less than two hours ago.

The final bell pealed and Beck rose from his chair. "He's local," he said. "The son of a bitch lives right here in Serenity Heights." Dammit, he'd missed it. It'd been right there the whole time and he'd missed it.

"We've already figured that much," Mitch said, frowning.

"Yeah," Beck said as he walked to the window. He yanked on the cord, drawing up the miniblinds, then pointing to the red brick bell tower in the distance. "But he's close enough to hear those bells from *that* tower."

Mitch's frown deepened. "Yeah. So am I. Big deal. What's your point?"

"The UNSUB is close enough that the bells can be picked up on a recording device."

Mitch smacked the table with his hand. "The audio files."

"Two bells were definitely in one of those recordings," Beck said. "It's distant, but it's there. Where do Pomeroy and McElvoy live?"

"Pomeroy lives about two blocks from here," Charlie told them. "That'd be close enough to hear the bells."

"And McElvoy?" Gage asked. "Where's Harrington Farm?"

"What's left of it abuts U property."

Beck yanked his keys from his pocket.

"Where are you going?" Mitch asked.

"To wake up a judge," Beck said, then stopped cold when one of the telephones in front of Charlie rang.

Charlie answered, then looked over at Beck, his expression grim. "He's on his way," Charlie said, then hung up. "That was one of the BCI agents. Ainsley's on the phone with the UNSUB now."

THERE WASN'T A limb on her body that wasn't shaking. Her knees felt weak, but she couldn't sit still, so she anxiously paced between the sofa and the living room window, waiting for Beck to arrive. Paris and Paige sat together on the sofa, looking equally distraught, while the two BCI agents did their thing with the recording equipment or frantically jotted notes on a yellow legal pad.

You've disappointed me, Ainsley.

She'd tried to keep him on the phone long enough for the BCI agents to pick up a trace, but the bastard had ended the call too soon for them to zero in on his exact location. All they'd been able to determine was that he was using a disposable Trac Phone, and that he was close. Close enough for them to trace the signal to one of the local towers, but that's where the trail ended.

I expected better from you. I expected the truth.

What truth? She didn't know him. All she knew was that he had her sister and if she got her hands of the son of a bitch, he was a dead man. What he did to Tara Iverson and Sloan Westin would be minor in comparison to what she wanted to do to him right now.

Even the anger coursing through her couldn't melt the

bone coldness inside her. She'd hoped for numbness earlier, but all she felt now was cold. Icy, as if everything inside her had been frozen solid.

She feared she'd never thaw.

Paris remained on the sofa next to Paige. The younger girl was hunched over and staring down at the carpet. She kept rocking back and forth, twisting the ties of her hoodie around her finger, then pulling it off and repeating the process again and again.

Hugging the sweater she'd put on earlier tighter around her, Ainsley turned to the window.

"Lee," Paige said. "Sit down. You're not helping."

Ainsley pulled the curtain back, but couldn't see anything except the empty porch furniture. "I can't," she said, turning to face her sister. Paige didn't look to be in any better shape than the rest of them with those dark circles underscoring her eyes. She must've broken every speed limit in the state considering she'd made the four-hour drive from Cinci in just under three hours.

Paris covered her face with her hands and started to cry again, quiet sobs that shook her shoulders. Paige slipped her arm around Paris and made soothing noises in an effort to comfort the girl.

"It's all my fault," Paris said. Her words were muffled, but still clear enough to be discernable. She looked up, her eyes still red from her earlier tears. "I wanted to go to the press conference and talked Cass into going. I thought it'd be cool to actually see one that wasn't on television."

"It's not your fault," Ainsley said. "So stop."

"If Cass didn't want to go, she wouldn't have," Paige told her. "No one talks her into anything. I know I never could."

That didn't seem to help, because Paris only cried harder. Paige tugged her close and Paris dropped her head on Paige's shoulder. It made sense that Paige would be the one to comfort Paris now. There was a reason her younger sister became an RN, since she was the one born with an over-abundance of the compassion gene. As a kid she'd nursed everything from baby birds fallen from their nests to litters of stray kittens and puppies.

Paris sniffled. "When the press conference started, every-one began pushing and shoving. We got separated. I looked for her, but just figured I'd find her afterward." She sat up straighter. "When I couldn't, I got worried."

"Paris, it's not your fault," Ainsley repeated. She turned and looked out the window again. Headlights flashed across the window signaling Beck's arrival as he pulled into the driveway. Two additional cars came screeching to a halt in front of the house, both police cruisers.

"I even looked for Mr. McElvoy, to see if he saw where Cass had gone, but he wasn't there, either."

"Who's McElvoy?" Paige asked.

"I work for him at the U," Paris said, her voice strained and raw from all the crying she'd done. "He was there, stand-ing behind us before it all got started." She wiped at the tears trailing down her face with the sleeve of her hoodie. "When I couldn't find Cass, I started looking around, but when I didn't see a blue van, I wasn't too worried at first. Then I came here and she wasn't home, so I ran back to the police station. That's when I found her cell phone in the planter and I knew. I just knew, because—"

"Because Cass never goes anywhere without her cell phone," Paige finished.

Ainsley dropped the curtain back in place as Beck bounded up the front porch steps. "What did you say?" she asked Paris.

Paris frowned. "What?"

"Why would you be looking for a blue van?" Ainsley asked her. She'd heard nothing about a blue van.

Beck knocked hard on the door. Ainsley didn't move, just kept staring at Paris, waiting for an answer.

"Would you mind getting that?" Paige asked the BCI agent closest to the door.

"Remember when Zach came here last night?" At Ainsley's nod, Paris said, "He told me he saw something out in the field where the body was found yesterday."

"Is that why you went to the station last night to see Beck?" Ainsley asked her, careful to keep the accusation she was feeling out of her voice. Her complaint wasn't with Paris, but with Beck. She couldn't believe he'd keep such a vital piece of information from not just her, but from the public. She'd even asked him why Paris had come to see him and he'd blown her off.

"Yeah," Paris said. "Zach wouldn't go, so I did and told him what Zach said he saw. I would've told you, but he asked me not to."

"Zach?"

Paris shook her head. "No. Chief Raines."

Ainsley merely nodded, not trusting herself to remain calm. None of this was Paris's fault. No, the man she held responsible had just walked in the room. The man who'd almost told her he loved her, but would never be able to trust her.

CHAPTER 21

AINSLEY BRUSHED PAST Beck without a word. She looked furious as she left the living room, and he was torn between going to her and doing his job. A choice he'd been faced with once before. Then, he'd made the wrong choice; he wasn't about to screw it up again.

"Take care of this," he said to Mitch and Gage. "I'll be right back."

He took off after Ainsley, but didn't see her in the kitchen or the family room beyond. He heard the slamming of her bedroom door, so he turned and started up the stairs after her. Without bothering to knock, he walked in and closed the door behind him.

She stood in front of her dresser, her hands tightly gripping the edge. "Are you all right?" he asked her.

She looked up and he caught her reflection in the mirror. She didn't look all right. She looked frazzled and worried, and ready to rip his head clean off his shoulders with her bare hands. "Get out."

The coldness in her voice chilled him. "What's going on, Ainsley?"

She spun around to face him. "I don't want to see you right now. In fact, I don't know if I ever want to see you again. Period."

"Look, I get it," he said, taking a few steps toward her. "You're under a lot of stress right now."

"You 'get it'?" she practically snarled at him. "You don't get shit."

Asshole.

She didn't say it, but the epithet was definitely hanging out there between them. Aimed right at him, in fact.

His patience slipped. "What's going on here?" he asked roughly.

"Why don't you tell me. Oh, wait," she said, her tone dripping with sarcasm. "That won't happen, because you don't trust me. Do you, Beck?"

Ah, hell. She'd found out about the van.

"I have told you repeatedly," she continued, her voice rising, "that anything you say to me is off the record, but apparently my word doesn't mean much to you, does it?"

"Ainsley—"

"Because if you did trust me, you wouldn't have withheld vital information from me."

"I did *not* withhold information from you," he argued. "Not intentionally."

"The hell you didn't. What about the blue van that was sighted? Ring a bell?"

"I didn't want the information made public."

"It's the only lead you have. Why the hell not?"

"If word got out, he could go into hiding and we'd never find him. If he ditched the van, we'd lose what little advantage we did have."

"But you didn't trust me to keep that information to myself, did you?"

"It wasn't intentional," he said again. He was not going to have this argument with her. Not now. Later, once they had her sister safely back home, she could rant and rail all she wanted at him. But for now, he was through.

"You can believe that or not," he said, his own tone hard. "The choice is yours."

"Why should I believe you?"

He let out a sigh and closed the distance between them. Taking hold of her shoulders, he looked into those pain-stricken eyes and said, "Because I love you."

She looked up at him, pain, hurt, and fear all warring within her gaze. "But you can't trust me." She shook off his touch. "You can't have one without the other, Beck. It just doesn't work that way. Not to me."

"We'll discuss this later."

"There's nothing more to discuss," she said. "Go. Bring my sister back to me."

There was nothing left for him to say, so he turned and left the room. Downstairs, the two BCI agents were huddled over the folding table set up with recording equipment.

"Got it," the older of the two agents, whose name Beck couldn't recall at the moment, said. He punched a button and played back Ainsley's conversation with their suspect.

The recording wasn't very long, since the UNSUB ended the call quickly, no doubt in hopes of avoiding a trace. Unfortunately, there was nothing in the recording that clued Beck in to the identity of the killer.

"Play it again," Beck suggested.

The agent punched the play button. *Hello, Ainsley. Are you ready for a new day?*

"Oh my God," Paris blurted. "That's Mr. McElvoy's voice."

The agent stopped the recording.

"Are you sure?" Beck asked her. Paris had been through the emotional ringer today. Her judgment could easily be skewed as a result.

"Yes," she said emphatically. "I'm positive. That's him."

"How do you know for sure?" he asked.

She had a disgusted look on her face. "The way he says

'hello, Ainsley,' all sleazy like. That's him," she said. "I *know* it's him."

"Thank you, Paris," Beck said.

"Sounds like enough for probable cause to me," Mitch said. "I'll call all available units."

"Make it a ten-forty," Beck told him. "We run silent, no lights so we don't alert him. And make sure both ends of the street are barricaded once we're in."

"Done," Mitch said, then made the call to dispatch.

Gage had his cell phone out and was dialing. "I'll alert SWAT to be on standby."

"What's going on?"

Beck turned at the sound of Ainsley's voice. "We've got him," he said. "It's McElvoy."

"I'm going with you."

"No," he said. "You're not."

She shot him a sour look, then spun around and left the room, only to return seconds later. She slapped something onto his chest, then held it against him with her index finger, using enough force to drill a hole through his chest. "This says I have a right to be there."

He took the plastic-coated press pass from her and tossed it on the table. "I don't think it's a good idea."

"I really don't care what you think any longer," she said, her voice as cold as the steely look in her eyes. "As a member of the press, I have a right to be present. So unless you're planning to trample all over my Constitutional rights, I'm going. If you want to stop me, you'll just have to arrest me."

To say he was tempted to do just that if it meant keeping her safe was nothing short of an understatement.

HARRINGTON FARM ABUTTED unused university grounds at the far, southern edge of town. There were no streetlights in this remote area, and the road was essentially deserted, with only one other farmhouse about a half mile further down the road and out of the city's jurisdiction.

Beck had requested Steve Jonas to stay with Ainsley's sister and Paris, while all other available units were already on scene and awaiting his word to go. Mitch had even called in half of the off-duty patrolmen, and between him, Gage, and the two additional BCI agents, they had the place surrounded.

Ainsley had promised him she'd wait in the Durango until she received an all clear from him. He prayed she kept her word, because the irony of it was he really had no other choice but to trust her.

After quickly determining the house was deserted, they concentrated on the barn. A light shown from beneath the barn door, which hadn't been completely closed. Beck tried the side door entrance, and it too was unlocked. With Gage backing him up, weapons drawn, together they pushed through the door.

The inside of the barn was enormous, and as deserted as the house had been, save the dark blue cargo van and a silver import sedan parked at the far end. Since Beck had ordered radio silence, he retraced his steps and motioned for Mitch and three others to come inside and begin searching. The remaining officers and the two BCI agents were to remain on standby, watching all possible exits. Beck had given them instructions to take McElvoy alive, and to shoot to wound and disable if fired upon first. One way or the other, McElvoy's reign of terror ended here and now.

Working in pairs, each team systematically searched the barn. There were dozens of smaller rooms, most of them dusty, empty except for cobwebs. That is, until Officer Gardocki suddenly appeared at Beck's side and motioned for him to follow.

Beck, with Gage following close behind, traced Gardocki's footsteps to a room at the western end of the barn. Gardocki flashed his light into the room and Beck had all the confirmation he needed that McElvoy was their suspect.

Lining the wall were a dozen shallow, glass-enclosed freezers. Inside the first freezer hung the mutilated corpse of Mattie Davenport, dressed in a sparkling gown, her wide blue eyes transfixed and unseeing. Four other freezers contained similar atrocities, but thankfully none of them matched the description of Megan Conner, or were Cassidy Brennan.

In the center of the room stood a single chair. A place where Beck easily imagined McElvoy sitting for hours, enjoying the horror show he'd created.

He'd witnessed a lot of ugliness in his job, but nothing, in all his years as a cop, could have prepared him for what he'd just seen. Anger like he'd never known boiled up inside him, and for the first time in his career, he thought he just might lose it. If McElvoy were in front of him right now, he honestly couldn't say he wouldn't fill the bastard full of lead.

He turned and stalked out of the room. Angrily, he signaled to Mitch and Gage to follow him. He was going to find the son of a bitch, even if he had to tear the place apart to do it.

They continued their silent search, and just when Beck was certain McElvoy had somehow slipped through their fingers, he spied a heavy wooden sliding door at the end of a row of three doors. The only difference in the doors being that the final one held no heavy lock securing it.

He slid it back and peered inside. At first glance, it looked to be no more than an empty storage bin, until he caught sight of a large meat hook hanging from a heavy chain. Using his flashlight, he searched further and found a piece of carpet rolled back and a heavy metal ring in the floorboard. He bent, tugged on the ring, and the board lifted, revealing a narrow stone staircase.

Light spilled out at the bottom of the stairs, partially illuminating the way. Keeping their backs to the wall, Beck,

Gage, and Mitch slowly descended the staircase, which opened into a large underground room.

Brilliant light flooded the area from the large surgical lamps hanging from the beams. Standing next to a physician's table stood Devin McElvoy. He very gently and calmly stroked Cassidy's long blond hair with a hairbrush. She was fully conscious and held down with restraints, and still wearing her own clothes.

Beck leveled his weapon on McElvoy. "Step away from the girl," Beck told him. Gage and Mitch moved from behind Beck, each with his weapon aimed at McElvoy.

McElvoy ignored the command and continued to run the brush through Cassidy's hair. "She's quite pretty, don't you agree?"

"Now, McElvoy," Beck ordered.

Mitch inched further away from Beck, carefully moving slowly toward McElvoy's left flank.

"It's always the pretty ones, you know," McElvoy said, still drawing the brush through Cassidy's hair. "They think because they're so pretty that everyone owes them. They don't care who they hurt to get what they want."

Beck chanced a quick glance at Cassidy. She couldn't move her head as McElvoy had some sort of device around her throat. Beck tried to get a better look, and quickly determined McElvoy had secured her head in place with piano wire, not tight enough to strangle her, but enough to cause her to choke if she moved. He'd expected tears, even fear, but instead, Cassidy had her sister's grit and determination, evident in the fury blazing in her eyes as she glared at McElvoy.

"It's over, McElvoy," Beck said. "Now step away from Cassidy and no one will die here tonight."

McElvoy very calmly set the brush down on the surgical tray at his elbow. His hand hovered over a syringe, drawn and filled with an unknown substance. His fingers flexed.

"Don't do it," Beck warned.

McElvoy grabbed the syringe. Mitch plowed into him from the left. The two of them hit the ground from the force of Mitch's unexpected blow.

The tray clattered to the floor. Glass vials smashed against the concrete floor, others rolled under the surgical table, where Cassidy was strapped down.

McElvoy rolled and stabbed Mitch in the side of the neck with the syringe.

Mitch howled in pain.

Beck moved in fast. He stood over McElvoy with his Glock pointed right at the bastard's heart. "Fucking breathe wrong, and I'll end you right now."

Gage stepped in and secured McElvoy, slapping a pair of handcuffs on him, then roughly hauling him to his feet. Beck grabbed hold of McElvoy's shirt and pulled him close enough to see the coldness in his eyes. "Where's Megan Conner?"

"She wasn't right," McElvoy said. "She was all wrong, and not like the others."

Beck let go of his shirt with a shove. "Get him out of my sight," he told Gage, then turned his back on McElvoy and started loosening the bonds that held Cassidy prisoner, starting with the wires wrapped around her neck.

"Call an ambulance," he yelled to Gage, who was leading McElvoy from the room. "Two of them."

"Three," Cassidy croaked as soon as the wires were loosened from around her neck. "Megan's in there." She tried to point, but her hands were still secured to the table.

Beck quickly got Cassidy untied. She started trembling, no doubt from shock. He radioed for Charlie, and searched for a blanket to cover Cassidy, but when he couldn't find one, he ripped off his jacket and settled it around her shoulders.

On the floor, Mitch swore a blue streak and pulled the syringe from his neck. He tried to stand, but quickly lost his balance and stumbled backward, sliding back to the cold concrete floor. "Fucker poisoned me," he muttered, his words slurring.

Beck bent and inspected the vials, several each of morphine and Narcon. One to knock his victims out cold, the other to bring them violently out of their drug-induced stupor. From the glassy eyed look Mitch was giving him, Beck suspected the captain had been injected with the former.

"It's morphine, old man," he told Mitch. "EMTs are on the way. You're going to be stoned for a while, but fine."

Charlie showed up and Beck directed him to search the rooms for Megan Conner, while he stayed with Cassidy. Charlie returned seconds later. The girl was alive, but unconscious.

Beck left Cassidy for only a moment to assure himself that the Conner girl was indeed alive and essentially unharmed. Leaving her in Charlie's capable hands, Beck returned to Cassidy. He tugged his jacket tighter around her slender shoulders.

"How did you find me?" Cassidy asked him, her voice raspy.

"Paris," Beck told her. "She recognized McElvoy's voice."

"Did she find my cell phone?" Cass asked, then coughed. "I threw it into the planter when McElvoy grabbed me. She knows I never go anywhere without my cell."

"As a matter of fact," he said, and gave her a grin, "she did."

"She's smart. You should hire her."

The kid deserved a medal, as far as he was concerned. Without her, it could've been hours before they'd gotten to Cassidy, and he didn't want to think about what they might have found.

"Maybe I will," he said, then stepped aside when the EMTs rushed into the room.

IT WAS HOURS before Beck was finally able to get away. The crime scene technicians would be at Harrington Farm for days collecting evidence. The bodies had been taken to the morgue, and with the exception of the Davenport girl, Beck suspected it could be days before the other victims were properly identified.

They'd processed McElvoy, and with District Attorney Sol Ayres and ADA Eisner observing through the one-way glass, Beck and Gage had interrogated McElvoy, who'd given them a full confession. He hadn't even bothered to lawyer up, which had made their job a hell of a lot easier. In Beck's opinion, McElvoy was two Bud Lights short of a twelve-pack, but when he'd expressed concern about an insanity plea to Ayers and Eisner, neither believed the insanity defense would wash. McElvoy didn't meet the legal definition of insane, at least in their opinion.

McElvoy had been transported to the county lockup to await arraignment on seven counts of murder in the first, kidnapping, and a host of other charges the DA was confident would result in a conviction. They would ask for the death penalty, but in the end, it would all depend on the jury whether or not McElvoy spent the rest of his life behind bars without the possibility of parole, or live out only a handful of years on death row, exhausting appeals.

After what Beck and his men had witnessed at Harrington Farm, his money was on the latter.

He walked through the doors of Grace Hospital and headed straight for the bank of elevators that would take him up to the floor where Cassidy was being kept for twenty-four hours of observation. His visit this afternoon was strictly a personal one, as evidenced by the bouquet of flowers and the teddy bear tucked under his arm.

Ainsley would be there, and probably her other sister, Paige, as well as Paris. Whether or not Ainsley would bother to speak to him remained to be seen.

He'd given the issue more thought once he'd finally been able to get some time to himself, and came to the conclusion that while he might have issues with trusting the press, he did trust Ainsley. As he'd told her last night, whether or not she chose to believe him was up to her. He hadn't intentionally kept the information from her, but even if he had, he was under no obligation to reveal every last fact about an ongoing investigation to her or anyone outside of law enforcement. If she had known about the tip they'd gotten, he had little doubt she'd have been out trying to track down that damn van herself once McElvoy took Cassidy, and possibly even getting herself and her sister killed in the process.

What's done is done, he thought as he stepped off the elevator. He couldn't turn back time. He could only hope that she came to understand that while he did trust her, there would be times when he couldn't, or wouldn't, talk about his job. Such was the lot of a cop's girlfriend, or wife, and one she'd have to accept if they were to have a future together.

AS BECK WALKED INTO the hospital room Ainsley's heart did that crazy little flip when she looked up from the magazine she hadn't really been reading while Cassidy slept. He looked more than a little ragged around the edges, the lines bracketing his eyes more pronounced, and a tiredness clung to him. Against her better judgment, she couldn't help worrying that he hadn't bothered to eat or sleep since she'd last seen him over fourteen hours ago.

Beck set the bouquet of flowers on the bedside table along with a cute white teddy bear dressed in a pink gingham dress. "How is she?" he asked quietly.

"Better than I expected," she said. "She'll have some bruising around her neck for a while, but no lasting physical damage. Her voice is a little raw yet, though."

"So what happens now?"

She wasn't certain whether he was referring to Cass or something else, so she opted for the path of least resistance.

"I'll be able to take her home in the morning," she told him. "Whether or not she goes back to U, I don't know. She and Paris were already talking about transferring to Florida State."

A half smile quirked his lips. "Do you blame them?"

She shook her head. "Not really. I'll miss her, and it goes without saying that I'll worry. Especially after . . ." She set the magazine on the mobile tray. "No, I don't blame them. If it were me, I'd want to get as far away from the memories as possible, too."

There were so many things she wanted to ask him. What happened with McElvoy? Did he confess? Do they know what made him do such horrible things to those poor girls? Would he forgive her for being such a bitch when all he'd been doing was his job?

She opted for a safer topic. "You just missed Agent Zimmerman. He left here about half an hour ago."

Beck circled the bed and sat in one of the dark green visitor chairs lined up against the wall, the one directly next to Ainsley's. He leaned forward, forearms braced on his knees, and turned his head to look at her. "He mentioned he'd be stopping by on his way home."

"He offered me a job."

Beck frowned. "Doing what?"

"Press liaison. Apparently I impressed the hell out of him at our press conference last night," she said with a quick grin. "It's not a done deal, though. I'd still have to go through all the clearance checks with Homeland Security and the state, plus complete a formal interview."

"So you're thinking about taking it, then?"

"I think so," she said. "The money is a lot more than I'm making now, plus benefits, which includes a very nice retirement plan. With everything at the paper up in the air now that Dylan's sold the *Sentinel* to Tricor, I don't think this is an opportunity I should walk away from."

288 Jamie Denton

He shifted his gaze and stared at the speckled linoleum tile between his feet. "Does this mean you'll be moving?"

"I don't know," she said honestly. Her insides started quivering and suddenly she felt entirely way too nervous. She fisted her hands, then flexed them and gripped the arms of the chair until her knuckles ached.

"With Cass considering moving to Florida, if I take the job with BCI, I'll be based in Cleveland but will have to travel around the state, so it is a possibility." She drew in a long breath and let it out slowly. "That's a lot of house to maintain for one person."

He looked at her, his gaze steady, but unreadable. "I thought Serenity Heights was home."

"Serenity Heights will always be my hometown," she said. "But as someone told me recently, sometimes you just have to let go and move on."

"And you're ready to move on?"

She gripped the arms of the chair even tighter. "Unless you can think of some other reason for me to stay in Serenity Heights?"

That half smile made a perfectly timed reappearance. "One or two come to mind."

Relief flooded her. She'd been all but certain she'd completely blown it with him. She'd essentially berated him for choosing his job over her, and that was just wrong.

"Beck, I am sorry about last night. I said things I shouldn't have," she admitted.

He grabbed her hand and pried it from the arm of the chair, then laced their fingers together. "I can't always talk about my job. You have to understand that."

"I do," she said. "I do now. I was too upset earlier to see—"

"Shhh," he murmured, cutting her off. He brought their joined hands to his mouth and gently brushed his lips over her fingers. "It's over and forgotten. Okay?"

"Okay," she agreed, thankful he wasn't going to make her grovel. Not that she didn't deserve to for her hideous behavior, at least in her opinion. But she'd make it up to him. Later, when they were finally alone and maybe could even enjoy one of those lazy mornings in bed they'd talked about.

Three months later

HAPPY WITH HER progress for the night, Ainsley pulled the pages from the printer, then shut down her laptop and pushed away from the old rolltop desk that now resided in the den at Beck's place. She stopped to add another couple of logs to the fireplace, then went to the kitchen to check on the progress of the banana bread she had baking in the oven. Thanksgiving was in two days and she still had pies to bake and the two spare bedrooms to ready before Paige, Cassidy, and Paris arrived tomorrow. Unless something went haywire at work and she was called in to deal with the press, she had an extra day off, giving her a nice long five-day weekend to work on her manuscript.

She loved her new job at BCI as a liaison to the press, but she quickly discovered she missed actual reporting. Digging up facts and reporting on them had been such an integral part of her life, she'd started toying with the idea of attempting to write a true crime book about the events that had occurred in Serenity Heights. Who knew if the book, once finished, would ever see publication, but she couldn't live with herself if she at least didn't give it a shot.

Devin McElvoy had turned out to be one interesting subject. Not that she planned to glorify the twisted serial killer who had terrorized their sleepy little town, but the story was one, she felt, worth reporting. He hadn't had an easy childhood, not by a long shot. What he'd suffered at the hands of his cruel and often sadistic nurse mother and dentist father was an exercise in extreme favoritism of one child over another, and enough to give her nightmares for the rest of her life. None of it excused McElvoy's crimes, but at least she understood, or thought she did, what had driven him to the depths of his own depravity.

It would be months yet before the case went to trial, and she was certain there would be more revealed on the atrocities McElvoy suffered and those that he inflicted on others. The number of lives destroyed was simply astounding.

The U was surviving the aftermath, but enrollment had dropped by a full third in the wake of McElvoy's reign of terror on the once quiet and serene campus. Not only had Cass and Paris finagled a midterm transfer to Florida State, with the assistance of the U's President Rhoades and Dean Chesterfield, but Megan Conner had dropped out of school to return to her hometown in Oklahoma. Zach Toomey, Paris's ex-boyfriend, still attended the U, and Ainsley had spied him hanging out at the Pizza Pit with a group of students from the U just two days ago. The chip on his shoulder was still as present as ever.

As Mona had predicted, Tricor had closed down the *Sentinel* within six weeks of taking it over. The building had been put up for sale, but in the current real estate market, she imagined it'd remain vacant for quite some time. Mona's early retirement had lasted roughly a week. On her way home from work one night, Ainsley had stopped in at the Cast Off to pick up some sock yarn, and Mona was there, teaching beginning knitting classes to a small group of high school girls. Lisa had taken a job as a receptionist in Doc Turner's office, and Dylan and his wife had relocated to North Carolina within two weeks of the sale of the paper.

She heard the garage door opener kick on, then the sound of Beck's truck being pulled inside. Moving in with him hadn't been an easy decision for her. She wasn't too worried about small town gossip, but of leaving the only home she'd ever known. Those concerns were quickly quashed by Paige and Cassidy, who both felt it was time to sell the house and move on, so she'd listed the house and was still hoping it'd sell sometime soon. With the real estate market a shambles, she wasn't holding her breath, seeing as they hadn't had a reasonable offer worth accepting yet.

Beck came through the door and her heart swelled, as it did every time she saw him. He balanced two pies in his hands and carefully set them on the counter. She crossed her arms and looked pointedly at the pies. "What do I have to do? Take out a full page spread in the *Plain Dealer* to let these nutty women know that you're spoken for?"

Beck chuckled, then hauled her into his arms for a long, slow, toe-curling kiss. "The pies are from Rose," he said, when he came up for air. "And for the record, I haven't seen so much as a stray cupcake since you started carting that rock around on your finger."

She held up the ring in question, and admired the full carat, princess-cut solitaire engagement ring he'd given her a month after they'd moved in together. "And such a lovely ring, at that."

The timer on the oven buzzed. She slipped out of his arms and went to pull out the banana bread. "You're home early," she said, setting the loaves on the wire rack to cool. Since Chief Munson's medical retirement, Beck had been appointed chief of police by the mayor. Beck had offered the deputy chief position to Mitch, who'd passed and recommended Charlie Gabriel for the post. "Wasn't there supposed to be a city council meeting tonight?"

"It was postponed until next week," he said, shrugging out of his coat. "I guess some of the council members thought it was a little too close to the holiday."

"No doubt," she said absently, admiring the play of muscle beneath his shirt as he slipped off his shoulder holster and slung it over the back of the chair. "Goodness, whatever will you do with all that spare time you have on your hands tonight?"

He looked over his shoulder at her, a lascivious light dancing in those intense green eyes that never failed to start her temperature rising and her blood humming in her veins.

"One or two ideas come to mind," he said, his voice all low and deep and sexy.

She laughed, then braced her hands behind her and hopped up on the counter. "Wanna come tell me about them?"

He crossed the short distance between them. He slid his hands up her legs and settled them on her waist. She widened her legs and he stepped between her thighs. "How about I show you instead?"

"I thought you'd never ask," she said, then wreathed her arms around his neck and kissed him senseless.

There's nothing more irresistible than EVERLASTING BAD BOYS. This sexy anthology from Shelly Laurenston, Cynthia Eden, and Noelle Mack is available now from Brava.
Check out Shelly's story, "Can't Get Enough."

"Ailean," she somehow managed to squeak out. "Good morn to you."

"And to you, Shalin. You look awfully beautiful today."

The fact that he could say that and sound like he meant it was probably why so many females fell under his spell. Yet Shalin couldn't be fooled. She had mirrors, did she not?

"Thank you. So why are you—"

"Och!" he cut in as he always did. The dragon rarely took a breath, it seemed. "You won't believe my morning, Shalin. You truly won't. Mind if I sit?"

"Uh—"

"Good. Thanks." He dropped down beside her. All that dragon as naked human male. It took every ounce of her strength not to reach out and touch him. Like that solid thigh brushing against her robe-covered leg, to see how it felt under her human hands. She'd never been with a male as human. She'd heard it could be . . . entertaining.

"So there I am, taking a bath, as she said I could, when suddenly her father comes in."

"Oh, that must have been—"

"Horrible, right. Because she told me that we were alone in that house. But apparently not. I think she wanted me to claim her or marry her or whatever they call it."

"Even though you're—"

"A dragon, right. She doesn't know that bit, you see. Best to keep her in the dark about that, don't you think?"

"Well—"

"Especially for just a night of entertainment. Why she'd want me as a mate, I have no idea. So what are you reading?"

It took her a moment to realize he'd asked her a question he expected her to answer. "*Alchemic Formulas from the Nolwenn Witches of Alsandair.*"

"Is it interesting?"

"A—"

"I don't know how you can read so many books. I get bored after a few pages."

"So," Shalin found the courage to ask, "you've never read the books about yourself?"

Ailean groaned, rested his elbows on his raised knees, and dropped his head in his hands. "Tell me you haven't read those."

Read them? She'd devoured them.

"Well—"

"Because I didn't authorize those to be written."

The books had begun to show up among humans and dragons nearly ten years before. She'd only just finished reading volume three the previous night and word of volume four being available soon had her nearly breathless. Each volume had two editions. One for humans and one for dragons written in the ancient language of their people. A language the humans of this world could never hope to learn with their much weaker minds, ensuring the fact dragons roamed among them freely remained a well-kept secret.

"The books aren't true, then?"

Based on his wince, she knew they were as true as they could be.

"I never said those things didn't happen. I just said I never authorized them being written about." He turned his head and looked at her, those silver eyes hot on her face. "I don't want you to think I run around telling tales about my relationships, Shalin. I can keep a secret quite well."

And how tempted she was to take him up on his unspoken offer, but that would be cutting her own throat. She'd officially be an enemy of Adienna then, and she simply wouldn't risk her life for any male.

"I—"

"Perhaps I could tempt you away from your interesting book with promise of a delicious meal at one of the nearby taverns?"

Shocked, Shalin gripped the book in her lap tightly. He wanted to take her out? In public?

What should she say? *I'd love to? How about dinner in my room? Forget that, let's go for it right here, right now?*

Instead what she heard herself stuttering was, "I . . . I can't."

"Can't or won't?"

"Both." She shot to her feet, the book still in her hands. "I have to go."

He stood and towered over her as no human could. "Don't go, Shalin. Spend the night with me."

She should be insulted. He'd just left another female's bed and now, still naked and wet from the woman's bath, he'd asked Shalin to warm his bed. But this was Ailean the Whore. He wasn't doing anything out of character. She actually felt kind of proud he'd asked her at all. Although she knew that to be pathetic. And she'd never admit it out loud.

Shalin focused on the book in her hands. "That's very kind of you, but . . . but I . . . I—"

Big fingers lightly gripped her chin and tilted her face up to his.

"Gods, Shalin. You do so tempt me."

She nearly melted at his words. Melted right into a big puddle at his feet.

"Ailean, I—"

Shalin stopped talking when she realized guards stood behind him.

"There you are," one of them said, slapping his hand down on Ailean's shoulder.

Ailean gave a short snort. "And such a good job finding me, since I've been standing here for the last twenty minutes."

With a snarl, the guard motioned to the others and large steel manacles were locked onto Ailean's wrists.

"Don't look so, Shalin." Ailean grinned. "I have every intention of coming back for you."

Shalin opened her mouth to say something, but no words would come out. He'd rendered her completely speechless. But since he really didn't let her get a word in edgewise, this wasn't exactly an incredible feat. Holding the book close to her chest and pulling the hood of her acolyte robe down over her face, she nodded, turned, and fled.

Here's a sneak peek at Kathy Love's
I WANT YOU TO WANT ME
Available now from Brava!

Just as she raised her hand to knock again, the door jerked open, her fisted hand coming close to bopping him in the nose. In the dim light, Vittorio grimaced at her through sleep-heavy eyes. His long hair was tangled and shoved haphazardly back from his face. Bare, muscled chest and flat stomach appeared over sweatpants slung low on his narrow hips.

"I'm sorry," Erika immediately said, even as her heart skipped wildly. An image of him lying in bed filled her mind, quickly morphing to a picture of her in bed with him. "I—I didn't think you'd be sleeping," she managed to mumble.

He frowned, blinking, then peered over her shoulder at the evening sky, which now nearly left them in darkness.

"I keep weird hours." His tone was flat, yet his voice still lent the words a beauty with its deep baritone timbre.

Erika stared at him, unable to keep from studying the shadows emphasizing the muscles of his chest and stomach. Chiseled and perfect. She immediately wanted to capture that perfection with her art.

But she managed to stop gaping and move her gaze up to his face, which was also a study in shadows and beauty.

Clearing her throat, she managed a smile. "I keep odd hours too."

He lifted an eyebrow, but didn't say anything. Instead he

leaned on the doorframe, crossing his arms over his chest. The movement caused his muscles to come to life. Erika's fingers twitched with the longing to shape her hand over them like she would the smooth clay of one of her sculptures.

"I'm guessing you didn't come up here to discuss our sleep habits."

Erika's eyes returned to his, as did the sense of dread she'd been experiencing at the bottom of the stairs. Cool disdain—that was what she was getting. Crap.

"No." She offered him another small smile. "No, I came up to see how your head is." She reached forward to brush aside his hair to see the wound, but he caught her wrist, stopping her. His cool fingers curled a tad too tightly on her skin.

"It's fine."

Erika nodded at the clipped response that didn't invite further questioning. Yet she didn't move, nor did he release her. Although his hold loosened and she could have sworn his thumb slid on the outside of her wrist like the briefest, faintest caress.

Crazy. She made a small noise in the back of her throat at the silly notion. The soft sound seemed to make Vittorio aware that he still held her, because he promptly dropped his fingers away from her.

Erika fought the urge to touch the place where his hand had been. Instead she stepped back from him. She should leave.

"Okay," she said feeling disoriented. "I just wanted to check." Check Philippe's theory, but as before she seemed to be the only one affected by Vittorio's nearness. Vittorio's expression was still remote, hardly filled with overwhelming attraction.

"I guess I should go, then," she added. She took another step backwards, then remembered the plate of treats she still held.

"Oh and I made you these," she said, shoving the plate toward him. "You know, as a peace offering."

He stared down at the plastic wrap-covered squares as if he expected them to crawl off the plate and attack, perhaps sticking in his beautiful long hair.

Her fingers held the plate, tightening with the desire to touch the silky-looking locks. Was she utterly mad? This man was not interested in her—in the least—and she was fantasizing about touching his hair.

"I—" He still regarded the cookies with consternation. "I don't eat—sweets."

"Oh." She pulled the plate away from him. "Okay. Well, I did just want to say I'm sorry."

He nodded, saying nothing.

"About last night, I mean," she said, watching his expression.

A muscle in his jaw worked as if he was clenching his teeth. "As you've already said," he stated.

Erika nodded, not sure what else to say. It certainly didn't appear he was any more willing to forgive her tonight than he was last night.

Suddenly that uncharacteristic feeling of irritation swelled inside her again. Why did he dislike her so much? Okay, she had hit him with a cell phone, but it had been in an unusual circumstance. And she did feel truly awful about it.

But instead of just accepting that he wasn't going to warm up to her, she heard herself saying, "I know this is going to sound weird, but I'm actually trying to figure out if you are someone that my psychic told me I'd meet."

Vittorio straightened, and the remote look in his eyes shifted, but it wasn't to an expression she liked any better. His eyes widened with amused disbelief.

"Your psychic?"

Erika had had this reaction before. More than once. And she immediately regretted her honesty.

"I'm sure this sounds a little strange to you."

He tilted his head. "What did this psychic say?"

She hesitated. Was he genuinely curious, or did he intend to mock her?

"He's been predicting that I would meet someone who at least physically fits your description."

He nodded, his gaze leaving hers as if he was considering the idea. She still couldn't quite decipher what he might be thinking.

"And what else did this psychic say?"

Erika again debated what to tell him. But the lopsided, not altogether kind, slant of his lips made her stop. He just thought she was nuts. And he didn't appear to like her any better for her nuttiness.

"Forget it." She raised a hand in a gesture of defeat. "I just wanted to be sure your head was all right."

She started to leave, when his voice stopped her. "Thanks."

Get in the holiday spirit with TO ALL A GOOD NIGHT,
a sexy anthology from Donna Kauffman, Jill Shalvis, and
HelenKay Dimon.
Check out Donna's story, "Unleashed"!

An hour later, she was quite thankful for the addendum maps, as she'd be hopelessly lost without them. Actually, even with them she'd gotten herself somewhat turned around, out at the end of the west wing—at least she was pretty sure it was west. Even the dogs had given up on the adventure and trotted off after some time, to God knew where. She was sure they'd find her when they got hungry or wanted to go out, so she wasn't too concerned about that. But she was getting hungry herself and she had no idea how to get back to the kitchen, much less the garage, or the rooms she'd been assigned to stay in.

She was stumbling down a dark corridor, unable to find the hall light switch, when a very deep male voice said, "If you're a burglar, then might I direct your attention downstairs to the formal dining room. The silver tea set alone would keep you in much better stealth gear for at least the next decade. At the very least, you'd be able to afford a flashlight."

Emma let out a strangled yelp as her heart leapt straight to her throat, then she froze in the darkness. Except for the animals, she was supposed to be completely alone. Not so much as a valet or sous chef was to be on the premises for the next twelve days. Of course, the notebook did say that

Cicero had a lengthy and amazing vocabulary. But he was at least two floors away. And she doubted he knew how to use the house speaker system. Armed with the notebook and not much else, Emma decided offense was the best defense. "Please state who you are and how you got in here. Security has already been alerted, so you'd best—"

Rich male laughter cut her off. "You must be the sitter."

"Which must make you the burglar, then," she shot back, nerves getting the better of her.

More laughter. Which, despite being sexy as all hell, did little to calm her down. Because, though she'd been joking, the idea that she'd been on the job for less than two hours and had already allowed a thief into the house was just a perverse enough thing that would actually happen to her.

The large shadow moved closer and she was deep into the fight-or-flight debate when a soft click sounded and the hallway was illuminated with a series of crystal wall sconces. Emma's first glance at her unexpected guest did little to balance her equilibrium.

Whoever he was, he beat her five-foot-nine height by a good half foot, which made the fight thing rather moot. Flight probably wasn't going to get her very far, either. He had the kind of broad shoulders, tapered waist and well-built legs her defensive line coach dad would recruit in a blink, and charming rascal dimples topped by twinkling blue eyes her Irish mother would swoon over as she served him beef stew and biscuits.

Emma, on the other hand, had absolutely no idea what to do with him.

And keep an eye out
for Katherine Garbera's latest,
BARE WITNESS
Coming next month from Brava!

Justine arched an eyebrow at him. "Are you making fun of me?"

"Never. I was trying—trying to tease a smile back on your lips."

"Why?"

"I like your smile."

"You do?"

"Yes."

"Why?"

Nigel shook his head this time. "You mustn't get many compliments."

She shrugged. "Honestly, I don't trust them."

"Why not?"

"What's with you and all the questions?"

"I'm a CEO; I thrive on information."

"So do bodyguards," she said.

The teasing note was back in her voice and he felt a little thrill of victory at having done that. "Why are you a bodyguard?"

"Well, to be honest, I'm usually more of a weapons expert and marksman. For most assignments we take on, Charity functions as the bodyguards."

"Why is that?"

"She's tall and gorgeous, just the sort of person that makes most assailants think they don't have a thing to worry about."

"And you're not."

She gestured to her short frame. "Height is one thing I've never needed."

"No?"

"No," she said. "I learned early on that if I don't quit, I can take anyone."

"Can you take me?"

"Easily," she said.

He took two steps toward her. The plane rocked and bucked and all the playfulness that she'd had a second ago disappeared as she used her body to take him down to the floor and braced both of their bodies.

When the plane leveled itself out she knew it had to be turbulence and not an engine out or any other danger. But her heart was racing and it had nothing at all to do with the security of Nigel Carter or his daughter.

Justine closed her eyes but that just made everything . . . better. All of her other senses came to life. The feel of his hard body under hers, the scent of his spicy aftershave, the sound of each exhalation of his minty breath against her cheek.

She opened her eyes as Nigel's hands settled low on her waist. This time it wasn't different. His hand was in the exact same spot that had worried her when they'd been standing toe-to-toe. But now it didn't bother her.